Three Short Novels of Dostoevsky

FYODOR DOSTOEVSKY, born in Moscow in 1821, was the son of an impoverished noble who had a position as resident doctor in the Mariinsky Hospital for the Poor. After a childhood spent in the family's house on the hospital grounds, he was sent in 1837 to the St. Petersburg School for Military Engineers, but resigned his military position in 1844 to devote himself to writing. His first novel, later translated under the title of *Poor Folk*, appeared two years later, the same year that *The Double* was published. Arrested in 1849 for his membership in the radical Petrashevsky Society, Dostoevsky received a death sentence and was actually standing before the firing squad when a messenger arrived from the tsar, commuting his punishment to four years in Siberia. After his imprisonment he went into the army, and it was not until 1859 that he finally returned to St. Petersburg where, until his death in 1881, he lived and wrote the novels for which he is famous.

CONSTANCE GARNETT (1862–1946) was an Englishwoman whose translations of Chekhov, Tolstoy, Turgenev, and Dostoevsky were largely responsible for introducing the works of these Russian masters to the English-speaking world. Her work was done in a Victorian idiom, and some of her translations have been recently revised. Avrahm Yarmolinsky, Russian-born and a resident of this country since 1913, is one of the best-known modern American translators from the Russian.

Three Short Novels of
DOSTOEVSKY

Translated by
Constance Garnett
Revised and Edited by
Avrahm Yarmolinsky

ANCHOR BOOKS
DOUBLEDAY & COMPANY, INC.
GARDEN CITY, NEW YORK

Library of Congress Catalog Card Number 60–5734
ISBN: 0-385-09435-3
Copyright © 1960 by Avrahm Yarmolinsky
All Rights Reserved
Printed in the United States of America

Contents

THE DOUBLE
A Petersburg Epic

Chapter I

IT was a little before eight o'clock in the morning when Yakov Petrovich Golyadkin, a titular councilor, woke up from a long sleep. He yawned, stretched, and at last opened his eyes completely. For some two minutes, however, he lay in his bed without moving, like a man who is not yet quite certain whether he is awake or still asleep, whether all that is going on around him is real and actual, or the continuation of his confused dreams. Very soon, however, Mr. Golyadkin's senses began to receive their habitual, everyday impressions more clearly and more distinctly. The dirty green, smoke-begrimed, dusty walls of his little room, his mahogany chest of drawers and imitation mahogany chairs, the table painted red, the ottoman upholstered in reddish oilcloth with little green flowers on it, and finally the clothes taken off in haste overnight and flung in a crumpled heap on the sofa, all looked at him familiarly. At last the gray autumn day, dull and dirty, peeped into the room through the dingy windowpane with such a sour grimace that Mr. Golyadkin could not possibly doubt any longer that he was not in the never-never land, but in the capital city of Petersburg, in his own flat on the fourth story

3

of a huge tenement house in Shestilavochny Street. Having made this important discovery, Mr. Golyadkin closed his eyes, as though regretting his dream and convulsively wanting to bring it back for a moment. But a minute later he leaped out of bed at one bound, probably all at once grasping the idea about which his scattered and wandering thoughts had been revolving until then. From his bed he ran straight to a little round looking glass that stood on the chest of drawers. Though the sleepy, weak-sighted countenance and rather bald head reflected in the mirror were of such an insignificant character that at first sight they would certainly not have attracted anyone's particular attention, yet the owner of the countenance was satisfied with all that he saw in the looking glass. "What a thing it would be," said Mr. Golyadkin in an undertone, "what a thing it would be if I were not up to the mark today, if something were amiss, if some unauthorized pimple had made its appearance, or anything else unpleasant had happened; so far, however, there's nothing wrong, so far all goes well."

Greatly delighted that all went well, Mr. Golyadkin put the looking glass back in its place and, although he was barefoot and in the attire in which he was accustomed to go to bed, he ran to the window and with great interest began looking for something in the courtyard, which the windows of his flat fronted. Apparently what he was looking for in the yard quite satisfied him too; his face beamed with a self-satisfied smile. Then, after first peeping, however, behind the partition into his valet Petrushka's cubicle and making sure that Petrushka was not there, he tiptoed to the table, unlocked the drawer in it, and, fumbling in the farthest corner of it, took from under old yellowed papers and all sorts of rubbish a shabby green pocketbook, opened it cautiously, and with care and relish peeped into the remotest, secret fold of it. Probably the wad of green, gray, blue, red, and particolored notes looked at Golyadkin, too, affably and approvingly: with a radiant face he laid the open pocketbook before him and rubbed his hands vigorously in token of the greatest pleasure. Finally, he took it out—his comforting wad of notes—and, for the hundredth time since the previous day, counted them over, carefully rubbing every note between forefinger and thumb.

"Seven hundred and fifty roubles in notes," he concluded at last, in a half-whisper. "Seven hundred and fifty roubles, a notable sum! It's an agreeable sum," he went on, in a trembling voice somewhat weak with gratification, as he squeezed the wad with his fingers and smiled significantly; "a very agreeable sum! A sum agreeable to anyone! I should like to see the man to whom that would be a trivial sum! There's no knowing how far a sum like that may lead a man. . . . What's the meaning of it, though?" thought Mr. Golyadkin; "where's Petrushka?" And still in the same attire he peeped behind the partition again. Again there was no sign of Petrushka; and alone the samovar standing on the floor was beside itself, fuming and raging, threatening every minute to boil over, chattering in its queer lisping, burring language, probably telling Mr. Golyadkin something like, "Take me, good people, I'm perfectly ripe and ready."

"Damn the fellow," thought Mr. Golyadkin. "That lazy brute might really drive a man out of all patience; where's he dawdling now?"

In righteous indignation he went out into the hall, which consisted of a little corridor at the end of which was a door into the entry, and saw his servant surrounded by a good-sized group of lackeys, a mixed rabble of local domestics and outsiders. Petrushka was holding forth, the others were listening. Apparently both the subject of the conversation and the conversation itself were not to Mr. Golyadkin's liking. He promptly called Petrushka and returned to his room, displeased and even upset. "That beast would sell a man for a halfpenny, and especially his master," he thought to himself: "and he has sold me, he certainly has. I bet he has sold me for next to nothing. Well?"

"They've brought the livery, sir."

"Put it on, and come here."

When he had put on his livery, Petrushka, with a stupid

5

grin on his face, came into the room. His costume was as strange as can be. He had on a much-worn green livery, with frayed gold braid on it, apparently made for a man a yard taller than Petrushka. In his hand he held a hat also trimmed with gold braid and with green feathers in it, and at his hip hung a footman's sword in a leather sheath. Finally, to complete the picture, Petrushka, who had a weakness for informal attire, was barefoot. Mr. Golyadkin examined Petrushka from all sides and was apparently satisfied. The livery had evidently been hired for some solemn occasion. It was also noticeable that during his master's inspection Petrushka watched him with strange expectancy, and with marked curiosity followed every movement he made, which extremely embarrassed Mr. Golyadkin.

"Well, and what about the carriage?"

"The carriage is here too."

"For the whole day?"

"For the whole day. Twenty-five roubles."

"And have the boots been sent?"

"Yes."

"Dolt! Can't even say, 'Yes, sir.' Bring them here."

Having expressed his satisfaction that the boots fitted, Mr. Golyadkin asked for his tea, and for water to wash and shave. He shaved with great care and washed as scrupulously, hurriedly sipped his tea and proceeded to the principal final ceremony of attiring himself: he put on an almost new pair of trousers; then a shirtfront with brass studs, and a very bright and agreeably flowered waistcoat; about his neck he tied a particolored silk cravat, and finally drew on his full-dress coat, which was also brand-new and carefully brushed. As he dressed, he more than once looked lovingly at his boots, lifted up first one leg and then the other, admiring the shape of his footwear, kept muttering something to himself, and from time to time made expressive grimaces in response to his thoughts. Mr. Golyadkin was, however, extremely absent-minded that morning, for he scarcely noticed the little smiles and grimaces made at his expense by Petrushka, who was helping him dress. At last, having arranged everything properly and having finished dressing, Mr. Golyadkin put his wallet in his pocket, took a final admiring look at Petrushka, who had put on his boots and was therefore also quite ready, and, noticing that everything was done and that there was nothing left to wait for, he ran hurriedly and fussily down the stairs, with a slight throbbing at his heart.

The light-blue hired carriage with a crest on it came thundering up to the steps. Petrushka, exchanging winks with the driver and some loiterers, helped his master into the carriage; and, hardly able to suppress an idiotic laugh, shouted in an unnatural voice, "Go ahead!" jumped on the footboard, and the whole turnout, clattering and rumbling noisily, rolled in the direction of the Nevsky Prospect.

As soon as the light-blue carriage passed the gate, Mr. Golyadkin rubbed his hands convulsively and went off into a quiet, noiseless chuckle, like a man of a cheerful disposition who has succeeded in playing a splendid trick, and is himself as pleased as Punch with the performance. Immediately after his access of gaiety, however, laughter was replaced by a strange, anxious expression on the face of Mr. Golyadkin. Though the day was damp and cloudy, he let down both windows of the carriage and began carefully scrutinizing the passers-by to the left and to the right, at once assuming a decorous and sedate air when he thought anyone was looking at him. At the corner of Liteyny Street and Nevsky Prospect he was startled by a most unpleasant sensation and, frowning like some poor devil whose corn has been accidentally stepped on, he huddled hastily, even fearfully, into the darkest corner of his carriage.

The fact is that he had noticed two of his colleagues, two young clerks employed in the same government department as he. The clerks, on their part, were also, it seemed to Mr. Golyadkin, extremely perplexed at encountering their colleague in this way; one of them, in fact, pointed out Mr. Golyadkin to the other. Mr. Golyadkin even fancied that the latter actually hailed him loudly by name, which, of course, was very unseemly in the street. Our hero concealed himself and did not respond. "The silly youngsters!" he began to reason with himself. "Why, what is there strange about it? A man in a carriage, a man needs to be in a carriage, and so he hires a carriage. They're simply trash! I know them—simply urchins, who still want thrashing! Playing pitch-and-toss when they're flush and gadding about—that's all they think about. I'd like to tell them a thing or two, but . . ."

Mr. Golyadkin broke off suddenly, petrified. A smart pair of Kazan horses, very familiar to Mr. Golyadkin, hitched to a fashionable droshky, drove rapidly by on the right side of his carriage. The gentleman sitting in the droshky, happening to catch a glimpse of Mr. Golyadkin, who had rather incautiously poked his head out of the carriage window, also appeared to be extremely astonished at the unexpected sight and, bending out as far as he could, looked with the greatest curiosity and interest into the corner of the carriage in which our hero made haste to conceal himself. The gentleman in the droshky was Andrey Filippovich, section head of the office in which Mr. Golyadkin was employed as assistant to the chief clerk. Mr. Golyadkin, seeing that Andrey Filippovich recognized him, that he was looking at him open-eyed, and that it was impossible to hide, flushed to the roots of his hair.

"To bow or not to bow? To hail him or not? To recognize him or not?" our hero wondered in indescribable anguish, "or shall I pretend that I am not myself, but somebody else strikingly like me, and look as though nothing were the matter? Just . . . not me, not me and that's all," said Mr. Golyadkin, taking off his hat to Andrey Filippovich, and keeping his eyes fixed upon him. "Don't . . . don't mind me," he whispered with an effort; "just don't mind me. It's not me at all, Andrey Filippovich, it's not me at all, not me, and that's all."

Soon, however, the droshky passed the carriage, and the magnetism of his chief's eyes was at an end. Yet he went on blushing, smiling, and muttering something to himself. . . .

"I was a fool not to have hailed him," he thought at last. "I ought to have taken a bolder line and behaved with gentlemanly frankness. I ought to have said, 'This is how it is, Andrey Filippovich. I too have a dinner invitation,' and that's all!"

Then, suddenly recalling that he had flunked out, our hero flushed as hot as fire, frowned, and cast a terrible, defiant glance at the front corner of the carriage, a glance calculated to reduce instantly all his foes to ashes. At last, he was suddenly inspired to pull the cord attached to the driver's elbow, and stopped the carriage, telling him to drive back to Liteyny Street. The fact was that Mr. Golyadkin, probably for the sake of his own peace of mind, found it urgently necessary to say something very interesting to his doctor, Krestyan Ivanovich. True, he had made Krestyan Ivanovich's acquaintance quite recently, having, indeed, paid him only a single visit the previous week to consult him about some matter. But a doctor, as they say, is like a confessor, and it would be stupid for him to avoid Krestyan Ivanovich, who was indeed in duty bound to know his patients. "Will it be all right, though," our hero went on, getting out of the carriage at the entrance to a five-story house on Liteyny Street, at which he had told the driver to stop: "Will it be all right? Will it be proper? Will it be appropriate? After all, though," he went on, as he mounted the stairs out of breath and trying to check the palpitation of his heart, which had the habit of palpitating on other people's staircases. "After all, I am on my own business and there's nothing reprehensible in it. . . . It would be stupid to avoid him. Why, I'll make believe that I am all right, and have simply looked in as I passed. . . . He will see that it's all just as it should be."

Reasoning like this, Mr. Golyadkin mounted to the second story and stopped before flat number five, on the door of which there was a handsome copper plate with the inscription:

KRESTYAN IVANOVICH RUTENSPITZ
Doctor of Medicine and Surgery

Stopping at the door, our hero made haste to assume an air of propriety, undue familiarity, and even of a certain amiability, and prepared to pull the cord of the bell. As he was about to do so he promptly and rather appropriately reflected that it might be better to come tomorrow, and that there was no very pressing need for the moment. But as he suddenly heard footsteps on the stairs, he immediately changed his mind again and, while he was about it, rang Krestyan Ivanovich's bell—with an air, moreover, of great determination.

Chapter II

The doctor of medicine and surgery, Krestyan Ivanovich Rutenspitz, a very hale though elderly man, endowed with thick eyebrows and whiskers that were beginning to turn gray, expressive and sparkling eyes by means of which alone he routed every disease, and, lastly, with a distinguished order on his breast, was sitting in his consulting room that morning in his comfortable armchair. He was drinking coffee, which his wife had brought him with her own hand, smoking a cigar, and from time to time writing prescriptions for his patients. After prescribing a medicine for an old man who was suffering from hemorrhoids and seeing the aged patient out by the side door, Krestyan Ivanovich sat down to await the next visitor. Mr. Golyadkin walked in.

Apparently Krestyan Ivanovich did not in the least expect or desire to see Mr. Golyadkin, for he was suddenly taken aback for a moment, and his countenance involuntarily assumed a strange and, one may almost say, a displeased expression. As Mr. Golyadkin, on his part, almost always inappropriately sagged and lost his presence of mind whenever he approached anyone about his own little affairs, on this occasion, too, he was thrown into considerable confusion. Having neglected to get ready his first sentence, which was invariably a stumbling block for him on such occasions, he muttered something—apparently an apology—and, not knowing what to do next, took a chair and sat down. But, realizing that he had sat down without being asked to do so, he was immediately conscious of his lapse, and made haste to efface his offense against etiquette and good breeding by promptly getting up again from the seat he had taken uninvited. Then, collecting himself and dimly perceiving that he had committed two stupid blunders at once, he immediately decided to commit a third— that is, tried to right himself, muttered something, smiled, blushed, was overcome with embarrassment, sank into expressive silence, and finally sat down for good and did not get up again. Only, to be on the safe side, he secured his position by fixing the doctor with that defiant look which had an extraordinary power of figuratively crushing Mr. Golyadkin's enemies and reducing them to ashes. This glance, moreover, expressed to the full Mr. Golyadkin's independence—that is, said plainly that there was nothing the matter with Mr. Golyadkin, that he was by himself, like everybody else, and that, in any event, he minded his own business. Krestyan Ivanovich coughed, grunted, apparently in token of approval and assent to all this, and bent an inquisitorial, questioning gaze upon his visitor.

"I have come to trouble you a second time, Krestyan Ivanovich," Mr. Golyadkin began with a smile, "and now I venture to ask your indulgence a second time. . . ." He was obviously at a loss for words.

"H'm . . . Yes!" Krestyan Ivanovich brought out, sending forth a jet of smoke from his mouth and putting down his cigar on the table, "but you must follow the treatment prescribed; I explained to you that what would be beneficial to your health is a change of habits. . . . Well, amusements, and visits to friends and acquaintances; also, no hostility to the bottle; likewise, cheerful company."

Mr. Golyadkin, still smiling, hastened to observe that he

thought he was like everyone else, that he was at his own place, that he had amusements like everyone else . . . that, of course, he might go to the theater, for he had the means like everyone else, that he spent the day at the office and the evenings at home, that he was quite all right; he even observed, in passing, that he was, so far as he could see, as good as anyone, that he lived at home, and, finally, that he had Petrushka. At this point Mr. Golyadkin stopped short.

"H'm, no, that is not the proper order, and that is not at all what I wanted to ask you about. I am interested to know, in general, if you, a great lover of cheerful company, a jolly time have, and if your mode of life melancholy or gay is."

"Krestyan Ivanovich, I . . ."

"H'm . . . I tell you," interrupted the doctor, "that you must a radical change of your entire life have, must, in a certain sense, your character break." (Krestyan Ivanovich laid special stress on the word "break," and paused for a moment with a very significant air.) "Must not shun gaiety, must see plays and visit club, and, in any case, to the bottle not hostile be. Staying at home is not good for you. . . . You must by no means stay at home."

"I like quiet, Krestyan Ivanovich," said Mr. Golyadkin, with a significant look at the doctor and evidently seeking words to express his thought most aptly. "In my flat there's only me and Petrushka . . . I mean my man, Krestyan Ivanovich. I mean to say, Krestyan Ivanovich, that I go my way, my own way, Krestyan Ivanovich. I keep myself to myself, and so far as I can see am not dependent on anyone. I go for walks, too, Krestyan Ivanovich."

"What's that? Yes! Well, nowadays there's no pleasure in walking; the climate's extremely bad."

"Quite so, Krestyan Ivanovich. Though I'm a peaceable man, Krestyan Ivanovich, as I've had the honor of explaining to you already, yet my way lies apart, Krestyan Ivanovich. The road of life is broad . . . I mean . . . I mean to say, Krestyan Ivanovich. . . . Excuse me, Krestyan Ivanovich, I'm a poor hand at speaking eloquently."

"H'm . . . you say . . ."

"I say, you must excuse me, Krestyan Ivanovich, that as far as I can see I am no great hand at eloquence in speaking," Mr. Golyadkin articulated in a half-offended tone, going somewhat astray and getting confused. "In that respect, Krestyan Ivanovich, I'm not quite like other people," he added, with a peculiar smile. "I can't talk much, and have never learned to embellish my style. But then, I act, Krestyan Ivanovich. But then, I act, Krestyan Ivanovich."

"H'm . . . How do you mean . . . you act?" responded Krestyan Ivanovich.

Then a moment's silence followed. The doctor looked somewhat strangely and mistrustfully at his visitor. Mr. Golyadkin, for his part, too, stole a rather mistrustful glance at the doctor.

"Krestyan Ivanovich," he began, going on in the same tone as before, somewhat irritated and puzzled by the doctor's extreme obstinacy, "I like tranquillity and not the noisy gaiety of fashionable society. Among them, I mean, in high society, Krestyan Ivanovich, one must know how to polish the floor with one's boots . . ." (here Mr. Golyadkin made a slight scrape on the floor with his foot); "they expect it, and they expect puns too . . . one must know how to make a perfumed compliment, sir . . . that's what they expect there. And I've not learned to do it, Krestyan Ivanovich, I've never learned all those tricks, I've never had the time. I'm a simple person, and not ingenious, and I've no external polish. In that respect, I surrender, Krestyan Ivanovich, I lay down my arms, speaking in that sense."

All this Mr. Golyadkin delivered with an air which made it perfectly clear that our hero by no means regretted that he was laying down his arms in that sense and that he had not learned these tricks; quite the contrary, indeed. As Krestyan Ivanovich listened to him, he looked down with a very unpleasant grimace on his face, seeming to have a presentiment of some sort. Mr. Golyadkin's tirade was followed by a rather long and significant silence.

"You have, I think, departed a little from the subject," Krestyan Ivanovich said at last, in a low voice. "I confess I cannot quite understand you."

"I'm not a great hand at fine phrases, Krestyan Ivanovich; I've had the honor to inform you, Krestyan Ivanovich, already that I'm a poor hand at speaking eloquently," said Mr. Golyadkin, this time in a sharp and resolute tone.

"H'm!"

"Krestyan Ivanovich!" began Mr. Golyadkin again in a low but significant and somewhat solemn style, emphasizing every point. "Krestyan Ivanovich, when I came in here I began with apologies. I repeat the same thing again, and again ask your indulgence for a while. I have nothing to conceal from you, Krestyan Ivanovich. I'm a little man, as you know; but, fortunately for me, I do not regret being a little man. Quite the contrary, Krestyan Ivanovich; and, to be perfectly frank, I'm proud that I'm not a great man but a little man. I'm no intrigant and I'm proud of that too. I don't act on the sly, but openly, without wiles, and although I could do harm too, and a great deal of harm, indeed, and know to whom and how to do it, Krestyan Ivanovich, yet I won't sully myself, and in that sense I wash my hands. In that sense, I say, I wash them, Krestyan Ivanovich!" Mr. Golyadkin paused expressively for a moment; he had been speaking with mild fervor.

"I go my way, Krestyan Ivanovich," our hero continued, "directly, openly, by no devious paths, for I disdain them, and leave them to others. I do not try to humiliate those who are perhaps more blameless than you and I . . . that is, I mean, I and they, Krestyan Ivanovich—I didn't mean you. I don't like insinuations; I've no taste for contemptible duplicity; gossip and slander I disdain. I only put on a mask at a masquerade, and don't wear one before people every day. I only ask you, Krestyan Ivanovich, how would you revenge yourself upon your enemy, your most spiteful enemy—the one you would consider such?" Mr. Golyadkin concluded with a challenging glance at Krestyan Ivanovich.

Though Mr. Golyadkin uttered all this most distinctly and clearly, weighing his words with a self-confident air and reckoning on their probable effect, yet meanwhile he was looking at Krestyan Ivanovich with anxiety, with great anxiety, with extreme anxiety. Now he was all eyes, and timidly waited for the doctor's answer with irritable and agonized impatience. But, to the perplexity and complete rout of our hero, Krestyan Ivanovich only muttered something to himself under his breath; then he moved his arm-chair up to the table, and rather dryly, though politely, announced something to the effect that his time was valuable, and that he did not quite understand; that he was ready, however, to be of service to him as far as he was able, but he would not go into anything further that did not concern him. At this point he took the pen, drew a piece of paper toward him, cut out of it the usual long strip, and announced that he would immediately prescribe what was necessary.

"No, sir, it's not necessary, Krestyan Ivanovich! No, sir, that's not necessary at all!" said Mr. Golyadkin, getting up from his seat, and clutching Krestyan Ivanovich's right hand. "That isn't what's wanted, Krestyan Ivanovich."

And, while he said this, a queer change came over him. His gray eyes gleamed strangely, his lips began to quiver, all the muscles, all the features of his face began moving and working. He was trembling all over. After stopping the doctor's hand, Mr. Golyadkin followed his first movement by standing motionless, as though he had no confidence in himself and were waiting for some inspiration for further action.

Then followed a rather strange scene.

Somewhat taken aback, Krestyan Ivanovich seemed for a moment rooted to his chair and gazed in open-eyed bewilderment at Mr. Golyadkin, who looked at him in exactly the same way. At last Krestyan Ivanovich stood up, gently holding on to the lapel of Mr. Golyadkin's coat. For some seconds they both stood like that, motionless, with their eyes fixed on each other. Then, however, in an extraordinarily strange way came Mr. Golyadkin's second movement. His lips trembled, his chin began twitching, and our hero quite unexpectedly burst into tears. Sobbing, shaking his head, and beating his breast with his right hand, while with his left clutching the lapel of the doctor's coat, he tried to say something and to offer some explanation without delay, but could not utter a word.

At last Krestyan Ivanovich recovered from his amazement.

"Come, calm yourself, sit down!" he brought out at last, trying to make Mr. Golyadkin sit down in an armchair.

"I have enemies, Krestyan Ivanovich, I have enemies; I have malicious enemies who have sworn to destroy me . . ." Mr. Golyadkin answered in a frightened whisper.

"Come, come, why enemies? You mustn't talk about enemies! You really mustn't. Sit down, sit down," Krestyan Ivanovich went on, finally getting Mr. Golyadkin into the armchair.

Mr. Golyadkin sat down at last, still keeping his eyes fixed on the doctor. With an extremely displeased air, Krestyan Ivanovich began to pace his consulting room. A long silence followed.

"I'm grateful to you, Krestyan Ivanovich, I'm very grateful, and I'm very sensible of all you've done for me now. To my dying day I shall never forget your kindness, Krestyan Ivanovich," said Mr. Golyadkin, getting up from his seat with an offended air.

"Enough of this! I tell you, enough of this!" Krestyan Ivanovich responded rather sternly to Mr. Golyadkin's outburst, making him sit down again.

"Well, what's the matter? Tell me what is worrying you now?" Krestyan Ivanovich went on. "What enemies are you talking about? What is wrong?"

"No, Krestyan Ivanovich, we'd better leave that now," answered Mr. Golyadkin, casting down his eyes; "let us put all that aside for the present . . . till another time,

Krestyan Ivanovich, till a more convenient moment, when everything will be revealed, and the mask will fall off certain faces, and something will come to light. But, meanwhile, now, of course, after what has passed between us . . . you will agree yourself, Krestyan Ivanovich. . . . Allow me to wish you good morning, Krestyan Ivanovich," said Mr. Golyadkin, getting up gravely and resolutely and taking his hat.

"Oh, well . . . as you like . . . h'm . . ." (A moment of silence followed.) "For my part, you know . . . whatever I can do . . . and I sincerely wish you well."

"I understand you, Krestyan Ivanovich, I understand; I understand you perfectly now. . . . In any case excuse me for having troubled you, Krestyan Ivanovich."

"H'm, no, I didn't mean to tell that. However, as you please; go on taking the medicines as before. . . ."

"I will go on with the medicines as you say, Krestyan Ivanovich. I will go on with them, and I will get them at the same chemist's . . . To be even a chemist nowadays, Krestyan Ivanovich, is an important business. . . ."

"How so? In what sense do you mean?"

"In a very ordinary sense, Krestyan Ivanovich. I mean to say that nowadays that's the way of the world. . . ."

"H'm . . ."

"That every silly youngster, not only a chemist's boy, turns up his nose at respectable people."

"H'm. How do you mean?"

"I'm speaking of a certain person, Krestyan Ivanovich . . . of a common acquaintance of ours, Krestyan Ivanovich, of Vladimir Semyonovich, for instance. . . ."

"Ah!"

"Yes, Krestyan Ivanovich: and I know certain people, Krestyan Ivanovich, who don't quite keep to the general rule of telling the truth, sometimes."

"Ah! How so?"

"Why, that's how it is: but that's beside the point: they sometimes manage to treat you to an egg in juice."

"Treat you to what?"

"An egg in juice, Krestyan Ivanovich. It's a Russian saying. They know how to congratulate someone at the right moment, for instance; there are people like that."

"Congratulate?"

"Yes, congratulate, Krestyan Ivanovich, as someone with whom I am on very friendly terms did the other day!"

"Someone you are on very friendly terms with? . . . Ah! How's that?" said Krestyan Ivanovich, looking attentively at Mr. Golyadkin.

"Yes, someone I am very well in with indeed congratulated someone else who is a close acquaintance, and, what's more, a friend, a 'bosom friend,' as the saying goes, on his promotion, on his receiving the rank of assessor. This was how he put it: 'I am exceedingly glad of the opportunity to offer you, Vladimir Semyonovich, my congratulations, my *sincere* congratulations, on your receiving the rank. And I'm the more pleased, as all the world knows that nowadays there are no more grannies who tell fortunes.'"

At this point Mr. Golyadkin gave a sly nod, and, screwing up his eyes, looked at Krestyan Ivanovich. . . .

"H'm. So he said that. . . ."

"He did, Krestyan Ivanovich, he said it and then and there glanced at Andrey Filippovich, the uncle of our darling, Vladimir Semyonovich. But what is it to me, Krestyan Ivanovich, that he has been made an assessor? What is it to me? But he wants to get married, and he is still wet behind the ears, if I may be allowed the expression. And I said as much. Vladimir Semyonovich, said I! I've said everything now; allow me to withdraw."

"H'm . . ."

"Yes, Krestyan Ivanovich, allow me now, I say, to withdraw. But, to kill two birds with one stone, as I twitted the young fellow by mentioning the grannies, I turned to Klara Olsufyevna (it all happened the day before yesterday at Olsufy Ivanovich's), and she had only just sung a romance full of feeling. 'You've been pleased to sing songs full of feeling, madam,' said I, 'but they've not been listened to with a pure heart.' And by that I hinted plainly, Krestyan Ivanovich, hinted plainly, that they were not currying favor with her now, but looking higher. . . ."

"Ah! And what did he say?"

"He bit into a lemon, Krestyan Ivanovich, as the saying goes."

"H'm . . ."

"Yes, Krestyan Ivanovich. To the old man himself, too, I said, 'Olsufy Ivanovich,' said I, 'I know how much I'm indebted to you, I appreciate to the full all the kindness you've showered upon me since I was almost a child. But open your eyes, Olsufy Ivanovich,' I said. 'Look about you. I myself do things openly and aboveboard, Olsufy Ivanovich.' "

"Oh, really!"

"Yes, Krestyan Ivanovich. Really . . ."

"Well, what did he say?"

"Yes, what, indeed, Krestyan Ivanovich? He mumbled one thing and another, saying, 'I know you,' and 'his Excellency is a beneficent man'—he rambled on, he spun it out. . . . You know, he's begun to be a bit shaky, as they say, with old age."

"Ah! So that's how it is now!"

"Yes, Krestyan Ivanovich. And that's how we all are! Poor old man! He has one foot in the grave, as they say, but whenever a bit of old wives' gossip is being cooked up, he is right there, listening; without him it is impossible; without him they wouldn't . . ."

"Gossip, you say?"

"Yes, Krestyan Ivanovich, they've cooked up some gossip. Our bear, too, had a finger in it, and so did his nephew, our darling. They've joined hands with the old women and, of course, cooked up the affair. Would you believe it? What do you think they trumped up to murder a man?"

"To murder a man?"

"Yes, Krestyan Ivanovich, to murder a man, to murder

him morally. They spread about . . . I'm speaking of a close friend of mine."

Krestyan Ivanovich nodded.

"They spread a rumor about him. . . . I confess I'm ashamed to speak of it, Krestyan Ivanovich."

"H'm . . ."

"They spread a rumor that he had signed a marriage promise, that he was already engaged . . . and would you believe it, Krestyan Ivanovich, to whom?"

"Really?"

"To a disreputable German woman, the proprietress of an eating house, from which he gets his dinners; instead of paying what he owes her, he offers her his hand."

"Is that what they say?"

"Would you believe it, Krestyan Ivanovich? A German woman, a low, nasty, shameless German woman, Karolina Ivanovna, if you know . . ."

"I confess, for my part . . ."

"I understand you, Krestyan Ivanovich, I understand, and for my part I feel it. . . ."

"Tell me, please, where are you living now?"

"Where am I living now, Krestyan Ivanovich?"

"Yes . . . I want . . . I believe, you used to live . . ."

"Yes, Krestyan Ivanovich, I did, I used to. To be sure, I lived!" answered Mr. Golyadkin, accompanying his words with a little laugh, and somewhat disconcerting Krestyan Ivanovich by his answer.

"No, you misunderstood me; I mean, for my part . . ."

"I, too, meant for my part, Krestyan Ivanovich, I meant it too," Mr. Golyadkin continued, laughing. "But I've kept you far too long, Krestyan Ivanovich. I hope you will allow me now to wish you good morning."

"H'm . . ."

"Yes, Krestyan Ivanovich, I understand you; I fully understand you now," said our hero, slightly showing off before Krestyan Ivanovich. "And so permit me to wish you good morning. . . ."

At this point our hero scraped his foot and walked out

of the room, leaving Krestyan Ivanovich in the utmost amazement. As he went down the doctor's stairs he smiled and rubbed his hands gleefully. On the steps, breathing the fresh air and feeling himself at liberty, he was even actually prepared to acknowledge himself the happiest of mortals, and thereupon go straight to his office—when suddenly his carriage rumbled up to the door: he glanced at it and remembered everything. Petrushka was already opening the carriage door. An odd and extremely unpleasant sensation gripped all of Mr. Golyadkin. He blushed, as it were, for a moment. Something seemed to stab him. He was just about to raise his foot to the carriage step when he suddenly turned around and looked toward Krestyan Ivanovich's window. Sure enough! Krestyan Ivanovich was standing at the window, stroking his whiskers with his right hand and staring with some curiosity at the hero of our story.

"That doctor is stupid," thought Mr. Golyadkin, huddling out of sight in the carriage; "extremely stupid. He may treat his patients all right, but still . . . he's a blockhead all the same."

Mr. Golyadkin sat down, Petrushka shouted, "Go ahead!" and the carriage rolled toward Nevsky Prospect again.

Chapter III

Mr. Golyadkin spent the whole morning madly bustling about. On reaching Nevsky Prospect our hero told the driver to stop at Gostiny Dvor.[1] Jumping out of his carriage, he ran to the arcade, accompanied by Petrushka, and went straight to a shop where gold and silver articles were for sale. One could see from his very air that he had his hands full and a terrible amount of business to transact. Having arranged by dint of much bragging to buy a complete set of dinner dishes, a tea service, a cigar case of in-

[1] A row of shops opening on an arcade.—A.Y.

genious shape, and a silver shaving set—all for the sum of fifteen hundred roubles—and finally, having priced some other articles, useful and agreeable in their own way, he ended by promising to come without fail next day, or to send for his purchases the same day. He took the number of the shop, and, listening attentively to the shopkeeper, who kept pressing for a deposit, said that he should have it in good time. After that he hurriedly took leave of the perplexed shopkeeper and, followed by a regular flock of salesmen, walked along the arcade, continually looking round at Petrushka and diligently seeking out new shops. On the way he dropped into a money-changer's and changed all his big notes into small ones, and though he lost on the exchange, his pocketbook was considerably fatter, which evidently afforded him extreme satisfaction. Finally, he stopped at a shop for ladies' dress materials. Here, too, after he picked out goods for a large sum, Mr. Golyadkin promised to come again, took the number of the shop, and, on being asked for a deposit, assured the shopkeeper that he should have a deposit too, in good time. Then he visited several other shops, picking out merchandise in each of them, pricing various items, sometimes haggling a long time with the shopkeeper, going out of the shop and returning two or three times—in fact he displayed exceptional activity. From Gostiny Dvor our hero went to a well-known furniture shop, where he ordered furniture for six rooms; he admired a fashionable and very fanciful ladies' dressing table in the latest style, and, assuring the shopkeeper that he would certainly send for all these things, walked out of the shop, as usual promising a deposit. Then he went off somewhere else and ordered more goods. In short, there seemed to be no end to the business he had to get through. At last, Mr. Golyadkin himself seemed to grow very tired of it all, and he began, goodness knows why, to be tormented by remorse. Nothing would have induced him now, for instance, to meet Andrey Filippovich, or even Krestyan Ivanovich.

Finally the town clock struck three. When Mr. Golyad-

kin at last took his seat in the carriage, a pair of gloves
and a bottle of scent that cost a rouble and a half were all
the purchases he had made that morning. As it was still
rather early, he ordered his coachman to stop near a well-
known restaurant on Nevsky Prospect which he only knew
by hearsay, got out of the carriage, and hurried in to have
a bite, to rest, and to kill time.

Having eaten as a man who has the prospect of a sumptuous dinner eats, that is, having a snack in order to still
the pangs, as they say, and having downed one small glass
of vodka, Mr. Golyadkin established himself in an armchair and, modestly looking about him, peacefully settled
down to a lean nationalist paper. After reading a couple
of lines he stood up and looked in the mirror, set himself
to rights, and smoothed himself down; then he went to the
window to see whether his carriage was there . . . then he
sat down again in his place and took up the paper. It was
noticeable that our hero was extremely agitated. Glancing
at his watch and seeing that it was only a quarter past
three and that he had consequently a long time to wait
and, at the same time, thinking that to sit like that was
unseemly, Mr. Golyadkin ordered a chocolate, though he
felt no particular inclination for it at the moment. Having
had the chocolate and noticing that the time had moved
on a little, he went up to pay his check. Suddenly someone
slapped him on the shoulder.

He turned around and saw facing him two of his colleagues, the same two he had met that morning on Liteyny
Street, young men, very much his juniors both in age and
in rank. Our hero's relations with them were neither one
thing nor the other, neither friendly nor openly hostile.
Proprieties were, of course, observed on both sides; there
was nothing like intimacy, nor could there be. The meeting
at this moment was extremely distasteful to Mr. Golyadkin.
He frowned a little, and grew confused for an instant.

"Yakov Petrovich, Yakov Petrovich!" chirped the two
registering clerks, "you here? What brings you?"

"Ah, it is you, gentlemen," Mr. Golyadkin interrupted

hurriedly, somewhat embarrassed and scandalized by the clerks' amazement and by the familiarity of their address, but willy-nilly assuming the free and easy manner of a fellow who is up to the mark. "So you've deserted the office, gentlemen, he—he—he. . . ." Then, to keep up his dignity and to patronize the youths, in dealing with whom he never overstepped certain limits, he attempted to slap one of the youths on the shoulder; but this attempt at good fellowship did not succeed and, instead of being a gesture of well-bred familiarity, turned out to be something entirely different.

"Well, and our bear, is he still at the office?"

"Who's that, Yakov Petrovich?"

"Why, the bear. Do you mean to say you don't know whose name that is?" Mr. Golyadkin laughed and turned to the cashier to take his change.

"I mean Andrey Filippovich, gentlemen," he went on, when he was through with the cashier, turning to the clerks this time with a very serious face. The two registrars winked at one another.

"He's still at the office and he asked for you, Yakov Petrovich," answered one of them.

"At the office, eh! In that case, let him stay, gentlemen. And he asked for me, eh?"

"He was asking for you, Yakov Petrovich; but what's up with you, scented, pomaded, and such a dandy?"

"Nothing, gentlemen, nothing! Leave off," answered Mr. Golyadkin, looking away with a strained smile. Seeing that Mr. Golyadkin was smiling, the clerks guffawed. Mr. Golyadkin was a little offended.

"I'll tell you as friends, gentlemen," our hero said, after a brief silence, as though deciding that he might as well reveal something to them. "You all know me, gentlemen, but hitherto you've known only one side of me. No one is to blame for that and I'm conscious that the fault has been partly my own."

Mr. Golyadkin compressed his lips and looked significantly at the clerks. The clerks winked at one another again.

"Hitherto, gentlemen, you have not known me. To explain myself here and now would not be quite appropriate. I shall only say something casually in passing. There are people, gentlemen, who dislike roundabout ways and only mask themselves at masquerades. There are people who do not see man's direct purpose in the adroit ability to polish the floor with their boots. There are people, gentlemen, who will not say that they are happy and that they enjoy a full life when, for instance, their trousers fit well. There are people, finally, who dislike dashing and whirling about to no purpose, fawning, and flirting, and above all, gentlemen, poking their noses where they are not wanted. . . . I've said almost everything, gentlemen; now allow me to withdraw. . . ."

Mr. Golyadkin paused. As the clerks had now got all that they wanted, both of them with extreme rudeness burst into shouts of laughter. Mr. Golyadkin flared up.

"Laugh away, gentlemen, laugh away for the time being! But when you are a bit older, you will see," he said, with a feeling of offended dignity, taking his hat and retreating to the door.

"But I will say more, gentlemen," he added, turning for the last time to the clerks, "I will say more—you are both here with me face to face. These are my rules, gentlemen: if I fail I don't lose heart, if I succeed I hold on, and in any case I don't try to trip up anyone. I'm not one to intrigue— and I'm proud of it. I'm not fit to be a diplomat. They say, too, gentlemen, that the ball comes to the player. It's true and I'm ready to admit it; but who's the player, and who's the ball in this case? That is still the question, gentlemen!"

Mr. Golyadkin subsided into eloquent silence, and, with a most significant air, that is, raising his eyebrows and compressing his lips as tight as possible, he bowed to the clerks and walked out, leaving them in utmost amazement.

"What are your orders now?" Petrushka asked rather gruffly; he was probably weary of staying out in the cold. "What are your orders?" he asked Mr. Golyadkin, meeting the terrible, withering glance with which our hero had protected himself twice already that morning, and to which he had recourse now for the third time as he came down the steps.

"To Izmailovsky Bridge."

"To Izmailovsky Bridge! Go ahead!"

"Dinner will not begin till after four, or perhaps at five o'clock," thought Mr. Golyadkin; "isn't it early now? I can be a little early, though; besides, it's only a family dinner. And so I can come *sans-façon,* as well-bred people put it. Why shouldn't I come *sans-façon?* The bear told us, too, that it would all be *sans-façon,* and so I too . . ." Such were Mr. Golyadkin's reflections; meanwhile his excitement grew more and more acute. It was obvious that he was preparing himself for something very troublesome, to say the least; he muttered to himself, gesticulated with his right hand, continually looked out of his carriage window, so that, seeing Mr. Golyadkin, no one would have said that he was on his way to a good dinner, and only a simple dinner in his family circle—*sans-façon,* as they say among well-bred people. Finally, just close to Izmailovsky Bridge, Mr. Golyadkin pointed out a house; and the carriage rolled noisily through the gateway and stopped at the first entrance on the right. Noticing a feminine figure at the second-story window, Mr. Golyadkin kissed his hand to her. He had, however, not the slightest idea what he was doing, for he felt more dead than alive at the moment. He got out of the carriage pale, distraught; he mounted the steps, took off his hat, mechanically set himself to rights, and, though feeling a slight tremor in his knees, went upstairs.

"Olsufy Ivanovich?" he inquired of the man who opened the door.

"At home, sir; that is, he's not at home, sir, his honor's not at home, sir."

"What? What do you mean, my good man? I—I've come to dinner, brother. You know me, don't you?"

"To be sure I know you! I've orders not to admit you, sir."

"You . . . you, brother . . . you must be making a mistake. It's me. I'm invited, old man; I've come to dinner,"

Mr. Golyadkin announced, taking off his coat and display-ing an unmistakable intention of going into the apartment.

"Allow me, sir, you can't, sir. I've orders not to admit you. I've orders to forbid you the house. That's how it is."

Mr. Golyadkin turned pale. At that very moment the door leading into the inner rooms opened and Gerasimych, Olsufy Ivanovich's old valet, came out.

"Here's the gentleman trying to go in, Emelyan Gera-simych, he wants to go in, and I . . ."

"And you're a fool, Alexeich. Go inside and send the rascal Semyonych here. It's impossible, sir," he said po-litely but firmly, addressing Mr. Golyadkin. "It's quite im-possible, sir. His honor begs you to excuse him, sir, he can't see you, sir."

"His honor said he couldn't see me?" Mr. Golyadkin asked uncertainly. "Excuse me, Gerasimych, why is it im-possible?"

"It's quite impossible, sir. His honor said, 'Ask him to excuse us.' His honor can't see you, sir."

"Why not? How's that? Why?"

"Allow me, allow me!"

"How is it, though? It isn't right! Announce me. . . . How is that? I've come to dinner. . . ."

"Allow me, allow me!"

"Ah, well, that's a different matter, his honor asked to be excused; but, allow me, Gerasimych; how is that, Gerasimych?"

"Allow me, allow me!" replied Gerasimych, very firmly brushing aside Mr. Golyadkin with his hand and making way for two gentlemen who walked into the entry that very instant. The gentlemen in question were Andrey Filippo-vich and his nephew, Vladimir Semyonovich. Both of them gave Mr. Golyadkin a puzzled look. Andrey Filippovich was on the point of saying something, but Mr. Golyadkin had by now made up his mind; he was by now walking out of Olsufy Ivanovich's entry, blushing and smiling, with eyes cast down and a countenance showing helpless bewilderment.

"I will come afterward, Gerasimych; I will have it out: I hope that all this will without delay be explained in due time," he said as he was crossing the threshold.

"Yakov Petrovich, Yakov Petrovich!" called Andrey Filippovich behind him.

Mr. Golyadkin was by that time on the first landing. He turned quickly to Andrey Filippovich.

"What can I do for you, Andrey Filippovich?" he said in a rather resolute voice.

"What's wrong with you, Yakov Petrovich? How do you . . . ?"

"No matter, Andrey Filippovich. I'm here on my own account. This is my private life, Andrey Filippovich."

"What's that?"

"I say, Andrey Filippovich, that this is my private life, and that, as far as I can see, there's nothing reprehensible to be found here touching my official relations."

"What? Touching your official . . . What's the matter with you, my good sir?"

"Nothing, Andrey Filippovich, absolutely nothing; an impudent hussy, and nothing more. . . ."

"What! What?" Andrey Filippovich was stupefied with amazement. Mr. Golyadkin, who, talking to Andrey Filippovich from below, had till then looked as though he would fly into Andrey Filippovich's face, seeing that the section head became somewhat flustered, almost unwittingly moved up a tread. Andrey Filippovich drew back. Mr. Golyadkin went up one step and then another. Andrey Filippovich looked about him uneasily. Mr. Golyadkin mounted the stairs rapidly. Still more rapidly Andrey Filippovich darted into the flat and slammed the door behind him.

Mr. Golyadkin was left alone. Everything went black before his eyes. He was utterly nonplused, and stood now in a sort of stupor, as though recalling something extremely preposterous that had happened quite recently. "Oh, oh!" he muttered, with a strained smile. Meanwhile, there was the sound of steps and voices from the stairs below, prob-

ably of other guests invited by Olsufy Ivanovich. Mr.
Golyadkin collected himself to some extent, put up his raccoon collar, concealing himself behind it as far as possible,
and began going downstairs mincing, limping, and stumbling in his haste. He felt weak and numb. His confusion
was such that, when he came out on the steps, he did not
even wait for his carriage but walked across the muddy
court to it. When he reached his carriage and was about
to get into it, Mr. Golyadkin inwardly betrayed a desire to
sink through the ground or to hide in a mousehole together
with his carriage. It seemed to him that everything in
Olsufy Ivanovich's house was looking at him now out of
every window. He knew that he would certainly die on the
spot if he were to turn round.

"What are you laughing at, blockhead?" he said in a
patter to Petrushka, who was on the point of helping him
into the carriage.

"What should I laugh at? I'm doing nothing; where to
now?"

"We'll go home. Drive on. . . ."

"Home! Go ahead!" shouted Petrushka, climbing on to
the footboard.

"What a crow's gullet!" thought Mr. Golyadkin. Meanwhile, the carriage had driven a good distance from Izmailovsky Bridge. Suddenly our hero pulled the cord with all
his might and shouted to the driver to turn back at once.
The coachman turned his horses and within two minutes
was driving into Olsufy Ivanovich's yard again.

"No, no, you fool, drive back!" shouted Mr. Golyadkin
—and, as though he were expecting this order, the coachman made no reply but, without stopping at the entrance,
drove all around the courtyard and out into the street again.

Mr. Golyadkin did not go home, but, after passing the
Semyonovsky Bridge, told the driver to turn into a side
street and stop near a restaurant of rather modest appearance. Getting out of the carriage, our hero paid off the
driver and so got rid of the carriage at last. He told Petrushka to go home and await his return, while he went into

the restaurant, took a private room, and ordered dinner. He felt very ill and his brain was in a state of utmost confusion and chaos. For a long time he paced the floor in agitation; at last he sat down in a chair, propped up his brow with his hands, and began trying his best to reflect on and settle some aspects of his present situation.

Chapter IV

The solemn day, the birthday of Klara Olsufyevna, the only daughter of the councilor of state, Berendeyev, Mr. Golyadkin's quondam benefactor was celebrated by a brilliant and sumptuous dinner party, such as had not been seen for many a long day within the walls of the functionaries' flats in the neighborhood of Izmailovsky Bridge—a dinner more like some Belshazzarian feast than an ordinary dinner, with a suggestion of something Babylonian in its brilliance, luxury, and decorum, with Veuve-Clicquot champagne, oysters and fruit from Eliseyev's and Milyutin's, with all sorts of fatted calves, and the entire table of ranks. This festive day was to conclude with a brilliant ball, a small family birthday ball, but yet brilliant in its taste, its cultural distinction, and decorum. Of course, I am willing to admit that similar balls do take place sometimes, though rarely. Such balls, more like family festivities than balls, can only be given in houses like that of the councilor of state.

I will say more: I even doubt if such balls could be given in the houses of all state councilors. Oh, if I were a poet! Such as Homer or Pushkin, I mean, of course; with any lesser talent one must not butt in—I should certainly have painted that entire glorious day for you, oh, my readers, with a broad brush and brilliant colors! No, I should have begun my epic with the dinner, I should have stressed that striking and solemn moment when the first goblet was raised to honor the queen of the fete. I should have first depicted to you the guests plunged in expectation, and a reverent silence more like the eloquence of Demosthenes than ordinary silence. I should then have described for you Andrey Filippovich, who as the eldest of the guests has some right to take precedence. Adorned with gray hair and the orders that befit gray hair, he got up from his seat and raised above his head a glass of the sparkling wine that is brought from a distant kingdom expressly to down on such occasions and that is more like heavenly nectar than wine. I should have depicted for you the guests and the happy parents of the queen of the fete, as they too raised their glasses after Andrey Filippovich and fastened on him eyes full of expectation. I should have pictured for you how the oft-mentioned Andrey Filippovich, having first dropped a tear in the glass, offered his congratulations and good wishes, proposed a toast, and drank the young lady's health. But I confess fully I could not have done justice to the solemn moment when Klara Olsufyevna herself, the queen of the fete, blushing like a vernal rose with bliss and modesty and overcome by emotion, sank into the arms of her tender mother, whereat that tender mother gave way to tears, and the father, Olsufy Ivanovich, a venerable old man and a privy councilor, who had lost the use of his legs in the long years of service and been rewarded by destiny for his devotion with a bank roll, a house, lands, and a beautiful daughter—the father himself sobbed like a little child and announced through his tears that his Excellency was a beneficent man. I could not, I positively could not, describe the rapture that forthwith possessed every heart, a rapture clearly evinced in the conduct of a youthful registrar (though at that moment he was more like a councilor of state than a registering clerk), who was moved to tears, too, as he listened to Andrey Filippovich. In his turn, too, Andrey Filippovich was at that solemn moment quite unlike a collegiate councilor and section head in the department—yes, he was something else . . . what, exactly, I do not know, but not a collegiate councilor. He was something more exalted! Finally . . .

Oh, why do I not possess the secret of lofty, powerful style, the sublime style, to describe these grand and edifying moments of human life, which seem created expressly to prove that virtue sometimes triumphs over disloyalty, free-thinking, vice, and envy! I shall say nothing, but in silence —which will be better than any eloquence—I will point to that fortunate youth, just entering on his twenty-sixth spring—to Vladimir Semyonovich, Andrey Filippovich's nephew, who in his turn now rose from his seat, who in his turn proposed a toast, and upon whom were fastened the tearful eyes of the parents, the proud eyes of Andrey Filippovich, the bashful eyes of the queen of the fete herself, the enraptured eyes of the guests, and even the decorously envious eyes of some of the young man's youthful colleagues. I shall say nothing of that, though I cannot refrain from observing that everything in that young man— who was, indeed, speaking in a complimentary sense, more like an elderly than a young man—everything, from his ruddy cheeks to his assessorial rank at this solemn moment, seemed almost to proclaim aloud the lofty pinnacle a man can attain through good conduct!

I shall not describe how Anton Antonovich Syetochkin, a little old man hoary with age, the head clerk of a department, who was a colleague of Andrey Filippovich's and a quondam colleague of Olsufy Ivanovich's, as well as an old friend of the family and Klara Olsufyevna's godfather, in his turn proposed a toast, crowed like a cock, and recited some light verse; how by this extremely proper breach of propriety, if one may use such an expression, he made the whole company laugh till they cried, and how Klara Olsufyevna, at her parents' bidding, rewarded him for his hilarity and courtesy with a kiss. I shall only say that the guests, who after such a dinner could not but feel like kinsfolk and brothers, at last rose from the table, and that the elderly and the sedate guests, after a brief interval spent in friendly conversation, interspersed with some candid, though, of course, very polite and proper avowals, went decorously into the next room and, without losing valuable time, promptly divided into parties and, full of the sense of their own dignity, installed themselves at tables covered with green baize. Meanwhile, the ladies established in the drawing room suddenly became very affable and began talking about dress materials. At last the venerable host himself, who had lost the use of his legs while faithfully serving the state, and had been rewarded with all the blessings we have enumerated above, began walking on crutches among his guests, supported by Vladimir Semyonovich and Klara Olsufyevna, and he, too, suddenly becoming extremely affable, decided to improvise a modest little ball, regardless of expense; to that end a nimble youth (the one who was more like a councilor of state than a youth) was dispatched to fetch musicians, and musicians to the number of eleven arrived, and exactly at half-past eight struck up the inviting strains of a French quadrille, followed by various other dances. . . .

It is needless to say that my pen is too weak, dull, and spiritless to describe the ball improvised by the extraordinary hospitality of the gray-headed host. And how, I ask, can the modest chronicler of Mr. Golyadkin's adventures, extremely curious though they are in their own way, how can I depict this remarkable and refined amalgam of beauty, brilliance, seemliness, gaiety, amiable sedateness and sedate amiability, vivacity, joy, all the mirth and playfulness of these wives and daughters of officials, more like fairies than ladies—in a complimentary sense—with their lily shoulders and rosy faces, their ethereal figures, their playfully agile, homeopathic—to use exalted language—little feet? Finally, how can I describe to you these officials, their brilliant partners—the gay and the stolid, the young and the staid, the merry and the decorously vague, the ones who smoke a pipe in the intervals between the dances in a distant little green room, and those who do not smoke a pipe in the intervals between the dances—partners every one of whom has a respectable surname and rank. All of them are imbued with a taste for the elegant and a sense of their dignity, and almost all speak French to their ladies, or if Russian, use only the most well-bred expressions, compliments, and profound observations, and only in the smoking room permit themselves some genial lapses from this high tone, some phrases of cordial and friendly intimacy, such, for instance, as: "'Pon my soul, Pete, you rascal, you did kick off that polka in style," or, "I say, Vasya, you so-and-so, you did take your dame firmly in hand!" My pen is unequal to all this, as I've already had the honor of explaining to you, gentle reader! Therefore I keep silent. Let us rather return to Mr. Golyadkin, the true and only hero of our very truthful tale.

The fact is that he found himself now in a position that was very strange, to say the least. He was there also, gentlemen—that is, not at the ball, but almost at the ball; he was, all right though he was by himself, yet at this moment he was a little astray; he was standing at that moment— strange to say—on the back entry of Olsufy Ivanovich's flat. But it was all right, his standing there; he was so-so. He was standing in a corner, huddled in a place which was not very warm, but quite dark, partly hidden by a huge cupboard and an old screen, in the midst of rubbish, litter, and odds and ends of all sorts, concealing himself for the time being and watching the course of proceedings as a disinterested spectator. He was only looking on now, gentlemen; he, too, gentlemen, might go in, of course . . . why shouldn't he go in? He had only to take one step and he would go in, and would go in very adroitly. Just now, though he had been standing nearly three hours in the cold between the cupboard and the screen in the midst of the rubbish, litter, and odds and ends of all sorts, he was quoting, in his own justification, a phrase of the late lamented French minister, Villeyle: "All things come in time to him who has the gumption to wait." Mr. Golyadkin had read this sentence in some book on quite a different subject, but now very aptly recalled it. The phrase, to begin with, was exceedingly appropriate to his present position, and, indeed, why shouldn't it occur to a man who had been waiting for almost three hours in the cold and the dark in expectation of a happy denouement to his adventures. After quoting very appropriately the phrase of the French minister, Villeyle, as has been said, Mr. Golyadkin immediately recalled, for no known reason, the Turkish Vizier, Martzimiris, as well as the beautiful Margravine Luise, whose history he had read also in some book. Then the thought crossed his mind that the Jesuits made it their rule that the end justifies the means. Having fortified himself somewhat with this historical fact, Mr. Golyadkin said to himself: What were the Jesuits? The Jesuits were every one of them very great fools; that he could outdo all of them; that if only the pantry would be empty for one minute (the door of the pantry opened straight into the passage to the back stairs, where Mr. Golyadkin was in hiding now), he would, in spite of all the Jesuits in the world, go straight in, first from the pantry into the tearoom, then into the room where they were now playing cards, and then straight into the hall where they were now dancing the polka. And he would go in, he would certainly go in, in spite of anything he would go in—he would slip in—and that would be all, no one would notice him; and once there he would know what to do.

Well, so this is the position in which we find the hero of our perfectly true story, though, indeed, it is difficult to explain what was going on in his mind at that moment. The fact is that he had made his way to the back stairs and to the passage, on the ground that, as he said to himself, why shouldn't he? Everyone did; but he had not ventured to penetrate farther, evidently he did not dare to do so. . . . Not because he really did not dare, but just because he did not care to, because he preferred to act on the quiet. So here he was, waiting now for a chance to slip in, and he had been waiting for it two hours and a half. "Why not wait? Villeyle himself had waited. But what had Villeyle to do with it?" thought Mr. Golyadkin: "How does Villeyle come in? But how am I to . . . to go and penetrate? . . . Oh, you dummy!" said Mr. Golyadkin, pinching his benumbed cheek with his benumbed fingers; "you silly fool, you silly old Golyadkin—the fool of a surname!"

But these compliments paid to himself were only by the way and without any apparent aim. Now he was on the point of pushing forward and slipping in; the moment had come, the refreshment pantry was empty, and no one was in sight. Mr. Golyadkin saw all this through the window; with two steps he was at the door and began already to open it. "Should I go in or not? Come, should I or not? I'll go in . . . why not? To the bold all ways lie open!" Having reassured himself in this way, our hero suddenly and quite unexpectedly retreated behind the screen. "No," he thought. "What if somebody came in? Yes, they've come in; why did I dawdle when there were no people about? Even so, shall I go and slip in? . . . No, how slip in when a man has such a character! Fie, what a vile tendency! I got scared like a chicken! Being scared is our special line, that's the fact of the matter! Always playing scurvy tricks is our line; no need to ask us about that. Just stand here like a post, and that's all! At home I should be having a cup of tea. If I come in later Petrushka'll grumble, maybe. Shall I go home? Damnation take all this! I'll go and that'll be the end of it!"

Having settled the matter in this way, Mr. Golyadkin dashed forward as though someone had touched a spring in him; with two steps he found himself in the pantry, flung off his overcoat, took off his hat, hurriedly thrust these things into a corner, set himself to rights and smoothed himself down; then . . . then he moved on to the tearoom, and from the tearoom darted into the next room, slipped almost unnoticed among the excited card-players, then . . . Mr. Golyadkin forgot everything that was going on about him, and appeared like a bolt from the blue in the dance hall.

As ill-luck would have it, there was no dancing. The ladies were promenading up and down the room in picturesque groups. The gentlemen were standing about in groups or flitting about the room engaging partners. Mr.

Golyadkin noticed nothing of this. He saw only Klara Olsufyevna, near her Andrey Filippovich, then Vladimir Semyonovich, two or three officers, and, finally, two or three other young men who were also very interesting and, as anyone could see at a glance, promised well or actually had some achievements to their credit. . . . He saw some other people, too. Or, rather, he saw nobody and looked at nobody . . . but, moved by the same spring which had sent him dashing into the midst of a ball to which he had not been invited, he moved forward, and then on and on. On the way he jostled against a councilor and trod on his foot, and incidentally stepped on a very venerable old lady's dress and tore it a little, pushed against a servant with a tray, and then ran against somebody else, and, not noticing all this, or rather noticing it but at the same time looking at no one, prancing his way farther and farther forward, he suddenly found himself facing Klara Olsufyevna. There is no doubt whatever that he would, with the utmost delight, without winking an eye, have sunk through the floor at that moment; but what has once been done cannot be undone . . . can never be undone. What was he to do? "If I fail I don't lose heart, if I succeed I hold on." Mr. Golyadkin was, of course, not one to intrigue, nor accomplished in the art of polishing the floor with his boots. . . . And so, indeed, it proved. Besides, the Jesuits had a hand in it too . . . though Mr. Golyadkin had no thoughts to spare for them now! All the moving, noisy, talking, laughing groups were suddenly hushed as though at a signal and, little by little, crowded around Mr. Golyadkin. He, however, seemed to hear nothing, to see nothing, he could not look . . . he could not possibly look at anything; he kept his eyes on the floor and so stood, having vowed to himself, in passing, that he would shoot himself that same night. Having made this vow, Mr. Golyadkin inwardly said to himself, "Here goes!" and to his own great astonishment began unexpectedly to speak.

He began with congratulations and proper wishes. The congratulations went off well, but over the good wishes our hero stumbled. He had felt that should he stammer, all would be lost at once. And so it turned out—he stumbled and got stuck . . . having got stuck, he blushed crimson; having blushed, he was overcome with confusion. In his confusion he raised his eyes; having raised his eyes, he looked about him; having looked about him—he almost swooned. . . . Everyone stood still, everyone was silent, everyone was waiting; a little way off there was whispering; a little nearer there was laughter. Mr. Golyadkin darted a humble, imploring look at Andrey Filippovich. Andrey Filippovich responded with such a look that if our hero had not been utterly crushed already he certainly would have been crushed a second time—that is, if that were possible. There was a long silence.

"This rather concerns my domestic circumstances and my private life, Andrey Filippovich," our hero, half-dead, articulated in a scarcely audible voice; "it is not an official incident, Andrey Filippovich. . . ."

"For shame, sir, for shame!" Andrey Filippovich brought out in a half-whisper, with an indescribable air of indignation; he pronounced these words and, giving Klara Olsufyevna his arm, turned away from Mr. Golyadkin.

"I've nothing to be ashamed of, Andrey Filippovich," answered Mr. Golyadkin, also in a whisper, looking around miserably, trying helplessly to discover in the perplexed crowd something with which he could retrieve his social position.

"It's nothing, nothing, gentlemen! Why, what's the matter? It could happen to anyone," whispered Mr. Golyadkin, moving a little away and trying to escape from the crowd surrounding him.

They made way for him. Our hero passed through two rows of inquisitive and wondering spectators. Fate drew him on. It was fate, he himself felt, that was leading him on. He would have given a great deal, of course, for a chance to be back in the passage by the back stairs, without having committed a breach of propriety; but as that was utterly impossible he began trying to creep away into a corner and to stand there—modestly, decorously, apart, without interfering with anyone, without attracting special attention, but at the same time winning the favor of his host and the company. At the same time Mr. Golyadkin felt as though the ground were giving way under him, as though he were staggering, falling. At last he made his way to a corner and stood in it, like an outsider, a rather indifferent spectator, leaning his arms on the backs of two chairs, taking complete possession of them in that way, and trying, as far as he could, to glance briskly at the guests grouped about him. Standing nearest him was an officer, a tall and handsome fellow, beside whom Golyadkin felt himself a small insect.

"These two chairs, lieutenant, are intended, one for Klara Olsufyevna, and the other for Princess Chevchehanov who is dancing. I'm keeping these seats for them," said Mr. Golyadkin breathlessly, turning his imploring eyes on the officer. The lieutenant said nothing, but turned away with a murderous smile. Checked in this direction, our hero was about to try his luck in another quarter, and directly addressed an important councilor with a cross of great distinction on his neck. But the councilor looked him up and down with such a frigid stare that Mr. Golyadkin felt distinctly as though a whole tubful of cold water had been thrown over him. He subsided into silence. He made up his mind to keep quiet, not to open his mouth, to show that he was quite all right, that he was like everyone else, and that his situation, as far as he could see, was quite a proper one. With this object he riveted his gaze to the cuff of his coat, then raised his eyes and fixed them upon a very respectable-looking gentleman. "That gentleman has a wig on," thought Mr. Golyadkin; "and if he takes off that wig he will be bald, his head will be as bare as the palm of my hand." Having made this important discovery, Mr. Golyadkin thought of the Arab emirs, whose heads are left bare and shaven if they take off the green turbans they wear as a sign of their descent from the prophet Mahomet. Then, probably from some special association of his ideas with the Turks, he thought of Turkish slippers and at once, apropos of that, recalled the fact that Andrey Filippovich was wearing boots that were more like slippers than boots.

It was evident that Mr. Golyadkin had to some extent fitted himself into his situation. "If that chandelier," flashed through his mind, "were to come down from the ceiling and fall upon the company, I should rush at once to save Klara Olsufyevna. Having saved her, I'd say to her, 'Don't be alarmed, madam, it's nothing. I'm your rescuer.' Then . . ." At that moment Mr. Golyadkin looked about in search of Klara Olsufyevna, and saw Gerasimych, Olsufy Ivanovich's old valet. Gerasimych, with a most solicitous and solemnly official air, was making straight for him. Mr. Golyadkin started and frowned due to an unaccountable but most disagreeable sensation; he looked about him mechanically. If only he could somehow creep off somewhere, unobserved, on the sly, it occurred to him, simply efface himself, that is, behave as though he had nothing at all to do with it all! . . . But before our hero could make up his mind to do anything, Gerasimych was standing before him.

"You see, Gerasimych," said our hero, with a little smile, addressing Gerasimych; "go and tell them—do you see the candle there in the chandelier, Gerasimych—it will be falling down directly: so, you know, you must tell them to see to it; it really will fall down, Gerasimych. . . ."

"The candle? No, the candle's standing straight; but somebody is asking for you, sir."

"Who is asking for me, Gerasimych?"

"I really can't say, sir, who it is. A man with a message. 'Is Yakov Petrovich Golyadkin here?' says he. 'Then call him out,' says he, 'on very urgent and important business. . . .' That's how it is, sir."

"No, Gerasimych, you are making a mistake; there you are making a mistake, Gerasimych."

"I doubt it, sir."

"No, Gerasimych, it isn't doubtful; there's nothing doubtful about it, Gerasimych. Nobody's asking for me, but I'm quite at home here—that is, in my right place, Gerasimych."

Mr. Golyadkin took breath and looked about him. Yes! everyone in the room was staring at him and listening in a sort of solemn expectation. The men had crowded a little nearer and were all attention. A little farther away the ladies were whispering together anxiously. The master of the house made his appearance at no great distance from Mr. Golyadkin, and though it was impossible to tell from his expression that he, too, was taking a close and direct interest in Mr. Golyadkin's situation, for everything was being done with delicacy, nevertheless, it all made our hero feel that the decisive moment had come for him. Mr. Golyadkin saw clearly that the time had come for a bold stroke, the chance of bringing shame on his enemies. Mr. Golyadkin was agitated. He felt a sort of inspiration, and, in a quivering and impressive voice, he began again, addressing the waiting valet.

"No, my dear fellow, no one's calling for me. You are mistaken. I will say more: you were mistaken this morning, too, when you assured me . . . dared to assure me, I say," (he raised his voice), "that Olsufy Ivanovich, who has been my benefactor as long as I can remember and has, in a sense, been a father to me, was shutting his door upon me at the moment when a solemn family event rejoiced his paternal heart." (Mr. Golyadkin looked about him complacently, but with deep feeling. Tears welled up in his eyes.) "I repeat, my friend," our hero concluded, "you were mistaken, you were cruelly, unpardonably mistaken. . . ."

The moment was a solemn one. Mr. Golyadkin felt that the effect was quite certain. He stood with modestly downcast eyes, expecting Olsufy Ivanovich to embrace him. The guests showed signs of agitation and perplexity; even the inflexible and terrible Gerasimych faltered over the words "I doubt it . . ." when suddenly the ruthless orchestra, apropos of nothing, struck up a polka. All was lost, all was scattered to the winds. Mr. Golyadkin started; Gerasimych stepped back; everything in the room began billowing like

the sea; and Vladimir Semyonovich led the dance with
Klara Olsufyevna, while the handsome lieutenant followed
with Princess Chevchehanov. Onlookers, curious and delighted, crowded in to watch the couples dancing the
polka—an interesting, fashionable new dance which turned
everyone's head. Mr. Golyadkin was, for the time, forgotten.
But suddenly the company was thrown into excitement,
confusion, and commotion, the music ceased . . . a strange
incident occurred. Tired out with the dance, and almost
breathless with fatigue, Klara Olsufyevna, with glowing
cheeks and heaving bosom, sank into an armchair, completely exhausted. All hearts turned to the fascinating
charmer, all vied with one another in complimenting her
and thanking her for the pleasure conferred on them, when
suddenly there stood before her Mr. Golyadkin. He was
pale, extremely perturbed; he, too, seemed completely exhausted, he could scarcely move. He was smiling for some
reason, he stretched out his hand imploringly. Klara Olsufyevna was so taken aback that she had not time to withdraw hers and mechanically got up at the invitation. Mr.
Golyadkin lurched forward, first once, then a second time,
then lifted his leg, then made a scrape, then gave a sort of
stamp, then stumbled . . . he, too, wanted to dance with
Klara Olsufyevna. Klara Olsufyevna screamed; everyone
rushed to free her hand from Mr. Golyadkin's, and in a
moment our hero was carried almost ten paces away by
the rush of the crowd. A circle formed around him too.
Two old ladies, whom he had almost knocked down in his
retreat, raised a great squeal and outcry. The commotion
was awful; all were asking questions, shouting, arguing.
The orchestra lapsed into silence. Our hero was turning
around in his circle and mechanically, with a semblance
of a smile, muttering something to himself, such as, "Why
not?" The polka, so far, at least, as he could see, was a new
and very interesting dance, invented for the diversion of
the ladies . . . but since things had taken this turn, he was
ready to agree. But no one apparently thought of asking
Mr. Golyadkin's consent. Our hero became suddenly aware

that someone's hand was laid on his arm, that another hand pressed against his back, that he was with peculiar solicitude being guided in a certain direction.

At last he noticed that he was going straight to the door. Mr. Golyadkin wanted to say something, to do something. . . . But, no, he no longer wanted anything. He only mechanically kept tittering. At last he felt that they were putting his greatcoat on him, that his hat was pulled over his eyes; then he discovered that he was in the entry on the stairs in the dark and cold and finally on the stairs. At last he stumbled, and it seemed to him that he was falling down a precipice; he tried to cry out—and suddenly found himself in the courtyard. He felt a gust of fresh air and stood still for a minute; at that very instant, the strains of the orchestra striking up again reached his ears. Mr. Golyadkin suddenly recalled everything; all his flagging energies seemed to come back to him again. He had been standing as though riveted to the spot, but now he started off and rushed away headlong, anywhere, into the air, into the open, wherever chance might take him.

Chapter V

It was striking midnight from all the clock towers in Petersburg when Mr. Golyadkin, beside himself, ran out on the Fontanka quay, close to the Izmailovsky Bridge, fleeing from his foes, from persecution, from a hailstorm of fillips aimed at him, from the shrieks of excited old ladies, from the Ohs and Ahs of other women, and from the murderous eyes of Andrey Filippovich. Mr. Golyadkin was killed— killed entirely, in the full sense of the word, and if he still preserved the ability to run, it was simply through some sort of miracle, a miracle in which at last he himself refused to believe. It was an awful November night—wet, foggy, rainy, snowy, fraught with colds in the head, fevers, swollen faces, quinseys, inflammations of all kinds and descriptions

—fraught, in short, with all the gifts of a Petersburg November. The wind howled in the deserted streets, lifting up the black water of the canal above the rings, and perkily brushing against the lean lanterns on the embankment, so that they chimed in with the howling in a thin, shrill creak, keeping up the endless squeaky, jangling concert with which every inhabitant of Petersburg is so familiar. It was both snowing and raining. Lashed by the wind, the streams of rain water spurted almost horizontally, as though from a fireman's hose, pricking and stinging the face of the luckless Mr. Golyadkin like a thousand pins and needles. In the stillness of the night, broken only by the distant rumbling of carriages, the howl of the wind, and the creaking of the lanterns, there was the dismal sound of the splash and gurgle of water, streaming from every roof, every porch, every gutter, and every cornice, onto the granite of the pavement. There was not a soul, near or far, and, indeed, it seemed that there could not be any at such an hour and in such weather. And so only Mr. Golyadkin, alone with his despair, was trotting mincingly along the pavement of Fontanka, in haste to reach as soon as possible his flat on the fourth story in Shestilavochny Street.

Though the snow, the rain, and all the nameless horrors of a raging snowstorm and fog, under a Petersburg November sky, suddenly attacked Mr. Golyadkin, already shattered by misfortunes, showing him no mercy, giving him no rest, drenching him to the bone, glueing up his eyelids, blowing right through him from all sides, leading him astray and perplexing him—though all this was hurled upon Mr. Golyadkin at once, as though conspiring and combining with all his enemies to provide him with a grand day, evening, and night, in spite of all this Mr. Golyadkin was almost insensible to this final proof of the hostility of destiny: so violently had he been shaken and shocked by what had happened a few minutes before at Berendyev's! If any disinterested spectator could have glanced casually at Mr. Golyadkin's painful progress, he too would instantly have grasped the awful horror of his pitiful plight and would certainly have said that Mr. Golyadkin looked as though he wanted to hide somewhere from himself, as though he were trying to run away from himself! Yes! It was really so. One may say more: Mr. Golyadkin wanted not only to run away from himself, but to be obliterated, to cease to be, to turn into dust. At the moment he understood nothing of what was going on about him, paid no attention to his surroundings, and looked as though the miseries of the inclement night, of the long tramp, the rain, the snow, the wind, all the cruelty of the weather, did not exist for him. The galosh that slipped off the boot on Mr. Golyadkin's right foot was left behind in the snow and slush on the sidewalk of Fontanka, and Mr. Golyadkin did not think of turning back to get it, did not, in fact, notice that he had lost it. He was so perplexed that, in spite of everything around him, he stood several times stock-still in the middle of the sidewalk, completely possessed by the thought of his recent horrible downfall; at those moments he would die, vanish; then he would suddenly set off again like a madman and would run, run without looking back, as though he were pursued, as though he were fleeing from some still more awful calamity. . . . The position was truly awful! . . .

At last, completely exhausted, Mr. Golyadkin halted, leaned on the railing in the position of a man whose nose has suddenly begun to bleed, and began looking intently at the black, turbid waters of the canal. There is no telling how much time he was thus occupied. All that is known is that at that instant Mr. Golyadkin reached such a pitch of despair, was so harassed, so tortured, so exhausted, and so dispirited that he forgot everything, forgot the Izmailovsky Bridge, forgot Shestilavochny Street, forgot his present plight. . . . After all, what did it matter? It made no difference to him: the thing was done, finished, the verdict was confirmed and signed; what did he care?

All at once . . . all at once he started and involuntarily jumped aside a couple of paces. With unaccountable uneasiness he began gazing about him; but no one was there, nothing special had happened, and yet . . . and yet it seemed to him that just now, that very minute, someone was standing near him, beside him, also leaning on the railing, and—marvelous to relate!—had even said something to him, said something quickly, abruptly, not quite intelligibly, but something very close to him, something concerning him. "Well, was it only my imagination?" said Mr. Golyadkin, looking around once more. "But where am I standing? . . . Och, Och," he concluded, shaking his head. He began gazing with an uneasy, miserable feeling, indeed with fear, into the damp, murky distance, straining his vision and doing his utmost to pierce with his nearsighted eyes the wet expanse that stretched before him. There was nothing new, however, nothing special caught Mr. Golyadkin's eye. Everything seemed to be all right, as it should be, that is, the snow was falling more heavily, more thickly, and in larger flakes, nothing could be seen twenty paces away, the lanterns creaked more shrilly than ever, and the wind seemed to intone its melancholy song even more tearfully, more piteously, like an importunate beggar whining for a copper to get a crust of bread. "Oh, oh, what's the matter with me?" Mr. Golyadkin repeated, starting on his journey again and still looking around him. At the same time a new sensation took possession of Mr. Golyadkin's whole being: it was anguish and not anguish, fear and not fear . . . a feverish tremor ran through his veins. The moment was insufferable! "Well, no matter; perhaps it's no matter at all, and there's no stain on anyone's honor. Perhaps it's as it should be," he went on, without understanding what he was saying. "Perhaps it will all be for the best in the end, and there will be no cause for complaint and everyone will be acquitted."

Talking like this and comforting himself with words, Mr. Golyadkin shook himself a little, brought down the snow which had drifted in thick layers on his hat, his collar, his overcoat, his tie, his boots, and everything—but his strange feeling, his strange, dark misery he could not push away, could not shake off. Somewhere in the distance there was the boom of a cannon shot. "What weather!" thought our hero. "Is there going to be a flood? The water seems to have risen very high."

Mr. Golyadkin had hardly said or thought this when he saw a passer-by coming toward him, by chance, belated, no doubt, like himself. An unimportant, casual incident, one might suppose, but for some unknown reason Mr. Golyadkin was troubled, even scared, and rather flurried. Not that he was exactly afraid of some ill-intentioned man, but just so . . . "Who knows who this belated individual is?" flashed through Mr. Golyadkin's mind. "Maybe he too is . . . maybe he's the main thing in it, and isn't here for nothing, but is here with an object, crossing my path and provoking me." Possibly, however, he did not think this precisely, but only had a passing feeling of something like it—and something very unpleasant. There was no time for thinking and feeling though. The stranger was already within two paces. Mr. Golyadkin, as he invariably did, hastened to assume a quite peculiar air, an air which said clearly that he, Golyadkin, kept himself to himself, that he was all right, that the road was wide enough for all, and that he, Golyadkin, was not interfering with anyone. Suddenly he stopped dead in his tracks as though struck by lightning, and quickly turned around after the figure which had only just passed him—turned as though someone had tugged him from behind, as though the wind had turned him like a weathercock. The passer-by was quickly vanishing in the snowstorm. He, too, walked quickly; he was dressed just like Mr. Golyadkin and, like him, wrapped up from head to foot, and he, too, trotted along the pavement of Fontanka with rapid little steps which suggested that he was a little scared.

"What—what is it?" whispered Mr. Golyadkin, smiling mistrustfully, but he trembled all over. An icy shiver ran down his spine. Meanwhile, the stranger had vanished completely; even the sound of his steps was no longer heard.

But Mr. Golyadkin still stood and gazed after him. At last, however, he gradually came to himself.

"What's the meaning of it?" he thought with vexation. "Why, have I really gone out of my mind?" He turned and went on his way, walking faster and faster, and trying not to think of anything at all. He even closed his eyes at last with the same object. Suddenly, above the howling of the wind and the noise of the downpour, the sound of steps very close at hand reached his ears again. He started and opened his eyes. Again a rapidly approaching figure showed black before him, some twenty paces away. This little figure was hastening, tripping along, hurrying; the distance between them diminished rapidly. Mr. Golyadkin could by now get a full view of his second belated companion. He made him out, and screamed with amazement and horror; his legs gave way under him. It was the same pedestrian who had passed him ten minutes before, and who now quite unexpectedly appeared before him again. But this was not the only marvel that struck Mr. Golyadkin. He was so amazed that he stood still, cried out, was on the point of saying something, and rushed to overtake the stranger, even shouted something to him, probably anxious to stop him as quickly as possible. The stranger did, in fact, stop some ten paces from Mr. Golyadkin, so that the light from the lantern that stood nearby fell full upon his whole figure—stood still, turned to Mr. Golyadkin, and with an impatient and anxious air waited to hear what he would say.

"Excuse me, possibly I'm mistaken," our hero brought out in a quavering voice.

The stranger in silence, and with an air of annoyance, turned and rapidly went on his way, as though in haste to make up for the two seconds he had wasted on Mr. Golyadkin. As for the latter, he was quivering in every nerve, his knees shook and gave way under him, and with a moan he sat down on a sidewalk post. There really was reason, however, for his being so overwhelmed. The fact is that now this stranger somehow seemed to him familiar. That

48

would have been nothing, though. But he recognized, almost certainly recognized this man. He had often seen him,
that man, had seen him some time in the past, and very
lately too; where could it have been? Perhaps even yesterday? But, again, that Mr. Golyadkin had often seen him
before was not the chief thing; there was hardly anything
special about the man; at first sight the man would not
have aroused any special attention. He was just a man like
anyone else, a decent fellow like all other decent fellows,
of course, and perhaps he was a man of merit and considerable merit, too—in short, he was a man who was by
himself. Mr. Golyadkin did not ever harbor any hatred or
enmity, not even the slightest hostility toward this man—
indeed, quite the contrary, it would seem—and yet (and
this was the real point) he would not for any treasure on
earth have been willing to meet that man, and especially
to meet him as he had done now, for instance. We may
say more: Mr. Golyadkin knew that man perfectly well;
he even knew what his full name was; and yet nothing
would have induced him, and again, for no treasure on
earth would he have consented to name him, to consent to
acknowledge that he was called so-and-so, that his patro-
nymic was this and his surname was that.

Whether Mr. Golyadkin's quandary lasted a short time
or a long time, whether he was sitting for a long time on
the sidewalk post, I cannot say; but, recovering himself a
little at last, he suddenly fell to running, without looking
around, as fast as his legs could carry him; he was out of
breath, twice he stumbled and almost fell—and through
this circumstance his other boot was also orphaned of its
galosh. At last Mr. Golyadkin slackened his pace a little
to take breath, looked hurriedly around, and saw that he
had already, without being aware of it, run all along Fontanka, had crossed the Anichkov Bridge, had covered part
of Nevsky Prospect, and was now standing at the corner of
Liteyny Street. Mr. Golyadkin turned into Liteyny Street.
His condition at that instant was like that of a man standing at the edge of a fearful precipice, while the earth is

crumbling under him, is already shaking, moving, rocking for the last time, plunging downward, drawing him into the abyss, and yet the luckless wretch has not the vigor, or the strength of mind, to leap back to avert his eyes from the yawning chasm; the abyss draws him and at last he leaps into it, himself hastening the moment of his destruction.

Mr. Golyadkin knew, felt, and was firmly convinced that some other evil would certainly befall him on the way, that some unpleasantness would overtake him, that he would, for instance, meet his stranger once more: but, oddly enough, he positively desired this meeting, considered it inevitable, and all he asked was that it might all be quickly over, that his situation should be cleared up in one way or another, but as soon as possible. And meanwhile he ran on and on, as though moved by some external force, for he felt a weakness and numbness in his whole being; he could not think of anything, though his thoughts caught at everything like brambles. A little lost dog, soaked and shivering, attached itself to Mr. Golyadkin, and ran beside him, scurrying along with its tail between its legs and ears drooping, looking at him from time to time with timid comprehension. Some remote, long-forgotten idea—a memory of something that had happened long ago—came into his mind now, kept knocking at his brain as with a hammer, vexing him and refusing to be shaken off. "That horrid little curl!" whispered Mr. Golyadkin, not understanding himself.

At last he saw his stranger at the corner of Italyansky Street. But this time the stranger was not coming to meet him, but was going in the same direction as he was, and he, too, was running, a few steps ahead. At last they turned into Shestilavochny Street. This took Mr. Golyadkin's breath away. The stranger stopped right before the house in which Mr. Golyadkin lodged. He heard a ring at the bell and almost at the same time the grating of the iron bolt. The wicket gate opened, the stranger stooped, flashed by, and disappeared. Almost at the same instant Mr. Golyadkin reached the spot and like an arrow darted in at the gate. Heedless of the grumbling porter, he ran, gasping for breath, into the yard, and immediately saw his interesting companion, whom he had lost sight of for a moment.

The stranger appeared for a moment at the entrance to the staircase which led to Mr. Golyadkin's flat. Mr. Golyadkin rushed after him. The stairs were dark, damp, and dirty. At every turning there were heaps of all kinds of trash from the flats, so that an unaccustomed stranger who found himself on the stairs in the dark was forced to climb them for half an hour in danger of breaking his legs, cursing the stairs as well as the friends who lived in such an inconvenient place. But Mr. Golyadkin's companion seemed to be familiar with it, as though he were at home; he ran up lightly, without difficulty, showing a perfect knowledge of the locale. Mr. Golyadkin had almost overtaken him; in fact, once or twice the skirt of the stranger's coat flicked him on the nose. His heart stood still. The stranger stopped before the door of Mr. Golyadkin's flat, knocked on it, and (which would have surprised Mr. Golyadkin at any other time) Petrushka, as though he had been waiting up, opened the door at once and, with a candle in his hand, followed the stranger as the latter went in. Beside himself, the hero of our story dashed into his lodging; without taking off his hat or coat he walked the length of the little passage and stood still in the doorway of his room, as though thunderstruck. All his presentiments had come true. All that he had dreaded and surmised had come to pass in reality. His breath failed him, his head was in a whirl. The stranger, also in his coat and hat, was sitting before him on his bed, and with a faint smile and slightly screwed-up eyes, nodded to him in a friendly way. Mr. Golyadkin wanted to scream, but could not, to protest in some way, but his strength failed him. His hair stood on end, and he almost fell down with horror. And, indeed, there was good reason. He recognized his nocturnal friend. The nocturnal friend was none other than himself—Mr. Golyadkin himself, another Mr. Golyadkin, but absolutely the same as he himself—in short, what is called his double in every respect. . . .

Chapter VI

Precisely at eight o'clock next morning Mr. Golyadkin woke up in his bed. At once all the extraordinary incidents of the previous day and the wild, incredible night, with all its almost impossible adventures, presented themselves to his imagination and memory in all their terrifying fullness. Such intense, diabolical malice on the part of his enemies, and, above all, the final proof of that malice, froze Mr. Golyadkin's heart. But at the same time it was all so strange, incomprehensible, wild, it seemed so impossible, that it was really hard to credit the whole business. Mr. Golyadkin himself would have been indeed ready to admit that it was all incredible ravings, a passing derangement of the imagination, a darkening of the mind, if he had not fortunately known by bitter experience to what lengths spite will sometimes carry a man, what a pitch of ferocity an enemy may reach in avenging an injury to his honor and pride. Besides, Mr. Golyadkin's bruised limbs, heavy head, aching back, and bad cold bore vivid witness to the reality of his expedition of the previous night, and to some extent of all that had happened on that occasion. And, indeed, Mr. Golyadkin had known long, long before that *they* were getting up something, that there was someone else with *them*. But, having thought it over thoroughly, he made up his mind to keep quiet, to submit and not to protest against it for the time being. "Perhaps they only intend to frighten me," he reflected, "and when they see that I don't mind, that I make no protest, but keep perfectly quiet and bear with it meekly, they'll give it up, they'll give it up of themselves, give it up of their own accord."

Such, then, were the thoughts in Mr. Golyadkin's head as, stretching himself in his bed, resting his bruised limbs,

he waited for Petrushka to come into his room as usual.
. . . He waited for a full quarter of an hour, heard the
lazy scamp fiddling about with the samovar behind the
screen, and yet could not bring himself to call him. We
may say more: Mr. Golyadkin was a little afraid of confronting Petrushka.

"Why, goodness knows," he thought, "goodness knows
how that rascal looks at it all. He keeps on saying nothing,
but he is crafty."

At last the door creaked and Petrushka came in with a
tray in his hands. Mr. Golyadkin stole a timid glance at
him, impatiently waiting to see what would happen, waiting to see whether he would not say something about a
certain circumstance. But Petrushka said nothing; he was,
on the contrary, more taciturn, more glum and ill-humored
than usual; he looked sulkily at everything; altogether it
was evident that something very much displeased him; he
did not even once glance at his master, which, by the way,
rather piqued the latter. Setting all he had brought on the
table, he turned and went out of the room without a word.

"He knows, he knows, he knows all about it, the scoundrel!" Mr. Golyadkin grumbled to himself as he took his
tea. Yet our hero did not address a single question to his
servant, though Petrushka came into his room several
times afterward on various errands. Mr. Golyadkin was in
a greatly disturbed state of mind. He still dreaded going
to the office. He had a strong presentiment that just there
he would find something amiss. "You will go there," he
thought, "and you may be sure that you will run into something! Isn't it better to be patient? Isn't it better to wait a
bit now? Let them do what they like there; but I'd better
stay here a bit today, brace myself, put myself in order,
and think over the whole affair more thoroughly, then
afterward I could seize the right moment, take them by
surprise, and make a show of complete innocence."

Arguing thus with himself, Mr. Golyadkin smoked pipe
after pipe; time was flying. It was already nearly half-past
nine.

"Why, it's half-past nine already," thought Mr. Golyadkin; "it's late for me to make my appearance. Besides, I'm ill, of course I'm ill, I'm certainly ill; who will deny it? What's the matter with me? If they send someone to make inquiries, let the supervisor come; and isn't there something the matter with me really? My back aches, I have a cough, and a cold in the head; and, in fact, it's out of the question for me to go out in such weather, utterly out of the question. I might be taken ill and perhaps die; nowadays especially the death rate is so high. . . ."

With such arguments Mr. Golyadkin succeeded at last in setting his conscience at rest, and fortified himself beforehand against being raked over the coals by Andrey Filippovich for dereliction of duty. As a rule in such cases our hero was particularly fond of justifying himself in his own eyes with all sorts of irrefutable arguments, and so completely setting his conscience at rest. And so now, having completely soothed his conscience, he took up his pipe, filled it, and had no sooner settled down comfortably to smoke, when he jumped up quickly from the sofa, flung away the pipe, briskly washed, shaved, and brushed his hair, got into his uniform and so on, snatched up some papers, and ran at top speed to the office.

Mr. Golyadkin walked into his section timidly, in trembling expectation of something unpleasant—an expectation which was none the less disagreeable for being vague and unconscious; he sat timidly down in his usual place next the head clerk, Anton Antonovich Setochkin. Without looking at anything or allowing his attention to be distracted, he plunged into the contents of the papers that lay before him. He made up his mind and vowed to himself to avoid, as far as possible, anything provocative, anything that might badly compromise him, such as indiscreet questions, people's little jokes, and unseemly allusions to the incidents of the previous evening; he made up his mind also to abstain from the usual interchange of civilities with his colleagues, such as inquiries after health and the like. But evidently it was impossible, out of the question, to keep to this. Anxiety and lack of knowledge in regard to anything that might offend him always worried him far more than the offense itself. And that was why, in spite of his vow to refrain from entering into anything that might happen, and to shun everything, Mr. Golyadkin from time to time, on the sly, very, very quietly, raised his head and stealthily looked about him to right and to left, peeped at the countenances of his colleagues, and tried to gather whether there were not something new and particular in them that related to himself and that was concealed from him for improper purposes. He assumed that there must be a necessary connection between all that had happened yesterday and all that surrounded him now. At last, in his misery, he began to long for something—goodness knows what, even some calamity—that would put an end to it all—he did not care. At this point destiny trapped Mr. Golyadkin: he had hardly felt this desire when his doubts were settled in the strangest and most unexpected manner.

The door leading from the next room suddenly gave a soft and timid creak, as though to indicate that the person about to enter was a very unimportant one, and a figure, very familiar to Mr. Golyadkin, stood shyly before the very desk at which our hero was seated. The latter did not raise his head—no, he only stole a glance at him, the tiniest glance; but he knew all, he understood all, to the smallest details. He grew hot with shame, and buried his hapless head in his papers with precisely the same object with which the ostrich, pursued by hunters, hides his head in the burning sand. The new arrival bowed to Andrey Filippovich, and thereupon a voice was heard speaking in the officially sweet tone which all persons in authority use in addressing their subordinates in public offices.

"Take a seat here," said Andrey Filippovich, motioning the newcomer to Anton Antonovich's desk. "Here, opposite Mr. Golyadkin, and we'll soon give you something to do."

Andrey Filippovich ended by making a rapid, decorously admonitory gesture, and then immediately became engrossed in the papers that lay in a heap before him.

At last, Mr. Golyadkin lifted his eyes, and, if he did not faint, it was solely because he had had a foreboding of it all from the first, that he had been forewarned from the first, had guessed in his heart who the stranger was. Mr. Golyadkin's first movement was to look quickly about him, to see whether there were any whispering, any office joke on the subject being molded, whether anyone's face was distorted with wonder, whether indeed someone had not fallen under the table from fright. But to his intense astonishment there was no sign of anything of the sort. The behavior of his colleagues and companions amazed him. It seemed contrary to common sense. Mr. Golyadkin was positively scared by this extraordinary reticence. The fact spoke for itself; it was a strange, hideous, outrageous thing. It was enough to rouse anyone. All this, of course, only flashed through Mr. Golyadkin's mind. He himself was roasting on a slow fire. And, indeed, there was reason enough for him to be in such a state. The person who was sitting opposite Mr. Golyadkin now was his terror, was his shame, was his nightmare of the evening before; in short, was Mr. Golyadkin himself, not the Mr. Golyadkin who was sitting now in his chair with his mouth agape and a pen in his petrified hand, not the one who was assistant to the chief clerk, not the one who liked to efface himself and slink away in the crowd, not the one whose gait plainly said, "Don't touch me, and I won't touch you," or, "Don't touch me, you see I'm not touching you"; no, this was another Mr. Golyadkin, quite different, yet, at the same time, exactly like the first—the same height, the same figure, the same clothes, the same bald spot; in fact, nothing, absolutely nothing, was lacking to complete the likeness, so that if one were to set them side by side, nobody, absolutely nobody, could have undertaken to distinguish which was the real Golyadkin and which was the counterfeit one, which was the old one and which was the new one, which was the original and which was the copy.

Our hero was, as it were, in the position of a man upon

whom some practical joker had stealthily, in jest, turned a burning glass.

"What is this? Is it a dream?" he wondered. "Is it reality or the continuation of what happened yesterday? How is that? And by what right is all this taking place? Who has permitted the existence of such a clerk, who has authorized this? Am I asleep, am I dreaming?"

Mr. Golyadkin tried pinching himself, even tried to screw up his courage to pinch someone else. . . . No, it was not a dream, and that was all about it. Mr. Golyadkin felt that he was dripping with sweat; he felt that what was happening to him was something incredible, unheard of, and for that very reason something to complete his misery, utterly unseemly, for Mr. Golyadkin understood and felt all the disadvantage of being the first example of such a vile adventure. In the end he even began to doubt his own existence, and, though he was prepared for anything and had been longing for his doubts to be settled in any way whatever, yet the essence of the thing was certainly amazingly unexpected. Anguish oppressed and tormented him. At times he lost all power of thought and memory. Coming to himself after such a moment, he would notice that he was mechanically and unconsciously moving the pen over the paper. Distrusting himself, he began going over what he had written—and could make nothing of it. At last the other Mr. Golyadkin, who had been sitting discreetly and decorously at the table, got up and disappeared through the door into the other room to fetch some file. Mr. Golyadkin looked around—everything was quiet; nothing was heard but the scratching of pens, the rustle of sheets, and conversation in the corners farthest from Andrey Filippovich's seat. Mr. Golyadkin looked at Anton Antonovich, and as, in all probability, our hero's countenance fully reflected his present condition and harmonized with the whole situation, and was consequently, in some respects, very remarkable, good-natured Anton Antonovich, laying aside his pen, inquired after his health with uncommon sympathy.

"I'm very well, thank God, Anton Antonovich," said Mr. Golyadkin, stammering. "I am perfectly well, Anton Antonovich. I am all right now, Anton Antonovich," he added uncertainly, not yet fully trusting Anton Antonovich, whose name he had mentioned so often.

"I fancied you were not quite well: though that's not to be wondered at; no, indeed! Nowadays especially there's such a lot of illness going about. Do you know . . ."

"Yes, Anton Antonovich, I know there is such a lot of illness. . . . That isn't the reason, Anton Antonovich," Mr. Golyadkin went on, looking intently at Anton Antonovich. "You see, Anton Antonovich, I don't even know how you . . . that is, I mean to say, how to approach this matter, Anton Antonovich. . . ."

"How so, sir? I . . . do you know. . . . I must confess I don't quite follow you; you must . . . you must explain, you know, in what respect you are in difficulties," said Anton Antonovich, beginning to be in difficulties himself, seeing that there were actually tears in Mr. Golyadkin's eyes.

"Really, Anton Antonovich . . . I . . . there's a clerk here, Anton Antonovich. . . ."

"Well! I still don't understand."

"I mean to say, Anton Antonovich, there's a new clerk here."

"Yes, there is, sir, a namesake of yours."

"What?" cried Mr. Golyadkin.

"I say, a namesake of yours; his name's Golyadkin too. Is he a brother of yours?"

"No, Anton Antonovich, I . . ."

"H'm! you don't say so! And I thought he must be a near relation of yours. Do you know, there's a sort of family likeness."

Mr. Golyadkin was petrified with astonishment, and for the moment he lost his tongue. To treat so lightly such an abominable, unheard-of thing, a thing undeniably rare in its way, a thing which would have amazed even an unconcerned spectator, to speak of a family resemblance when he could see a mirror image of himself!

"Do you know, Yakov Petrovich, what I advise you to do?" Anton Antonovich went on. "Go and consult a doctor. Do you know, you look somehow quite indisposed. Your eyes especially . . . you know, there's a peculiar expression in them."

"No, Anton Antonovich, I feel, of course . . . that is, I keep wanting to ask about this clerk."

"Well, sir?"

"That is, have not you noticed, Anton Antonovich, something peculiar about him, something very marked?"

"That is?"

"That is, I mean, Anton Antonovich, a striking likeness with somebody, for instance; with me, for instance? You spoke just now, you see, Anton Antonovich, of a family likeness, you've made a casual remark. . . . You know there really are sometimes twins exactly alike, like two drops of water, so that they can't be told apart. Well, that's what I mean."

"To be sure," said Anton Antonovich, after a moment's thought, speaking as though he were struck by the fact for the first time; "yes, indeed, sir! You are right, there is a striking likeness, and you are quite right in what you say. You really might be mistaken for one another," he went on, opening his eyes wider and wider; "and, do you know, Yakov Petrovich, it's positively a marvelous likeness, fantastic, in fact, as the saying is; that is, just as you . . . Have you noticed it, Yakov Petrovich? I wanted to ask you to explain it; but, sir, I must confess, I didn't take proper notice at first. It's a marvel, really a marvel! And, you know, you are not a native of these parts, are you, Yakov Petrovich?"

"No, sir."

"He is not a native of these parts either, you know. Perhaps he hails from the same part of the country as you do. Where, may I make bold to inquire, did your mother live mostly?"

"You said . . . you said, Anton Antonovich, that he is not a native of these parts?"

"No, he is not. How strange it is, indeed!" continued the talkative Anton Antonovich, for whom it was a genuine treat to have a chat. "The matter may well arouse curiosity; and yet, you know, you might often pass the man by, brush, jostle against him, without noticing anything. But you mustn't be upset about it. It does happen. Do you know, the same thing, I must tell you, happened to my aunt on my mother's side; she saw her own double before her death. . . ."

"No, I—excuse my interrupting you, Anton Antonovich—I wanted to find out, Anton Antonovich, how that clerk . . . that is, on what grounds is he here?"

"In place of Semyon Ivanovich, to fill the vacancy left by his death; the post was vacant, so he was appointed. Do you know, I'm told poor Semyon Ivanovich left three children, all tiny tots. The widow fell at the feet of his Excellency. They do say she dissembles; she's got a bit of money, but she's hiding it."

"No, Anton Antonovich, I was still referring to that circumstance."

"You mean . . . ? To be sure! But why are you so interested in that? I tell you, do not upset yourself. All this is temporary to some extent. Why, after all, you know, you have nothing to do with it. It's God Almighty who has ordained it so, it's His will, and it is sinful to repine. His wisdom is apparent in it. And, as far as I can make out, Yakov Petrovich, you are not to blame in any way. There are all sorts of strange things in the world! Mother Nature is generous, and you will not be required to answer for it, you won't be responsible. You must have heard, for instance, I hope, of those—what's their name?—oh, the Siamese twins, whose backs are joined together, and so they live and eat and sleep together. It is said they earn good money."

"Allow me, Anton Antonovich. . . ."

"I understand, I understand! Yes! But what of it? It's no matter, I tell you, as far as I can see there's nothing for you to upset yourself about. After all, he's a clerk like any other clerk, he seems to be a capable man. He says his name is Golyadkin, that he's not a native of these parts, and that he's a titular councilor. He had a personal interview with his Excellency."

"And how did it go, sir?"

"It was all right; it is said he gave a satisfactory account of himself, presented his reasons. 'It's like this, your Excellency,' he said, 'being without means, I desire to enter the service, and would be particularly gratified to be serving under your Excellency . . .' and so on, all very properly; he expressed himself neatly, you know. He must be a man of sense. Well, of course, he came with a recommendation; you can't do without it, you know. . . ."

"Well, sir, from whom, then . . . that is, I mean, who is it has had a hand in this shameful business?"

"Yes, sir, it was a good recommendation, they say; his Excellency, I'm told, and Andrey Filippovich had a laugh together."

"A laugh, his Excellency and Andrey Filippovich?"

"Yes, his Excellency just smiled and said that it was all right, and that he had nothing against it, so long as he did his duty. . . ."

"Well, go on, sir. You are reviving me to some extent, Anton Antonovich; go on, I entreat you."

"Allow me, I again . . . Well, then come, it's nothing, it's a very simple matter; you mustn't upset yourself, I tell you, and there's nothing suspicious about it. . . ."

"No. I . . . that is, Anton Antonovich, I want to ask you, did his Excellency say anything more . . . about me, for instance?"

"Why, what do you mean? No, nothing of the sort; you can set your mind quite at rest. You know it is, of course, a rather striking circumstance, and at first . . . why, here, I, for instance, I scarcely noticed it. I really don't know why I didn't notice it till you mentioned it. But you can set your mind at rest entirely. He said nothing particular, absolutely nothing," added good-natured Anton Antonovich, getting up from his chair.

"So, then, Anton Antonovich, I . . ."

"Oh, you must excuse me. Here I've been chatting about these trivial matters, and I've business that is important and urgent. I must inquire about it."

"Anton Antonovich!" Andrey Filippovich's voice sounded, summoning him politely, "his Excellency has been asking for you."

"This minute, sir. I'm coming this minute, Andrey Filippovich." And Anton Antonovich, taking a pile of papers, flew off first to Andrey Filippovich and then into his Excellency's office.

"How is it?" wondered Mr. Golyadkin. "So that's the sort of game that's going on here! So the wind's in that quarter now. . . . That's not bad; so things have taken a most pleasant turn," our hero said to himself, rubbing his hands, and so delighted that he scarcely felt the chair under him. "So our affair is an ordinary thing. It turns out to be a trifling matter, it comes to nothing at all. No one has done anything really, and they don't say a word, the robbers, they are sitting busy with their work; that's splendid, splendid! I like the good-natured fellow; I've always liked him, and I'm always ready to respect him. . . . Come to think, though, who knows? . . . Take this Anton Antonovich. . . . I'm afraid to trust him; his hair's too gray, and he's tottering with old age. It's an immense and glorious thing, though, that his Excellency said nothing, and ignored the matter. It's a good thing! I approve! Only why does Andrey Filippovich interfere with his giggles? What's he got to do with it? The old dodger. Always on my track, always, like a black cat, on the watch to run across a man's path, always thwarting and annoying a man, always annoying and thwarting a man. . . ."

Mr. Golyadkin looked around him again, and was again revived by hopes. Yet he felt that he was troubled by one remote idea, an unpleasant idea. It even occurred to him that he might try somehow to make up to the clerks, even to forestall events (perhaps when leaving the office or approaching his colleagues as though about his work), by dropping a hint in the course of conversation to the effect that this was a really striking resemblance, a strange circumstance, a farcical caricature, that is, to treat it all lightly, and in this way fathom the danger. "One must remember that still waters run deep," our hero concluded inwardly. This was, however, only an idea of Mr. Golyadkin's. He thought better of it in time. He realized that this would be going too far. "That's your temperament," he said to himself, tapping himself lightly on the forehead; "as soon as you gain anything you break loose! You're a simple soul! No, you and I had better be patient, Yakov Petrovich; let us wait and be patient!"

Nevertheless, as we have mentioned already, Mr. Golyadkin was buoyed up with the most confident hopes, feeling as though he had risen from the dead.

"No matter," he thought, "it's as though five hundred pounds had been lifted off my chest! Here is a riddle, to be sure! But the solution was quite simple.[2] Krylov is right, a clever chap, a dodger, that Krylov, and a great fable-writer! And as for that fellow, let him work in the office, and good luck to him so long as he doesn't meddle or interfere with anyone; let him work in the office—I consent and approve!"

Meanwhile the hours were passing, flying by, and, without his noticing it, the clock struck four. The office closed. Andrey Filippovich took his hat, and, as usual, all followed his example. Mr. Golyadkin dawdled a little on purpose, long enough to be the last to go out when all the others had gone their several ways. Finding himself on the street, he felt as though he were in paradise, so that he even felt inclined to make a detour and take a stroll along Nevsky Prospect. "To be sure, this is destiny," thought our hero, "this unexpected turn of affairs. And the weather has cleared up, and there was a frost and sledges. And the frost suits the Russian, the Russian gets on capitally with

[2] The proverbial catch line of a fable by Krylov about futile attempts to open a casket in various ingenious ways, except the simple, which is also the right one.—A.Y.

the frost! I like the Russian. And the dear little snow, the first snow of the season, as the hunter would say; this is the time to go shooting hares with the first snow on the ground. Well, there, it doesn't matter."

This was how Mr. Golyadkin's enthusiasm found expression. Yet something was fretting him, not exactly anguish, but at times he had such a gnawing at his heart that he did not know how to find relief.

"Let us wait a day, though, and then we shall rejoice. What is this anyway? Come, let us think it over, let us look at it. Come, let us consider it, my young friend, let us consider it. Why, in the first place, a man's exactly like you, absolutely. Well, what is there in that? If there is such a man, why should I weep over it? What is it to me? I stand aside, I whistle to myself, and that's all! That's all there is to it! Let him work in the office! Well, it's strange and a marvel, they say, that the Siamese twins . . . But why bring in the Siamese twins? They are twins, of course, but even great men, you know, sometimes look like queer fish. In fact, we know from history that the famous Suvorov used to crow like a cock. . . . But there, he did all that for political reasons; and great generals . . . but what are generals, after all? But I keep myself to myself, that's all, and I don't care about anyone else, and, secure in my innocence, I scorn my enemies. I am not one to intrigue, and I'm proud of it. I am pure-hearted, straightforward, neat, pleasant, gentle."

All at once Mr. Golyadkin lapsed into silence, stopped short, and began trembling like a leaf; he even closed his eyes for a moment. Hoping, however, that the object of his terror was only an illusion, he opened his eyes at last and stole a timid glance to the right. No, it was no illusion! . . . The man whose acquaintance he had made that morning was mincing along by his side, smiling, peeping into his face, and apparently seeking an opportunity to begin a conversation with him. The conversation did not begin, however. They both walked like this for about fifty paces. All Mr. Golyadkin's efforts were concentrated on muffling himself up, hiding himself in his coat, and pulling his hat down as far as possible over his eyes. To complete his mortification, his companion's coat and hat were exactly like his own, as though they had been taken off Mr. Golyadkin.

"My dear sir," our hero brought out at last, trying to speak almost in a whisper, and not looking at his companion, "we are going different ways, I believe. . . . I am convinced of it, in fact," he said, after a brief pause. "Finally, I am sure I have made myself clear," he added, rather severely, in conclusion.

"I should like . . ." his companion spoke at last, "I should like . . . no doubt you will be magnanimous and pardon me . . . I don't know to whom to turn here . . . my circumstances . . . I trust you will pardon my impertinence. I fancied, indeed, that, moved by compassion, you showed some interest in me this morning. For my part, I felt drawn to you from the first moment. I . . ."

At this point Mr. Golyadkin inwardly wished that the earth would open under his companion's feet.

"If I might venture to hope," the stranger went on, "that you would accord me an indulgent hearing, Yakov Petrovich. . . ."

"We can . . . you . . . you had better come home with me," answered Mr. Golyadkin. "We will cross now to the other side of Nevsky Prospect, it will be more convenient for us there, and then take a little lane. . . . We'd better do that."

"Very well, sir, without fail, let us take the little lane," our hero's meek companion responded timidly, suggesting by the tone of his reply that it was not for him to choose, and that in his position he was quite prepared to be satisfied with the lane. As for Mr. Golyadkin, he was utterly unable to grasp what was happening to him. He did not trust himself. He hadn't yet recovered from his amazement.

Chapter VII

He recovered himself a little on the staircase as he went up to his flat.

"Oh, I'm a muttonhead," he railed at himself inwardly. "Where am I taking him? I am thrusting my head into the noose. What will Petrushka think, seeing us together? What will the scoundrel dare to imagine now? And he's suspicious. . . ."

But it was too late to regret it. Mr. Golyadkin knocked at the door; it was opened, and Petrushka began taking off the visitor's coat as well as his master's. Mr. Golyadkin looked askance, just stealing a glance at Petrushka, trying to read his countenance and guess what he was thinking. But to his intense astonishment he saw that his servant showed no trace of surprise, but seemed, on the contrary, to have been expecting something of the sort. Of course he did scowl, as it was; he kept his eyes turned away and looked as though he were about to eat someone alive.

"Can it be that somebody has bewitched them all today?" thought our hero. "Some devil must have called on them. There certainly must be something peculiar about the whole lot of them today. Damn it all, what a torture it is!"

Such were Mr. Golyadkin's thoughts and reflections as he led his visitor into his room and politely asked him to sit down. The visitor appeared to be greatly embarrassed, he was very shy, and humbly watched every move his host made, caught his glances, and seemed trying to guess his thoughts from them. There was something downtrodden, crushed, scared about all his gestures, so that—if the comparison may be allowed—he was at that moment rather like the man who for want of his own clothes, has put on somebody else's: the sleeves ride up, the waist is almost up to the back of his head, and every minute he keeps pulling down the short waistcoat; he wriggles sideways and edges away, tries to hide somewhere or peeps into every face, and listens whether people are talking of his circumstances, laughing at him or are ashamed of him—and the man blushes, loses his presence of mind, his pride is wounded. . . . Mr. Golyadkin put down his hat on the window sill and carelessly sent it flying to the floor. The visitor darted at once to pick it up, brushed off the dust, and carefully put it back, while he laid his own on the floor near a chair, on the edge of which he meekly seated himself.

This trivial incident partly opened Mr. Golyadkin's eyes; he realized that the man badly needed him, and so did not fret about how to open the conversation, very properly leaving all that to the guest. The visitor, for his part, did nothing to break the silence either; whether he was shy, a little ashamed, or from politeness was waiting for his host to take the lead is not certain and would be difficult to determine. At that moment Petrushka came in; he stood still in the doorway, and fixed his eyes in the direction farthest from where the visitor and his master were seated.

"Shall I bring in dinner for two?" he said carelessly, in a husky voice.

"I—I don't know . . . you . . . yes, bring dinner for two, my boy."

Petrushka went out. Mr. Golyadkin glanced at his visitor. The latter blushed up to his ears. Mr. Golyadkin was a kindhearted man, and so in the kindness of his heart he at once elaborated a theory. "The fellow's hard up," he thought. "Yes, and in his situation only one day. Most likely he's suffered in his time. Maybe his good clothes are all that he has, and not enough to buy a dinner. Ah, poor fellow, how crushed he seems! But no matter; in a way it's better so. . . . Excuse me," began Mr. Golyadkin, "allow me to ask what I may call you."

"I . . . I . . . I'm Yakov Petrovich," his visitor almost whispered, as though conscience-stricken, and ashamed, as though apologizing for being called Yakov Petrovich too.

"Yakov Petrovich!" repeated our hero, unable to conceal his confusion.

"Yes, just so, sir . . . I am your namesake, sir," responded Mr. Golyadkin's meek guest, venturing to smile and speak a little jocosely. But at once he drew back, assuming a very serious, though a little disconcerted, air, noticing that his host was in no joking mood.

"You . . . allow me to ask you, to what am I indebted for the honor . . . ?"

"Knowing your generosity and your benevolence," interposed the visitor in a rapid but timid voice, half-rising from his seat, "I have ventured to turn to you and to solicit your . . . acquaintance and protection . . ." he concluded, finding it difficult to express himself and choosing words not too flattering or servile, that he might not compromise his dignity and not so bold as to suggest an unseemly equality. In fact, one may say the visitor behaved like a well-born beggar with a darned dress coat, a gentleman's passport in his pocket, who has not yet learned how to hold out his hand properly.

"You perplex me," answered Mr. Golyadkin, gazing around at himself, his walls, and his visitor. "In what could I . . . that is, I mean, in precisely what way could I be of service to you?"

"I felt drawn to you, Yakov Petrovich, at first sight, and kindly forgive me, I built my hopes on you—I made bold to build my hopes on you, Yakov Petrovich. I . . . I'm completely at a loss here, Yakov Petrovich; I'm poor, I've had a great deal of trouble, Yakov Petrovich, and I'm a newcomer here. Learning that you, with your innate goodness and excellence of heart, bear the same name . . ."

Mr. Golyadkin frowned.

"The same name as myself and are a native of the same district, I made up my mind to turn to you, and to make known to you my difficult position."

"Very good, sir, very good; I really don't know what to say," Mr. Golyadkin responded in an embarrassed tone. "Well, we'll have a talk after dinner. . . ."

The guest bowed; dinner was brought in. Petrushka laid the table, and Mr. Golyadkin and his visitor proceeded to partake of it. The dinner did not last long, for they were both in a hurry, the host because he felt ill at ease, and was, besides, ashamed that the dinner was a poor one—he was ashamed partly because he wanted to give the visitor a good meal, and partly because he wanted to show him he did not live like a beggar. The guest, for his part, was in terrible confusion and extremely embarrassed. When he had finished the slice of bread he had taken, he was afraid to put out his hand to take another slice, was ashamed to help himself to the best morsels, and was continually assuring his host that he was not at all hungry, that the dinner was excellent, that he was absolutely satisfied with it, and should not forget it to his dying day. When the meal was over Mr. Golyadkin lighted his pipe, and offered another, which he kept for a friend, to the guest. They sat down facing each other, and the visitor began telling his adventures.

Mr. Golyadkin's story lasted three or four hours. His history was, however, composed of the most trivial and wretched, if one may say so, incidents; it had to do with details of service in some provincial board, with prosecutors and chairmen, some office intrigues, the depravity of a court clerk, with an inspector, and the sudden appointment of a new chief, with the sufferings inflicted on the second Mr. Golyadkin, quite without any fault on his part; with his aged aunt, Pelagea Semyonovna; with how, through various intrigues on the part of his enemies, he had lost his situation, and had come to Petersburg on foot; with the harassing and wretched time he had had here in Petersburg, how for a long time he had tried in vain to get a job, had spent all his money, had nothing left, had been living almost in the street, ate stale bread and washed it down with his tears, slept on the bare floor, and finally how some good man had exerted himself on his behalf, had given him an introduction, and had magnanimously got him into a new berth. Mr. Golyadkin's guest shed tears as he told his story, and wiped his eyes with a blue check handkerchief that looked like a piece of oilcloth. He ended by making a clean breast of it to Mr. Golyadkin, and confessing that he was not only for the time without means of subsistence and money for a decent lodging, but had not even the where-withal to fit himself out properly, so that he had not, he said in conclusion, been able to get together enough for a pair of wretched boots, and that he had to hire a uniform for a short time.

Mr. Golyadkin was moved, genuinely touched. Even though his visitor's story was of the most trivial variety, every word of it was like heavenly manna to his heart. The fact is that Mr. Golyadkin was forgetting his recent mis-givings, surrendered his heart to joy and freedom, and at last mentally dubbed himself a fool. It was all so natural! And what a thing to be so distressed about, what a thing to sound the alarm about! To be sure, there was, there really was, one ticklish circumstance—but, after all, it was no misfortune; it could not disgrace a man, it could not cast a slur on his honor or ruin his career, since he was innocent, since nature herself was mixed up in it. Moreover, the guest begged for protection, wept, railed at destiny, seemed such an artless, pitiful, insignificant person, with no wiles or malice to him, and he himself seemed now to be ashamed, though perhaps on different grounds, of the strange resemblance of his countenance to that of Mr. Golyadkin. His behavior was absolutely unimpeachable; his one desire was to please his host, and he looked as a man who is conscience-stricken and feels guilty toward someone else. If any doubtful point was touched upon, for instance, the visitor at once agreed with Mr. Golyadkin's opinion. If by mistake he advanced an opinion in opposition to Mr. Golyadkin's, and afterward noticed that he had made a slip, he immediately corrected his mistake, explained himself, and made it clear that he meant the same thing as his host, that he thought as he did and saw eye to eye with him in all things. In short, the man's conduct compelled Mr. Golyadkin to conclude at last that his visitor must be a very amiable person in every way.

Meanwhile, tea was brought in; it was nearly nine o'clock. Mr. Golyadkin was in excellent spirits, grew lively and skittish, let himself go a little, and finally plunged into a most animated and entertaining conversation with his guest. In his cheerful moments Mr. Golyadkin liked to talk about things of interest. So now he told the visitor a great deal about Petersburg, about its amusements and attractions, about the theater, the clubs, about Bryullov's picture,[3] and about the two Englishmen who came from England to Petersburg on purpose to look at the iron railing of the Summer Garden, and left immediately after they had seen it; about the office; about Olsufy Ivanovich and Andrey Filippovich; about the way Russia was every moment progressing toward a state of perfection, so that "Letters flourish here today"; about an anecdote he had lately read in the *Northern Bee* concerning a boa constrictor in India of immense strength; about Baron Brambeus,[4] and so on. In short, Mr. Golyadkin was quite happy, first, because his mind was at rest; secondly, because, so far from being afraid of his enemies, he was quite prepared now to challenge them all to mortal combat; thirdly, because he was now in the rule of patron and doing a good deed. Yet he confessed in his heart that he was not yet completely happy at the moment, that there was still a hidden worm gnawing at his heart, though it was only a tiny one. He was extremely tormented by the memory of the previous evening at Olsufy Ivanovich's. He would have given a great deal now for a chance to undo some of the things that had taken place there.

"It's no matter, though!" our hero decided at last, and he firmly resolved in his heart to behave well in future and not to commit such blunders again. As Mr. Golyadkin was

[3] "The Last Day of Pompeii," a painting which was exhibited in the Academy of Arts and attracted much attention.—A.Y.

[4] The pseudonym of a Russian novelist and critic of the period.—A.Y.

now fully worked up, and had suddenly become almost completely happy, the fancy took him to enjoy life a bit. Rum was brought in by Petrushka, and punch was prepared. The guest and the host drained a glass each, and then a second. The guest turned out to be even more amiable than before, and gave more than one proof of his frankness and happy character; he entered keenly into Mr. Golyadkin's pleasure, seemed only to rejoice in his rejoicing, and to look upon him as his one and only benefactor. Taking up a pen and a sheet of paper, he asked Mr. Golyadkin not to look at what he was going to write, and afterward showed his host what he had written. It turned out to be a quatrain, written with a good deal of feeling, in an excellent style, and in a fine hand, and evidently was the composition of the amiable guest himself. The lines were as follows:

> If thou wilt forget me,
> I shall not forget thee;
> Though all things may be,
> Do not thou forget me.

With tears in his eyes Mr. Golyadkin embraced his guest and, completely overcome by emotion, he himself initiated his guest into some of his secrets and private affairs, Andrey Filippovich and Klara Olsufyevna being prominent in his remarks.

"Well, you may be sure we shall get on together, Yakov Petrovich," said our hero to his guest. "You and I will take to each other like fish to water, Yakov Petrovich; we shall be like brothers; we'll be cunning, old chap, we'll scheme together; for our part, we'll play a deep game to spite them, to spite them we'll play a deep game. And don't you trust any of them. I know you, Yakov Petrovich, and I understand your character; you'll tell them everything straight out, you know, you're a guileless soul! You must shun them all, my boy."

The guest entirely agreed with him, thanked him, and, at last, he too grew tearful.

"Do you know, Yasha," Mr. Golyadkin went on in a

shaking voice, weak with emotion, "you must make your home here with me for a time, or forever. We shall get on together. What do you say, brother, eh? And don't you worry or repine because there's such a strange circumstance about us now; it's a sin to repine, brother; it's nature! And Mother Nature is liberal with her gifts, so there, brother Yasha! It's out of love for you that I speak, out of brotherly love. And we two will be cunning, Yasha, and, for our part, lay mines and get the better of them."

They reached their third and fourth glass of punch at last, and then Mr. Golyadkin began to be aware of two sensations; the one that he was extraordinarily happy, and the other that he could not stand on his feet. The guest was, of course, invited to stay the night. A bed was somehow made up on two rows of chairs. Mr. Golyadkin declared that under a friend's roof the bare floor was a soft bed, that for his part he could sleep anywhere, humbly and gratefully; that he was in paradise now, that he had been through a great deal of trouble and grief in his time; he had seen ups and downs, had all sorts of things to put up with, and—who knows what the future holds?—maybe he would have still more to put up with. Mr. Golyadkin protested against this, and began to argue that one must put one's faith in God. His guest entirely agreed, saying that there was, of course, no one like God. At this point Mr. Golyadkin observed that in certain respects the Turks were right in calling upon God even in their sleep. Then, while rejecting the aspersions cast by certain men of learning on the Turkish prophet Mahomet and recognizing him as a great politician in his way, Mr. Golyadkin passed to a very interesting description of an Algerian barbershop, which he had read in the miscellaneous section of a magazine. The friends laughed heartily at the simple-mindedness of the Turks, but paid due tribute to their fanaticism, which they ascribed to opium.

At last the guest began undressing, and, thinking in the kindness of his heart that very likely he hadn't even a decent shirt, Mr. Golyadkin went behind the partition to avoid embarrassing a man who had suffered enough, and partly to reassure himself as far as possible about Petrushka, to test him, to cheer him up if he could, to be kind to the fellow, so that everyone might be happy and that everything might be pleasant all around. It must be remarked that Petrushka still troubled Mr. Golyadkin somewhat.

"You go to bed now, Pyotr," Mr. Golyadkin said gently, coming into his servant's compartment; "you go to bed now and wake me up at eight o'clock. Do you understand, Petrusha?"[5]

Mr. Golyadkin spoke with exceptional softness and friendliness. But Petrushka remained silent. He was puttering about near his bed, and did not even turn around to face his master, which he ought to have done out of simple respect for him.

"Did you hear what I said, Pyotr?" Mr. Golyadkin went on. "You go to bed now and wake me tomorrow at eight o'clock; do you understand?"

"I know that; no use telling me!" Petrushka grumbled to himself.

"Well, that's right, Petrusha; I only mentioned it that you might be happy and at ease. Now we are all happy, so I want you, too, to be happy and at ease. And now I wish you good night. Sleep, Petrusha, sleep; we all have to work. . . . Don't get any wrong notions, my man . . ." Mr. Golyadkin began, but stopped short. "Isn't this too much?" he thought. "Haven't I gone too far? That's how it always is; I always overdo it."

Our hero felt much dissatisfied with himself as he left Petrushka. He was, besides, rather wounded by Petrushka's stubbornness and rudeness. "One makes advances to the rascal, his master does the rascal honor, and he does not feel it," reflected Mr. Golyadkin. "But there, that's the nasty way of all that sort of people!"

Somewhat staggering, he went back to the room, and,

[5] While the form "Petrushka" has a disparaging force, "Petrusha" carries a suggestion of endearment.—A.Y.

seeing that his guest had settled himself for the night, he
sat down on the edge of his bed for a minute.

"Come, confess, Yasha," he began in a whisper, "you're
a rascal, you know; you're guilty toward me, aren't you?
You've taken my name, you know, confess," he went on,
twitting his guest in a rather familiar way. At last, saying
a friendly good night to him, Mr. Golyadkin started preparing for the night. The guest meanwhile began snoring.
Mr. Golyadkin in his turn got into bed, laughing and
whispering to himself, "You are drunk today, my dear
fellow, Yakov Petrovich, you rascal, you old Golyadkin, you
—what a surname to have! Why, what are you so pleased
about? You'll burst into tears tomorrow, you know, you
sniveler; what am I to do with you?"

At this point a rather strange sensation pervaded Mr.
Golyadkin's whole being, something like doubt or repentance.

"I let myself go," he thought; "now there's a noise in my
head and I'm drunk; you couldn't restrain yourself, you
fool, you! And you came out with a poem of nonsense, and
you were planning to be so cunning, you scoundrel. Of
course, to forgive and forget injuries is the height of virtue;
but it's a bad thing, nevertheless! Yes, that's so!"

At this point Mr. Golyadkin got up, took a candle, and
went on tiptoe to look once more at his sleeping guest. He
stood over him for a long time, deep in thought. "An unpleasant picture! A libelous matter, a regular libel, and
that's what it is!"

At last Mr. Golyadkin settled down for good. There was
a humming, a buzzing, a ringing in his head. He began to
drop off . . . tried to think about something, to remember
something very interesting, to decide something very important, some delicate question—but could not. Sleep descended upon his hapless head, and he slept as people
generally sleep who are not used to drinking and have
downed five glasses of punch at some friendly gathering.

Chapter VIII

Mr. Golyadkin woke up next morning at eight o'clock as usual; as soon as he was awake he recalled all the adventures of the previous evening—and frowned as he recalled them. "Ugh, I did play the fool last night!" he said to himself, sitting up and glancing at his guest's bed. But what was his amazement when he saw in the room no trace, not only of his guest, but even of the bed on which his guest had slept!

"What is this?" Mr. Golyadkin almost shrieked. "What can it be? What does this new circumstance mean?"

While Mr. Golyadkin was gazing in open-mouthed bewilderment at the empty spot, the door creaked and Petrushka came in with the tea tray.

"Where, then, where?" our hero said in a hardly audible voice, pointing to the place which had been occupied by his guest the night before.

At first Petrushka made no answer and did not even look at his master, but fixed his eyes upon the corner at the right, so that Mr. Golyadkin himself felt compelled to look into that corner. After a brief silence, however, Petrushka in a rude and husky voice answered that his master was not at home.

"You idiot; why, I'm your master, Petrushka!" said Mr. Golyadkin in a broken voice, looking open-eyed at his servant.

Petrushka made no reply, but he gave Mr. Golyadkin such a look that the latter blushed to the roots of his hair. It was a look of insulting reproach, resembling open abuse. Mr. Golyadkin was disheartened. At last Petrushka explained that the *other one* had gone away an hour and a half ago, and would not wait. His answer, of course, was probable and plausible; it was evident that Petrushka was not lying, that his insulting look and the phrase the *other one* employed by him were only the result of the notorious circumstance. Nevertheless Mr. Golyadkin understood, though dimly, that something was wrong, and that destiny had still another surprise, not altogether a pleasant one, in store for him.

"All right, we shall see," he thought to himself. "We shall see; in due time we'll get to the bottom of all this. . . . Oh, Lord!" he moaned in conclusion, in quite a different voice. "And why did I invite him, to what end did I do all that? Why, I am thrusting my head into their thievish noose myself; I am tying the noose with my own hands. Oh, you fool, you fool! You can't resist fibbing like some silly boy, some clerk, some wretched creature of no rank at all, a milksop, a rotten rag; you gossip, you, you old woman! . . . Oh, all ye saints! And he wrote verses, the rogue, and made me a declaration of love! How can I . . . How can I show him the door in a polite way if he turns up again, the rogue? Of course, there are all sorts of ways and means. I can say this is how it is, my salary being so limited, etc. Or scare him off in some way saying that, taking this and that into consideration, I am forced to make clear . . . that he would have to pay an equal share of the cost of board and lodging, and pay the money in advance. H'm! No, damn it all, no! That would besmirch me. It's not quite tactful! Couldn't I do something like this: suggest to Petrushka that he should annoy him in some way, should be disrespectful, be rude, and get rid of him in that way? Set them against each other in some way. . . . No, damn it all, no! It's dangerous and again, looked at from a certain point of view—it's not the right thing at all! Not the right thing at all! But there, what if he doesn't come? Will that be bad too? I did fib last night! . . . Oh, it's a bad lookout, a bad lookout! Oh, we're in a bad way! Oh, I'm a cursed fool, a cursed fool! You just can't learn to behave, you can't conduct yourself reasonably. Well, what if he comes, and decides not to move in? God grant he may do so! I should be very glad if he did. I should give a good deal to have him do so. . . ."

Such were Mr. Golyadkin's reflections as he swallowed his tea and glanced continually at the clock on the wall.

"It's a quarter to nine; it's time to go. Something is going to happen! What will it be? I should like to know what exactly lies hidden in all this—that is, the object, the trend, and all the trickery. It would be a good thing to find out what exactly all these people are aiming at, and what will be their first step. . . ."

Mr. Golyadkin could endure it no longer. He threw down his unfinished pipe, dressed, and set off for the office, anxious to detect the danger if possible and to ascertain everything by his presence in person. There *was* danger; there was no doubt of that in his mind.

"Now, we will get to the bottom of it," said Mr. Golyadkin, taking off his coat and galoshes in the vestibule. "We'll go into all these matters immediately."

Having made up his mind to act in this way, our hero put himself to rights, assumed a correct and official air, and was just about to pass into the adjoining room, when suddenly, in the very doorway, he jostled against his acquaintance of the day before, his friend and crony. Mr. Golyadkin Jr. seemed not to notice Mr. Golyadkin Sr., though they met almost nose to nose. Mr. Golyadkin Jr. seemed to be busy, to be hastening somewhere, and was breathless; he had such an official air, such a businesslike air that it seemed as though anyone could read in his face: "Entrusted with a special commission."

"Oh, it's you, Yakov Petrovich!" said our hero, clutching the hand of his last night's guest.

"Later on, later on, excuse me, you'll tell me about it afterward," cried Mr. Golyadkin Jr., trying to dash on.

"But, excuse me; I believe, Yakov Petrovich, you wanted . . ."

"What is it? Make haste and explain, sir."

At this point his guest of the previous night halted as though reluctantly and against his will, and put his ear almost to Mr. Golyadkin's nose.

"I must tell you, Yakov Petrovich, that I am surprised

at your manner . . . a manner which to all appearance I could not have expected at all."

"There's a proper form for everything, sir. Report to his Excellency's secretary and then get in touch in the proper way with the head of the office. Have you got your petition?"

"You . . . I really don't know, Yakov Petrovich! You simply amaze me, Yakov Petrovich! I suppose you don't recognize me or, with your characteristic gaiety, you are joking."

"Oh, it's you," said Mr. Golyadkin Jr., seeming only now to recognize Mr. Golyadkin Sr. "So it's you? Well, have you had a good night?"

Then, smiling a little—a formal and conventional smile, by no means the sort of smile that was befitting (for, after all, he owed a debt of gratitude to Mr. Golyadkin Sr.)—smiling this formal and conventional smile, Mr. Golyadkin Jr. added that, for his part, he was very glad Mr. Golyadkin Sr. had had a good night; then he made a slight bow and, shuffling his feet a little, looked to the right, and to the left, then dropped his eyes to the floor, made for the side door, and, muttering in a hurried whisper that he had a special assignment, whisked into the next room, and vanished from sight.

"Well, that's a nice thing!" muttered our hero, petrified for a moment. "This is the circumstance I am up against."

At this point Mr. Golyadkin, for some reason, felt creepy all over.

"However," he went on saying to himself, as he made his way to his section, "however, I spoke long ago of such a circumstance: I had a presentiment long ago that he had a special commission. Why, I said just yesterday that the man must certainly be employed on some special commission."

"Have you finished copying out the document you had yesterday, Yakov Petrovich," Anton Antonovich Setochkin asked Mr. Golyadkin, when the latter was seated beside him. "Have you got it here?"

"Yes," murmured Mr. Golyadkin, glancing at the head clerk with a rather dejected air.

"Good! I mention it because Andrey Filippovich has asked for it twice. I'm afraid his Excellency may want it. . . ."

"Yes, it's finished, sir. . . ."

"Well, sir, that's all right then."

"I believe, Anton Antonovich, I have always performed my duties properly. I always scrupulously do the work entrusted to me by my superiors, I attend to it zealously."

"Yes. Well, what do you mean by that, sir?"

"I mean nothing, Anton Antonovich. I only want to explain, Anton Antonovich, that I . . . that is, I meant to express that disloyalty and envy sometimes spare no person whatever in their search for their daily abominable food. . . ."

"Excuse me, I don't quite understand you. What person are you alluding to?"

"That is, I only meant to say, Anton Antonovich, that I follow the straight path and scorn devious ways, that I am not one to intrigue, and that, if I may be allowed to say so, I can very justly be proud of it. . . ."

"Yes, sir. That's quite so, and, to the best of my understanding, I thoroughly endorse your remarks; but allow me to tell you, Yakov Petrovich, that personalities are not quite permissible in good society, that I, for instance, am ready to put up with anything behind my back—for everyone's abused behind his back—but to my face, if you please, my good sir, I don't allow anyone to be impudent. I've grown gray in the government service, sir, and I don't allow anyone to be impudent to me in my old age. . . ."

"No, Anton Antonovich . . . you see, Anton Antonovich . . . you haven't quite caught my meaning, sir. To be sure, Anton Antonovich, I for my part could only consider it an honor . . ."

"Well, then, I ask your pardon too. I've been taught in the old school. And it's too late for me to learn your new-fangled ways. I believe I've had wit enough for the service

of our country up to now. As you are aware, sir, I hav
order of merit for twenty-five years' irreproachable se
ice. . . ."

"I feel it, Anton Antonovich, for my part, I quite feel
all that. But I didn't mean that, I am speaking of a mask,
Anton Antonovich. . . ."

"A mask, sir?"

"Again you, that is . . . I fear that you are taking this,
too, in a wrong sense, that is the sense of my remarks, as
you say yourself, Anton Antonovich. I am simply developing a theory, that is, I am advancing the idea, Anton
Antonovich, that persons who wear a mask have become
far from uncommon, and that nowadays it is hard to recognize the man beneath the mask, sir. . . ."

"Well, do you know, it's not altogether so hard. Sometimes it's fairly easy, sir. Sometimes one need not go far
to look for it."

"No, you know, Anton Antonovich, I say, I say to myself, that I, for instance, do not put on a mask except when
there is need of it; that is, simply at carnival time or at
some festive gathering, speaking in the literal sense; but
that I do not wear a mask before people in daily life,
speaking in another, less obvious sense. That's what I
meant to say, Anton Antonovich."

"Well, we must drop all this for the present; I've no
time to spare," said Anton Antonovich, getting up from
his seat and collecting some papers in order to report to
his Excellency. "As for your business, I can imagine it will
be settled in due course. You will see for yourself whom
you should reproach and whom you should blame, and
thereupon I humbly beg you to spare me further private
explanations and arguments which interfere with my
work. . . ."

"No, Anton Antonovich," Mr. Golyadkin, turning a little
pale, began addressing the retreating figure of Anton
Antonovich; "I had no thought of the kind."

"What does it mean?" our hero went on saying to himself, when he was left alone; "what quarter is the wind in

now, and what is one to make of this new piece of chicanery?"

At the very time when our bewildered and half-crushed hero was on the point of preparing to solve this new problem, there was a noise and a bustling about in the next room, the door opened, and Andrey Filippovich, who had been on some business in his Excellency's study, appeared breathless in the doorway, and called to Mr. Golyadkin. Knowing what was wanted and anxious not to keep Andrey Filippovich waiting, Mr. Golyadkin leaped up from his seat, and, as was proper, immediately started fussing for all he was worth, getting the papers that were required finally neat and ready and preparing to follow them and Andrey Filippovich into his Excellency's study. Suddenly, almost slipping under the arm of Andrey Filippovich, who was standing right in the doorway, Mr. Golyadkin Jr. whisked into the room in breathless haste and bustle, with a solemn and resolutely official air; he bounded straight up to Mr. Golyadkin Sr., who was expecting nothing less than such an attack.

"The papers, Yakov Petrovich, the papers . . . his Excellency has been pleased to ask for them; have you got them ready?" Mr. Golyadkin Sr.'s friend chirped in a hurried undertone. "Andrey Filippovich is waiting for you. . . ."

"I know he is waiting without your telling me," said Mr. Golyadkin Sr., also in a hurried whisper.

"No, Yakov Petrovich, I did not mean that; I did not mean that at all, Yakov Petrovich, not that at all; I sympathize with you, Yakov Petrovich, and am moved by heartfelt interest."

"Which I most humbly beg you to spare me. Allow me, allow me. . . ."

"You'll put them in a folder, of course, Yakov Petrovich, and you'll place a mark at page three; allow me, Yakov Petrovich. . . ."

"You allow me, at last. . . ."

"But, I say, there's an ink blot here, Yakov Petrovich; have you noticed the ink blot?"

At this point Andrey Filippovich called Yakov Petrovich a second time.

"One moment, Andrey Filippovich, I'm only just . . . Do you understand Russian, sir?"

"It would be best to take it out with a penknife, Yakov Petrovich. You had better rely upon me; you had better not touch it yourself, Yakov Petrovich, rely upon me—I'll do it with a penknife. . . ."

Andrey Filippovich called Mr. Golyadkin a third time.

"But, allow me, where's the blot? I don't think there's a blot at all."

"It's a huge blot. Here it is! Here, allow me, I saw it here . . . you just let me, Yakov Petrovich, I'll just touch it with the penknife, out of sympathy, Yakov Petrovich, I'll scratch it out with the penknife out of heartfelt sympathy. There, like this; see, it's done."

At this point, and quite unexpectedly, Mr. Golyadkin Jr. overpowered Mr. Golyadkin Sr. in the momentary struggle that had arisen between them, and so, entirely against the latter's will, suddenly, without rhyme or reason, took possession of the document required by the authorities, and instead of scratching it out with the penknife out of heartfelt sympathy, as he had perfidiously assured Mr. Golyadkin Sr., hurriedly rolled it up, put it under his arm, in two bounds was beside Andrey Filippovich, who noticed none of his maneuvers, and flew with the latter into the Director's study. Mr. Golyadkin remained as though riveted to the spot, holding the penknife in his hand and apparently on the point of scratching something out with it. . . .

Our hero could not yet grasp his new situation. He had not yet come to his senses. He felt the blow, but thought that it was something of no consequence. In terrible, indescribable misery he tore himself at last from his seat, rushed straight to the Director's room, imploring Heaven on the way that everything might somehow all be arranged satisfactorily and so would be all right. . . . In the room, which adjoined the Director's private study, he ran straight into Andrey Filippovich and his namesake. Both of them were coming out of the study; Mr. Golyadkin moved aside. Andrey Filippovich was talking with a good-humored smile, Mr. Golyadkin Sr.'s namesake was smiling, too, fawning upon Andrey Filippovich and mincing along at a respectful distance from him, and was whispering something in his ear with a delighted air, to which Andrey Filippovich assented with a gracious nod. In a flash our hero grasped the whole situation. The fact is that the work had almost surpassed his Excellency's expectations (as Mr. Golyadkin learned afterward) and was finished punctually by the time it was needed. His Excellency was extremely pleased with it. It was even said that his Excellency had said "Thank you" to Mr. Golyadkin Jr., had thanked him warmly, had said that he would remember it on occasion, would certainly not forget it. . . . Of course, the first thing Mr. Golyadkin did was to protest, to protest with the utmost vigor of which he was capable. Pale as death, and almost beside himself, he rushed up to Andrey Filippovich. But the latter, hearing that Mr. Golyadkin's business was a private matter, refused to listen, observing firmly that he had not a minute to spare even for his own affairs.

The curtness of his tone and the abruptness of his refusal staggered Mr. Golyadkin. "I had better, perhaps, try in another quarter. . . . I had better appeal to Anton Antonovich," he said to himself. But, to his misfortune, Anton Antonovich was not available either: he, too, was busy with something somewhere.

"Ah, it was not without design that he asked me to spare him explanation and gossip!" thought our hero. "This was what the old rogue had in mind! In that case I shall simply make bold to implore his Excellency."

Still pale and feeling that his brain was in complete disorder, greatly perplexed as to what he ought to decide to do, Mr. Golyadkin sat down on the chair. "It would have been a great deal better if it had all turned out to be of no consequence," he kept incessantly saying to himself. "Indeed, such a shady business was utterly improbable. In the first place, it was nonsense, and secondly it could not happen. Most likely it was imagination, or something else happened, and not what really did happen; or perhaps I went there myself . . . and somehow mistook myself for someone else . . . in short, it's an utterly impossible thing."

Mr. Golyadkin had no sooner made up his mind that it was an utterly impossible thing than Mr. Golyadkin Jr. flew into the room with papers in both hands as well as under his arm. Saying two or three words about business to Andrey Filippovich as he passed, exchanging remarks with someone else, polite greetings with a second official, and familiarities with a third, Mr. Golyadkin Jr., having apparently no time to waste, seemed on the point of leaving the room, but luckily for Mr. Golyadkin Sr. he stopped in the doorway to say a few words as he passed two or three young clerks. Mr. Golyadkin Sr. rushed straight at him. As soon as Mr. Golyadkin Jr. saw Mr. Golyadkin Sr.'s movement he began immediately looking about him very uneasily. But our hero already held his last night's guest by the sleeve. The clerks surrounding the two titular councilors stepped back and waited with curiosity to see what would happen. The senior titular councilor realized that public opinion was not on his side, he realized that a plot was on foot against him; this made it all the more necessary for him to hold his own now. The moment was a decisive one.

"Well!" said Mr. Golyadkin Jr., looking rather insolently at Mr. Golyadkin Sr.

The latter could hardly breathe.

"I don't know," he began, "in what way to make plain to you the strangeness of your behavior toward me, sir."

"Well, sir. Go on." At this point Mr. Golyadkin Jr. turned around and winked to the clerks standing around, as though to give them to understand that a comedy was just now about to begin.

"The impudence and shamelessness of your manners with me, sir, in the present case, unmask your true character . . . better than any words of mine could do. Don't rely on your game; it is rather poor. . . ."

"Come, Yakov Petrovich, tell me now, how did you sleep?" answered Mr. Golyadkin Jr., looking Mr. Golyadkin Sr. straight in the eye.

"You forget yourself, sir," said the titular councilor, utterly at a loss, hardly able to feel the floor under his feet. "I trust that you will take a different tone. . . ."

"My darling!" exclaimed Mr. Golyadkin Jr., making a rather unseemly grimace at Mr. Golyadkin Sr., and suddenly, quite unexpectedly, under the pretense of fondling him, he pinched his chubby right cheek with two fingers.

Our hero blazed up. . . . As soon as Mr. Golyadkin Jr. noticed that his opponent, quivering in every limb, speechless with rage, as red as a lobster, and exasperated beyond all endurance, might actually be driven to attack him, he promptly and in the most shameless way hastened to forestall him. Having patted him two or three times on the cheek, tickled him two or three times, played with him for a few seconds in this way, while his victim stood rigid and beside himself with fury, to the not inconsiderable diversion of the young men standing around, Mr. Golyadkin Jr., with a most revolting shamelessness, gave Mr. Golyadkin Sr. a flick on his rather prominent paunch, and with a most venomous and suggestive smile said to him, "None of your tricks, brother Yakov, none of your tricks! We'll be sly, you and I, Yakov Petrovich, we'll be sly."

Then, before our hero could come to himself to the slightest extent after the last attack, Mr. Golyadkin Jr. (first giving a little smile to the spectators standing around) suddenly assumed a most businesslike, occupied, and official air, dropped his eyes to the floor, drew himself in, shrank together, and saying rapidly "on a special commission" cut a caper with his short legs and darted away into the next room. Our hero could not believe his eyes and was still in no condition to pull himself together. . . .

At last he came to his senses. Recognizing in a flash that he was ruined, annihilated, as it were, that he had disgraced himself and sullied his reputation, that he had been held up to ridicule and spat upon in the presence of strangers, that he had been treacherously abused by one whom he had considered only the day before as his greatest and most trustworthy friend, that he had, in fact, utterly failed, Mr. Golyadkin Sr. rushed in pursuit of his enemy. At the moment he would not even think of the witnesses of his ignominy.

"They're all in a conspiracy together," he said to himself; "they stand by each other and set each other on to attack me." After taking a dozen steps, however, our hero perceived clearly that all pursuit would be vain and useless, and so he turned back. "You won't get away," he thought, "you'll come a cropper in good time; the wolf will have to pay for the sheep's tears."

With ferocious composure and the most energetic determination, Mr. Golyadkin went up to his chair and sat down. "You won't get away," he said again. Now it was not a question of passive resistance; there was determination and aggression in the air, and anyone who had seen how Mr. Golyadkin at that moment, flushed and scarcely able to restrain his excitement, thrust his pen into the inkwell and with what fury he began scribbling on the paper, could be certain beforehand that the matter would not pass off like this, and could not end simply in some sort of a womanish way. In the depth of his soul he formed a resolution, and in his heart of hearts swore to carry it out. To tell the truth, he still did not quite know how to act, or rather did not know at all, but never mind, that did not matter!

"Imposture and shamelessness do not pay nowadays, sir. Imposture and shamelessness, sir, lead to no good, but lead to the halter. Grishka Otrepyev[6] was the only one, sir, who gained by imposture, deceiving a blind people, and even that not for long."

In spite of this last circumstance Mr. Golyadkin decided

[6] The pretender to the Russian throne who reigned in 1604–6 as (Pseudo-) Demetrius I.—A.Y.

to wait till such time as the mask should fall from certain persons and something should be made manifest. For this it was necessary, in the first place, that office hours should be over as soon as possible, and till then our hero decided to undertake nothing. Then, when office hours were over, he would take one step. He would know then how he must act after taking that step, how to arrange his whole plan of action, to shatter the horn of arrogance and crush the snake gnawing the dust in contemptible impotence. To allow himself to be treated like a rag used for wiping dirty boots, Mr. Golyadkin could not. He could not consent to that, especially in the present case. Had it not been for that last disgrace, our hero might have, perhaps, brought himself reluctantly to control his anger; he might, perhaps, have decided to hold his peace, to submit and not protest too obstinately; he would just have argued a little, have tentatively put in a claim, have proved that he was in the right, then he would have given way a little, then, perhaps, he would have given way a little more, then he would have come around altogether, then, especially when the opposing party solemnly admitted that he was in the right, perhaps, he would have made it up with his adversary, would even have been a little touched, there might even, perhaps—who could tell?—spring up a new, close, warm friendship, on an even broader basis than the friendship of last night, so that this friendship might, in the end, completely eclipse the unpleasantness of the rather unseemly resemblance of the two individuals, so that both the titular councilors might be highly delighted, and might go on living in this state till they were a hundred, and so on. To tell the whole truth, Mr. Golyadkin began to regret a little that he had stood up for himself and his rights, and had at once come in for unpleasantness in consequence.

"Should he give in," thought Mr. Golyadkin, "say he was joking, I would forgive him. I would forgive him even more if he would acknowledge it aloud. But I won't let myself be treated like a rag. I have not allowed even persons very different from him to treat me so, still less will I permit a depraved person to attempt it. I am not a rag. I am not a rag, sir!"

In short, our hero made up his mind. "It's your own fault, sir!" he thought. He made up his mind to protest, and to protest with all his might to the very last. That was the sort of man he was! He could not consent to allow himself to be insulted, still less to allow himself to be treated as a rag, and, above all, to allow a thoroughly vicious man to treat him so. No quarreling, however, no quarreling! Possibly if someone wanted, if someone, for instance, actually insisted on turning Mr. Golyadkin into a rag, he might have done so, might have done so without opposition or punishment (Mr. Golyadkin was himself conscious of this at times), and he would have been a rag and not Golyadkin—yes, a nasty, filthy rag; but it would not have been a simple rag, it would have been a rag possessed of pride, it would have been an animated rag possessed of feelings, even though neither his pride nor his feelings could assert themselves, and lay hidden deep down in the filthy folds of the rag, still the feelings were there. . . .

The hours dragged on for an incredibly long time; at last it struck four. Soon after, all got up and, following the chief, each one made for home. Mr. Golyadkin mingled with the crowd; he kept a vigilant lookout, and did not lose sight of the man he wanted. At last our hero saw that his friend ran up to the office attendants who handed the clerks their overcoats, and, while waiting for his, fawned on them in his usual nasty way. The minute was a decisive one. Mr. Golyadkin forced his way somehow through the crowd and, anxious not to be left behind, he, too, began fussing about his overcoat. But Mr. Golyadkin's friend was given his overcoat first because here, too, he had succeeded, as he always did, in getting around people by whispering something to them, wheedling them, fawning on them.

After putting on his overcoat, Mr. Golyadkin Jr. glanced ironically at Mr. Golyadkin Sr., doing this openly and obviously to spite him, looked about him with his characteristic insolence, finally walked mincingly about among the other clerks—no doubt in order to leave a good impression behind—said a word to one, whispered something to another, respectfully accosted a third, directed a smile at a fourth, gave his hand to a fifth, and gaily darted downstairs. Mr Golyadkin Sr. pursued him, and to his inexpressible delight overtook him on the last step and seized him by the collar of his overcoat. It seemed as though Mr. Golyadkin Jr. was a little disconcerted, and looked about him with a helpless air.

"What do you mean by this?" he whispered to Mr. Golyadkin at last, in a weak voice.

"Sir, if you are a gentleman, I trust that you will recall our friendly relations of yesterday," said our hero.

"Ah, yes! Well? Did you sleep well, sir?"

Fury rendered Mr. Golyadkin Sr. speechless for a moment.

"I slept well, sir . . . but allow me to tell you, sir, that you are playing a very intricate game. . . ."

"Who says so? My enemies say that," answered abruptly the man who called himself Mr. Golyadkin, and, saying this, he unexpectedly freed himself from the feeble hand of the real Mr. Golyadkin. As soon as he was free he rushed down the stairs, looked around him, saw a cab, ran up to it, got in, and in one moment vanished from Mr. Golyadkin Sr.'s sight. The despairing titular councilor, abandoned by all, gazed about him, but there was no other cab. He tried to run, but his legs gave way under him. With a look of open-mouthed astonishment on his countenance, feeling annihilated, shriveled up, he leaned helplessly against a lamppost, and remained so for some minutes in the middle of the pavement. It seemed as though all were lost for Mr. Golyadkin.

Chapter IX

Everything, apparently, even nature itself, seemed to be up in arms against Mr. Golyadkin; but he was still on his legs and unconquered; he had the feeling that he was unconquered. He was ready to do battle. He rubbed his hands with such feeling and such energy when he recovered from his first amazement that it could be deduced from his air alone that he would not give in. Yet the danger was imminent; evident; Mr. Golyadkin felt this too; but how to grapple with it, with this danger? That was the question. The thought even flashed through Mr. Golyadkin's mind for a moment, "Why not leave it just so, simply give it up? Why, what is it? It's just nothing. I'll keep apart as though it were not me," thought Mr. Golyadkin. "I'll let it all pass; it's not me, and that's all about it; he's apart too, maybe he'll give up too; he'll fuss about, the rascal, he'll fuss about, he'll fidget awhile and give up. That's how it will be! I'll succeed by dint of meekness. And, indeed, where is the danger? Come, what danger is there? I should like anyone to tell me where the danger lies in this business. It is a trivial affair. An everyday affair . . ."

At this point Mr. Golyadkin's tongue stopped short; the words died away on his lips; he even swore at himself for this thought; he exposed himself on the spot as a despicable coward for having this thought. This did not, however, advance him any farther. He felt that it was absolutely necessary for him at the moment to decide on some course of action. He even felt that he would give a great deal to anyone who could tell him what he must make up his mind to do. Yes, but how could he guess? Though, indeed, he had no time to guess. In any case, that he might lose no time he took a cab and dashed home.

"Well? How are you feeling now?" he wondered; "how are you pleased to be feeling, Yakov Petrovich? What are you going to do? What are you going to do now, you rogue, you, you rascal, you? You've brought yourself to this plight, and now you are weeping and whimpering!"

So Mr. Golyadkin taunted himself as he jolted along in the shaky vehicle. To taunt himself and so rub salt on his wounds was, at this time, an intense satisfaction to Mr. Golyadkin, almost a voluptuous delight.

"Well," he thought, "if some magician were to turn up now, or if it could come to pass in some official way and I were told, 'Give a finger of your right hand, Golyadkin —and we will be quits; there shall not be the other Golyadkin, and you will be happy, only you won't have your finger'—yes, I would give up my finger, I certainly would give it up without making a wry face. . . . The devil take it all!" the despairing titular councilor cried at last. "Why, what is it all for? Well, it all had to be; yes, it absolutely had to; yes, just this had to be, as though nothing else were possible! And it was all right at first. Everyone was pleased and happy. But there, it had to happen! There's nothing to be gained by talking, though one must act."

And so, almost resolved upon some action, Mr. Golyadkin reached home, and without a moment's delay snatched up his pipe, and, sucking at it with all his might and puffing out clouds of smoke to right and to left, began pacing up and down the room in a state of violent excitement. Meanwhile, Petrushka began laying the table. At last Mr. Golyadkin made up his mind completely, flung aside his pipe, put on his overcoat, said he would not dine at home, and ran out of the flat. Petrushka, panting, overtook him on the stairs with the hat he had forgotten. Mr. Golyadkin took his hat, wanted so incidentally to justify himself somewhat in Petrushka's eyes, so that the fellow might not get such ideas into his head as "queer thing, he forgetting his hat." But as Petrushka walked away at once and would not even look at him, Mr. Golyadkin put on his hat without further explanation, ran downstairs, and, repeating to himself that perhaps everything might be for the best, and that things would somehow come right, though he was conscious among other things of a cold chill right down to his heels, he went out into the street, took a cab, and hastened to Andrey Filippovich's.

"Would it not be better tomorrow, though?" thought Mr. Golyadkin, as he took hold of the bell rope of Andrey Filippovich's flat. "And, besides, what can I say in particular? There is nothing particular about the situation. It's such a wretched affair, yes, it really is wretched, paltry, that is, almost a paltry affair . . . yes, that's what it all is, this incident. . . ." Suddenly Mr. Golyadkin pulled at the bell; the bell rang; footsteps were heard within. . . . Mr. Golyadkin cursed himself on the spot for his hastiness and audacity. His recent unpleasant experiences, which he had almost forgotten because of other troubles, and his clash with Andrey Filippovich immediately came to his mind. But by now it was too late to run away; the door opened. Luckily for Mr. Golyadkin he was informed that Andrey Filippovich had not returned from the office and had not dined at home.

"I know where he dines: he dines near the Izmailovsky Bridge," thought our hero; and he was immensely relieved. To the footman's inquiry what message he would leave, he said, "It's all right, my good man, I'll look in later," and he even ran downstairs with a certain cheerful briskness. Going out into the street, he decided to dismiss the cab and paid the driver. When the man asked for a tip, saying he had been waiting in the street and had not spared his horse for his honor, he gave him five kopecks extra, and even willingly; and then walked on.

"It really is the sort of thing," thought Mr. Golyadkin, "that cannot be left like that; though, if one thinks it over, thinks it over sensibly, what am I to fuss about here, in reality? Well, I shall, however, go on discussing why I should make a fuss, toil, hustle, suffer, wear myself out. To begin with, the thing's done and there's no undoing it . . . of course, there's no undoing it! Let us put it like this: a man turns up with a satisfactory reference, said to be a capable clerk, of good conduct, only he is poor and has suffered many reverses—all sorts of difficulties. Well, poverty is no crime; so I must stand aside. Well, really, what nonsense it is! Well, the man is so made, so made by nature itself, that he and someone else are as like as two peas, that he is the spit and image of the other man; how could they refuse to take him into the department on that account? If it is fate, if it is only fate, if it is only blind chance that is to blame—is he to be treated like a rag, is he to be refused employment? Why, what would become of justice after that? He is a poor man, lost, cowed; it makes one's heart ache; compassion bids one care for him! Yes, indeed, our superiors would be fine fellows if they took the same view as a reprobate like me! What a noddle I have! It holds foolishness enough for a dozen! Yes, yes! They did right, and many thanks to them for being good to a poor, luckless fellow. . . . Why, let us assume for a moment that we are twins, that we had been born twin brothers, and nothing else—there it is! Well, what of it? Why, nothing! All the clerks can be trained to accept it. . . . And an outsider, coming into our office, would certainly find nothing unseemly or offensive in the circumstance. In fact, there is really something touching in it; to think that divine Providence has created two men exactly alike, and the beneficent head of the department, seeing the divine handiwork, has sheltered the twins.

"It would, of course," Mr. Golyadkin went on, taking breath and dropping his voice, "it would, of course, have been better if there had been . . . if there had been nothing of this touching kindness, and if there had been no twins either. . . . The devil take it all! And why did it have to be? And what was the particular and urgent necessity for it? My goodness! What a fine mess the devil has made of it! Besides, he has such a character, too, he's of such a playful, horrid disposition—he's such a scoundrel, a nimble fellow, a toady, a lickspittle; such a Golyadkin! I dare say he will misbehave and disgrace my name, the blackguard! And now I have to look after him and wait upon him! What a nuisance! However, what of it? Well, never mind! Granted, he's a scoundrel, well, let him be a scoundrel, but to make up for it, the other one's honest; so he will be a scoundrel and I'll be honest, and they'll say that this Golyadkin's a rascal, don't take any notice of him, and don't mix him up with the other who is honest, virtuous, meek, gentle, always to be relied upon in the service, and worthy of promotion; that's how it is! Well, very good. . . . But what if . . . what if they get us mixed up? . . . You can expect anything from him! Oh, Lord! . . . The rascal will not stop at cheating—he will pretend to be another, as though a man were a rag, without considering that a man is not a rag. Oh, Lord! Ough, what a calamity!"

Arguing and lamenting in this way, Mr. Golyadkin ran on without choosing his way, and not knowing where he was going. He came to his senses on Nevsky Prospect, only owing to the chance that he ran full-tilt into a passer-by, so that he saw stars. Mr. Golyadkin muttered his excuses without raising his head, and it was only after the passer-by, muttering something far from flattering, had walked a considerable distance away that he raised his nose and looked about to see where he was and how he had got there. Noticing that he was close to the restaurant in which he had rested while getting ready for the dinner party at Olsufy Ivanovich's, our hero was suddenly conscious of a pinching and nipping sensation in his stomach; he remembered that he had not dined; no, there was no prospect of a dinner party anywhere. And so, without losing precious time, he ran upstairs into the restaurant to have a snack as quickly as possible, and to avoid delay. And, though everything in the restaurant was rather expensive, that minor circumstance did not on this occasion make Mr. Golyadkin pause, and, indeed, he had no time to pause over such trifles. In the brightly lighted room the customers were crowded around the counter, heaped with all sorts of such tidbits as are consumed by well-bred persons. The attendant scarcely had time to fill glasses, hand out edibles, take money, and give change. Mr. Golyadkin waited for his turn and modestly stretched out his hand for an open-faced patty. Having retreated into a corner, turned his back on the company, and eaten the patty with appetite, he went back to the attendant, put down his plate, and, knowing the price, took out a ten-kopeck piece and laid the coin on the counter, trying to catch the shopman's eye and point out to him that there was the money for one patty.

"One rouble ten kopecks," the attendant said through clenched teeth.

Mr. Golyadkin was astounded.

"You are speaking to me? . . . I . . . I took one patty, I believe."

"You've had eleven," the man retorted confidently.

"You . . . so it seems to me . . . I believe, you're mistaken. . . . I really took only one patty, I think."

"I counted them; you took eleven. Since you've had them, you must pay for them. We don't give anything away free of charge."

Mr. Golyadkin was stunned. "Am I the victim of some sort of witchcraft?" he wondered. Meanwhile, the man waited for Mr. Golyadkin to make up his mind; people crowded around Mr. Golyadkin; he was already feeling in his pocket for a silver rouble, to pay the full amount at once in order to avoid further trouble.

"Well, if it was eleven, it was eleven," he thought, turning as red as a lobster. "Why, what does it matter if eleven patties have been eaten? Why, a man's hungry, so he eats eleven patties; well, let him eat, and may it do him good; and there's nothing to wonder at in that, and there's nothing to laugh at. . . ."

At that moment something seemed to stab Mr. Golyadkin. He raised his eyes and—at once he guessed the riddle, knew what the sorcery was; all his difficulties were solved. . . .

In the doorway to the next room, almost directly behind the attendant and facing Mr. Golyadkin, in the doorway which, till that moment, our hero had taken for a looking glass, a man was standing—he was standing, Mr. Golyadkin himself was standing—not the original Mr. Golyadkin, the hero of our story, but the other Mr. Golyadkin, the new Mr. Golyadkin. The second Mr. Golyadkin was apparently in excellent spirits. He smiled to Mr. Golyadkin the first, nodded to him, winked, minced a little, and looked as though in another minute he would vanish, would disappear into the next room, and then go out, maybe, by a back exit; and there it would be, and all pursuit would be in vain. In his hand he had the last morsel of the tenth patty, and before Mr. Golyadkin's very eyes he popped it into his mouth and smacked his lips.

"He has impersonated me, the scoundrel!" thought Mr. Golyadkin, flushing hot with shame. "He is not ashamed of the publicity of it! Do they see him? No one seems to notice him. . . ."

Mr. Golyadkin threw down his rouble as though it burned his fingers, and, without noticing the shopman's insolently significant grin, a smile of triumph and serene power, he extricated himself from the crowd, and rushed away without looking around. "I must be thankful that at least he has not completely compromised me!" thought Mr. Golyadkin Sr. "I must be thankful to the brigand, to him and to fate, that everything was satisfactorily settled. The waiter was rude, that was all. But, after all, he was in the right. One rouble and ten kopecks were owing; so he was in the right. 'We don't give anything away free of charge,' he said! He might have been more polite, though, the wafer!"

All this Mr. Golyadkin said to himself as he went downstairs to the entrance, but on the last step he stopped dead, and suddenly flushed till the tears came into his eyes at the insult to his dignity. After standing stock-still for half a minute, he stamped his foot resolutely, at one bound leaped from the porch step into the street, and, without looking around, rushed breathless and unconscious of fatigue back home to his flat in Shestilavochny Street. When he got home, without removing his overcoat, contrary to his habit, without even stopping to take his pipe, he sat down on the sofa, drew the inkwell toward him, took up a pen, got a sheet of notepaper, and, with a hand that trembled from inward excitement, began scribbling the following epistle:

Dear Yakov Petrovich!

I should not have taken up my pen if my circumstances, and you yourself, my dear sir, had not compelled me to do so. Believe me that necessity alone has induced me to enter upon such an explanation with you and therefore, first of all, I beg you to look upon this step of mine not as a premeditated intention to insult you, my dear sir, but as the inevitable consequence of the circumstances that are a bond between us now.

("I think that's all right, proper, courteous, though not lacking in force and firmness. . . . I don't think there is anything for him to take offense at. Besides, I'm fully within my rights," thought Mr. Golyadkin, reading over what he had written.)

Your strange and sudden appearance, my dear sir, on a stormy night, after the coarse and unseemly behavior toward me of my enemies, for whom I feel too much contempt even to mention their names, was the starting point of all the misunderstandings existing between us at the present time. Your obstinate desire to persist in your course of action, sir, and forcibly to enter the circle of my existence and all my relations in practical life, oversteps the limits imposed by the merest politeness and every rule of civilized society. I imagine there is no need, sir, for me to refer to your ravishing my papers, and my good name, in order to gain the favor of our superiors— a favor you have not deserved. There is no need to refer here either to your intentional and insulting refusal of the explanation necessitated by the circumstances. Finally, to omit nothing, I will not allude here to your last strange, one may even say, your incomprehensible behavior toward me at the coffeehouse. I am far from lamenting the needless—for me—loss of a rouble; but I cannot help expressing my indignation at the recollection of your open infringement upon my honor, and, what is more, perpetrated in the presence of several persons of good breeding, though not belonging to my circle of acquaintance.

("Am I not going too far?" wondered Mr. Golyadkin. "Isn't it too much; won't it be too insulting—that hint at good breeding, for instance? . . . But there, it doesn't matter! I must show him the firmness of my character. I might, however, to soften him, flatter him, and butter him up at the end. But there, we shall see.")

But I should not have wearied you with my letter, my dear sir, if I were not firmly convinced that the nobility of your sentiments and your open, candid character would suggest to you yourself a means for retrieving all lapses and restoring everything to the original state.

I venture to rest confidently assured that you will not take my letter in a sense derogatory to yourself, and at the same time that you will not refuse to explain yourself expressly on this occasion in writing, sending the letter by my man.

In expectation of your reply, I have the honor, dear sir, to remain,

Your obedient servant,
Y. Golyadkin

"Well, that is quite all right. The thing's done, it has come to letter-writing. But who is to blame for that? He himself is to blame; he himself reduces a man to the necessity of demanding written documents. And I am within my rights. . . ."

Having read over his letter for the last time, Mr. Golyadkin folded it up, sealed it, and called Petrushka. Petrushka came in looking, as usual, sleepy and extremely cross about something.

"You will take this letter, my boy . . . do you understand?" Petrushka was silent.

"You will take it to the office; there you must find the clerk on duty, provincial secretary Vahrameyev. He is the one on duty today. Do you understand that?"

"I understand."

"'I understand'! Can't you say, 'I understand, sir'? Ask for the secretary Vahrameyev, and tell him that your master greets him and humbly requests him to find out from the departmental address book where the titular councilor, Golyadkin, lives."

Petrushka remained mute, and, as Mr. Golyadkin fancied, smiled.

"Well, so you see, Pyotr, you will ask him for the address, and find out where the new clerk, Golyadkin, lives."

"Very good."

"You will ask for the address and then take this letter there. Do you understand?"

"I understand."

"If there . . . where you have to take the letter, that gentleman to whom you have to give it, I mean Golyadkin . . . What are you laughing at, you blockhead?"

"What is there to laugh at? What is it to me! I wasn't doing anything sir. It's not for the likes of us to laugh. . . ."

"Well, now . . . if that gentleman should ask, 'How is your master, how is he getting on?'; if he . . . well, if he should ask you anything—you hold your tongue, and answer, 'My master is all right, and begs you for an answer to his letter.' Do you understand?"

"Yes, sir."

"Well, then, say, 'My master is all right and quite well, and is just getting ready to pay a call; and he asks you for an answer in writing.' You got that?"

"Yes."

"Well, go along, then.

"Why, what a bother I have with this blockhead! He laughs to himself, and that's all. What's he laughing at? I've lived to see trouble. Here I've certainly lived to see trouble.

Though it may perhaps all turn out for the best. . . . That rascal will gad about for two hours now, I expect; he'll go off somewhere else. . . . There's no sending him anywhere. What misery it is! . . . What misery has come upon me!"

Feeling his misfortune to the full, our hero made up his mind to remain passive for two hours till Petrushka returned. For about an hour he walked about the room, smoked, then put aside his pipe and sat down to a book, then he lay down on the sofa, then took up his pipe again, then again began running about the room. He tried to think things over, but was absolutely unable to put his mind to anything. At last the agony of remaining passive reached its climax and Mr. Golyadkin made up his mind to take a certain step. "Petrushka will stay away another hour," he thought. "I can investigate the matter; I shall investigate the matter in my own way."

Without loss of time, in haste to investigate the matter, Mr. Golyadkin took his hat, left the room, locked up his flat, went in to the porter, gave him the key, together with ten kopecks—Mr. Golyadkin had become extraordinarily freehanded of late—and was off. Mr. Golyadkin went first on foot to the Izmailovsky Bridge. It took him half an hour to get there. When he reached the goal of his journey he went straight into the yard of the house so familiar to him, and glanced up at the windows of the councilor of state Berendyev's flat. Except for three windows with red curtains, all the rest were dark.

"Olsufy Ivanovich has no visitors today, I suppose," thought Mr. Golyadkin; "they must all be staying at home today."

After standing for some time in the yard, our hero was on the point of deciding on some course of action. But he was apparently not destined to reach a decision. Mr. Golyadkin changed his mind, and, giving up the idea as a bad job, went back into the street.

"No, it's not here that I should have come. What could

I do here? . . . No, I'd better, I mean . . . investigate the matter personally."

Having come to this conclusion, Mr. Golyadkin rushed off to his office. He had a long way to go. Besides, the streets were horribly muddy, and the wet snow came down in thick flakes. But it seemed as though difficulty did not exist for our hero at the moment. He was drenched through, it is true, and he was no little spattered with mud. "But that's no matter," he said to himself, "so long as the goal is reached." And Mr. Golyadkin certainly was nearing his goal. The dark mass of the huge government building stood up black before his eyes.

"Stay," he thought; "where am I going, and what am I going to do here? Suppose I do find out where he lives? Meanwhile, Petrushka will certainly have come back and brought me the answer. I am only wasting precious time, I have already wasted a lot of time. But no matter; all this can still be put right. Though shouldn't I, perhaps, go in and see Vahrameyev? But, no, I'll go later. . . . Oh! There was no need to have gone out at all. But, there, it's my character! I've a knack of always seizing a chance of rushing ahead of things, whether there is a need to or not. . . . H'm! . . . What time is it? It must be nine by now. Petrushka might have come and not found me at home. It was pure folly on my part to go out. . . . Oh, it is really a nuisance!"

Having thus sincerely acknowledged that he had done something exceedingly foolish, our hero ran back to Shestilavochny Street. He arrived there, weary and exhausted. From the porter he learned that Petrushka had not returned yet.

"To be sure! I had a foreboding it would be so," thought our hero; "and meanwhile it's nine o'clock. What a scoundrel! He's always tippling somewhere! Mercy on us! What a day has fallen to my miserable lot!"

Reflecting and lamenting in this way, Mr. Golyadkin unlocked his flat, got a light, took off his outdoor things, smoked his pipe and, tired, worn out, exhausted, and hungry, lay down on the sofa and waited for Petrushka. The candle burned dimly; the light flickered on the wall. . . . Mr. Golyadkin gazed and gazed, and thought and thought, and fell fast asleep at last.

It was late when he woke up. The candle had almost completely burned down, was smoking and on the point of going out. Mr. Golyadkin jumped up, shook himself, and remembered absolutely all. Behind the screen he heard Petrushka snoring lustily. Mr. Golyadkin rushed to the window—not a light anywhere. He opened the wicket—all was still; the city was asleep as though it were dead; so it must have been two or three o'clock—so it proved to be, indeed; the clock behind the partition made an effort and struck two. Mr. Golyadkin rushed behind the partition.

He succeeded, somehow, though only after great exertions, in rousing Petrushka, and making him sit up in his bed. At that moment the candle went out completely. About ten minutes passed before Mr. Golyadkin succeeded in finding another candle and lighting it. In the interval Petrushka had fallen asleep again.

"You scoundrel, you worthless fellow, you!" said Mr. Golyadkin, shaking him up again. "Will you get up, will you wake?" After half an hour of effort Mr. Golyadkin succeeded, however, in rousing his servant thoroughly, and dragging him out from behind the partition. Only then, our hero noticed that Petrushka was what is called dead-drunk and could hardly stand on his legs.

"You loafer, you!" cried Mr. Golyadkin; "you highway robber! You're the death of me! Good heavens! Whatever has he done with the letter? Oh, my God! Where is it? . . . And why did I write it? As though there were any need for me to have written it! I went scribbling away out of pride, like a booby! I've got myself into this fix because of conceit! That is what conceit does for you, you rascal, that is what! . . . Come, what have you done with the letter, you robber? To whom did you give it?"

"I didn't give anyone no letter; and I never had no letter . . . so there!"

Mr. Golyadkin wrung his hands in despair.

"Listen, Pyotr . . . listen to me, listen to me. . . ."

"I am listening . . ."

"Where have you been?—answer . . ."

"Where have I been? . . . I've been to see good people!
What is it to me!"

"Oh, Lord! Where did you go, to begin with? Did you
go to the office? . . . Listen, Pyotr, perhaps you're drunk?"

"Me drunk! May I be struck dead on the spot this minute! I haven't had a drop, not a drop—so there. . . ."

"No, no, it's no matter your being drunk. . . . I only
asked; it's all right your being drunk; I don't mind,
Petrusha, I don't mind. . . . Perhaps it's only that you have
forgotten, but you'll remember it all. Come, try to remember—have you been to see that clerk, Vahrameyev; have
you been to him or not?"

"I haven't been, and there ain't no such clerk. May I
be . . ."

"No, no, Pyotr! No, Petrusha, you know I don't mind.
Why, you see I don't mind. . . . Well, what does it matter! Well, it's cold and damp outside, and so a man has a
drop, and it's no matter. I am not angry. I've been drinking myself today, my boy. . . . Come, own up, try and
remember, did you go to Vahrameyev?"

"Well, then, now, this is how it was, it's the truth—I
did go, may I be . . ."

"Well, it's all right, Petrusha, that's quite all right. You
see, I'm not angry. . . . Come, come," our hero went on,
coaxing his servant more and more, patting him on the
shoulder and smiling to him, "come, you had a little nip,
you scoundrel. . . . You had two-penn'orth of something,
I suppose? You're a rogue! Well, that's no matter; come,
you see that I'm not angry. . . . I'm not angry, my boy,
I'm not angry. . . ."

"No, I'm not a rogue, say what you like. . . . I only
dropped in on some good people. I'm not a rogue, and I
never have been a rogue. . . ."

"Oh, no, no, Petrusha; listen, Pyotr, you know I wasn't

scolding when I called you a rogue. I said that to comfort you, I used the word in a higher sense. You see, Petrusha, it is sometimes a compliment to a man when you call him a rogue, a cunning fellow, that he knows what's what and would not let anyone take him in. Some men like it. . . . Well, well, it doesn't matter! Come, tell me, Petrusha, without keeping anything back, openly, as to a friend. . . . Did you go to Vahrameyev's, and did he give you the address?"

"He did give me the address, he did give me the address too. He's a fine gentleman! 'Your master,' says he, 'is a fine man,' says he, 'very fine man,' says he, 'give your master my regards,' says he, 'thank him and say that I like him,' says he—'that I do respect your master,' says he, 'because,' says he, 'your master, Petrusha,' says he, 'is a fine man, and you,' says he, 'Petrusha, are a good man, too. . . .'"

"But the address, the address! You Judas!" The last word Mr. Golyadkin uttered almost in a whisper.

"And the address . . . he did give the address too."

"He did? Well, where then does Golyadkin, the clerk Golyadkin, the titular councilor, live?"

"'Why,' says he, 'Golyadkin lives on Shestilavochny Street. When you get to Shestilavochny Street, take the stairs on the right and it's the fourth floor. And there,' says he, 'you'll find Golyadkin. . . .'"

"You scoundrel, you!" our hero cried, out of patience at last. "You highway robber! Why, that's my address; why, you are talking about me. But there's another Golyadkin; I'm talking of the other one, you scoundrel!"

"Well, that's as you please! What is it to me? Have it your own way. . . ."

"And the letter. The letter?"

"What letter? There wasn't any letter, and I didn't see no letter."

"But what have you done with it, you rascal?"

"I delivered the letter, I delivered it. 'Give him my regards,' says he, 'thank him. Your master's a nice man,' says he. 'Give my regards,' says he, 'to your master. . . .'"

"But who said that? Was it Golyadkin said it?"

Petrushka was silent for a moment, and then, with a broad grin, stared straight into his master's face. . . .

"Listen, you robber, you!" began Mr. Golyadkin, breathless, beside himself with fury; "listen, what have you done to me? Tell me what you've done to me? You've destroyed me, you villain, you've cut the head off my shoulders, you Judas!"

"Well, have it your own way! I don't care," said Petrushka in a resolute tone of voice, retreating behind the partition.

"Come here, come here, you robber. . . ."

"I'm not coming to you now, I'm not coming at all. What do I care? I'm going to good folk. . . . Good folk live honestly, good folk live without cheating, and they don't come double. . . ."

Mr. Golyadkin's hands and feet went ice cold, his breath failed him. . . .

"Yes, sir," Petrushka went on, "they never come in twos. They don't offend God and honest folk. . . ."

"You loafer, you are drunk! Go to sleep now, you robber, you! And tomorrow you'll catch it," Mr. Golyadkin added in a voice hardly audible. As for Petrushka, he muttered something more; then he could be heard getting into bed, making it creak. After a prolonged yawn, he stretched, and at last his snoring announced that he was sleeping the sleep of the just, as they say. Mr. Golyadkin was neither alive nor dead. Petrushka's behavior, his very strange, though vague, hints, at which it was useless to be angry, especially as they were uttered by a drunken man, and, finally, the sinister turn taken by the affair, all this shook Mr. Golyadkin to the depths of his being.

"And what on earth possessed me to go for him in the middle of the night?" said our hero, trembling all over from a sick sensation. "What the devil made me have anything to do with a drunken man! What could I expect from a drunken man? Whatever he says is a lie. But what was he hinting at, the robber? Good Lord! And why did I write all those letters? I'm my own enemy, I'm my own murderer! I couldn't hold my tongue! I had to go scribbling nonsense! And what now? You are going to rack and ruin, you are an old rag, and yet you worry about your pride; you say, 'It's a slur on my honor,' you must stick up for your honor! My own murderer, that is what I am!"

Thus spoke Mr. Golyadkin, sitting on his sofa and hardly daring to stir for terror. Suddenly his eyes fastened upon an object which excited his interest to the utmost. In terror lest the object that caught his attention should prove to be an illusion, a figment of his imagination, he stretched out his hand to it with hope, with dread, with indescribable curiosity. . . . No, it was no figment! No delusion! It was a letter, really a letter, undoubtedly a letter, and addressed to him. Mr. Golyadkin took the letter from the table. His heart beat terribly.

"No doubt that scoundrel brought it," he thought, "put it there, and then forgot it; no doubt, that is how it happened: no doubt, that is just how it happened. . . ."

The letter was from Vahrameyev, a young fellow-clerk who had once been his friend. "I had a presentiment of this, though," thought our hero, "and I had a presentiment of all that there would be in the letter. . . ."

The letter was as follows:

My dear Yakov Petrovich!

Your servant is drunk, and there is no getting any sense out of him. For that reason I prefer to reply by letter. I hasten to inform you that the commission you've entrusted to me—that is, to deliver a letter to a certain person known to you, I agree to carry out carefully and exactly. That person, who is very well known to you—he has replaced a friend for me—and whose name I will refrain from mentioning (because I do not wish unnecessarily to blacken the reputation of a perfectly innocent man), lodges with us at Karolina Ivanovna's, in the room which used to be occupied by the infantry officer from Tambov when you were here. That person, however, you can always find in the company of honest and open-hearted people, which is more than one can say for some individuals. From this day on I intend to break off all connection with you; it's impossible for us to remain on friendly terms and to keep up our former comradeship. And, therefore, I beg you, my dear sir, immediately on the receipt of this candid letter from me, to send me the two roubles you owe me for the razors of foreign make which I sold you seven months ago, if you will kindly remember, when you were still living with us in the lodgings of Karolina Ivanovna, a lady whom I respect from the bottom of my heart. I am acting in this way because you, by the accounts I hear from intelligent persons, have lost your dignity and reputation and have become a source of danger to the morals of the innocent and uncontaminated, for some persons are not straightforward, their words are fraudulent, and their show of good intentions is suspicious. One can always and everywhere find people capable of standing up for Karolina Ivanovna, who was always irreproachable in her conduct, and who is, in the second place, an honest woman, and, what's more, a maiden lady, no longer young, though, on the other hand, of a good foreign family—and certain persons have asked me to mention this fact in this letter both by the way and also speaking for myself. In any case you will learn all in due time, if you haven't learned it yet, though you've made yourself notorious from one end of the town to the other, according to the accounts I hear from intelligent people, and consequently might well have received intelligence relating to you, my dear sir, that this person, known to you, whose name I will not mention here for certain honorable reasons, is highly respected by right-thinking people, and is, moreover, of lively and agreeable disposition, and is equally successful in the service and in

the society of persons of common sense, keeps his word
and is true in friendship, and does not insult behind their
back those with whom he is on friendly terms to their
face.

In any case, I remain

Your obedient servant,
N. Vahrameyev

P.S. You had better dismiss your man: he is a drunkard and probably gives you a great deal of trouble; you
had better engage Yevstafy, who used to be in service
here, and is now without a situation. Your present servant is not only a drunkard, but, what's more, he's a thief,
for only last week he sold a pound of lump sugar to
Karolina Ivanovna at a low price, which, in my opinion,
he could not have done otherwise than by robbing you
in a very sly way, little by little, at various times. I write
this to you for your own good, although some people can
do nothing but insult and deceive everybody, especially
persons of honesty and good nature; what is more, they
revile them behind their back and misrepresent them,
simply from envy, and because they can't call themselves such.

V

After reading Vahrameyev's letter our hero remained for
a long time sitting motionless on his sofa. A new light
seemed to be breaking through the obscure and baffling fog
which had surrounded him for the last two days. Our hero
was beginning to reach a partial understanding. . . . He
tried to get up from the sofa to take a turn about the room,
to rouse himself, to collect his scattered thoughts, to fix
them upon a certain subject, and then, having set himself
straight a little, to think over his situation thoroughly. But
as soon as he tried to stand up he fell back again at once,
weak and helpless. "Yes, of course, I had a presentiment of
all that; how he writes, though, and what is the real meaning of his words? Of course, I do understand the meaning;

but what will it lead to? If he had said straight out: it is thus and so, such and such is wanted, I would have done it. Things have taken such a turn, things have come to such an unpleasant pass! Oh, if only tomorrow would make haste and come, and I could get to work! I know now what to do. I shall say this and that, I accept the reasons, but I won't sell my honor, and so on. . . . But he, that notorious person, that discreditable individual, how does he come to be mixed up in it? And why has he turned up just here? Oh, if tomorrow would make haste and come! They'll give me a bad name before then, they are intriguing, they are working to spite me! The great thing is not to lose time, and now, for instance, to write a letter, and only to intimate this and that and that I agree to such and such. And at daybreak tomorrow to send it off, before he can do anything . . . and so checkmate them, get in before them, the darlings. . . . They will defame me, and that's the fact of the matter!"

Mr. Golyadkin drew the paper to him, took up a pen, and wrote the following missive in answer to the letter of the provincial secretary, Vahrameyev:

My dear Nestor Ignatyevich!

With amazement that distressed my heart have I perused your insulting letter to me, for I see clearly that you mean me when you speak of certain discreditable persons and falsely well-intentioned people. I see with genuine sorrow how rapidly the calumny has spread and how deeply it has taken root, to the detriment of my welfare, my honor, and my good name. And this is the more deplorable and insulting, since even honest people of a genuinely noble way of thinking, and, above all, of straightforward and open disposition, abandon the interests of honorable men and with all the best qualities of their hearts attach themselves to the pernicious rottenness, which in our difficult and immoral age has multiplied so greatly and so inauspiciously. In conclusion, I will say that the debt of two roubles of which you remind me I regard as a sacred duty to return to you in its entirety.

As for your hints, sir, concerning a certain person of the female sex, concerning the intentions, calculations, and various designs of that person, I can only tell you, my dear sir, that I have but a very dim and obscure understanding of those insinuations. Permit me, my dear sir, to preserve my honorable way of thinking and my good name undefiled. In any case, I am ready to stoop to an explanation in person, preferring a personal to a written explanation as more secure, and I am, moreover, ready to come to various peaceable agreements, mutual, of course. To that end I beg you, my dear sir, to convey to that person my readiness for a personal arrangement and, moreover, to beg her to fix the time and place of the interview. It grieved me, sir, to read your hints at my having insulted you, having been treacherous to our pristine friendship, and having spoken ill of you. I ascribe all this to misunderstanding, to the abominable calumny, envy, and ill-will of those whom I may justly call my bitterest enemies. But I suppose they do not know that innocence is strong through its very innocence, that the shamelessness, insolence, and revolting familiarity of some persons sooner or later gain the stigma of universal contempt; and that such persons will perish through nothing but their own indecency and the corruption of their hearts. In conclusion, I beg you, my dear sir, to convey to those persons that their strange pretension and dishonorable and fantastic desire to squeeze others out of the position which those others occupy, through their existence in this world, and to take their place, deserve amazement, pity, and, moreover, the madhouse; that, moreover, such efforts are strictly prohibited by law, which in my opinion is perfectly just, for everyone ought to be satisfied with his own place. There is a limit to everything and, if this is a joke, it is a joke in very bad taste. I will say more: it is an utterly immoral joke, for,

I make bold to assure you, sir, my own views which I have expounded above in regard to keeping *one's own place*, are purely moral.

In any case I have the honor to remain,

Your humble servant,
Y. Golyadkin

Chapter X

Altogether, it may be said that the adventure of the previous day had thoroughly unnerved Mr. Golyadkin. Our hero passed a very bad night; that is, he was unable to get five minutes' sleep; as though some practical joker had scattered bristles in his bed. He spent the whole night half-asleep, half-awake, tossing from side to side, from right to left, moaning and groaning, dozing off for a moment, waking up again a minute later, and all this was accompanied by a strange misery, vague memories, hideous visions—in short, everything disagreeable that can be imagined. . . .

At one moment the figure of Andrey Filippovich appeared before him in a strange, mysterious half-light, a frigid, wrathful figure, with a cold, harsh gaze and a stiffly polite expression of disapproval. . . . And as soon as Mr. Golyadkin was on the point of going up to Andrey Fillipovich to defend himself in some way and to prove to him that he was not at all what his enemies represented him, that he was like this and like that, that he even possessed this and that in addition to his ordinary innate virtues—at once a person only too well known for his discreditable behavior appeared on the scene, and by some most revolting means instantly frustrated poor Mr. Golyadkin's efforts; on the spot, almost before the latter's eyes, he blackened his reputation, trampled his dignity in the mud, and then immediately usurped his place in the service and in society. At another time Mr. Golyadkin's head itched from a fillip lately received and humbly accepted—received either in docility or somehow in the performance of his duties, a fillip against which it was difficult to protest. . . .

And while Mr. Golyadkin was racking his brains over the question why it was so difficult to protest even against such a fillip, this idea of a fillip gradually assumed a different form—the form of some well-known, trifling, or fairly sizable piece of nastiness which he had seen, heard, or even himself committed—and frequently committed, indeed, and not on nasty grounds, not from any nasty impulse, even, but just so—sometimes, for instance, out of delicacy, another time owing to his absolute defenselessness—finally because . . . because, in short, Mr. Golyadkin knew perfectly well *because of what!* At this point Mr. Golyadkin blushed in his sleep, and, smothering his blushes, muttered to himself that in this case, for instance, he ought to be able to show in this case the remarkable strength of his character; and then he wound up by asking himself, "What, after all, is strength of character? Why mention it now?" But what irritated and enraged Mr. Golyadkin most of all was that invariably, at such a moment, and on the spot, a person well known for his undignified libelous behavior turned up uninvited, and, regardless of the fact that the matter was apparently settled, he, too, would begin muttering, with an unseemly little smile, "What's the use of strength of character! How could you and I, Yakov Petrovich, have strength of character? . . ."

Or Mr. Golyadkin would dream that he was in the company of a number of persons distinguished for their wit and good breeding; that he, Mr. Golyadkin, too, was conspicuous for his wit and courtesy, that everybody liked him, even some of his enemies who were present began to like him, which pleased Mr. Golyadkin very much; that everyone gave him precedence, and that at last Mr. Golyadkin himself, with gratification, overheard the host, drawing one of the guests aside, speak in his, Mr. Golyadkin's, praise . . . and all of a sudden, apropos of nothing, there appeared again the person, notorious for his evil intentions and brutal impulses, in the form of Mr. Golyadkin Jr., and on the spot at once, in one moment, by his very appearance on the scene, Mr. Golyadkin Jr. would destroy all the triumph and glory of Mr. Golyadkin Sr., eclipse Mr. Golyadkin Sr., trample him in the mud, and, at last, prove clearly that Golyadkin Sr.—that is, the genuine one—was not the genuine at all but the spurious, and that he, Golyadkin Jr., was the real one; that, in fact, Mr. Golyadkin Sr. was not at all what he appeared to be, but someone very disgraceful, and that consequently he had no right to move in the society of honorable and well-bred people. And all this was done so quickly that Mr. Golyadkin had not time to open his mouth before all of them adhered, body and soul, to the wicked, sham Mr. Golyadkin, and with deepest contempt rejected him, the real and innocent Mr. Golyadkin. There was not one person left whose opinion the infamous Mr. Golyadkin had not changed around. There was not left one person, even the most insignificant of the company, to whom the false and worthless Mr. Golyadkin would not make up in his sweetest manner, upon whom he would not fawn in his own way, before whom he would not burn sweet and agreeable incense, so that the person thus treated simply sniffed and sneezed till the tears came, in token of the intensest pleasure. And the worst of it was that all this was done in a flash; the speed with which the suspicious and worthless Mr. Golyadkin moved was amazing!

He scarcely had time, for instance, to make up to one person and win his favor—and before one could wink an eye he was at another. He would stealthily fawn on him, pluck a smile of benevolence, shake his short, round, though rather wooden-looking leg, and already he would be at a third, wooing him, making up to him in a friendly way; before one had time to open one's mouth, before one had time to feel surprised, he would be at a fourth, on the same terms with him—it was horrible: sorcery and nothing else! And everyone was pleased with him and everybody liked him, and everyone was extolling him, and all were proclaiming in chorus that his courtesy and sarcastic wit were superior to the courtesy and sarcastic wit of the real Mr. Golyadkin and putting the real and innocent Mr. Golyadkin to shame thereby and rejecting the vivacious Mr. Golyadkin, and shoving and pushing out the well-intentioned Mr. Golyadkin, and showering blows on the man so well known for his love of his neighbors—the real Mr. Golyadkin!

Miserable, terrified, furious, the cruelly treated Mr. Golyadkin ran out into the street and tried to take a cab in order to drive straight to his Excellency's, or, at any rate, to Andrey Filippovich's, but—horror! the cabmen absolutely refused to take Mr. Golyadkin, saying, "We cannot drive two gentlemen exactly alike, sir; a good man tries to live honestly, your honor, and never comes double." Beside himself with shame, the perfectly honest Mr. Golyadkin looked around and did, in fact, assure himself with his own eyes that the cabmen and Petrushka, who was in league with them, were all quite right, for the depraved Mr. Golyadkin was actually on the spot, beside him, close at hand, and with his characteristic nastiness was again, at this critical moment, certainly preparing to do something very unseemly, and quite out of keeping with that refinement which is usually acquired by good breeding—that refinement of which the loathsome Mr. Golyadkin the second was always boasting at every opportunity. Beside himself with shame and despair, the utterly ruined though perfectly just Mr. Golyadkin plunged headlong, ready to go wherever fate might lead him; but at every step he took, at every tap of his foot on the granite of the pavement, there leaped up as though out of the earth a Mr. Golyadkin precisely the same, perfectly alike, and of a revolting depravity of heart. And all these precisely similar Golyadkins set to running after one another as soon as they appeared, and stretched in a long chain like a file of geese, hobbling after the real Mr. Golyadkin, so there was nowhere to escape from these duplicates—so that Mr. Golyadkin, who was in every way deserving of compassion, was breathless with terror; so that at last a terrible multitude of duplicates had sprung into being; so that the whole capital was at last chock-full of duplicate Golyadkins, and the police officer, seeing such a breach of decorum, was obliged to seize all these duplicates by the collar and to put them into the station house, which happened to be nearby. . . . Numb and frozen with horror, our hero would wake up, and, numb and frozen with horror, feel that his waking state was hardly more cheerful. . . . It was painful and harrowing. . . . He was overcome by such anguish that he felt as though someone were gnawing at his heart.

At last Mr. Golyadkin could endure it no longer. "This shall not be!" he cried, resolutely sitting up in bed, and after this exclamation he was fully awake.

It was apparently rather late in the day. It was unusually light in the room. The sunshine filtered through the frozen panes and flooded the room with light, which surprised Mr. Golyadkin not a little, for it was only at noon that the sun looked into his room; and at least, so far as Mr. Golyadkin could remember, the heavenly luminary had scarcely ever before deviated from its course. Our hero had hardly time to wonder at this when he heard the clock buzzing behind the partition and getting ready to strike. "Now," thought Mr. Golyadkin, and he prepared to listen with painful suspense. . . . But, to complete Mr. Golyadkin's astonishment, the clock put its back into the job and only struck once.

"What does this mean?" cried our hero, finally leaping out of bed. And, unable to believe his ears, he rushed behind the screen just as he was. It actually was one o'clock. Mr. Golyadkin glanced at Petrushka's bed; but the room did not even smell of Petrushka: his bed had long been made and left, his boots were nowhere to be seen either— an unmistakable sign that Petrushka was not in. Mr. Golyadkin rushed to the door: the door was locked. "But where is Petrushka?" he went on in a whisper, conscious of intense excitement and feeling a perceptible tremor all over him. . . . Suddenly a thought flashed through his mind. . . . Mr. Golyadkin rushed to the table, looked all over it, felt all around—yes, his letter of the night before to Vahrameyev was not there. Petrushka was nowhere behind the screen either, the clock had just struck one, and some new points were evident to him in Vahrameyev's letter, points that were obscure at first sight, though now they were fully explained. Finally Petrushka, he had evidently been bribed! "Yes, yes, that was so!"

"So this is where the main plot was hatched!" cried Mr. Golyadkin, slapping himself on the forehead and opening his eyes wider and wider. "So in that niggardly German woman's den the main power of the evil spirit lies hidden now! So she was only making a strategic diversion in directing me to the Izmailovsky Bridge—she was distracting my attention, confusing me (the worthless witch), and in that way laying her mines! Yes, that is so! If one only looks at the thing from that point of view, all of this is bound to be so, and the scoundrel's appearance on the scene is also fully explained: it's all part and parcel of the same thing. They've kept him in reserve a long while, they have had him in readiness for the rainy day. This is how it has all turned out! This is what it has come to. But there, never mind. No time has been lost as yet."

At this point Mr. Golyadkin recollected with horror that it was past one in the afternoon. "What if they have succeeded by now? . . ." He uttered a moan. . . . "But, no, they are lying, they've not had time—we shall see. . . ." He dressed after a fashion, seized paper and a pen, and scribbled the following missive:

My dear Yakov Petrovich!

Either you or I, but both together we cannot be! And so I must inform you that your strange, absurd, and at the same time impossible desire to appear to be my twin and to give yourself out as such will serve no other purpose than to bring about your complete disgrace and discomfiture. And so I beg you, for the sake of your own advantage, to step aside and make way for really honorable and well-intentioned men. Otherwise I am ready to determine upon taking extreme measures. I lay down my pen and await. . . . I remain, though, ready to be of service—even with pistols.

Y. Golyadkin

Our hero rubbed his hands energetically when he had finished the note. Then, pulling on his greatcoat and putting on his hat, he unlocked his flat with a spare key and set off for the office. He reached it but could not make up his mind to go in—it was by now too late: it was half-past two by Mr. Golyadkin's watch. All at once a circumstance of apparently little importance settled certain doubts in Mr. Golyadkin's mind: a flushed and breathless figure suddenly made its appearance from behind the corner of the office building and with a rat's stealthy gait darted up the steps and into the entry. It was a copying clerk called Ostafyev, a man Mr. Golyadkin knew very well, who was rather useful and ready to do anything for a ten-kopeck piece. Knowing Ostafyev's weak spot and surmising that after his brief visit to a certain indispensable place he would probably be greedier than ever for tips, our hero made up his mind not to be sparing of them, and immediately darted up the steps, and then into the entry after him, called to him and, with a mysterious air, drew him aside into a convenient corner behind a huge iron stove. And, having led him there, our hero began questioning him.

"Well, my dear fellow, how are things going in there . . . you understand me?"

"Yes, your honor, I wish you good health, your honor."

"All right, my good man, all right; but I'll make it worth your while, my good fellow. Well, you see, so how are things?"

"What is your honor pleased to inquire about?" At this point Ostafyev held his hand before his mouth that had opened as if by accident.

"You see, my dear fellow, it's this way . . . but don't you imagine anything. . . . Come, is Andrey Filippovich here?"

"Yes, he is, sir."

"And are the clerks here?"

"Yes, sir, they are here as usual."

"And his Excellency too?"

"And his Excellency too, sir." Here the man held his hand before his mouth that opened again, and looked rather curiously and strangely at Mr. Golyadkin. So at least our hero fancied.

"And there's nothing special there, my good man?"

"No, sir, certainly not, sir."

"So there's nothing concerning me, my friend? Is there nothing going on there—that is, nothing more than . . . eh? Just like that, you understand, my friend?"

"No, sir, nothing has been heard so far, sir." Again the man put his hand before his mouth and again looked rather strangely at Mr. Golyadkin. The fact is, Mr. Golyadkin was trying to penetrate into Ostafyev's countenance to discover whether he was not keeping something back. And, in fact, the man did seem to be hiding something: the fact is that Ostafyev was becoming somehow colder and more churlish, and did not enter into Mr. Golyadkin's interests with the same sympathy as at the beginning of the conversation. "He is to some extent justified," thought Mr. Golyadkin. "After all, what am I to him? Perhaps his palm has already been greased by the other side, and that's why he had just visited the indispensable place. But, here, I'll try him. . . ." Mr. Golyadkin realized that the moment for ten kopecks had arrived.

"Here, my dear fellow. . . ."

"I'm deeply grateful to your honor."

"I'll let you have more."

"Yes, your honor."

"I'll give you some more directly, and when the business is over I'll give you as much again. Do you understand?"

The clerk was silent, stood at attention, and stared fixedly at Mr. Golyadkin.

"Come, tell me now: has anything been said about me? . . ."

"I think, so far, nothing . . . so to say . . . nothing so far, sir." Ostafyev, like Mr. Golyadkin, spoke deliberately and preserved a mysterious air, twitching his eyebrows a little, looking at the ground, trying to fall into the suitable tone, and, in fact, doing his very utmost to earn what had been promised him, for what he had received already he reckoned as already earned.

"And so nothing is known?"

"So far, nothing, sir."

"Listen . . . I mean . . . perhaps there will be something in the wind. . . ."

"Later on, of course, there may be something."

"That's bad," thought our hero. "Listen, here's something more, my dear fellow."

"I am deeply grateful to your honor."

"Was Vahrameyev here yesterday?"

"Yes, sir."

"And . . . somebody else? . . . Was he? . . . Try and remember, brother."

The man ransacked his memory for a moment, and could think of nothing appropriate.

"No, sir, there wasn't anybody else."

"H'm!" A silence followed.

"Listen, brother, here's some more; tell me everything, all you know."

"Yes, sir." Ostafyev had now become as meek as a lamb, which was just what Mr. Golyadkin needed.

"Explain to me now, my good man, what footing is he on?"

"All right, sir, a good one, sir," answered the man, staring open-eyed at Mr. Golyadkin.

"How do you mean, a good one?"

"I mean, just so, sir." Here Ostafyev twitched his eyebrows significantly. He was utterly nonplused, though, and didn't know what more to say.

"That's bad," thought Mr. Golyadkin. "Hasn't anything more happened . . . to Vahrameyev, I mean?"

"Everything is just as usual, sir."

"Think a little."

"There is, they say, sir . . ."

"Come, what?"

Ostafyev put his hand in front of his mouth.

"Isn't there a letter from them to me?"

"This morning Miheyev, the watchman, went to Vahrameyev's lodging, the German woman's place, so I'll go and ask him, if you like."

"Do me the favor, brother, for goodness' sake! . . . I only mean . . . you mustn't imagine anything, brother, I only mean . . . Yes, you make inquiries, brother, find out whether they are not getting up something against me. How is he acting? That is what I want to know; that is what you must find out, my dear fellow, and then I'll make it worth your while, my good man. . . ."

"I will, your honor, and Ivan Semyonovich sat in your place today, sir."

"Ivan Semyonovich? Oh, really! You don't say so."

"Andrey Filippovich told him to sit there, sir."

"Really! How did that happen? You must find out about it, brother; for God's sake find out, brother; find it all out —and I'll make it worth your while, my dear fellow; that's what I want to know . . . and don't you imagine anything, brother. . . ."

"At your service; I'll go at once. And aren't you going in today, sir?"

"No, my friend; I only came to have a look around, my friend, and I'll make it worth your while afterward, my friend."

"At your service, sir." The man ran rapidly and eagerly up the stairs, and Mr. Golyadkin was left alone.

"That's bad!" he thought. "Oh, it's a bad business, a bad business! Oh! Things are in a bad way with us now! What does it all mean? What did that drunkard's insinuations mean, for instance, and whose trickery is it? Ah! I know

now who is back of it. There is what it comes to. No doubt
they found out and made him sit there. . . . But, after all,
did they seat him there? It was Andrey Filippovich seated
him there, he seated Ivan Semyonovich there himself; why
did he make him sit there and with what object? Probably
they found out. . . . That is Vahrameyev's work—that is,
not Vahrameyev's; he is as stupid as an ashen log, Vahrameyev is, and they are all at work in his behalf, and they
egged that scoundrel on to come here for the same purpose, and the German woman brought up her grievance,
the one-eyed hussy. I always suspected that this intrigue
was not without an object, and that in all this old-womanish
gossip there is certainly something, and I said as much to
Krestyan Ivanovich, telling him they'd sworn to cut a man's
throat—in a moral sense, of course—and so they pounced
upon Karolina Ivanovna. No, there are masters at work
here, one can see! Yes, sir, there is a master's hand at work
here, and not Vahrameyev's. I've said already that Vahrameyev is stupid, but . . . I know who it is does all the
work, it's that rascal, that impostor! That's what he relies
upon, which is partly proved by his successes in the best
society. And it would certainly be desirable to know on
what footing he is now. What sort of a figure does he cut
among them? Only, why have they taken Ivan Semyonovich? What the devil do they want with Ivan Semyonovich?
As though they could not have found anyone else. It
would have come, however, to the same thing, no matter
whom they would have seated; and the only thing I know
is that I have suspected Ivan Semyonovich for a long time
past. I noticed long ago what a nasty, horrid old man he
was—they say he lends money at Jewish interests. To be
sure, the bear's the leading spirit in the whole affair. The
bear is mixed up in the whole affair. It began in this way.
It began at the Izmailovsky Bridge; that's how it began. . . ."

At this point Mr. Golyadkin made a wry face, as though
he had taken a bite out of a lemon, probably remembering
something very unpleasant. "But, there, it doesn't matter,"

he thought. "I keep harping on my own troubles. But what is keeping Ostafyev? Most likely he is staying on or has been delayed somehow. It is a good thing, in a sense, that I am intriguing like this, and am laying mines on my side too. All I have to do is to give Ostafyev ten kopecks and he's . . . so to speak, on my side. Only the point is, is he really on my side? Perhaps they've got him on their side too . . . and they are carrying on an intrigue by means of him on their side too. He looks a brigand, the swindler, a regular brigand; he's hiding something, the rogue. 'No, nothing,' says he, 'and I am deeply grateful to your honor,' says he. You brigand, you!"

He heard a noise. . . . Mr. Golyadkin shrank together and jumped behind the stove. Someone came downstairs and went out into the street. "Who could that be going away now?" our hero thought to himself. A minute later someone's footsteps were heard again. . . . At this point Mr. Golyadkin could not resist poking the very tip of his nose out beyond his breastwork—he poked it out and instantly withdrew it, as though someone had pricked it with a pin. This time someone he knew well was coming—that is the scoundrel, the plotter and the profligate—he was approaching with his usual foul, tripping little step, mincing and prancing as though he were going to kick someone.

"The rascal," said our hero to himself.

Mr. Golyadkin could not, however, help observing that the rascal had under his arm a huge green briefcase belonging to his Excellency. "He's on a special assignment again," thought Mr. Golyadkin, flushing crimson and shrinking into himself more than ever from vexation.

As soon as Mr. Golyadkin Jr. had slipped past Mr. Golyadkin Sr. without observing him in the least, footsteps were heard for the third time, and this time Mr. Golyadkin thought that they were Ostafyev's. In fact, a sleek copying clerk did look in on him behind the stove. It was not, however, Ostafyev, but another clerk, Pisarenko by name. This surprised Mr. Golyadkin. "Why had he mixed up other people in the secret?" our hero wondered. "What barbarians! Nothing is sacred to them! Well, my friend?" he brought out, addressing Pisarenko. "Who sent you, my friend?"

"I've come about your business, sir. There's no news so far from anyone, sir. But should there be any we'll let you know."

"And Ostafyev?"

"It was quite impossible for him to come, your honor. His Excellency has walked through the section twice, and I, too, have no time to stay."

"Thank you, my good man, thank you . . . only, tell me . . ."

"Upon my word, sir, I can't stay. . . . They are asking for us every minute. . . . But if your honor will stay here a while longer, we'll let you know if anything happens concerning your little affair."

"No, my friend, you just tell me . . ."

"Excuse me, I've no time to stay, sir," said Pisarenko, tearing himself away from Mr. Golyadkin, who had clutched him by his coat. "I really can't. If your honor will stay a while longer here, we'll let you know."

"In a minute, my good man, in a minute! In a minute, my good fellow! I tell you what, here's a letter; and I'll make it worth your while, my good man."

"Yes, sir."

"Try and give it to Mr. Golyadkin, my dear fellow."

"Golyadkin?"

"Yes, my man, to Mr. Golyadkin."

"Very good, sir; as soon as I get off I'll take it to him, and you stay here, meanwhile. No one will see you here. . . ."

"No, my good man, don't imagine. . . . I'm not standing here to avoid being seen. But I'm not going to stay here now, my friend. . . . I'll be close by, in the side street. There's a coffeehouse there; so I'll wait there, and if anything happens, you let me know about everything, you understand?"

"Very good, sir. Only let me go; I understand."

"And I'll make it worth your while," Mr. Golyadkin called after Pisarenko, who had at last got free.

"The rogue seemed to be getting rather rude," our hero reflected as he stealthily emerged from behind the stove. "There's some other dodge here. That's clear. . . . At first it was one thing and another. . . . He really was in a hurry, though; perhaps there's a great deal to do in the office. And his Excellency had been through the section twice. . . . What was the occasion? . . . Ugh! But never mind! It may mean nothing, perhaps; but now we shall see. . . ."

At this point Mr. Golyadkin was about to open the door, intending to go out into the street, when suddenly, at that very instant, his Excellency's carriage thundered up to the porch. Before Mr. Golyadkin had time to recover from the shock, the door of the carriage was opened from within and a gentleman jumped out on the porch. It was none other than Mr. Golyadkin Jr., who had only gone out ten minutes before. Mr. Golyadkin Sr. remembered that the Director's quarter was but a couple of paces away. "He has been out on a special assignment," our hero thought to himself.

Meanwhile, Mr. Golyadkin Jr. took out of the carriage a thick green briefcase and also some papers. Finally, giving some orders to the coachman, he opened the door, almost pushing Mr. Golyadkin Sr., purposely avoided noticing him in order to spite him in this way, and mounted the office staircase at a run.

"That's bad!" thought Mr. Golyadkin. "This is what it has come to now! Oh, good Lord! Look at him."

For half a minute our hero remained motionless. At last he made up his mind. Without pausing to think, aware of a violent palpitation of the heart and a tremor in all his limbs, he ran up the stairs after his enemy. "Here goes; what does it matter to me? I have nothing to do with the case," he thought, taking off his hat, his greatcoat, and his galoshes in the entry.

When Mr. Golyadkin walked into his office, it was al-

ready dark. Neither Andrey Filippovich nor Anton Antonovich was in the room. Both of them were in the Director's
room, handing in reports. His Excellency, so it was ru-
mored, was in haste to report to his superior. In consequence of this, and also because dusk had set in, and the
office hours were almost over, several of the clerks, especially the younger ones, were, at the moment when our
hero entered, enjoying a period of inactivity; gathered together in groups, they were talking, arguing, and laughing,
and some of the most youthful—that is, belonging to the
lowest grades in the service—had got up a game of pitch
and toss in a corner by the window. Knowing what was
proper, and feeling at the moment a special need to con-
ciliate and get on with them, Mr. Golyadkin immediately
approached those with whom he used to get on best, in
order to wish them good evening, and so on. But his colleagues answered his greetings rather strangely. He was un-
pleasantly struck by a certain general coldness, even curtness, one might almost say severity, in their manner. No
one shook hands with him. Some simply said, "How do you
do" and walked away; others barely nodded; one simply
turned away and pretended not to notice him; at last some
of them—and what mortified Mr. Golyadkin most of all,
some of the youngsters in the lowest grades, mere lads who,
as Mr. Golyadkin justly observed about them, were capable
of nothing but gadding about and playing pitch and toss
at every opportunity—little by little collected around Mr.
Golyadkin, formed a group round him and almost barred
his way. They all looked at him with a sort of insulting
curiosity.

It was a bad sign. Mr. Golyadkin felt this, and very prudently prepared for his part not to notice it. Suddenly a
quite unexpected event dealt him the final blow, as they
say, and utterly crushed him.

At the moment most trying to Mr. Golyadkin Sr., suddenly, as though by design, there appeared in the group
of fellow-clerks surrounding him Mr. Golyadkin Jr., gay as
ever, smiling his little smile as ever, nimble, too, as ever;

in short, the playboy, skipping and tripping, chuckling and fawning, with sprightly tongue and sprightly toe, as always, precisely as he had been, for instance, the day before at a very unpleasant moment for Mr. Golyadkin Sr.

Grinning, mincing, and fidgeting, with a smile that seemed to say "Good evening" to everyone, he wormed his way into the group of clerks, shaking hands with one, slapping another on the shoulder, putting his arm around yet another, explaining to a fourth how he had come to be employed by his Excellency, where he had been, what he had done, what he had brought with him; to the fifth, probably his most intimate friend, he gave a resounding kiss—in fact, everything happened as it did in Mr. Golyadkin's dream. When he had skipped about to his heart's content, polished them all off in his usual way, disposed them all in his favor, whether he needed them or not, when he had lavished his blandishments on all the clerks, Mr. Golyadkin Jr. suddenly, and most likely by mistake, for he had not yet had time to notice his oldest friend, held out his hand to Mr. Golyadkin Sr. also. Probably also by mistake—though he had had time to observe the unseemly Mr. Golyadkin Jr. thoroughly, our hero at once eagerly seized the hand so unexpectedly held out to him and pressed it in the warmest and friendliest way, pressed it with a strange, quite unexpected inner feeling, with a kind of tearful emotion. Whether our hero was misled by the first movement of his worthless foe, or was taken unawares, or, without recognizing it, felt at the bottom of his heart how defenseless he was—it is difficult to say. The fact remains that Mr. Golyadkin Sr., in full possession of his senses, of his own free will, before witnesses, solemnly shook hands with him whom he called his mortal foe. But what was the amazement, the frenzy and fury, what was the horror and the shame of Mr. Golyadkin Sr., when his enemy and mortal foe, the ignoble Mr. Golyadkin Jr., noticing the mistake of that persecuted, innocent man he had perfidiously deceived, without a trace of shame, of feeling, of compassion, or of conscience, pulled his hand out of Mr. Golyadkins' with insufferable rudeness and insolence. Moreover, he shook the hand as though it had been soiled with something horrid; what was worse, he spat aside with disgust, accompanying this with a most insulting gesture; worse still, he drew out his handkerchief and, in the most outrageous way, wiped all his fingers that had rested for one moment in the hand of Mr. Golyadkin Sr. While he did this Mr. Golyadkin Jr. looked about him on purpose in his characteristic horrid way, took care that everyone should see what he was doing, glanced into people's eyes, and evidently tried to impress on all everything that was most unpleasant in regard to Mr. Golyadkin Sr. Mr. Golyadkin Jr.'s revolting behavior seemed to arouse general indignation among the clerks that surrounded them; even the frivolous youngsters showed their displeasure. A murmur of protest rose on all sides. Mr. Golyadkin could not help hearing it; but suddenly—an appropriate witticism that bubbled from the lips of Mr. Golyadkin Jr. shattered, annihilated our hero's last hopes, and inclined the balance again in favor of his deadly and useless foe.

"He's our Russian Faublas,[7] gentlemen; allow me to introduce the youthful Faublas," piped Mr. Golyadkin Jr., with his characteristic insolence, mincing and threading his way among the clerks, and directing their attention to the petrified and at the same time frantic Mr. Golyadkin. "Let us kiss, darling," he went on with insufferable familiarity, moving close to the man he had so treacherously insulted. The useless Mr. Golyadkin Jr.'s jest seemed to touch a responsive chord, for it contained an insidious allusion to a circumstance with which all were apparently familiar. Our hero became painfully conscious of the hand of his enemy on his shoulders. But he had made up his mind by now. With blazing eyes, pale face, and a fixed smile, he somehow managed to get out of the crowd and with uneven, hurried steps made straight for his Excellency's study. In

[7] Hero of the novel, *Les amours du chevalier de Faublas,* by Louvet de Couvray, translated into Russian late in the eighteenth century.

the room next to it he was met by Andrey Filippovich,
who had just come out from his Excellency's study, and,
although there were present in the room at the moment a
good number of persons who were strangers to Mr. Golyadkin, yet our hero did not care to take such a fact into
consideration. Boldly, resolutely, directly, almost wondering at himself and inwardly admiring his own courage,
without loss of time he accosted Andrey Filippovich, who
was a good deal surprised by this unexpected attack.

"Ah! . . . What is it . . . what do you want?" asked the
section head, not listening to Mr. Golyadkin's faltering
words.

"Andrey Filippovich, I . . . may I, Andrey Filippovich,
have a conversation with his Excellency at once and in
private?" our hero said resolutely and distinctly, fixing the
most determined glance on Andrey Filippovich.

"What, sir? Of course not." Andrey Filippovich scanned
Mr. Golyadkin from head to foot.

"I say all this, Andrey Filippovich, because I am surprised that no one here has unmasked the impostor and
scoundrel."

"Wha-a-at!"

"Scoundrel, Andrey Filippovich!"

"Of whom are you pleased to speak in those terms?"

"Of a notorious person, Andrey Filippovich; I'm alluding, Andrey Filippovich, to a notorious person; I have the
right . . . I think, Andrey Filippovich, that the authorities
ought to encourage such a step," added Mr. Golyadkin,
evidently hardly knowing what he was saying. "Andrey
Filippovich . . . no doubt you see yourself, Andrey Filippovich, that this honorable step is a mark of my complete
loyalty—of my regarding my superior as a father, Andrey
Filippovich; I as much as say that I regard my beneficent
superior as a father and blindly entrust my fate to him.
It's as much as to say . . . you see . . ." At this point Mr.
Golyadkin's voice trembled, his face flushed, and two tears
welled up on his eyelashes.

As Andrey Filippovich listened to Mr. Golyadkin he was

so astonished that he could not help stepping back a couple of paces. Then he looked about him uneasily. . . . It is difficult to say how the matter would have ended. But suddenly the door of his Excellency's study opened, and he himself came out, accompanied by several officials. All the people in the room followed in a string. His Excellency called Andrey Filippovich and walked beside him, opening a conversation about some business matters. When all had set off and gone out of the room, Mr. Golyadkin came to his senses. Growing calmer, he took refuge under the wing of Anton Antonovich, who came last in the procession and who, Mr. Golyadkin fancied, looked stern and anxious. "I've been talking nonsense, I've been making a mess of it again," he thought to himself, "but there, never mind."

"I hope, at least, that you, Anton Antonovich, will consent to listen to me and to enter into my situation," he said quietly, in a voice that still trembled a little with excitement. "Rejected by all, I appeal to you. I am still at a loss to understand what Andrey Filippovich's words mean, Anton Antonovich. Explain them to me if you can. . . ."

"Everything will be explained in due time, sir," Anton Antonovich replied sternly and emphatically, and as it seemed to Mr. Golyadkin with an air that gave him plainly to understand that Anton Antonovich had no desire whatever to continue the conversation. "You will soon know all about it. You will be officially informed about everything today."

"What do you mean by officially informed, Anton Antonovich? Why officially?" our hero asked timidly.

"It is not for you and me to discuss what our superiors decide upon, Yakov Petrovich."

"Why our superiors, Anton Antonovich?" said our hero, still more intimidated; "why our superiors? I don't see what reason there is to trouble our superiors, Anton Antonovich. . . . Perhaps you mean to say something about yesterday's doings, Anton Antonovich?"

"Oh, no, nothing to do with yesterday; there's something else amiss with you."

"What is there amiss, Anton Antonovich? I believe, Anton Antonovich, that I have done nothing amiss."

"And with whom did you intend to be crafty?" Anton Antonovich cut in sharply, completely dumbfounding Mr. Golyadkin. Mr. Golyadkin started, and turned as white as a handkerchief.

"Of course, Anton Antonovich," he said, in a voice hardly audible, "if one harks to the voice of calumny and listens to our enemies' tales, without heeding what the other side has to say in its defense, then, of course . . . then, of course, Anton Antonovich, one may suffer innocently and for nothing."

"To be sure; and what of your unseemly conduct, in damaging the reputation of a wellborn maiden belonging to the virtuous and well-known family who had befriended you?"

"What conduct do you mean, Anton Antonovich?"

"Yes, sir, and about your praiseworthy conduct in regard to that other maiden who, though poor, is of honorable foreign extraction, you know nothing either?"

"Allow me, Anton Antonovich . . . listen to me, Anton Antonovich. . . ."

"And your treacherous behavior and slander of another person, your charging another person with your own sins. Eh? What do you call that?"

"I did not turn him out, Anton Antonovich," said our hero, trembling; "and I've never instructed Petrushka, my man, to do anything of the sort. . . . He ate my bread, Anton Antonovich, he took advantage of my hospitality," our hero added significantly and with deep emotion, so much so that his chin started quivering a little and tears were ready to well up again.

"That is only your talk, that he has eaten your bread," answered Anton Antonovich, grinning, and there was a perfidious note in his voice which sent a pang to Mr. Golyadkin's heart.

"Allow me most humbly to ask you again, Anton Antonovich: is his Excellency aware of all this business?"

"Of course! But you must let me go now, though. I've no time for you. . . . You'll know everything you need to know this very day."

"Allow me, for God's sake, one more minute, Anton Antonovich."

"You'll tell it to me afterward. . . ."

"No, Anton Antonovich; I . . . you see, Anton Antonovich . . . only listen . . . I am not one for freethinking, Anton Antonovich; I shun freethinking; I am quite ready for my part . . . and, indeed, I've entertained the idea that . . ."

"Very good, very good. I've heard that already, sir."

"No, you have not heard that, Anton Antonovich. It is something else, Anton Antonovich; it's a good thing, really, a good thing and pleasant to hear. . . . As I've explained to you, Anton Antonovich, I admit the idea, as I have said before, that the divine Providence has created two men exactly alike, and that the beneficent authorities, seeing the hand of Providence, have provided a berth for the twins. That is a good thing, Anton Antonovich. You see that it is a very good thing, Anton Antonovich, and that I am very far from freethinking. I regard my beneficent superior as a father; I say beneficent, of course . . . a young man must be in the service. . . . Stand up for me, Anton Antonovich, take my part, Anton Antonovich. . . . I am all right . . . Anton Antonovich, for God's sake, one little word more . . . Anton Antonovich. . . ."

But by now Anton Antonovich was far away from Mr. Golyadkin. . . . As for our hero, he was so bewildered and overcome by all that had happened and all that he had heard that he did not know where he was standing, what he had heard, what he had done, what had happened to him, and what was still going to happen to him.

With imploring eyes he sought for Anton Antonovich in the crowd of clerks, that he might justify himself further in his eyes and say something to him extremely well-intentioned and agreeable and creditable to himself. . . . By degrees, however, a new light began to break upon our hero's bewildered mind, a new and awful light that revealed at once a whole perspective of hitherto unknown and utterly unsuspected circumstances. . . . At that moment somebody gave our bewildered hero a poke in the ribs. He looked around. Pisarenko was standing before him.

"A letter, your honor."

"Ah, you've gone and fetched it, then, my good man?"

"No, it was brought at ten o'clock this morning, sir. Sergey Miheyev, the watchman, brought it from Mr. Vahrameyev's lodging."

"Very good, my friend, very good, and I'll make it worth your while, my dear fellow."

Saying this, Mr. Golyadkin thrust the letter in the side pocket of his uniform and buttoned up every button of it; then he looked around him, and, to his surprise, found that he was by now in the vestibule of the office, in a group of clerks crowding at the exit, for office hours were over. Mr. Golyadkin had not only failed till that moment to observe this circumstance, but had no notion how he suddenly came to be wearing his greatcoat and galoshes and to be holding his hat in his hand. All the clerks were standing motionless, in reverential expectation. As a matter of fact, his Excellency was standing at the bottom of the stairs waiting for his carriage, which was for some reason late in arriving, and was carrying on a very interesting conversation with Andrey Filippovich and two councilors. At a little distance from Andrey Filippovich stood Anton Antonovich and several other clerks, who were all smiles, seeing that his Excellency was pleased to joke and laugh. The clerks who were crowded at the top of the stairs were smiling too, in expectation of his Excellency's laughing again. The only one who was not smiling was Fedosyeyich, the corpulent doorman, who stood stiffly at attention, holding the handle of the door and waiting impatiently for his daily portion of pleasure, which consisted in flinging a leaf of the door wide open with a swing of his arm, and then, with a low bow, reverentially making way for his Excellency. But the one who seemed to be more pleased and delighted than any was the worthless and ignoble enemy of Mr. Golyadkin. At that instant he positively forgot all his colleagues, and even gave up tripping and mincing in his usual odious way; he even forgot to make up to anybody. He was all eyes and ears, he even strangely shrank together, no doubt the better to hear, and never took his eyes off his Excellency, and only from time to time his arms, legs, and head twitched with faintly perceptible tremors that betrayed the secret emotions of his soul.

"Isn't he in a state!" thought our hero; "he looks like a minion, the rascal! I should like to know how it is that he takes in people of the best society. He has neither brains nor character, neither education nor feeling; he's a lucky rogue! Good Lord! How can a man, when you think of it, go and make friends with everyone so quickly! And he'll get on, I swear the fellow will get on, the rogue will make his way—he's a lucky rascal! I should like to know, too, what he keeps whispering to everyone—what plots he is hatching with all these people, and what secrets they are talking about. My God, if only I could . . . get on with them a little too . . . say this and that. Perhaps I had better ask him . . . tell him I won't do it again; I'm at fault, a young man must serve nowadays, your Excellency. I am not in the least put out by my obscure position—so there! I am not going to protest in any way, either; I shall bear it all with meekness and patience, so there! Shouldn't I do that? . . . You can't get at the rascal, though; you can't reach him with anything you say; you can't hammer reason into his head. . . . We'll try, though. I may happen to hit on a good moment, so I'll try. . . ."

Feeling in his uneasiness, his misery, and his bewilderment that he couldn't leave things like this, that the critical moment was coming, that he must explain himself to someone, our hero began to move a little toward the place where his worthless and enigmatic enemy stood; but at that very moment his Excellency's long-expected carriage rolled up thunderingly to the entrance, Fedosyeyich flung open the door, and, bending double, let his Excellency pass. All the waiting clerks at once streamed out toward the door, and for a moment separated Mr. Golyadkin Sr. from Mr. Golyadkin Jr.

"You shan't get away!" said our hero, forcing his way through the crowd while he kept his eyes fixed on the man he wanted. At last the crowd dispersed. Our hero felt he was free and rushed in pursuit of his enemy.

Chapter XI

Mr. Golyadkin's breath failed him; he flew as on wings after his rapidly retreating enemy. He was conscious of possessing immense energy. Yet, in spite of this terrible energy, he might safely have held that at that moment a mere gnat—had a gnat been able to live in Petersburg at that time of the year—could very easily have knocked him down with its wing. He felt, too, that he was crestfallen and utterly weak again, that he was carried along by a peculiar outside force, that it was not he himself who was running, but, on the contrary, that his legs were giving way under him and refused to obey him. All this might turn out for the best, however. "Whether it is for the best or not for the best," thought Mr. Golyadkin, almost breathless from running so quickly, "but that the game is lost there cannot be the slightest doubt now; that I am utterly done for is certain, definite, settled, and signed."

In spite of all this our hero felt as though he had risen from the dead, as though he had endured a battle, won a victory when he succeeded in clutching the overcoat of his enemy, who had already raised one foot to get into the cab he had engaged.

"My dear sir! My dear sir!" he shouted to the infamous Mr. Golyadkin Jr. "My dear sir, I hope that you . . ."

"No, please do not hope for anything," Mr. Golyadkin's heartless enemy answered evasively, standing with one foot on the step of the cab, vainly waving the other leg in the air, in his efforts to get in, and trying to preserve his equilibrium. At the same time he endeavored with all his might to wrench his coat away from Mr. Golyadkin Sr., while the latter held on to it with all the means that had been vouchsafed to him by nature.

"Yakov Petrovich, only ten minutes. . . ."

"Excuse me, I've no time, sir. . . ."

"You must admit, Yakov Petrovich . . . please, Yakov Petrovich . . . for God's sake, Yakov Petrovich . . . let us have it out—boldly. . . . One little second, Yakov Petrovich . . ."

"Darling, I can't stay," answered Mr. Golyadkin's ignoble enemy, with uncivil familiarity, disguised as good-natured heartiness; "another time, believe me, with all my heart and soul; but now I really can't . . ."

"The scoundrel!" thought our hero. "Yakov Petrovich," he cried miserably. "I have never been your enemy. But spiteful people have described me as such unjustly. . . . I am ready, for my part . . . Yakov Petrovich, shall we go in here together, at once, Yakov Petrovich? And with all my heart, as you have so justly put it just now, and in straightforward, honorable language—here into this coffee-house? Then everything will explain itself, just like that, Yakov Petrovich. Then everything will certainly explain itself. . . ."

"Into the coffeehouse? Very good, sir. I am not against it. Let us go into the coffeehouse on one condition, only, my dear sir, on one condition—that all these things shall be cleared up. So be it, my love," said Mr. Golyadkin Jr., getting out of the cab and shamelessly slapping our hero on the shoulder. "For your sake, Yakov Petrovich, my dear friend, I am ready to go by the lane (as you were pleased to observe so aptly on one occasion, Yakov Petrovich). Why, what a rogue he is! Upon my word, he does just what he likes with one!" Mr. Golyadkin's false friend went on, fawning upon him and cajoling him with a little smile.

The coffeehouse which the two Mr. Golyadkins entered was remote from the main streets and was at the moment quite empty. A rather stout German woman made her appearance behind the counter as soon as the bell rang. Mr. Golyadkin and his unworthy enemy went into the second room, where a puffy-looking boy with closely cropped hair was busy with a bundle of chips at the stove, trying to revive the smoldering fire. At Mr. Golyadkin Jr.'s request chocolate was served.

"An appetizing little wench," said Mr. Golyadkin Jr., with a sly wink at Mr. Golyadkin Sr.

Our hero blushed and said nothing.

"Oh, yes, I forgot, I beg your pardon. I know your taste. We are sweet on slim little Fräuleins, sir; you and I are sweet on little German women, slim, and still attractive, aren't we, you upright soul? We rent their lodgings, corrupt their morals. We dedicate our hearts to them for their beer soup and their milk soup, and give them all sorts of written promises, that's what we do, you Faublas, you deceiver!"

All this Mr. Golyadkin Jr. said, making a completely useless, though villainously artful allusion to a certain personage of the female sex, while he fawned upon our hero, smiled at him with an amiable air, and a deceitful show of being delighted with him and pleased to have met him. Seeing that Mr. Golyadkin Sr. was by no means so stupid and deficient in breeding and the manners of good society as to believe him, the ignoble man resolved to change his tactics and to make an open attack upon him. After uttering his disgusting remark, the false Mr. Golyadkin ended by slapping the real Mr. Golyadkin on the shoulder, with a revolting effrontery and familiarity. Not content with that, he began playing pranks utterly unfit for well-bred society; he took it into his head to repeat his old, infamous trick—that is, regardless of the resistance and faint cries of the indignant Mr. Golyadkin Sr., he pinched the latter's cheek. At the spectacle of such depravity our hero flew into a rage and was silent . . . only for the time being, however.

"That is the talk of my enemies," he answered at last,

in a trembling voice, prudently restraining himself. At the same time our hero looked around uneasily toward the door. The fact is that Mr. Golyadkin Jr. seemed in excellent spirits, and ready for all sorts of little jokes, unseemly in a public place, and, speaking generally, not permissible by the laws of the world, especially in well-bred society.

"Oh, well, in that case, as you please," Mr. Golyadkin Jr. gravely responded to our hero's remark, setting down upon the table the empty cup which he had gulped down with unseemly greed. "Well, there's no need for me to stay long with you, however. . . . Well, how are you getting on now, Yakov Petrovich?"

"There's only one thing I can tell you, Yakov Petrovich," our hero answered, with *sang-froid* and dignity; "I've never been your enemy."

"H'm . . . Well, what about Petrushka? Petrushka is his name, isn't it? Yes, it is! Well, how is he? All right? The same as ever?"

"He, too, is the same as ever, Yakov Petrovich," answered Mr. Golyadkin Sr., somewhat amazed. "I don't know, Yakov Petrovich . . . for my part . . . from a candid, honorable standpoint, Yakov Petrovich, you must admit, Yakov Petrovich . . ."

"Yes, but you know yourself, Yakov Petrovich," Mr. Golyadkin Jr. answered in a soft and expressive voice, posing falsely as a sad man overcome with remorse and deserving compassion. "You know yourself we live in difficult times. . . . I call you to witness, Yakov Petrovich; you are an intelligent man and a just one," Mr. Golyadkin Jr. interposed, flattering Mr. Golyadkin Sr. basely. "Life is not a plaything, you know yourself, Yakov Petrovich," Mr. Golyadkin Jr. added significantly, thus pretending to be a clever and learned man who is capable of discoursing on lofty subjects.

"For my part, Yakov Petrovich," our hero answered warmly, "for my part, scorning to be roundabout and speaking boldly and openly, using forthright, honorable language and putting the whole matter on an honorable footing, I tell you I can openly and honorably assert, Yakov Petrovich, that I am absolutely blameless, and that, you know it yourself, Yakov Petrovich, the error is mutual—everything is possible—the world's verdict, the opinion of the servile crowd. . . . I speak openly, Yakov Petrovich, everything is possible. I will add, too, Yakov Petrovich, if you judge it in this way, if you look at the matter from a lofty, noble point of view, then I will boldly say, without false shame I will say, Yakov Petrovich, that it will positively be a pleasure for me to discover that I have been in error, it will positively be a pleasure for me to avow it. You know yourself, you are an intelligent man and, what is more, you are a high-minded one. Without shame, without false shame, I am ready to confess it," he wound up with dignity and nobility.

"It is fate, destiny, Yakov Petrovich . . . but let us drop all this," said Mr. Golyadkin Jr. with a sigh. "Let us rather use the brief moments of our meeting for a more pleasant and profitable conversation, as is only suitable between two colleagues. . . . Really, I have not succeeded in saying two words to you all this time. . . . I am not to blame for that, Yakov Petrovich. . . ."

"Nor I," answered our hero heatedly, "nor I, either! My heart tells me, Yakov Petrovich, that I'm not to blame in all this matter. Let us blame fate for all this, Yakov Petrovich," added Mr. Golyadkin Sr., in a completely conciliatory tone. His voice was beginning, little by little, to soften and to quaver.

"Well! How is your health?" said the aberrant fellow in a sweet voice.

"I have a little cough," answered our hero, even more sweetly.

"Take care of yourself. There is so much illness going about, you may easily get quinsy; for my part I confess I've begun to wrap myself up in flannel."

"One may, indeed, Yakov Petrovich, very easily get quinsy," our hero brought out after a meek silence; "Yakov Petrovich, I see that I was mistaken. I remember with tender emotion those happy moments which we managed to spend together, under my poor, though I venture to say, hospitable roof. . . ."

"In your letter, however, you wrote something very different," said Mr. Golyadkin Jr. reproachfully, speaking on this occasion—though only on this occasion—quite justly.

"Yakov Petrovich, I was in error. . . . I see clearly now that I was in error in my unhappy letter too. Yakov Petrovich, I am ashamed to look at you, Yakov Petrovich, you wouldn't believe it. . . . Give me that letter that I may tear it to pieces before your eyes, Yakov Petrovich, and if that is in no way possible I entreat you to read it the other way around—altogether the other way around—that is, on purpose, with a friendly intention, giving the opposite sense to all the words in my letter. I was in error. Forgive me, Yakov Petrovich, I was quite . . . I was grievously in error, Yakov Petrovich."

"You say so?" Mr. Golyadkin's perfidious friend inquired, rather casually and indifferently.

"I say that I was quite in error, Yakov Petrovich, and that for my part, quite without false shame, I am . . ."

"Ah, well, that's all right! That's a good thing that you were in error," answered Mr. Golyadkin Jr. rudely.

"I even had an idea, Yakov Petrovich," our candid hero answered in a gentlemanly way, completely failing to observe the horrible perfidy of his false friend; "I even had an idea that here were two people created exactly alike."

"Ah, is that your idea?"

At this point the notoriously useless Mr. Golyadkin took up his hat. Still failing to notice his teacher, Mr. Golyadkin Sr., too, got up, smiling nobly and open-heartedly at his false friend, and trying in his innocence to be tender to him, to encourage him, and in that way to form a new friendship with him.

"Good-by, your Excellency," Mr. Golyadkin Jr. called out suddenly. Our hero started, noticing in his enemy's face something positively Bacchanalian, and, solely to get rid of him, put two fingers into the immoral fellow's outstretched hand; but then . . . then his enemy's impudence passed all bounds. Seizing the two fingers of Mr. Golyadkin's hand, and at first squeezing them, the worthless fellow on the spot, before Mr. Golyadkin's eyes, brought himself to repeat the shameful joke of the morning. The measure of human patience was exceeded.

He was already hiding in his pocket the handkerchief with which he had wiped his fingers when Mr. Golyadkin Sr. recovered from the shock and dashed after him into the next room, into which his irreconcilable foe had in his usual nasty way hastened to decamp. As though completely guiltless, he was standing at the counter eating patties, and with perfect composure, like a virtuous man, paying compliments to the German woman behind the counter.

"Not before ladies," thought our hero, and he, too, went up to the counter, so agitated that he hardly knew what he was doing.

"The wench is certainly not bad! What do you think?" Mr. Golyadkin Jr. started his scurvy tricks again, reckoning, no doubt, upon Mr. Golyadkin's infinite patience. The stout German woman, for her part, looked at both her visitors with pewtery, vacant-looking eyes, smiling affably and evidently not understanding a syllable of Russian. Our hero flared up at the words of the shameless Mr. Golyadkin Jr., and, unable to control himself, rushed at him with the evident intention of tearing him to pieces and finishing him off completely, but Mr. Golyadkin Jr., in his usual mean way, was already far off; he took to his heels, he was already on the steps. It goes without saying that, after the first moment of stupefaction with which Mr. Golyadkin Sr. was naturally overcome, he recovered himself and rushed full speed after the offender. The latter had already got into a cab, whose driver was obviously in collusion with him. But at that very instant the stout German woman, seeing both her customers make off, shrieked and rang her bell with all her might. Our hero, in mid-flight, as it were, turned back, and, without asking for change, flung her money for himself and for the shameless man who had left without paying, and although thus delayed he managed, again in mid-flight, to catch up with his enemy. Clutching at the wing of the cab with all the force bestowed on him by nature, our hero scudded for some time along the street, trying to clamber upon the vehicle, while Mr. Golyadkin Jr. did his utmost to prevent him from doing so. Meanwhile the cabman, with whip, reins, kicks, and shouts urged on his jaded nag which quite unexpectedly dropped into a gallop, taking the bit between its teeth, and kicking with its hind legs at every third step, according to its horrid habit. At last our hero succeeded in climbing into the cab. His back against the driver's, he was facing his enemy, their knees touching and his right hand grasping the very shabby fur collar of his depraved and bitter foe.

The enemies were borne along for some time in silence. Our hero could scarcely breathe. It was a bad road and he was jolted at every step and in peril of breaking his neck. Moreover, his obdurate foe still refused to acknowledge himself vanquished and was trying to shove him off into the mud. To complete the unpleasantness of his position the weather was detestable. The snow was falling in heavy flakes and doing its utmost to creep under the unfastened overcoat of the genuine Mr. Golyadkin. It was foggy and pitch dark. It was difficult to tell through what streets and in what direction they were dashing. . . . It seemed to Mr. Golyadkin that there was something familiar about what was happening to him. At one moment he tried to remember whether he had had a presentiment of it the day before, in a dream, for instance. . . .

At last his wretchedness reached the utmost pitch of agony. Throwing himself upon his merciless opponent, he began to shout. But his cries died away upon his lips. . . . There was a moment when Mr. Golyadkin forgot everything, and decided that all this was of no consequence and that it was all nothing, that it was happening in some inexplicable manner, and that, therefore, to protest was a superfluous and completely hopeless effort. . . . But suddenly, and almost at the same instant that our hero was drawing this conclusion, an unexpected jolt gave quite a new turn to the affair. Mr. Golyadkin fell off the cab like a sack of flour and rolled on the ground, quite correctly confessing, at the moment of his fall, that he had got into a temper inopportunely. Jumping up at last, he saw that they had stopped; the cab was standing in the middle of some courtyard, and at first sight our hero noticed that it was the courtyard of the house in which Olsufy Ivanovich lodged. At the same instant he noticed that his enemy was mounting the steps, probably on his way to Olsufy Ivanovich's. In indescribable misery he was about to pursue his enemy, but, fortunately for himself, prudently thought better of it in time. Not forgetting to pay the cabman, Mr. Golyadkin rushed into the street and ran with all his might along it, following his nose. The snow was falling heavily as before; as before it was misty, wet, and dark. Our hero did not walk, but flew, toppling over everyone on the way —men, women, and children, and himself rebounding from everyone—men, women, and children. About him and after him resounded frightened voices, squeals, screams . . . but Mr. Golyadkin seemed unconscious and would pay no heed to anything. . . .

He came to himself, however, on Semyonovsky Bridge, and then only because he succeeded in brushing awkwardly against and upsetting two peasant women and the wares they were selling, and, at the same time, tumbling himself. "That's no matter," thought Mr. Golyadkin, "that can easily turn out for the best," and he felt in his pocket at once, intending to make up for the cakes, apples, nuts, and various trifles he had scattered with a rouble. Suddenly a new light dawned upon Mr. Golyadkin; in his pocket he felt the letter given him in the morning by the clerk. Remembering that there was a tavern he knew close by, he dropped in at it, without a moment's delay, settled himself at a little table lighted by a tallow candle, and, taking no notice of anything, paying no heed to the waiter who came to ask for his orders, broke the seal and began reading the following letter, which firmly staggered him:

To the noble man, who suffers for my sake, and is ever dear to my heart!

I am suffering, I am perishing—save me! The slanderer, the intriguer, notorious for the uselessness of his tendency, has entangled me in his snares, and I have perished! I am lost! But he is abhorrent to me, while you, my darling! . . . They have tried to separate us, they have intercepted my letters to you—and all this has been the work of the vicious man who has taken advantage of his one good quality—his resemblance to you. In any case, a man can always be plain in appearance, yet fascinate by his intelligence, his strong feelings, and his agreeable manners. . . . I am perishing! I am being married against my will, and the chief part in this intrigue is taken by my parent and benefactor, the state councilor, Olsufy Ivanovich, probably desirous of securing for me a place and connections in fashionable society. . . . But I have made up my mind and I protest by all the means bestowed on me by nature. Be waiting for me with your carriage at nine o'clock this evening at the windows of Olsufy Ivanovich's flat. We are having another ball and the handsome lieutenant is coming. I will come out and we will fly away. Moreover, there are other government offices in which one can be of service to one's country. In any case, remember, my friend, that innocence is strong by virtue of its very innocence. Farewell. Wait with the carriage at the entrance. I shall throw myself into the protection of your arms at two o'clock in the night.

> Yours till death,
> Klara Olsufyevna

After reading the letter our hero remained for some minutes dumbfounded. In terrible anxiety, in terrible agitation, white as a sheet, with the letter in his hand, he walked several times up and down the room; to complete the unpleasantness of his position, though our hero failed to observe it, he was at that moment the object of the exclusive attention of everyone in the room. Probably the disorder of his attire, his unrestrained excitement, his walking, or rather running about the room, his gesticulating with both hands, perhaps some enigmatic words unconsciously spoken at random, probably all this discredited Mr. Golyadkin in the opinion of the customers, and even the waiter began to look at him suspiciously. Coming to himself, Mr. Golyadkin noticed that he was standing in the middle of the room and was in an almost unseemly, discourteous manner staring at an old man of very respectable appearance who, having dined and said grace before the ikon, had sat down again and, for his part, also fixed his eyes upon Mr. Golyadkin. Our hero looked vaguely about him and noticed that everyone, positively everyone, was looking at him with a hostile and suspicious air. All at once a retired military man with a red collar asked loudly for the *Police Bulletins.* Mr. Golyadkin started and turned crimson; he happened to look down and saw that he was in such disorderly attire as it was improper for him to wear even at home, let alone in a public place. His boots, his trousers, and the whole of his left side were covered with mud; the right footstrap was torn off, and even his coat was torn in many places. In extreme misery our hero went up to the table at which he had read the letter, and saw that the waiter was coming up to him with a strange and impertinently urgent expression on his face. Utterly disconcerted and crestfallen, our hero began to examine the table at which he was now standing. On the table were dirty plates left from somebody's dinner, a soiled table napkin and a knife, fork, and spoon that had just been used. "Who, then, has been having dinner?" thought our hero. "Can it have been I? Well, anything is possible! I must have had dinner without noticing it; what am I to do?"

Raising his eyes, Mr. Golyadkin again saw beside him the waiter who was about to address him.

"What do I owe you, my lad?" our hero inquired, in a trembling voice.

A loud laugh sounded around Mr. Golyadkin; the waiter

himself grinned. Mr. Golyadkin realized that he had blundered again, and had done something dreadfully stupid. He was overcome by confusion, and to avoid standing there with nothing to do he put his hand in his pocket to get out his handkerchief; but to the indescribable amazement of himself and all surrounding him, he pulled out instead of his handkerchief the bottle of medicine which Krestyan Ivanovich had prescribed for him four days earlier. "Get the medicine at the same chemist's," flashed through Mr. Golyadkin's brain. . . .

Suddenly he started and almost cried out in horror. A new light dawned. . . . The dark reddish, repulsive liquid flashed with a sinister gleam in Mr. Golyadkin's eyes. . . . The bottle dropped from his hands and was instantly smashed. Our hero cried out and stepped back a pace to avoid the spilled liquid. . . . He was trembling in every limb, and drops of sweat came out on his forehead and temples. "So my life is in danger!" Meanwhile there was a stir, a commotion in the room; all the people surrounded Mr. Golyadkin, everyone talked to Mr. Golyadkin, some even caught hold of Mr. Golyadkin. But our hero was dumb and motionless, seeing nothing, hearing nothing, feeling nothing. . . . At last, as though tearing himself from the place, he rushed out of the tavern, pushing away all and each who tried to detain him; almost unconscious, he got into the first cab that passed him and drove to his flat.

In the entry of his flat he met Miheyev, the watchman from the office, with an official envelope in his hand.

"I know, my good man, I know all about it," our exhausted hero answered, in a weak, miserable voice; "it's official. . . ."

The envelope did, in fact, contain instructions to Mr. Golyadkin, signed by Andrey Filippovich, to hand over the papers in his hands to Ivan Semyonovich. Taking the envelope and giving a ten-kopeck piece to the man, Mr. Golyadkin went into his flat and saw that Petrushka was collecting his trash, all his things into a heap, evidently intending to abandon Mr. Golyadkin and move to the flat of Karolina Ivanovna, who had enticed him to take the place of Yevstafy.

Chapter XII

Petrushka came in swaggering, with a strangely casual manner and an air of servile solemnity on his face. It was evident that he was planning something, that he felt thoroughly within his rights, and he looked like an unconcerned outsider—that is, as though he were anybody's servant rather than Mr. Golyadkin's.

"Well, my good lad," our hero began breathlessly, "what time is it, now, my lad?"

Without speaking, Petrushka went behind his partition, then returned, and in a rather independent tone announced that it was nearly half-past seven.

"Well, that's all right, my lad, that's all right. Well, you see, my boy . . . allow me to tell you, my lad, that everything seems to be at an end between us."

Petrushka said nothing.

"Well, now that everything is over between us, tell me openly, as to a friend, where were you?"

"Where I was? To see good people, sir."

"I know, my friend, I know. I have always been satisfied with you, and I'll give you a character. . . . Well, what are you going to do there now?"

"Why, sir, you know yourself. Sure, a good man won't teach you anything bad."

"I know, my dear fellow, I know. Nowadays good people are rare, my lad; prize them, my friend. Well, how are they?"

"To be sure, they . . . Only I can't be your servant any longer, sir; as your honor must know."

"I know, my dear fellow, I know your zeal and devotion; I have seen it all, my lad, I've noticed it. I respect you, my friend. I respect a good and honest man, even if he's a lackey."

"Why, yes, to be sure! The likes of us, of course, as you know yourself, look for what is best for them. That's so. We all know, sir, that there's no getting on without a good man."

"Very well, very well, my boy, I'm aware of it. . . . Come, here's your money and here's your character. Now we'll kiss and say good-by, brother. . . . Come, now, my lad, I'll ask one service of you, one last service," said Mr. Golyadkin, in a solemn tone. "You see, my dear boy, all sorts of things happen. Sorrow, my friend, dwells even in gilded palaces, and there's no escaping it. You know, my boy, I've always been kind to you, my boy."

Petrushka remained mute.

"I believe I've always been kind to you, my dear fellow. . . . Come, how much linen have we now, my dear boy?"

"Well, it's all there, sir. Six linen shirts, three pairs of socks, four shirtfronts, a flannel jersey; of underwear, two sets. You know, sir, yourself, that's all there is. I've got nothing of yours, sir. . . . I look after my master's belongings, sir. I am satisfied with you, sir . . . we all know . . . and I've never been guilty of anything, sir, you know yourself, sir. . . ."

"I trust you, my lad, I trust you. I didn't mean that, my friend, I didn't mean that, you know, my lad; I tell you what . . ."

"To be sure, sir, we know that already. Why, when I used to be in service at General Stolbnyakov's . . . they let me go when the family went away to Saratov . . . they've an estate there. . . ."

"No; I didn't mean that, my lad, I didn't mean that; don't think anything of the sort, my dear fellow. . . ."

"To be sure. It's easy, as you know yourself, sir, to take away the character of folks like us. And I've always given satisfaction—to ministers, generals, senators, counts—I've served them all, sir—Prince Svinchatkin, Colonel Pereborkin,

General Nedobarov—he would visit my master, come to his estate. It is known. . . ."

"Yes, my lad, very good, my lad, very good. And now I too am going away, my friend. . . . A different path lies before each man, no one can tell what road he may have to take. Come, my lad, help me get dressed now, pack my uniform too . . . and my other trousers, my sheets, quilts, and pillows. . . ."

"Am I to tie them all up in a bundle?"

"Yes, my lad, yes; in a bundle, please. Who knows what may happen to us. Come, my dear boy, you go and find a carriage. . . ."

"A carriage, sir?"

"Yes, my lad, a carriage; a roomy one, and take it by the hour. And don't you imagine anything. . . ."

"And are you meaning to go far, sir?"

"I don't know, my lad, I don't know that either. I think you had better pack my feather bed too. What do you think, my lad? I am relying on you, my dear fellow. . . ."

"Is your honor setting off at once?"

"Yes, my friend, yes! Circumstances have turned out so . . . so it is, my dear fellow, so it is. . . ."

"Yes, sir; in our regiment the same thing happened to the lieutenant, sir; he carried off a country gentleman's . . ."

"Eloped? . . . How, my dear fellow?"

"Yes, sir, eloped, and they were married in another manor house. Everything was got ready beforehand. They were pursued; the late prince took their part, and so the affair was settled. . . ."

"They were married, yes. . . . But how is it, my dear fellow. . . . How did you come to know, my boy?"

"Why, the earth is full of rumors, sir. We know, sir, we all know. . . . To be sure, there's no one without sin. Only I'll tell you now, sir, let me speak plainly, in the words of servants, sir; since it has come to this, I must tell you, sir; you have an enemy—you've a rival, sir, a powerful rival, so there. . . ."

"I know, my dear fellow, I know; you know yourself,

my dear fellow. . . . So, you see, I'm relying upon you. What are we to do now, my friend! What do you advise me?"

"Well, sir, if you are in that way now, if you've come, so to say, to such a pass, sir, you'll have to make some purchases, sir—say some sheets, pillows, another feather bed, a double one, a good quilt. Here, a neighbor downstairs—she's a townswoman, sir—she has got a good fox-fur woman's coat, so you might look at it and buy it, you might have a look at it at once. You'll need it now, sir; it's a good coat, sir, a satin coat, lined with fox fur. . . ."

"Very good, my friend, very good, I agree, my friend, I rely upon you, I rely upon you entirely; a coat, too, my lad. . . . Only hurry, hurry! For God's sake, hurry! I'll buy the coat too—only, please, make haste! It will soon be eight o'clock, hurry, for God's sake, my friend! Hurry up, my friend!"

Petrushka dropped the bundle of linen, pillows, quilt, sheets, and all sorts of odds and ends which he had started to collect and tie up, and rushed headlong out of the room. Meanwhile, Mr. Golyadkin seized the letter once more, but was unable to read it. Clutching his hapless head, he leaned against the wall in a state of stupefaction. He could think of nothing, he could do nothing either, he could not even tell what was happening to him. At last, seeing that time was passing and neither Petrushka nor the coat had made their appearance, Mr. Golyadkin made up his mind to go out himself. Opening the door into the entry, he heard belowstairs noise, talk, disputing. . . . Several of the women of the neighboring flats were shouting, talking, arguing about something—Mr. Golyadkin knew what. Petrushka's voice was heard; then there was a sound of footsteps. "My goodness! They'll bring all the world in here," moaned Mr. Golyadkin, wringing his hands in despair and rushing back into his room.

Finding himself in his room, he fell almost senseless on the sofa with his face in the pillow. After lying a minute in this way, he jumped up, and, without waiting for Petrushka, put on his galoshes, his hat, and his greatcoat, snatched up his wallet, and ran headlong downstairs. "Nothing is wanted, nothing, my dear fellow! I will manage myself—everything myself. I don't need you for the present, and, meantime, things may take a better turn," Mr. Golyadkin muttered to Petrushka, meeting him on the stairs; then he ran into the yard, out into the street. His heart sank, he was in two minds. What was he to do, how was he to act in the present critical situation?

"Yes, how am I to act, my God? And that all this should have happened!" he cried out at last in despair, tottering along the street at random; "that all this should have happened! Why, but for this, but for just this, everything would have been in a fair way; at one stroke, at one skillful, vigorous, firm stroke it would have been set right! I bet my finger that it would have been set right! And I know, indeed, how it would have been settled. This is how it would have been managed: I'd have said, 'With your permission, sir, it's all one to me;' I would have said, 'Things aren't done like that, my dear sir, no, things aren't done like that; among us imposture will get you nowhere; an impostor, my dear sir, is a man who is worthless and of no benefit to the fatherland. Do you understand that? Do you understand that, my dear sir?' That's what I would have said. That's how it would have been. . . . But no . . . things are not like that . . . not a bit like that. . . . I am talking nonsense, like a fool! I am a suicidal fool, I am! It's not like that at all, you suicide, you. . . . This is how things are done, though, you debauchee, you! . . . Well, where am I to go now? Well, what am I going to do with myself now? What am I fit for now? Come, what are you fit for now, for instance, you, Golyadkin, you, you worthless fellow! Well, what next? I must get a carriage; 'hire a carriage and bring it here,' says she, 'we shall get our feet wet without a carriage,' says she. . . . And who could ever have thought it? Fie, fie, my young lady! Fie, fie, young lady of exemplary behavior! And this is the girl we all thought so much of! You've distinguished yourself!

. . . And it all comes from immoral education. And now that I've looked into it and got to the core of it all, I see that it is due to nothing else but immorality. Instead of looking after her as a child . . . and using the rod at times . . . they stuff her with sweets and dainties, and the old man dotes on her, saying, 'My dear, my love, my beauty, we'll marry you to a count!' . . . And now she has come forward and shown us her hand, as though to say, 'That's my little game!' Instead of keeping her at home as a child, they sent her to a boarding school to a French madame, and *émigrée*, a Madame Falbalas⁸ or something, and she learned all sorts of things at that Madame Falbalas', and this is how it turns out. 'Come,' says she, 'and be happy! Be in a carriage,' she says, 'at such and such a time, under the windows, and sing a sentimental romance in the Spanish style; I await you and I know you love me, and we will run away together and live in a hut.' But, lastly, it's not allowed; since it has come to that, madam, it's not allowed, it is against the law to abduct an innocent, respectable girl from her parents' home without their consent! And, finally, why, what for, and what need is there to do it? Come, she should marry a suitable person, the man marked out by destiny, and that would be the end of it. As for me, I'm in the government service, I might lose my berth through it; I might be prosecuted for it, madam! I tell you that, as if you did not know it! It's that German woman's doing. She's at the bottom of it all, the witch; she was the spark that set the forest on fire. For they've slandered a man, for they've invented a bit of womanish gossip about him, a cock-and-bull story, at the advice of Andrey Filippovich, that's what it all came from. Otherwise how could Petrushka be mixed up in it? What has he to do with it? What need for that rogue to be in it? No, I cannot, madam, I cannot possibly, not on any account. . . . No, madam, this time you must really excuse me. It's all your doing, madam, it's not all the German woman's

⁸ Madame Falbalas kept the *pension* attended by the heroine of Pushkin's *Count Nulin.*—A.Y.

doing, it's not the witch's doing at all, but simply yours. For the witch is a good woman, for the witch is not to blame in any way; it's your fault, madam; it's you who are to blame, that's how it is! It's you, you, madam, who are getting me into trouble. . . . Here a man is being ruined, a man is losing sight of himself, is unable to restrain himself—a wedding indeed! And how is it all going to end? And how will it all be arranged? I would give a great deal to know all that!"

So our hero reflected in his despair. Coming to himself suddenly, he observed that he was standing somewhere in Liteyny Street. The weather was awful: thaw had set in; it was snowing and raining—just as at that memorable time when in the dread hour of midnight all Mr. Golyadkin's troubles had begun. "What a night for a journey!" thought Mr. Golyadkin, looking at the weather. "It's death all around. . . . Good Lord! Where am I to find a carriage, for instance? I believe there's something black looming there at the corner. We'll see, we'll investigate. . . . My God!" our hero went on, bending his neck and tottering steps in the direction in which he saw something that looked like a cab.

"No, I know what I'll do; I'll go straight there, fall on my knees, if I can, and humbly beg for help, saying, 'I put my fate in your hands, in the hands of my superiors. Your Excellency, protect me and show me your favor'; and then I'll say this and that, and explain that it is an unlawful act; 'Do not destroy me, I look upon you as my father, do not abandon me . . . save my dignity, my honor, my name . . . save me from a miscreant, a vicious man. . . . He's another person, your Excellency, and I'm another person too; he's by himself and I am by myself too; I am really by myself, your Excellency; really by myself,' that's what I shall say. 'I cannot be like him. Change him, please, give orders for him to be changed and the godless, willful impersonation abolished . . . that it may not be an example to others, your Excellency. I look upon you as a father'; those in authority over us, our benefactors and protectors, are bound, of course, to encourage such impulses. . . . There's something chivalrous about it. 'I look upon you, my beneficent superior, as a father, and I commit my fate in trust to you, and I will not say anything against it; I trust in you, and myself retire' . . . that's what I would say."

"Well, my friend, are you a cabby?"

"I am. . . ."

"I want a cab for the evening. . . ."

"And does your honor want to go far?"

"For the evening, for the evening; wherever I have to go, my good man, wherever I have to go."

"Does your honor want to drive out of town?"

"Yes, my friend, out of town, perhaps. I don't quite know myself yet, I can't tell you for sure, my friend. You see, maybe it will all be settled for the best. We all know, my friend. . . ."

"Yes, sir, of course we all know. Please God it may."

"Yes, my friend, yes; thank you, my dear fellow; come, what's your fare, my good man?"

"Do you want to set off at once?"

"Yes, at once, that is, no, you will have to wait at a certain place. . . . A little while, not long, you'll have to wait. . . ."

"Well, if you hire me for the whole time, I couldn't ask less than six roubles in weather like this, sir. . . ."

"Oh, very well, my friend, very well; and I will make it worth your while, my dear fellow. So, come, you can drive me now, my good man."

"Get in; allow me, I'll put it straight a bit—now you will get in, if you please. Where shall I drive?"

"To Izmailovsky Bridge, my friend."

The driver climbed up on the box, with difficulty tore his pair of lean nags from the trough of hay, and set off for Izmailovsky Bridge. But suddenly Mr. Golyadkin pulled the cord, stopped the cab, and besought him in an imploring voice not to drive to Izmailovsky Bridge, but to turn back into another street. The driver turned into another street, and ten minutes later Mr. Golyadkin's newly hired vehicle was standing before the house in which his Excellency had a flat. Mr. Golyadkin got out of the carriage, begged the driver to be sure to wait, and with a sinking heart ran upstairs to the first story and pulled the bell; the door opened and our hero found himself in the entry of his Excellency's flat.

"Is his Excellency pleased to be at home?" asked Mr. Golyadkin, addressing the man who opened the door.

"What do you want, sir?" asked the servant, scrutinizing Mr. Golyadkin from head to foot.

"I, my friend . . . I am Golyadkin, an official, the titular councilor, Golyadkin. To say . . . to explain . . ."

"Wait; you cannot, sir. . . ."

"My friend, I cannot wait; my business is important, it's business that admits of no delay. . . ."

"But from whom have you come? Have you brought papers? . . ."

"No, my friend, I have come on my own account. Announce me, my friend, say so and so to—explain. I'll make it worth your while, my good man. . . ."

"Impossible, sir. His Excellency does not receive visitors, he has guests. Come at ten o'clock in the morning, sir. . . ."

"Announce me, my good man, I can't wait—it is impossible. . . . You'll have to answer for it, my good man."

"Why, go and announce him! What's the matter with you; want to save your shoe leather?" said another lackey, who was lolling on the bench and had not uttered a word till then.

"Shoe leather! I was told not to show anyone in, you know; the gentleman's time is the morning."

"Announce him. Will your tongue fall off, eh?"

"I'll announce him all right. My tongue will not fall off. Those are not my orders; I've told you, those are not my orders. Step inside."

Mr. Golyadkin went into the outermost room; there was a clock on the table. He glanced at it: it was half-past eight. His heart ached within him. Already he wanted to turn back, but at that very moment the lanky footman standing at the door of the next room had already boomed out Mr. Golyadkin's name. "Oh, what lungs!" thought our hero in indescribable misery. "Why, you ought to have said, 'He has come most humbly and meekly to make an explanation . . . have the kindness to see him.' . . . Now the whole business is ruined; all my hopes are scattered to the winds. But . . . however . . . never mind. . . ."

There was no time to think, though. The lackey, returning, said, "Please," and led Mr. Golyadkin into the study.

When our hero went in, he felt as though he were blinded, for he could see nothing at all. . . . Two or three figures flitted before his eyes, though. "Oh, yes, they are the guests," flashed through Mr. Golyadkin's mind. At last our hero could distinguish clearly the star on the black dress coat of his Excellency, then by degrees advanced to seeing the black coat, and finally gained the power of complete vision. . . .

"What is it, sir?" said a familiar voice above Mr. Golyadkin.

"The titular councilor, Golyadkin, your Excellency."

"Well?"

"I have come to make an explanation. . . ."

"How? . . . What's that?"

"Why, yes. This is how it is. I've come to have it out, your Excellency. . . ."

"But you . . . but who are you? . . ."

"M—m—mist—er Golyadkin, your Excellency, titular councilor."

"Well, what is it you want?"

"Why, this is how it is, I look upon you as a father; I myself retire . . . defend me from my enemy!"

"What's this?"

"It is known. . . ."

"What is known?"

Mr. Golyadkin was silent: his chin began twitching a little.

"Well?"

"I thought it chivalrous, your Excellency. . . . 'There's something chivalrous about it,' I said, 'and I look upon my superior as on a father. Protect me, I b—b—beg you with t—t—tears in my eyes. . . . Such impulses sh—sh—should b—b—be encouraged. . . .'"

His Excellency turned away. For some moments our hero could distinguish nothing. There was a weight on his chest. His breathing was labored. He did not know where he was standing. . . . He felt ashamed and sad. God knows what followed. . . .

When he recovered, our hero noticed that his Excellency was talking with his guests, and seemed to be sharply and forcefully arguing about something with them. One of the guests Mr. Golyadkin recognized at once. This was Andrey Filippovich; the other one he did not recognize. Yet there was something familiar about him—a tall, thick-set figure, elderly, possessed of very thick eyebrows and whiskers and an expressive, keen gaze. On his neck was an order and in his mouth a cigar. The stranger was smoking and without taking the cigar out of his mouth was nodding significantly and glancing from time to time at Mr. Golyadkin.

Mr. Golyadkin began to feel awkward; he turned away his eyes and immediately caught sight of another very odd visitor. In a doorway, which our hero had taken for a looking glass, just as he had done once before—*he* made his appearance—we know who: a very close acquaintance and friend of Mr. Golyadkin's. Mr. Golyadkin Jr. had actually been till then in a little room close by, hurriedly writing something; now, apparently because he was needed, he came in with papers under his arm, went up to his Excellency, and, while awaiting the latter's exclusive attention to his person, succeeded very adroitly in insinuating himself into the talk and consultation, taking his place a little behind Andrey Filippovich's back and partly screened by the cigar-smoking stranger. Mr. Golyadkin Jr. clearly took an extreme interest in the conversation, which he was eavesdropping on now in a gentlemanly way, nodding his head, fidgeting with his feet, smiling, glancing every minute at his Excellency—as if beseeching him with his eyes to be allowed to put his word in.

"The scoundrel!" thought Mr. Golyadkin, and involuntarily took a step forward. At this moment his Excellency turned around, and came rather hesitatingly toward Mr. Golyadkin.

"Well, that's all right, that's all right; well, run along, now. I'll look into your case, and I'll have someone show you out. . . ."

At this point his Excellency glanced at the gentleman with the thick whiskers. The latter nodded in assent.

Mr. Golyadkin felt and clearly understood that they were taking him for someone he wasn't and not at all treating him as they ought to.

"In one way or another I must explain myself," he thought; "I must say, 'This is how it is, your Excellency.'"

At this point in his perplexity he dropped his eyes to the floor, and to his great astonishment he saw a good-sized white patch on his Excellency's boots.

"Can they have split?" thought Mr. Golyadkin. Soon, however, he discovered that his Excellency's boots had not split, but were only strong reflectors—a phenomenon fully explained by the fact that they were made of patent leather and highly polished.

"It is what they call a *high light*," thought our hero; "the term is used particularly in artists' studios; elsewhere such a reflection is called a *rib of light*."

At this point Mr. Golyadkin raised his eyes and saw that the time had come to speak, for things might easily end badly. . . . Our hero took a step forward.

"I say this is how it is, your Excellency," he said, "and nowadays imposture will get you nowhere."

The general made no answer, but rang the bell violently. Our hero took another step forward.

"He is a vile, vicious man, your Excellency," said our hero, beside himself and faint with terror, though still pointing boldly and resolutely at his unworthy twin, who at the moment was fidgeting about near his Excellency. "I say this is how it is, and I am alluding to a notorious person."

Mr. Golyadkin's words produced a general commotion. Andrey Filippovich and the stranger started nodding their heads; his Excellency impatiently tugged at the bell rope to summon the servants. At this juncture Mr. Golyadkin Jr. came forward in his turn.

"Your Excellency," he said, "I humbly beg permission to speak." There was something very resolute in Mr. Golyadkin Jr.'s voice; everything about him showed that he felt himself completely within his rights.

"Allow me to ask you," he began again, anticipating his Excellency's reply in his eagerness, and this time addressing Mr. Golyadkin; "allow me to ask you, in whose presence you are making this explanation? Before whom are you standing, in whose study are you?"

Mr. Golyadkin Jr. was in a state of extraordinary excitement, flushed and burning with wrath and indignation; there were even tears in his eyes.

"Mr. and Mrs. Bassavryukov!" roared a lackey at the top of his voice, appearing in the doorway.

"A good aristocratic name, they hail from Little Russia," thought Mr. Golyadkin, and at that moment he felt someone lay a very friendly hand on his back, then a second hand was laid on his back. Mr. Golyadkin's infamous twin was bustling about in front leading the way; and our hero saw clearly that he was being steered to the big doors of the study.

"Just as it was at Olsufy Ivanovich's," he thought, and he found himself in the hall. Looking around, he saw beside him two of his Excellency's lackeys and his twin.

"The greatcoat, the greatcoat, the greatcoat, my friend's greatcoat! The greatcoat of my best friend!" chirped the depraved man, snatching the coat from one of the servants, and by way of a nasty and inauspicious joke flinging it straight over Mr. Golyadkin's head. As he was extricating himself from under his coat, Mr. Golyadkin distinctly heard the two lackeys snigger. But without listening to anything, or paying attention to what was going on, he walked out of the hall and found himself on the lighted stairs. Mr. Golyadkin Jr. followed him.

"Good-by, your Excellency!" he shouted after Mr. Golyadkin Sr.

"Scoundrel!" our hero exclaimed, beside himself.

"Well, scoundrel, then . . ."

"Depraved man!"

"Well, depraved man, then . . ." answered Mr. Golyadkin's unworthy enemy, and with his characteristic baseness he looked down from the top of the stairs straight into Mr. Golyadkin's face without blinking, as though begging him to keep up the name-calling. Our hero spat with indignation and ran out on the steps. He was so crushed that he had no recollection of how he got into the cab or who helped him in. Coming to himself, he found that he was being driven along the Fontanka. "We must be on our way to Izmailovsky Bridge, then," thought Mr. Golyadkin. At this point Mr. Golyadkin tried to think of something else, but could not; it was something so terrible that it defied explanation. . . . "Well, never mind," our hero concluded, and proceeded to Izmailovsky Bridge.

Chapter XIII

It seemed as though the weather meant to change for the better. The wet snow, which had till then been coming down in regular clouds, began by degrees to abate, and at last almost ceased. The sky became visible, and here and there tiny stars sparkled in it. It was only wet, muddy, damp, and stifling, especially for Mr. Golyadkin, who could hardly breathe as it was. His greatcoat, soaked and grown heavy, sent a sort of unpleasant warm dampness all through him and made his weakened legs buckle under its weight. A feverish sensation made him feel creepy all over; he was in a cold sick sweat from utter exhaustion, so much so that

Mr. Golyadkin even forgot to repeat on this suitable occasion with his characteristic firmness and resolution his favorite phrase that it would all maybe somehow most likely, certainly turn out for the best. "Still, all this does not matter for the time being," our sturdy and undaunted hero repeated, wiping from his face the cold drops that streamed in all directions from the brim of his round hat, which was so soaked that it could hold no more water. Adding that all this was nothing for the present, our hero tried to sit down on a rather thick stump which was lying near a pile of firewood in Olsufy Ivanovich's yard.

Of course, it was no good thinking of Spanish serenades and silken ladders, but it was quite necessary to think of a modest corner, snug and private, if not altogether warm. He felt greatly tempted, we may mention in passing, by that corner in the back entry of Olsufy Ivanovich's flat in which he had once, almost at the beginning of this true story, stood for two hours between a cupboard and an old screen among all sorts of domestic odds and ends and useless rubbish. The fact is that now too Mr. Golyadkin had stood waiting for two whole hours in Olsufy Ivanovich's yard. But as regards that modest and snug little corner, there were now certain drawbacks which had not existed before. The first drawback was the fact that it was probably now a marked place and that certain precautionary measures had been taken in regard to it since the scandal at Olsufy Ivanovich's last ball. Secondly, he had to wait for a signal from Klara Olsufyevna, for there was bound to be some such signal. That's how it always was, and, as he said, "It didn't begin with us and it won't end with us."

At this point Mr. Golyadkin very appropriately remembered, by the way, a novel he had read long ago in which the heroine, in precisely similar circumstances, signaled to her Alfred by tying a pink ribbon to her window. But now, at night, in the climate of Petersburg, notorious for its dampness and unreliability, a pink ribbon was hardly appropriate and, in short, utterly out of the question.

"No, this is no time for silk ladders," thought our hero,

"and I had better stay here quietly and comfortably. . . . I had better stand right here, for instance."

And he selected a place in the yard exactly opposite the window, near the stack of firewood. Of course, many postilions and coachmen and other people were walking about the yard, and there was, besides, the rumbling of wheels and the snorting of horses and so on; yet it was a convenient place, whether he was observed or not; but now, anyway, there was the advantage of being to some extent in the shade, and no one could see Mr. Golyadkin while he himself could see everything. The windows were brightly lit up, there was some sort of grand party at Olsufy Ivanovich's. No music was as yet heard, though.

"So it's not a ball, but a gathering of some other sort," thought our hero, his heart sinking. "Is it today?" flashed through his mind. "Perhaps there is a mistake in the date. It's possible; anything is possible. . . . Perhaps a letter was written yesterday, but it didn't reach me, and perhaps it did not reach me because Petrushka got mixed up in the affair, the rascal! Or it was written tomorrow, that is, that everything was to be done tomorrow, that is—waiting with a carriage. . . ."

At this point our hero turned cold all over and felt in his pocket for the letter, to make sure. But to his surprise the letter was not in his pocket.

"How's this?" whispered Mr. Golyadkin, more dead than alive. "Where did I leave it? Then I must have lost it. That is the last straw!" he moaned at last in conclusion. "What if it falls into evil hands? (Perhaps it already has.) Good Lord! What may it not lead to? It may lead to . . . Oh, my miserable fate!" Here Mr. Golyadkin began trembling like a leaf at the thought that perhaps his indecent twin had thrown the greatcoat over him with the express object of stealing the letter of which he had somehow got wind from Mr. Golyadkin's enemies.

"What's more, he's stolen it," thought our hero, "as evidence . . . but evidence of what?"

After the first shock of horror, the blood rushed to Mr.

Golyadkin's head. Moaning and gnashing his teeth, he clutched his burning head, sank down on his block of wood, and relapsed into brooding . . . but he could form no coherent thoughts. Faces kept flitting through his mind, incidents came back to his memory, now vaguely, now distinctly, the tunes of some foolish songs kept ringing in his ears. . . . He was in distress, in unnatural distress!

"My God, my God!" our hero thought, recovering a little, and suppressing a muffled sob, "give me fortitude of spirit in the immeasurable depths of my afflictions! That I am done for, that I have vanished there can be no doubt any longer, and this is all in the natural order of things, since it cannot be otherwise. To begin with, I've lost my berth, I've certainly lost it, I couldn't but lose it. . . . Well, suppose things are set right somehow. Let us assume that my money will suffice for a start. I must have another lodging, furniture of some sort. . . . In the first place, I shan't have Petrushka. I can get on without the rascal . . . perhaps as a lodger. Well, that will be all right! I can come and go when I like, and Petrushka won't grumble at my coming in late—yes, that is so; that's why it's a good thing to be a lodger. . . . Well, all this may be fine, but how is it that I am talking about something irrelevant, completely irrelevant?"

Here the thought of his real situation again dawned upon Mr. Golyadkin. He looked around.

"Oh, my God, my God! What have I just been talking about?" he thought, growing utterly bewildered and clutching his burning head in his hands. . . .

"Won't you soon be going, sir?" a voice sounded above Mr. Golyadkin. Our hero started; before him stood his cabman, who was also drenched through and chilled to the bone; growing impatient, and, having nothing to do, he had thought fit to take a look at Mr. Golyadkin behind the woodstack.

"I am all right, my friend . . . I am coming soon, very soon; you wait. . . ."

The cabman walked away, grumbling to himself. "What

is he grumbling about?" Mr. Golyadkin wondered through his tears. "Why, I have hired him for the evening, I'm within my rights now . . . that's how it is! I've hired him for the evening, and that's the end of it. Even if he stands still all the time, it's just the same. That's for me to decide. I am free to drive or not to drive. And my standing here behind the woodstack is nothing . . . and don't you dare to say anything; if a gentleman wants to stand behind the woodstack, he stands there . . . and he is not sullying anyone's reputation. So that's how it is! That's how it is! Madam, if you care to know, as for living in a hut, madam, nowadays no one does that. That's how it is! And in our industrial age there's no getting anywhere without good behavior, a fact of which you are a fatal example, madam. . . . You say, work as a court clerk and live in a hut on the seashore. In the first place, madam, there are no court clerks on the seashore, and, in the second place, you can't get a job as a court clerk. For suppose that, for example, I submit an application, present myself, saying, 'Give me the post of a court clerk . . . and defend me from my enemy.' . . . They'll tell you, madam, they'll say that there are lots of court clerks, and here you are not at Madame Falbalas', where you learned the rules of good behavior, of which you are such a fatal example. Good behavior, madam, means staying at home, honoring your father, and not thinking about suitors prematurely. Suitors will come in good time, madam, that's so! Of course, you are bound to have some talents, such as playing the piano a little sometimes, speaking French, have a knowledge of history, geography, scripture, and arithmetic, that's so! And that's all you need. Cooking, too, cooking certainly forms part of the education of a well-behaved girl! But what do we find? In the first place, my fair lady, they won't let you go. They'll chain you, and then they'll play their trump, and lock you up in a nunnery. How will it be then, madam? What will you have me do then? Would you have me, madam, emulate the heroes of some silly novels, and melt into tears on a neighboring hill, gazing at the cold walls of

your prisonhouse, and finally die, following the example of
some wretched German poets and novelists? Is that it,
madam? But, to begin with, allow me to tell you, as a
friend, that things are not done like that, and, in the second
place, I would have given you and your parents, too, a
good thrashing for letting you read French books; for
French books teach you no good. There's poison in them
. . . pernicious poison, madam! Or do you imagine, allow
me to ask you, or do you imagine that we shall elope with
impunity, and have a hut on the shore of the sea; and that
we shall begin billing and cooing and discussing various
feelings, and so spend the rest of our lives in happiness
and contentment? Then there will be a little one—so we
shall go to our father, the councilor of state, Olsufy Ivanovich, and say, 'We've got a little one, and so, on this propi-
tious occasion, remove your curse and bless the couple.' No,
madam, I tell you again, that's not the way things are
done, and in the first place there'll be no billing and cooing,
please don't reckon on it. Nowadays, madam, the husband
is the master and a good, well-brought-up wife must try
and please him in every way. And endearments, madam,
are not liked, nowadays, in our industrial age; the day of
Jean Jacques Rousseau is over. The husband comes home,
for instance, hungry from the office, and asks, 'Can't I have
something before dinner, my love, a drop of vodka to drink,
a bit of herring to eat?' So then, madam, you must have
the vodka and the herring ready. Your husband will down
the snack with relish, and won't so much as look at you.
'Run into the kitchen, kitten,' he'll say, 'and look after the
dinner,' and at most, once a week, he'll kiss you, even then
perfunctorily. . . . That's what it will be like, my lady!
Yes, even then, perfunctorily. . . . That's how it will be, if
it comes to looking at the thing in that way. . . . And
how do I come in? Why, madam, have you mixed me up
in your caprices? 'To the beneficent man who suffers for my
sake and who is in every way dear to my heart,' and so
on. But in the first place, madam, I am not suited to you,
you know yourself, I'm not a great hand at compliments,

I'm not fond of uttering perfumed trifles for the ladies. I don't like lady-killers, and I must own I've never been a good-looker. You won't find any swagger or false shame in me, and I tell you so now in all sincerity. A straightforward, open character and common sense is all I possess; I have nothing to do with intrigues. I am not one to intrigue, I say so and I'm proud of it—that's a fact! . . . I wear no mask among good people, and to tell you the whole truth . . ."

Suddenly Mr. Golyadkin started. The soaked red beard of his cabman appeared over the woodstack again. . . .

"I am coming directly, my friend. I'm coming at once, you know, at once," Mr. Golyadkin responded in a trembling and weak voice.

The cabman scratched the back of his head, stroked his beard, and moved a step forward . . . then stood still and looked at Mr. Golyadkin.

"I am coming directly, my friend; you see, my friend . . . I . . . just a little, you see, only a second . . . you see, my friend. . . ."

"Won't you be going anywhere at all?" the cabman asked, at last resolutely confronting Mr. Golyadkin.

"I'm coming directly, my friend, I am waiting, you see, my friend. . . ."

"Yes, sir. . . ."

"You see, my friend, I . . . What village do you come from, my friend?"

"We are under a master. . . ."

"And have you a kind master?"

"He's not bad. . . ."

"Yes, my friend; you stay here, my friend, you see. . . . Have you been in Petersburg long, my friend?"

"I've been driving a cab for a year now. . . ."

"And are you getting on all right, my friend?"

"Not bad."

"To be sure, my friend, to be sure. You ought to thank Providence, my friend. You should look for a good man. Good people are none too common nowadays, my friend.

A good man would wash you, give you food and drink, my good fellow, a good man would. But sometimes you see tears shed by the wealthy, my friend—a lamentable example; that's how it is, my friend. . . ."

The cabman seemed to feel sorry for Mr. Golyadkin.

"Well, your honor, I'll stay on. Will your honor be waiting long?"

"No, my friend, no; I . . . you know . . . er . . . I won't wait any longer, my good man. . . . What do you think, my friend? I rely upon you. I won't stay here any longer."

"Aren't you going to drive anywhere?"

"No, my friend, no; and I'll make it worth your while, my friend . . . that's how it is. How much do I owe you, my dear fellow?"

"What you hired me for, please, sir. I've been waiting here a long time; you won't wrong a man, sir."

"Well, here, my friend, here."

At this point Mr. Golyadkin gave six whole roubles to the cabman, and made up his mind in earnest to waste no more time, that is, to clear off with a whole skin, especially since the matter had been settled and the cabman dismissed, and there was nothing more to wait for. He walked out of the yard, through the gate, turned left and, without looking around, took to his heels, breathless and rejoicing. "Perhaps it will all be for the best," he thought, "and perhaps in this way I've steered clear of trouble." Indeed, Mr. Golyadkin suddenly, all at once, felt unusually light-hearted. "Oh, if only it could turn out for the best!" thought our hero, though he put little faith in his own words. "I know what I'll do . . ." he thought. "No, I'd better try the other tack. . . . Or wouldn't it be better to do this?" In this way, hesitating and seeking for the solution of his doubts, our hero ran as far as Semyonovsky Bridge; but, having reached it, he rationally, prudently, and conclusively decided to return.

"It will be better so," he thought. "I had better try another tack. This is what I'll do: I'll look on simply as an outsider, and that will be the end of it; I am simply an on-looker, an outsider—and nothing more, whatever happens—it's not my fault. That's how it is! That's how it shall be now."

Having decided to return, our hero actually did return, the more readily because with this happy thought of his he considered himself now quite an outsider.

"It's the best thing; you're not responsible for anything, and you'll see all that's necessary . . . that's the fact of the matter!"

It was a safe plan and there was an end to it all. Reassured, he crept back into the peaceful shelter of his soothing and protecting woodstack, and began gazing intently at the windows. This time he was not destined to gaze and wait for long. Suddenly a strange commotion became apparent at all the windows. Figures appeared and vanished, curtains were drawn back, Olsufy Ivanovich's windows were crowded with whole groups of people who peered out and were looking for something in the yard. From the security of his woodstack, our hero, too, began watching the general commotion with curiosity and craning his neck with interest to right and to left, at least as far as the short shadow of the woodstack, which screened him, would allow. Suddenly he started, grew numb, and almost caved in with horror. It seemed to him—in short, he realized, that they were not looking for anything or for anybody, but simply for him, Mr. Golyadkin! Everyone was looking and pointing in his direction. It was impossible to escape; they would see him. . . . Dumbfounded, Mr. Golyadkin huddled as closely as he could to the woodstack, and only then noticed that the treacherous shadow had betrayed him, that it did not cover him completely. Our hero would have been delighted at that moment to creep into a mouse-hole in the woodstack, and there meekly to remain, if only it had been possible. But it was absolutely impossible. In his agony he began at last staring openly and boldly at the windows; it was the best thing to do. . . . And suddenly he was burned up with shame. He had been seen, had been seen by all at once, everyone, they were all waving their hands, nodding their heads at him, calling to him; then several wickets clicked as they opened, several voices shouted something to him at once. . . .

"I wonder why they don't whip these naughty girls when they are children," our hero muttered to himself, losing his head completely. Suddenly without his hat and greatcoat, breathless, bustling, capering, perfidiously displaying intense joy at seeing Mr. Golyadkin, at last, came down the steps *he* (we know who).

"Yakov Petrovich," twittered this individual, so notorious for his worthlessness, "Yakov Petrovich, are you here? You'll catch cold. It's chilly here, Yakov Petrovich. Come indoors."

"Yakov Petrovich! No, I'm all right, Yakov Petrovich," our hero muttered in a submissive voice.

"No, you must come, Yakov Petrovich; they beg you, they most humbly beg you, they are waiting for us. 'Make us happy,' they say, 'and bring in Yakov Petrovich.' That's how things stand."

"No, Yakov Petrovich, you see, I'd better . . . I had better go home, Yakov Petrovich . . ." said our hero, roasting on a slow fire and freezing at the same time with shame and terror.

"No—no—no—no!" twittered the loathsome person. "No—no—no, on no account! Come along," he said resolutely, and he dragged Mr. Golyadkin Sr. to the steps. Mr. Golyadkin Sr. did not at all want to go, but, as everyone was looking at them, it would have been stupid to balk and resist; so our hero went—though, indeed, one cannot say that he went, because he did not know in the least what was happening to him. Though it made no difference!

Before our hero had time to recover and come to his senses, he found himself in the drawing room. He was pale, disheveled, harassed; with lusterless eyes he scanned the crowd—horror! The drawing room, all the rooms—were full to overflowing. There were masses of people, a whole galaxy of ladies; and all were crowding around Mr.

Golyadkin, all were pressing toward Mr. Golyadkin, all were bearing Mr. Golyadkin on their shoulders, and he perceived clearly that they were all forcing him in one direction.

"Not toward the door," was the thought that flashed through Mr. Golyadkin's mind.

They were, in fact, forcing him not toward the door but straight toward Olsufy Ivanovich's easy chair. On one side of the armchair stood Klara Olsufyevna, pale, languid, melancholy, but gorgeously dressed. Mr. Golyadkin was particularly struck by the wonderful effect of the tiny white flowers on her black hair. On the other side of the armchair stood Vladimir Semyonovich in a black dress coat with his new order in his buttonhole. Mr. Golyadkin was led, as has been stated above, straight up to Olsufy Ivanovich—on one side of him Mr. Golyadkin Jr., who had assumed an air of great decorum and propriety, to the immense relief of our hero, while on the other side was Andrey Filippovich, with a very solemn expression on his face.

"What can it mean?" Mr. Golyadkin wondered.

When he saw that he was being led to Olsufy Ivanovich, an idea struck him like a flash of lightning. The thought of the intercepted letter darted through his brain. In great agony our hero stood before Olsufy Ivanovich's chair.

"How shall I act now?" he wondered to himself. "Of course, I shall speak boldly and with an honorable frankness; I shall say this and that, and so on."

But what our hero apparently feared did not happen. Olsufy Ivanovich seemed to have received Mr. Golyadkin very warmly, and, though he did not hold out his hand to him, yet as he gazed at our hero, he shook his gray and venerable head—shook it with an air of solemn melancholy and at the same time of goodwill. So, at least, it seemed to Mr. Golyadkin. He even fancied that a tear glittered in Olsufy Ivanovich's lusterless eyes; he raised his eyes and saw that there seemed to be tears, too, on the eyelashes of Klara Olsufyevna, who was standing by—that there seemed to be something of the same sort even in the eyes of Vladimir Semyonovich—that the unruffled and composed dignity of Andrey Filippovich was in harmony with the general tearful sympathy—that even the young man who at one time looked very much like an important councilor, seizing the opportunity, was sobbing bitterly. . . . Though perhaps this was only all Mr. Golyadkin's fancy, because he was so much removed himself, and distinctly felt the hot tears running down his cold cheeks. . . .

Reconciled with mankind and his destiny, and at the moment filled with love, not only for Olsufy Ivanovich, not only for the guests as a whole, but even for his noxious twin (who seemed now to be by no means noxious, and not even to be his twin at all, but a person very agreeable in himself and in no way connected with him), our hero, in a voice broken with sobs, tried to express his feelings to Olsufy Ivanovich, but was too much overcome by all that he had gone through, and could not utter a word; he could only, with an expressive gesture, point silently at his heart. . . .

At last, probably to spare the feelings of the old man, Andrey Filippovich led Mr. Golyadkin a little away, though he seemed to leave him free to do as he liked. Smiling, muttering something to himself, somewhat bewildered, yet almost completely reconciled with fate and his fellow-creatures, our hero began to make his way through the dense crowd of guests. Everyone made way for him, everyone looked at him with strange curiosity and with mysterious, unaccountable sympathy. Our hero went into the next room; he met with the same attention everywhere; he was vaguely conscious of a whole crowd closely following him, noting every step he took, talking in undertones among themselves of something very interesting, shaking their heads, arguing and discussing in whispers. Mr. Golyadkin wanted very much to know what they were discussing in whispers. Looking around, he saw near him Mr. Golyadkin Jr. Feeling it necessary to seize his hand and draw him aside, Mr. Golyadkin begged the other

Yakov Petrovich most urgently to assist him in all his future
undertakings, and not to abandon him at a critical moment.
Mr. Golyadkin Jr. nodded his head gravely and warmly
pressed the hand of Mr. Golyadkin Sr. Our hero's heart
thrilled with the intensity of his emotion. He was gasping
for breath, however; he felt such a weight on his chest; all
those eyes fastened upon him were oppressing and crushing him. . . . In passing, Mr. Golyadkin caught a glimpse
of the councilor who wore a wig. The latter was looking
at him with a stern, searching eye, not in the least softened
by the general sympathy. Our hero made up his mind to
go straight up to him in order to smile at him and have an
immediate explanation, but this somehow did not come off.
For one instant Mr. Golyadkin became almost unconscious,
losing both memory and sensation.

When he came to himself again he noticed that he was
revolving in a large circle formed by the rest of the party
around him. Suddenly Mr. Golyadkin's name was called
from the next room; the shout was at once taken up by
the whole crowd. Excitement and uproar followed; all
rushed to the door of the drawing room, almost carrying
our hero along with them. The hardhearted councilor in
the wig found himself side by side with Mr. Golyadkin.
Finally, taking our hero by the hand, he made him sit
down beside him opposite Olsufy Ivanovich, at a considerable distance from the latter, however. Arranged in rows
around Mr. Golyadkin and Olsufy Ivanovich, all the guests
sat down. Everything was hushed; everyone preserved a
solemn silence; everyone was watching Olsufy Ivanovich,
evidently expecting something rather out of the ordinary.
Mr. Golyadkin noticed that beside Olsufy Ivanovich's chair
and directly facing the councilor sat Mr. Golyadkin Jr.,
with Andrey Filippovich. The silence was prolonged; they
were evidently expecting something.

"Just as it is in a family when someone is setting off on a
long journey. We've only to get up and say a prayer now,"
thought our hero.

Suddenly there was a general stir which interrupted

Mr. Golyadkin's reflections. Something long expected happened.

"He is coming, he is coming!" passed from one to another in the crowd.

"Who is it that is coming?" flashed through Mr. Golyadkin's mind, and a strange sensation made him shudder. "High time too!" said the councilor, looking intently at Andrey Filippovich. Andrey Filippovich, for his part, glanced at Olsufy Ivanovich. Olsufy Ivanovich gravely and solemnly nodded his head.

"Let us stand up," said the councilor, and made Mr. Golyadkin get up. All rose to their feet. Then the councilor took Mr. Golyadkin Sr. by the hand, and Andrey Filippovich took Mr. Golyadkin Jr. by the hand, and they solemnly brought together the two identical persons surrounded by the expectant crowd. Our hero looked about him in perplexity, but was at once checked and his attention was called to Mr. Golyadkin Jr., who was holding out his hand to him.

"They want to reconcile us," thought our hero, and, deeply moved, held out his hand to Mr. Golyadkin Jr.; and then—then offered his cheek. The other Mr. Golyadkin did the same. . . .

At this point it seemed to Mr. Golyadkin Sr. that his perfidious friend was smiling, that he gave a sly, hurried wink to the crowd of onlookers, and that there was something sinister in the face of the unseemly Mr. Golyadkin Jr., that he even made a grimace as he gave his Judas kiss. . . .

There was a ringing in Mr. Golyadkin's ears, and darkness before his eyes; it seemed to him that a multitude, a whole series of identical Golyadkins were noisily bursting in at every door of the room; but it was too late. . . . The resounding, treacherous kiss was given, and. . . .

Then something quite unexpected occurred. . . . The door opened noisily, and on the threshold stood a man, the very sight of whom turned Mr. Golyadkin's heart to ice. He stood rooted to the spot. A cry of horror died away in his choking throat. Yet, Mr. Golyadkin had known it all beforehand, and had had a presentiment of something of the sort for a long time. The stranger went up to Mr. Golyadkin gravely and solemnly. Mr. Golyadkin knew this personage very well. He had seen him before, had seen him very often, had seen him that day. . . . It was a tall, thick-set man in a black dress coat, with a good-sized cross about his neck, and was possessed of thick, very black whiskers; nothing was lacking but the cigar in the mouth to complete the picture. The stranger's eyes, as we have mentioned already, sent a chill of horror to Mr. Golyadkin's heart. With a grave and solemn air this terrible man approached the pitiable hero of our tale. . . . Our hero held out his hand to him; the stranger took his hand and drew him along with him. . . . With a bewildered, crushed air our hero looked about him.

"It's . . . it's Krestyan Ivanovich Rutenspitz, doctor of medicine and surgery; your old acquaintance, Yakov Petrovich!" a detestable voice twittered in Mr. Golyadkin's ear. He looked around: it was Mr. Golyadkin's twin, so revolting in the despicable meanness of his soul. A malicious, indecent joy shone in his countenance; he was rubbing his hands with rapture, turning his head from side to side in ecstasy, mincing around all and sundry in delight, and seemed ready to dance with glee. At last he pranced forward, took a candle from one of the servants, and walked in front, lighting the way to Mr. Golyadkin and Krestyan Ivanovich. Mr. Golyadkin heard the whole party in the drawing room rush out after him, crowding and squeezing one another, and all beginning to repeat after Mr. Golyadkin, "It is all right, don't be afraid, Yakov Petrovich; this is your old friend and acquaintance, you know, Krestyan Ivanovich Rutenspitz. . . ."

At last they came out on the brightly lighted stairs; there was a crowd of people on the stairs too. The front door was thrown open noisily, and Mr. Golyadkin found himself on the steps, together with Krestyan Ivanovich. Standing at the entrance was a carriage with four horses that were snorting with impatience. The malicious Mr. Golyadkin Jr. in three bounds flew down the stairs and opened the carriage door himself. Krestyan Ivanovich, with an admonishing gesture, asked Mr. Golyadkin to get in. There was no need of the admonishing gesture, however; there were plenty of people to help him in. . . . Faint with horror, Mr. Golyadkin looked back. The whole of the brightly lighted staircase was crowded with people; inquisitive eyes were looking at him from all sides; Olsufy Ivanovich himself was sitting in his easy chair on the top landing and watching all that took place with deep interest. Everyone was waiting. A murmur of impatience ran through the crowd when Mr. Golyadkin looked back.

"I hope there is nothing here . . . nothing reprehensible . . . or that can call for severity . . . and general attention in regard to my official relations," our hero brought out in his bewilderment. A clamor of talk rose all around him, all were shaking their heads. Tears started from Mr. Golyadkin's eyes.

"In that case I'm ready . . . I have full confidence . . . and I entrust my fate to Krestyan Ivanovich. . . ."

No sooner had Mr. Golyadkin declared that he entrusted his fate to Krestyan Ivanovich than a dreadful, deafening shout of joy came from those around him and was repeated in a sinister echo by the whole of the waiting crowd. Then Krestyan Ivanovich on one side and Andrey Filippovich on the other helped Mr. Golyadkin into the carriage; his double, in his usual nasty way, was helping to get him in from behind. The unhappy Mr. Golyadkin Sr. took his last look at everyone and everything, and, shivering like a kitten that has been drenched with cold water—if the comparison may be permitted—got into the carriage. Krestyan Ivanovich followed him in immediately. The carriage door slammed. There was a swish of the whip on the horses' backs . . . the horses started off. . . . The crowd dashed after Mr. Golyadkin. The shrill, furious shouts of his enemies pursued him by way of farewell. For some time several persons were still flashing around the

carriage that bore away Mr. Golyadkin; but by degrees
they were left behind, till at last they had all disappeared.
Mr. Golyadkin's unseemly twin kept up longer than anyone.
With his hands in the side pockets of his green uniform
trousers, he ran on with a satisfied air, skipping first to
one and then to the other side of the carriage, sometimes
catching hold of the windowframe and hanging from it,
poking his head in at the window, and throwing farewell
kisses to Mr. Golyadkin. But he too began to get tired, he
was less and less often to be seen, and at last vanished altogether. There was a dull ache in Mr. Golyadkin's heart;
a hot rush of blood set Mr. Golyadkin's head throbbing; he
was suffocating, he longed to unbutton himself—to bare his
breast, to cover it with snow and pour cold water on it. He
fell at last into a doze. . . .

When he came to himself, he saw that the horses were
taking him along an unfamiliar road. Dark woods wound
to the right and the left of it; the place was desolate and
deserted. Suddenly he almost swooned: two fiery eyes were
staring at him in the darkness, and those two eyes were
glittering with malignant, hellish glee. "That's not Krestyan
Ivanovich! Who is it? Or is it he? It is. It is Krestyan
Ivanovich, but not the old Krestyan Ivanovich, it's another
Krestyan Ivanovich! It's a terrible Krestyan Ivanovich!"

"Krestyan Ivanovich, I . . . I believe . . . I'm all right,
Krestyan Ivanovich," our hero was beginning timidly in a
trembling voice, hoping by his meekness and submissiveness to propitiate the terrible Krestyan Ivanovich a little.

"You will get quarters at public expense, viz. firewood,
light, and service, which you don't deserve," Krestyan
Ivanovich's answer rang out, stern and terrible as a judge's
sentence.

Our hero cried out and clutched his head. Alas! He had
had a presentiment of this for a long time.

NOTES FROM
THE UNDERGROUND
A Tale

Part I: The Underground[1]

I

I AM a sick man. . . . I am a spiteful man. I am an un-
attractive man. I believe my liver is diseased. However,
I know nothing at all about my disease, and do not
know for certain what ails me. I don't consult a doctor for
it, and never have, though I have a respect for medicine

[1] The author of the Notes and the Notes themselves are, of
course, imaginary. Nevertheless it is clear that such persons as
the writer of these notes not only may, but positively must,
exist in our society, when we consider the circumstances under
which our society was formed. I have tried to expose to the view
of the public more distinctly than is commonly done one of the
characters of the recent past. He is one of the representatives of
a generation still living. In this fragment, entitled "The Underground," this person introduces himself and his views, and, as
it were, tries to explain the causes owing to which he has made
his appearance and was bound to make his appearance in our
midst. In the second fragment there will appear the actual notes
of this person concerning certain events in his life.—Author's
Note.

and doctors. Besides, I am extremely superstitious, sufficiently so to respect medicine, anyway (I am well educated enough not to be superstitious, but I am superstitious). No, I refuse to consult a doctor from spite. That you probably will not understand. Well, I understand it, though. Of course, I can't explain who it is precisely that I am mortifying in this case by my spite: I am perfectly well aware that I cannot "pay out" the doctors by not consulting them; I know better than anyone that by all this I am only injuring myself and no one else. But still, if I don't consult a doctor it is from spite. My liver is bad, well—let it get worse!

I have been going on like that for a long time—twenty years. Now I am forty. I used to be in the government service, but am no longer. I was a spiteful official. I was rude and took pleasure in being so. I did not take bribes, you see, so I was bound to find a recompense in that, at least. (A poor jest, but I will not scratch it out. I wrote it thinking it would sound very witty; but now that I have seen myself that I only wanted to show off in a despicable way, I will not scratch it out on purpose!)

When petitioners used to come for information to the table at which I sat, I used to grind my teeth at them, and felt intense enjoyment when I succeeded in making anybody unhappy. I almost always did succeed. For the most part they were all timid people—of course, they were petitioners. But of the uppish ones there was one officer in particular I could not endure. He simply would not be humble, and clanged his sword in a disgusting way. I carried on a feud with him for eighteen months over that sword. At last I got the better of him. He left off clanking it. That happened in my youth, though.

But do you know, gentlemen, what was the chief point about my spite? Why, the whole point, the real sting of it lay in the fact that continually, even in the moment of the acutest spleen, I was inwardly conscious with shame that I was not only not a spiteful but not even an embittered man, that I was simply scaring sparrows at random and amusing myself by it. I might foam at the mouth, but bring me a doll to play with, give me a cup of tea with sugar in it, and maybe I might be appeased. I might even be genuinely touched, though probably I should grind my teeth at myself afterward and lie awake at night with shame for months after. That was my way.

I was lying when I said just now that I was a spiteful official. I was lying from spite. I was simply amusing myself with the petitioners and with the officer, and in reality I never could become spiteful. I was conscious every moment in myself of many, very many elements absolutely opposite to that. I felt them positively swarming in me, these opposite elements. I knew that they had been swarming in me all my life and craving some outlet, but I would not let them, would not let them, purposely would not let them come out. They tormented me till I was ashamed: they drove me to convulsions and—sickened me, at last, how they sickened me! Now, are not you fancying, gentlemen, that I am expressing remorse for something now, that I am asking your forgiveness for something? I am sure you are fancying that. . . . However, I assure you I do not care if you are. . . .

It was not only that I could not become spiteful, I did not know how to become anything: neither spiteful nor kind, neither a rascal nor an honest man, neither a hero nor an insect. Now, I am living out my life in my corner, taunting myself with the spiteful and useless consolation that an intelligent man cannot become anything seriously, and it is only the fool who becomes anything. Yes, a man in the nineteenth century must and morally ought to be pre-eminently a characterless creature; a man of character, an active man is pre-eminently a limited creature. That has been my conviction these forty years. I am forty years old now, and you know forty years is a whole lifetime; you know it is extreme old age. To live longer than forty years is bad manners, is vulgar, immoral. Who does live beyond forty? Answer that, sincerely and honestly. I will tell you who do: fools and worthless fellows. I tell all old men that to their face, all these venerable old men, all these silver-haired and reverend seniors! I tell the whole world that to its face! I have a right to say so, for I shall go on living to sixty myself. To seventy! To eighty! . . . Stay, let me take breath. . . .

You imagine no doubt, gentlemen, that I want to amuse you. You are mistaken in that, too. I am by no means such a mirthful person as you imagine, or as you may imagine; however, irritated by all this babble (and I feel that you are irritated), you think fit to ask me who I am—then my answer is, I am a collegiate assessor. I was in the service that I might have something to eat (and solely for that reason), and when last year a distant relation left me six thousand roubles in his will I immediately retired from the service and settled down in my corner. I used to live in this corner before, but now I have settled down in it. My room is a wretched, horrid one on the outskirts of the town. My servant is an old countrywoman, ill-natured from stupidity, and, moreover, there is always a nasty smell about her. I am told that the Petersburg climate is bad for me, and that with my small means it is very expensive to live in Petersburg. I know all that better than all these sage and experienced counselors and monitors. . . . But I am remaining in Petersburg; I am not going away from Petersburg! I am not going away because . . . ech! Why, it is absolutely no matter whether I am going away or not going away.

But what can a decent man speak of with most pleasure? Answer: Of himself.

Well, so I will talk about myself.

II

I want now to tell you, gentlemen, whether you care to hear it or not, why I could not even become an insect. I tell you solemnly that I have many times tried to become an insect. But I was not equal even to that. I swear, gentlemen, that to be too conscious is an illness—a real thoroughgoing illness. For man's everyday needs, it would have been quite enough to have the ordinary human consciousness, that is, half or a quarter of the amount which falls to the lot of a cultivated man of our unhappy nineteenth century, especially one who has the fatal ill-luck to inhabit Petersburg, the most abstract and premeditated town on the whole terrestrial globe. (There are premeditated and unpremeditated towns.) It would have been quite enough, for instance, to have the consciousness by which all so-called direct persons and men of action live. I bet you think I am writing all this from affectation, to be witty at the expense of men of action; and, what is more, that from ill-bred affectation, I am clanking a sword like my officer. But, gentlemen, whoever can pride himself on his diseases and even swagger over them?

Though, after all, everyone does do that; people do pride themselves on their diseases, and I do, maybe, more than anyone. We will not dispute it; my contention was absurd. But yet I am firmly persuaded that a great deal of consciousness, every sort of consciousness, in fact, is a disease. I stick to that. Let us leave that, too, for a minute. Tell me this: why does it happen that at the very, yes, at the very moments when I am most capable of feeling every refinement of all that is "good and beautiful," as they used to say at one time, it would, as though of design, happen that I not only felt but did such ugly things, such that. . . . Well, in short, actions that all, perhaps, commit; but which, as though purposely, occurred to me at the very time when I was most conscious that they ought not to be committed. The more conscious I was of goodness and of all that was "lofty and beautiful,"[2] the more deeply I sank into my mire and the more ready I was to sink in it altogether. But the chief point was that all this was, as it were, not accidental in me, but as though it were bound to be so. It was as though it were my most normal condition, and not in the least disease or depravity, so that at last all desire in me to struggle against this depravity passed.

[2] The phrase goes back to the essay, "Of the Lofty and the Beautiful," by Immanuel Kant.—A.Y.

It ended by my almost believing (perhaps actually believing) that this was perhaps my normal condition. But at first, in the beginning, what agonies I endured in that struggle! I did not believe it was the same with other people, and all my life I hid this fact about myself as a secret. I was ashamed (even now, perhaps, I am ashamed): I got to the point of feeling a sort of secret, abnormal, despicable enjoyment in returning home to my corner on some disgusting Petersburg night, acutely conscious that that day I had committed a loathsome action again, that what was done could never be undone, and secretly, inwardly gnawing, gnawing at myself for it, tearing and consuming myself till at last the bitterness turned into a sort of shameful accursed sweetness, and at last—into positive real enjoyment! Yes, into enjoyment, into enjoyment! I insist upon that. I have spoken of this because I keep wanting to know for a fact whether other people feel such enjoyment? I will explain; the enjoyment was just from the too intense consciousness of your own degradation; it was that you yourself felt that you had reached the last barrier; that it was horrible, but it could not be otherwise; that there was no escape for you; that you never could become a different man; that even if time and faith were still left you to change into something different, you would most likely not wish to change; or if you did wish to, even then you would do nothing; because perhaps in reality there was nothing for you to change into.

And the worst of it was, and the root of it all, that it was all in accord with the normal fundamental laws of overacute consciousness, and with the inertia that was the direct result of those laws, and that consequently one was not only unable to change but could do absolutely nothing. Thus it follows, as the result of acute consciousness, that one is not to blame for being a scoundrel; as though that were any consolation to the scoundrel once he has come to realize that he actually is a scoundrel. But enough. . . . Ech, I have talked a lot of nonsense, but what have I explained? How is enjoyment of this to be explained? But I will explain it. I will get to the bottom of it! That is why I have taken up my pen. . . .

I, for instance, have a great deal of *amour-propre*. I am as suspicious and prone to take offense as a humpback or a dwarf. But upon my word I sometimes have had moments when if I had happened to be slapped in the face I should, perhaps, have been positively glad of it. I say, in earnest, that I should probably have been able to discover even in that a peculiar sort of enjoyment—the enjoyment, of course, of despair; but in despair there are the most intense enjoyments, especially when one is very acutely conscious of the hopelessness of one's position. And when one is slapped in the face—why then the consciousness of being rubbed into a pulp would positively overwhelm one. The worst of it is, look at it which way one will, it still turns out that I was always the most to blame in everything. And what is most humiliating, to blame through no fault of my own, but, so to say, through the laws of nature. In the first place, to blame because I am cleverer than any of the people surrounding me. (I have always considered myself cleverer than any of the people surrounding me, and sometimes, would you believe it, have been positively ashamed of it. At any rate, I have all my life, as it were, turned my eyes away and never could look people straight in the face.) To blame, finally, because even if I had had magnanimity, I should only have suffered more from the sense of its uselessness. I should certainly never have been able to do anything from being magnanimous—neither to forgive, for my assailant would perhaps have slapped me due to the laws of nature, and one cannot forgive the laws of nature; nor to forget, for even if it were owing to the laws of nature, it is insulting all the same. Finally, even if I had wanted to be anything but magnanimous, had desired on the contrary to revenge myself on my assailant, I could not have revenged myself on anyone for anything because I should certainly never have made up my mind to do anything, even if I had been able to. Why should I not have made up my mind? About that in particular I want to say a few words.

III

There are people who know how to revenge themselves and to stand up for themselves in general; how do they do it? Why, when they are possessed, let us suppose, by the feeling of revenge, then for the time there is nothing else but that feeling left in their whole being. Such a gentleman simply dashes straight for his object like an infuriated bull with its horns down, and nothing but a wall will stop him. (By the way: facing the wall, such gentlemen—that is, the "direct" persons and men of action—are genuinely nonplused. For them a wall is not an evasion, as for us people who think and consequently do nothing; it is not an excuse for turning aside, an excuse for which we are always very glad, though we scarcely believe in it ourselves, as a rule. No, they are nonplused in all sincerity. The wall has for them something tranquilizing, morally soothing, final—maybe even something mysterious . . . but of the wall later.)

Well, such a direct person I regard as the real normal man, as his tender Mother Nature wished to see him when she graciously brought him into being on the earth. I envy such a man till I am green in the face. He is stupid. I am not disputing that, but perhaps the normal man should be stupid, how do you know? Perhaps it is very beautiful, in fact. And I am the more persuaded of that suspicion, if one can call it so, by the fact that if you take, for instance, the antithesis of the normal man, that is, the man of acute consciousness, who has come, of course, not out of the lap of nature but out of a retort (this is almost mysticism, gentlemen, but I suspect this, too), this retort-made man is sometimes so nonplused in the presence of his antithesis that with all his exaggerated consciousness he genuinely thinks of himself as a mouse and not a man. It may be an acutely conscious mouse, yet it is a mouse, while the other is a man, and therefore, et cetera, et cetera. And the worst of it is, he himself, his very own self, looks on himself as a mouse; no one asks him to do so; and that is an important point.

Now let us look at this mouse in action. Let us suppose, for instance, that it feels insulted, too (and it almost always does feel insulted), and wants to revenge itself, too. There may even be a greater accumulation of spite in it than in *l'homme de la nature et de la vérité*. The base and nasty desire to vent that spite on its assailant rankles perhaps even more nastily in it than in *l'homme de la nature et de la vérité*. For through his innate stupidity the latter looks upon his revenge as justice pure and simple; while in consequence of his acute consciousness the mouse does not believe in the justice of it. To come at last to the deed itself, to the very act of revenge. Apart from the one fundamental nastiness, the luckless mouse succeeds in creating around it so many other nastinesses in the form of doubts and questions, adds to the one question so many unsettled questions, that there inevitably works up around it a sort of fatal brew, a stinking mess, made up of its doubts, emotions, and of the contempt spat upon it by the direct men of action who stand solemnly about it as judges and arbitrators, laughing at it till their healthy sides ache. Of course the only thing left for it is to dismiss all that with a wave of its paw, and, with a smile of assumed contempt in which it does not even itself believe, creep ignominiously into its mousehole. There in its nasty, stinking, underground home our insulted, crushed, and ridiculed mouse promptly becomes absorbed in cold, malignant, and, above all, everlasting spite. For forty years together it will remember its injury down to the smallest, most ignominious details, and every time will add, of itself, details still more ignominious, spitefully teasing and tormenting itself with its own imagination. It will itself be ashamed of its imaginings, but yet it will recall it all, it will go over and over every detail, it will invent unheard-of things against itself, pretending that those things might happen, and will forgive nothing. Maybe it will begin to revenge itself, too, but, as it were, piecemeal, in trivial ways, from behind the stove, incognito, without believing either in its own right to vengeance, or in the success of its revenge, knowing that from all its efforts at revenge it will suffer a hundred times more than he on whom it revenges itself, while he, I daresay, will not even scratch himself. On its deathbed it will recall it all over again, with interest accumulated over all the years and . . .

But it is just in that cold, abominable half-despair, half-belief, in that conscious burying oneself alive for grief in the underground for forty years, in that acutely recognized and yet partly doubtful hopelessness of one's position, in that hell of unsatisfied desires turned inward, in that fever of oscillations, of resolutions determined forever and repented of again a minute later—that the savor of that strange enjoyment of which I have spoken lies. It is so subtle, so difficult of analysis, that persons who are a little limited, or even simply persons of strong nerves, will not understand a single atom of it. "Possibly," you will add on your own account with a grin, "people will not understand it either who have never received a slap in the face," and in that way you will politely hint to me that I, too, perhaps, have had the experience of a slap in the face in my life, and so I speak as one who knows. I bet that you are thinking that. But set your minds at rest, gentlemen, I have not received a slap in the face, though it is absolutely a matter of indifference to me what you may think about it. Possibly, I even regret, myself, that I have given so few slaps in the face during my life. But enough . . . not another word on that subject of such extreme interest to you.

I will continue calmly concerning persons with strong nerves who do not understand a certain refinement of enjoyment. Though in certain circumstances these gentlemen bellow their loudest like bulls, though this, let us suppose, does them the greatest credit, yet, as I have said already, confronted with the impossible, they subside at once. The impossible means the stone wall! What stone wall? Why, of course, the laws of nature, the deductions of natural science, mathematics. As soon as they prove to you, for instance, that you are descended from a monkey, then it is no use scowling, accept it for a fact. When they prove to you that in reality one drop of your own fat must be dearer to you than a hundred thousand of your fellow-creatures, and that this conclusion is the final solution of all so-called virtues and duties and all such prejudices and fancies, then you have just to accept it, there is no help for it, for twice two is a law of mathematics. Just try refuting it.

"Upon my word," they will shout at you, "it is no use protesting: it is a case of twice two makes four! Nature does not ask your permission, she has nothing to do with your wishes, and whether you like her laws or dislike them, you are bound to accept her as she is, and consequently all her conclusions. A wall, you see, is a wall . . . and so on, and so on."

Merciful heavens! but what do I care for the laws of nature and arithmetic, when, for some reason, I dislike those laws and the fact that twice two makes four? Of course I cannot break through the wall by battering my head against it if I really have not the strength to knock it down, but I am not going to be reconciled to it simply because it is a stone wall and I have not the strength.

As though such a stone wall really were a consolation, and really did contain some word of conciliation, simply because it is as true as twice two makes four. Oh, absurdity of absurdities! How much better it is to understand it all, to recognize it all, all the impossibilities and stone walls; not to be reconciled to one of those impossibilities and stone walls if it disgusts you to be reconciled; by the way of the most inevitable logical combinations to reach the most revolting conclusions on the everlasting theme that even for the stone wall you are yourself somehow to blame, though again it is as clear as day you are not to blame in the least, and therefore grinding your teeth in silent impotence to sink voluptuously into inertia, brooding on the fact that there is no one even for you to feel vindictive against, that you have not, and perhaps never will have, an object for your spite, that it is a sleight of hand, a bit of juggling, a card-sharper's trick, that it is simply a mess, no knowing what and no knowing who, but, in spite of all these uncertainties and jugglings, still there is an ache in you, and the more you do not know, the worse the ache.

IV

"Ha, ha, ha! You will be finding enjoyment in toothache next," you cry with a laugh.

"Well? Even in toothache there is enjoyment," I answer. I had toothache for a whole month and I know there is. In that case, of course, people are not spiteful in silence, but moan; but they are not candid moans, they are malignant moans, and the malignancy is the whole point. The enjoyment of the sufferer finds expression in those moans; if he did not feel enjoyment in them he would not moan. It is a good example, gentlemen, and I will develop it. Those moans express in the first place all the aimlessness of your pain, which is so humiliating to your consciousness; the whole legal system of nature on which you spit disdainfully, of course, but from which you suffer all the same, while she does not. They express the consciousness that you have no enemy to punish, but that you have pain; the consciousness that in spite of all possible Wagenheims[3] you are in complete slavery to your teeth; that if someone wishes it, your teeth will leave off aching, and if he does not, they will go on aching another three months; and that finally if you are still contumacious and still protest, all that is left you for your own gratification is to thrash yourself or beat your wall with your fist as hard as you can, and absolutely nothing more. Well, these mortal insults, these jeers on the part of someone unknown, end at last in an enjoyment which sometimes reaches the highest degree of voluptuousness. I ask you, gentlemen, listen sometimes to

[3] Dentists who advertised in the Petersburg papers in 1864. —A.Y.

the moans of an educated man of the nineteenth century suffering from toothache, on the second or third day of the attack, when he is beginning to moan, not as he moaned on the first day, that is, not simply because he has tooth-ache, not just as any coarse peasant, but as a man affected by progress and European civilization, a man who is "divorced from the soil and the national elements," as they express it nowadays. His moans become nasty, disgustingly malignant, and go on for whole days and nights. And of course he knows that he is doing himself no sort of good with his moans; he knows better than anyone that he is only lacerating and harassing himself and others for noth-ing; he knows that even the audience before whom he is making his efforts, and his whole family, listen to him with loathing, do not put a groat's worth of faith in him, and inwardly understand that he might moan differently, more simply, without trills and flourishes, and that he is only amusing himself like that from ill-humor, from malignancy. Well, it is in all these recognitions and disgraces that there lies a voluptuous pleasure. As though he would say, "I am worrying you, I am lacerating your hearts, I am keeping everyone in the house awake. Well, stay awake then, you, too, feel every minute that I have toothache. I am not a hero to you now, as I tried to seem before, but simply a nasty person, an impostor. Well, so be it, then! I am very glad that you see through me. It is nasty for you to hear my despicable moans: well, let it be nasty; here I will let you have a nastier flourish in a minute. . . ." You do not understand even now, gentlemen? No, it seems our develop-ment and our consciousness must go farther to understand all the intricacies of this pleasure. You laugh? Delighted. My jests, gentlemen, are of course in bad taste, jerky, in-volved, lacking self-confidence. But of course that is because I do not respect myself. Can a man of perception respect himself at all?

V

Come, can a man who attempts to find enjoyment in the very feeling of his own degradation possibly have a spark of respect for himself? I am not saying this now from any mawkish kind of remorse. And, indeed, I could never endure saying, "Forgive me, Papa, I won't do it again," not because I am incapable of saying that—on the contrary, perhaps just because I have been too capable of it, and in what a way, too! As though of design I used to get into trouble in cases when I was not to blame in any way. That was the nastiest part of it. At the same time I was genuinely touched and penitent, I used to shed tears and, of course, deceived myself, though I was not acting in the least and there was a sick feeling in my heart at the time. . . . For that one could not blame even the laws of nature, though the laws of nature have continually and all my life offended me more than anything. It is loathsome to remember it all, but it was loathsome even then. Of course, a minute or so later I would realize wrathfully that it was all a lie, a revolting lie, an affected lie, that is, all this penitence, this emotion, these vows of reform. You will ask why did I worry myself with such antics. Answer: Because it was very dull to sit with one's hands folded, and so one began cutting capers. That is really it. Observe yourselves more carefully, gentlemen, then you will understand that it is so. I invented adventures for myself and made up a life, so as at least to live in some way. How many times it has happened to me—well, for instance, to take offense simply on purpose, for nothing; and one knows oneself, of course, that one is offended at nothing, that one is putting it on, but yet one brings oneself, at last, to the point of being really offended. All my life I have had an impulse to play such pranks, so that in the end I could not control it in myself. Another time, twice, in fact, I tried hard to fall in love. I suffered, too, gentlemen, I assure you. In the depth of my heart there was no faith in my suffering, only a faint stir of mockery, but yet I did suffer, and in the real, orthodox way; I was jealous, beside myself . . . and it was all from ennui, gentlemen, all from ennui; inertia overcame me.

You know the direct, legitimate fruit of consciousness is inertia, that is, conscious sitting-with-the-hands-folded. I have referred to this already. I repeat, I repeat with emphasis: all "direct" persons and men of action are active just because they are stupid and limited. How explain that? I will tell you: in consequence of their limitation they take immediate and secondary causes for primary ones, and in that way persuade themselves more quickly and easily than other people do that they have found an infallible foundation for their activity, and their minds are at ease and you know that is the chief thing. To begin to act, you know, you must first have your mind completely at ease and no trace of doubt left in it. Why, how am I, for example, to set my mind at rest? Where are the primary causes on which I am to build? Where are my foundations? Where am I to get them from? I exercise myself in reflection, and consequently with me every primary cause at once draws after itself another still more primary, and so on to infinity. That is just the essence of every sort of consciousness and reflection. It must be a case of the laws of nature again. What is the result of it in the end? Why, just the same. Remember I spoke just now of vengeance. (I am sure you did not take it in.) I said that a man revenges himself because he sees justice in it. Therefore he has found a primary cause, that is, justice. And so he is at rest on all sides, and consequently he carries out his revenge calmly and successfully, being persuaded that he is doing a just and honest thing. But I see no justice in it, I find no sort of virtue in it either, and consequently if I attempt to revenge myself, it is only out of spite. Spite, of course, might overcome everything, all my doubts, and so might serve quite successfully in place of a primary cause, precisely because it is not a cause. But what is to be done if I have not even spite (I began with that just now, you know). In consequence again of those accursed laws of consciousness, anger in me is subject to chemical disintegration. You look into it, the object flies off into air, your reasons evaporate, the criminal is not to be found, the wrong becomes not a wrong but a phantom, something like the toothache, for which no one is to blame, and consequently there is only the same outlet left again—that is, to beat the wall as hard as you can. So you give it up with a wave of the hand because you have not found a fundamental cause. And try letting yourself be carried away by your feelings, blindly, without reflection, without a primary cause, repelling consciousness at least for a time; hate or love, if only not to sit with your hands folded. The day after tomorrow, at the latest, you will begin despising yourself for having knowingly deceived yourself. Result: a soap bubble and inertia. Oh, gentlemen, do you know, perhaps I consider myself an intelligent man, only because all my life I have been able neither to begin nor to finish anything. Granted I am a babbler, a harmless vexatious babbler, like all of us. But what is to be done if the direct and sole vocation of every intelligent man is babble, that is, the intentional pouring of water through a sieve?

VI

Oh, if I had done nothing simply from laziness! Heavens, how I should have respected myself, then. I should have respected myself because I should at least have been capable of being lazy; there would at least have been one quality, as it were, positive in me, in which I could have believed myself. Question: What is he? Answer: A sluggard; how very pleasant it would have been to hear that of oneself! It would mean that I was positively defined, it would mean that there was something to say about me. "Sluggard"—why, it is a calling and vocation, it is a career. Do not jest, it is so. I should then be a member of the best club by right, and should find my occupation in continually respecting myself. I knew a gentleman who prided himself all his life on being a connoisseur of Lafite. He considered this as his positive virtue, and never doubted himself. He died, not simply with a tranquil, but with a triumphant, conscience, and he was quite right, too. Then I should have chosen a career for myself, I should have been a sluggard and a glutton, not a simple one, but, for instance, one with sympathies for everything good and beautiful. How do you like that? I have long had visions of it. That "good and beautiful" weighs heavily on my mind at forty. But that is at forty; then—oh, then it would have been different! I should have found for myself a form of activity in keeping with it, to be precise, drinking to the health of everything "good and beautiful." I should have snatched at every opportunity to drop a tear into my glass and then to drain it to all that is "good and beautiful." I should then have turned everything into the good and the beautiful; in the nastiest, unquestionable trash, I should have sought out the good and the beautiful. I should have exuded tears like a wet sponge. An artist, for instance, paints a picture worthy of Gué. At once I drink to the health of the artist who painted Gué's picture,[4] because I love all that is "good and beautiful." An author has written As You Like It: at once I drink to his health because I love all that is "good and beautiful."

I should claim respect for doing so. I should persecute anyone who would not show me respect. I should live at ease, I should die with dignity, why, it is charming, perfectly charming! And what a good round belly I should have grown, what a treble chin I should have established, what a ruby nose I should have colored for myself, so that everyone would have said, looking at me, "Here is an asset! Here is something real and solid!" And, say what you like, it is very agreeable to hear such remarks about oneself in this negative age.

[4] Apparently "The Last Supper," by N. N. Gué, which was exhibited in Petersburg in 1863. It was attacked in the press as too realistic a treatment of a religious subject.—A.Y.

VII

But these are all golden dreams. Oh, tell me, who was it first announced, who was it first proclaimed, that man only does nasty things because he does not know his own interests; and that if he were enlightened, if his eyes were opened to his real normal interests, man would at once cease to do nasty things, would at once become good and noble because, being enlightened and understanding his real advantage, he would see his own advantage in the good[5] and nothing else, and we all know that not one man can, consciously, act against his own interests, consequently, so to say, through necessity, he would begin doing good? Oh, the babe! Oh, the pure, innocent child! Why, in the first place, when in all these thousands of years has there been a time when man has acted only from his own interest? What is to be done with the millions of facts that bear witness that men, *consciously*, that is fully understanding their real interests, have left them in the background and have rushed headlong on another path, to meet peril and danger, compelled to this course by nobody and by nothing, but, as it were, simply disliking the beaten track, and have obstinately, willfully, struck out another difficult, absurd way, seeking it almost in the darkness. So, I suppose, this obstinacy and perversity were pleasanter to them than any advantage. . . . Advantage! What is advantage? And will you take it upon yourself to define with perfect accuracy in what the advantage of man consists? And what if it so happens that a man's advantage, *sometimes*, not only may, but even must, consist in his desiring in certain cases what is harmful to himself and not advantageous? And if so, if there can be such a case, the whole principle falls into dust. What do you think—are there such cases? You laugh; laugh

[5] The author here attacks the radical essayist Chernyshevsky, who in his "Anthropological Principle in Philosophy" (1860) wrote: "Only good deeds are prudent; he alone is reasonable who is kind and only to the extent to which he is kind."—A.Y.

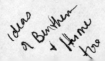
ideas
2 Bentham
+ Hume
too

away, gentlemen, but only answer me: have man's advantages been reckoned up with perfect certainty? Are there not some which not only have not been included but cannot possibly be included under any classification? You see, you gentlemen have, to the best of my knowledge, taken your whole register of human advantages from the averages of statistical figures and politico-economic formulas. Your advantages are prosperity, wealth, freedom, peace—and so on, and so on. So that the man who should, for instance, go openly and knowingly in opposition to all that list would, to your thinking, and indeed mine, too, of course, be an obscurantist or an absolute madman: wouldn't he? But, you know, this is what is surprising: why does it so happen that all these statisticians, sages, and lovers of humanity, when they reckon up human advantages, invariably leave out one? They don't even take it into their reckoning in the form in which it should be taken, and the whole reckoning depends upon that. It would be no great matter, they would simply have to take it, this advantage, and add it to the list. But the trouble is that this strange advantage does not fall under any classification and is not in place in any list. I have a friend, for instance . . . Ech! gentlemen, but of course he is your friend, too; and indeed there is no one, no one, to whom he is not a friend! When he prepares for any undertaking this gentleman immediately explains to you, elegantly and clearly, exactly how he must act in accordance with the laws of reason and truth. What is more, he will talk to you with excitement and passion of the true normal interests of man; with irony he will upbraid the shortsighted fools who do not understand their own interests, nor the true significance of virtue; and, within a quarter of an hour, without any sudden outside provocation, but simply through something inside him which is stronger than all his interests, he will go off on quite a different tack—that is, act in direct opposition to what he has just been saying about himself, in opposition to the laws of reason, in opposition to his own advantage, in fact in opposition to everything. . . . I warn you that my friend is a compound personality, and therefore it is difficult to blame him as an individual. The fact is, gentlemen, it seems there must really exist something that is dearer to almost every man than his greatest advantages, or (not to be illogical) there is a most advantageous advantage (the very one omitted of which we spoke just now) which is more important and more advantageous than all other advantages, for the sake of which a man if necessary is ready to act in opposition to all laws; that is, in opposition to reason, honor, peace, prosperity—in fact, in opposition to all those excellent and useful things, if only he can attain that fundamental, most advantageous advantage which is dearer to him than all.

"Yes, but it's advantage all the same," you will retort. But excuse me, I'll make the point clear, and it is not a case of playing upon words. What matters is that this advantage is remarkable from the very fact that it breaks down all our classifications, and continually shatters every system constructed by lovers of mankind for the benefit of mankind. In fact, it upsets everything. But, before I mention this advantage to you, I want to compromise myself personally, and therefore I boldly declare that all these fine systems, all these theories for explaining to mankind their real normal interests, in order that inevitably striving to pursue these interests that they may at once become good and noble—are, in my opinion, so far, mere logical exercises! Yes, logical exercises. Why, to maintain this theory of the regeneration of mankind by means of the pursuit of his own advantage is to my mind almost the same thing as . . . as to affirm, for instance, following Buckle, that through civilization mankind becomes softer, and consequently less bloodthirsty and less fitted for warfare. Logically it does seem to follow from his arguments. But man has such a predilection for systems and abstract deductions that he is ready to distort the truth intentionally, he is ready to deny the evidence of his senses only to justify his logic. I take this example because it is the most glaring instance of it. Only look about you: blood is being spilled in streams, and in the merriest way, as though it were champagne. Take the whole of the nineteenth century in which Buckle lived. Take Napoleon—the Great and also the present one. Take North America—the eternal union.[6] Take the farce of Schleswig-Holstein.[7] . . . And what is it that civilization softens in us? The only gain of civilization for mankind is the greater capacity for variety of sensations—and absolutely nothing more. And through the development of this many-sidedness man may come to finding enjoyment in bloodshed. In fact, this has already happened to him. Have you noticed that it is the most civilized gentlemen who have been the subtlest slaughterers, to whom the Attilas and Stenka Razins could not hold a candle, and if they are not so conspicuous as the Attilas and Stenka Razins, it is simply because they are so often met with, are so ordinary, and have become so familiar to us. In any case civilization has made mankind if not more bloodthirsty, certainly more vilely, more loathsomely bloodthirsty. In former days he saw justice in bloodshed and with his conscience at peace exterminated those he thought proper to kill. Now we do think bloodshed abominable and yet we engage in this abomination, and with more energy than ever. Which is worse? Decide that for yourselves. They say that Cleopatra (excuse an instance from Roman history) was fond of sticking gold pins into her slave girls' breasts and derived gratification from their screams and writhings. You will say that that was in comparatively barbarous times; that these are barbarous times too, because, also comparatively speaking, pins are stuck in even now; that though man has now learned to see more clearly than in barbarous ages, he is still far from having learned to act as reason and science would dictate. But yet you are fully convinced that he will be sure to learn when he gets rid of certain old bad habits, and when common sense and science have completely re-educated human nature and turned it in a normal direction. You are confident that then man will cease from *intentional* error and will,

[6] The irony is directed at the U. S. Civil War.—A.Y.
[7] The allusion is to the war between Denmark, on the one hand, and Austria and Prussia, on the other (1863–64).—A.Y.

so to say, be compelled not to want to set his will against his normal interests. That is not all; then, you say, science itself will teach man (though to my mind it's a superfluous luxury) that he never has really had any caprice or will of his own, and that he himself is something in the nature of a piano key or the stop of an organ, and that there are, besides, things called the laws of nature; so that everything he does is not done by his willing it, but is done of itself, by the laws of nature. Consequently we have only to discover these laws of nature, and man will no longer have to answer for his actions and life will become exceedingly easy for him. All human actions will then, of course, be tabulated according to these laws, mathematically, like tables of logarithms up to 108,000, and entered in an index; or, better still, there will be published certain well-intentioned works in the nature of encyclopedic dictionaries, in which everything will be so clearly calculated and noted that there will be no more deeds or adventures in the world.

Then—this is all what you say—new economic relations will be established, all ready-made and worked out with mathematical exactitude, so that every possible question will vanish in the twinkling of an eye, simply because every possible answer to it will be provided. Then the "Crystal Palace"[8] will be built. Then . . . In fact, those will be halcyon days. Of course there is no guaranteeing (this is my comment) that it will not be, for instance, frightfully dull then (for what will one have to do when everything will be calculated according to tables), but, on the other hand, everything will be extraordinarily rational. Of course boredom may lead you to anything. It is boredom sets one sticking gold pins into people, but all that does not matter. What is bad (this is my comment again) is that I dare say people will be thankful for the gold pins then. Man is stupid, you know, phenomenally stupid; or rather he is not at all stupid, but he is so ungrateful that you could not find

[8] The "pigiron-crystal" palace figures in the picture of the future socialist society (in Chernyshevsky's novel *What's to Be Done?*).—A.Y.

another like him in all creation. I, for instance, would not be in the least surprised if all of a sudden, apropos of nothing, in the midst of general prosperity a gentleman with an ignoble, or rather with a reactionary and ironical, countenance were to arise and, putting his arms akimbo, say to us all, "I say, gentlemen, hadn't we better kick over the whole show here and scatter rationalism to the winds, simply to send these logarithms to the devil, and to enable us to live once more at our own sweet foolish will!" That again would not matter; but what is annoying is that he would be sure to find followers—such is the nature of man. And all that for the most foolish reason, which, one would think, was hardly worth mentioning; that is, that man everywhere and at all times, whoever he may be, has preferred to act as he chose and not in the least as his reason and advantage dictated. And one may choose what is contrary to one's own interests, and sometimes one *positively ought* (that is my idea). One's own free unfettered choice, one's own caprice, however wild it may be, one's own fancy worked up at times to frenzy—is that very "most advantageous advantage" which we have overlooked, which comes under no classification and against which all systems and theories are continually being shattered to atoms. And how do these wiseacres know that man wants a normal, a virtuous choice? What has made them conceive that man must want a rationally advantageous choice? What man wants is simply *independent* choice, whatever that independence may cost and wherever it may lead. And choice, of course, the devil only knows what choice. . . .

VIII

"Ha! ha! ha! But you know there is no such thing as choice in reality, say what you like," you interpose with a chuckle. "Science has succeeded in so far analyzing man that we know already that choice and what is called freedom of will is nothing else than——"

Stay, gentlemen, I meant to begin with that myself. I

confess I was rather frightened. I was just going to say that the devil only knows what choice depends on, and that perhaps that was a very good thing, but I remembered the teaching of science . . . and pulled myself up. And here you have begun upon it. Indeed, if there really is some day discovered a formula for all our desires and caprices—that is, an explanation of what they depend upon, by what laws they arise, how they develop, what they are aiming at in one case and in another and so on, that is, a real mathematical formula—then, most likely, man will at once cease to feel desire, indeed, he will be certain to. For who would want to choose by rule? Besides, he will at once be transformed from a human being into an organ stop or something of the sort; for what is a man without desire, without free will, and without choice, if not a stop in an organ? What do you think? Let us reckon the chances—can such a thing happen or not?

"H'm!" you decide. "Our choice is usually mistaken from a false view of our advantage. We sometimes choose absolute nonsense, because in our foolishness we see in that nonsense the easiest means for attaining a supposed advantage. But when all that is explained and worked out on paper (which is perfectly possible, for it is contemptible and senseless to suppose that some laws of nature man will never understand), then certainly so-called desires will no longer exist. For if a desire should come into conflict with reason, we shall then reason and not desire, because it will be impossible retaining our reason to be *senseless* in our desires, and in that way knowingly act against reason and desire to injure ourselves. And as all choice and reasoning can be really calculated—because there will some day be discovered the laws of our so-called free will—so, joking apart, there may one day be something like a table constructed of them, so that we really shall choose in accordance with it. If, for instance, some day they calculate and prove to me that I made a long nose at someone because I could not help making a long nose at him and that I had to do it in that particular way, what *freedom* is left me, especially if I am a learned man and have taken my degree somewhere? Then I should be able to calculate my whole life for thirty years beforehand. In short, if this could be arranged, there would be nothing left for us to do; anyway, we should have to understand that. And, in fact, we ought unwearyingly to repeat to ourselves that at such and such a time and in such and such circumstances nature does not ask our leave; that we have got to take her as she is and not fashion her to suit our fancy, and if we really aspire to formulas and tables of rules, and well, even . . . to the chemical retort, there's no help for it, we must accept the retort too, or else it will be accepted without our consent. . . ."

Yes, but here I come to a stop! Gentlemen, you must excuse me for being overphilosophical; it's the result of forty years underground! Allow me to indulge my fancy. You see, gentlemen, reason is an excellent thing, there's no disputing that, but reason is nothing but reason and satisfies only the rational side of man's nature, while will is a manifestation of the whole life, that is, of the whole of human life including reason and all the impulses. And although our life, in this manifestation of it, is often worthless, yet it is life and not simply extracting square roots. Here I, for instance, quite naturally want to live, in order to satisfy all my capacities for life, and not simply my capacity for reasoning, that is, not simply one-twentieth of my capacity for life. What does reason know? Reason only knows what it has succeeded in learning (some things, perhaps, it will never learn; this is a poor comfort, but why not say so frankly?), and human nature acts as a whole, with everything that is in it, consciously or unconsciously, and, even if it goes wrong, it lives. I suspect, gentlemen, that you are looking at me with compassion; you tell me again that an enlightened and developed man, such, in short, as the future man will be, cannot consciously desire anything disadvantageous to himself, that that can be proved mathematically. I thoroughly agree, it can—by mathematics. But I repeat for the hundredth time, there is one case, one only, when man may consciously, purposely, desire what is injurious to himself, what is stupid, very stupid—simply in order to have the right to desire for himself even what is very stupid and not to be bound by an obligation to desire only what is sensible. Of course, this very stupid thing, this caprice of ours, may be in reality, gentlemen, more advantageous for us than anything else on earth, especially in certain cases. And in particular it may be more advantageous than any advantage even when it does us obvious harm, and contradicts the soundest conclusions of our reason concerning our advantage—for in any circumstances it preserves for us what is most precious and most important—that is, our personality, our individuality. Some, you see, maintain that this really is the most precious thing for mankind; choice can, of course, if it chooses, be in agreement with reason; and especially if this be not abused but kept within bounds. It is profitable and sometimes even praiseworthy. But very often, and even most often, choice is utterly and stubbornly opposed to reason . . . and . . . and . . . do you know that that, too, is profitable, sometimes even praiseworthy?

Gentlemen, let us suppose that man is not stupid. (Indeed one cannot refuse to suppose that, if only from the one consideration, that, if man is stupid, then who is wise?) But if he is not stupid, he is monstrously ungrateful! Phenomenally ungrateful. In fact, I believe that the best definition of man is the ungrateful biped. But that is not all, that is not his worst defect; his worst defect is his perpetual moral obliquity, perpetual—from the days of the Flood to the Schleswig-Holstein period. Moral obliquity and consequently lack of good sense; for it has long been accepted that lack of good sense is due to no other cause than moral obliquity. Put it to the test and cast your eyes upon the history of mankind. What will you see? Is it a grand spectacle? Grand, if you like. Take the Colossus of Rhodes, for instance, that's worth something. With good reason Mr. Anayevsky[9] testifies of it that some say that it

[9] A third-rate novelist who was the butt of criticism in the fifties and sixties.—A.Y.

is the work of man's hands, while others maintain that it has been created by nature herself. Is it many-colored? Maybe it is many-colored, too: if one takes the dress uniforms, military and civilian, of all peoples in all ages—that alone is worth something, and if you take the undress uniforms you will never get to the end of it; no historian would be equal to the job. Is it monotonous? Maybe it's monotonous too; it's fighting and fighting; they are fighting now, they fought before and they fought after—you will admit that it is almost too monotonous. In short, one may say anything about the history of the world—anything that might enter the most disordered imagination. The only thing one can't say is that it's rational. The very word sticks in one's throat. And, indeed, this is the odd thing that is continually happening: there are continually turning up in life moral and rational persons, sages and lovers of humanity who make it their object to live all their lives as morally and rationally as possible, to be, so to speak, a light to their neighbors simply in order to show them that it is possible to live morally and rationally in this world. And yet we all know that those very people sooner or later have been false to themselves, playing some queer trick, often a most unseemly one. Now I ask you: what can be expected of man since he is a being endowed with such strange qualities? Shower upon him every earthly blessing, drown him in a sea of happiness, so that nothing but bubbles of bliss can be seen on the surface; give him economic prosperity, such that he should have nothing else to do but sleep, eat cakes, and busy himself with the continuation of his species, and even then, out of sheer ingratitude, sheer spite, man would play you some nasty trick. He would even risk his cakes and would deliberately desire the most fatal rubbish, the most uneconomic absurdity, simply to introduce into all this positive good sense his pernicious fantastic element. It is just his fantastic dreams, his vulgar folly that he will desire to retain, simply in order to prove to himself—as though that were necessary—that men still are men and not the keys of a piano, which the laws of nature threaten to control so completely that soon one will be able to desire nothing but by the calendar. And that is not all: even if man really were nothing but a piano key, even if this were proved to him by natural science and mathematics, even then he would not become reasonable, but would purposely do something perverse out of simple ingratitude, simply to gain his point. And if he does not find means, he will contrive destruction and chaos, will contrive sufferings of all sorts, only to gain his point! He will launch a curse upon the world, and as only man can curse (it is his privilege, the primary distinction between him and other animals), maybe by his curse alone he will attain his object—that is, convince himself that he is a man and not a piano key! If you say that all this, too, can be calculated and tabulated— chaos and darkness and curses, so that the mere possibility of calculating it all beforehand would stop it all, and reason would reassert itself, then man would purposely go mad in order to be rid of reason and gain his point! I believe in it, I answer for it, for the whole work of man really seems to consist in nothing but proving to himself every minute that he is a man and not a piano key! It may be at the cost of his skin, it may be by cannibalism! And this being so, can one help being tempted to rejoice that it has not yet come off, and that desire still depends on something we don't know?

You will scream at me (that is, if you condescend to do so) that no one is touching my free will, that all they are concerned with is that my will should of itself, of its own free will, coincide with my own normal interests, with the laws of nature and arithmetic.

Good heavens, gentlemen, what sort of free will is left when we come to tabulation and arithmetic, when it will all be a case of twice two makes four? Twice two makes four without my will. As if free will meant that!

IX

Gentlemen, I am joking, and I know myself that my jokes are not brilliant, but you know one can't take everything as a joke. I am perhaps jesting while I gnash my teeth. Gentlemen, I am tormented by questions: answer them for me. You, for instance, want to cure men of their old habits and reform their will in accordance with science and good sense. But how do you know, not only that it is possible, but also that it is *desirable*, to reform man in that way? And what leads you to the conclusion that man's inclinations *need* reforming? In short, how do you know that such a reformation will be a benefit to man? And, to go to the root of the matter, why are you so positively convinced that not to act against his real normal interests guaranteed by the conclusions of reason and arithmetic is certainly always advantageous for man and must always be a law for mankind? So far, you know, this is only your supposition. It may be the law of logic, but not the law of humanity. Perhaps you think, gentlemen, that I am mad. Allow me to defend myself. I agree that man is pre-eminently a creative animal, predestined to strive consciously for an object and to engage in engineering—that is, incessantly and eternally to make new roads, *wherever they may lead*. But the reason why he wants sometimes to go off at a tangent may just be that he is *predestined* to make the road, and perhaps, too, that, however stupid the "direct" practical man may be, the thought sometimes will occur to him that the road almost always does lead *somewhere*, and that the destination it leads to is less important than the process of making it, and that the chief thing is to save the well-conducted child from despising engineering, and so giving way to the fatal idleness, which, as we all know, is the mother of all the vices. Man likes to make roads and to create, that is a fact beyond dispute. But why has he such a passionate love for destruction and chaos also? Tell me that! But on that point I want to say a couple of words myself. May it not be that he loves chaos and destruction (there can be no disputing that he does sometimes love it) because he is instinctively afraid of attaining his object and completing the edifice he is constructing? Who knows, perhaps he only loves that edifice from a distance, and is by no means in love with it at close quarters; perhaps he only loves building it and does not want to live in it, but will leave it, when completed, for the use of *les animaux domestiques*—such as the ants, the sheep, and so on. Now the taste of the ants is quite different. They have a marvelous edifice of that pattern which endures forever—the ant-heap.

With the ant-heap the respectable race of ants began and with the ant-heap they will probably end, which does the greatest credit to their perseverance and good sense. But man is a frivolous and incongruous creature, and perhaps, like a chess player, loves the process of the game, not the end of it. And who knows (there is no saying with certainty), perhaps the only goal on earth to which mankind is striving lies in this incessant process of attaining, in other words, in life itself, and not in the thing to be attained, which must always be expressed as a formula, as positive as twice two makes four, and such positiveness is not life, gentlemen, but is the beginning of death. Anyway, man has always been afraid of this mathematical certainty, and I am afraid of it now. Granted that man does nothing but seek that mathematical certainty, he traverses oceans, sacrifices his life in the quest, but to succeed, really to find it, he dreads, I assure you. He feels that when he has found it there will be nothing for him to look for. When workmen have finished their work they do at least receive their pay, they go to the tavern, then they are taken to the police station—and there is occupation for a week. But where can man go? Anyway, one can observe a certain awkwardness about him when he has attained such objects. He loves the process of attaining, but does not quite like to have attained, and that, of course, is very absurd. In fact, man is a comical creature; there seems to be a kind of jest in it all. But yet mathematical certainty is, after all, something insufferable.

Twice two makes four seems to me simply a piece of insolence. Twice two makes four is a pert coxcomb who stands with arms akimbo barring your path and spitting. I admit that twice two makes four is an excellent thing, but if we are to give everything its due, twice two makes five is sometimes a very charming thing too.

And why are you so firmly, so triumphantly, convinced that only the normal and the positive—in other words, only what is conducive to welfare—is for the advantage of man? Is not reason in error as regards advantage? Does not man, perhaps, love something besides well-being? Perhaps he is just as fond of suffering? Perhaps suffering is just as great a benefit to him as well-being? Man is sometimes extraordinarily, passionately, in love with suffering, and that is a fact. There is no need to appeal to universal history to prove that; only ask yourself, if you are a man and have lived at all. As far as my personal opinion is concerned, to care only for well-being seems to me positively ill-bred. Whether it's good or bad, it is sometimes very pleasant, too, to smash things. I hold no brief for suffering nor for well-being either. I am standing for . . . my caprice, and for its being guaranteed to me when necessary. Suffering would be out of place in vaudevilles, for instance; I know that. In the "Palace of Crystal" it is unthinkable; suffering means doubt, negation, and what would be the good of a "palace of crystal" if there could be any doubt about it? And yet I think man will never renounce real suffering, that is, destruction and chaos. Why, suffering is the sole origin of consciousness. Though I did lay it down at the beginning that consciousness is the greatest misfortune for man, yet I know man prizes it and would not give it up for any satisfaction. Consciousness, for instance, is infinitely superior to twice two makes four. Once you have mathematical certainty there is nothing left to do or to understand. There will be nothing left but to bottle up your five senses and plunge into contemplation. While if you stick to consciousness, even though the same result is attained, that is, there is nothing left to do, you can at least flog yourself at times, and that will, at any rate, liven you up. Reactionary as it is, it is better than nothing.

X

You believe in a crystal palace that can never be destroyed —a palace at which one will not be able to put out one's tongue or make a long nose on the sly. And perhaps that is just why I am afraid of this edifice, that it is of crystal and can never be destroyed and that one cannot put one's tongue out at it even on the sly.

You see, if it were not a palace, but a henhouse, I might creep into it to avoid getting wet, and yet I would not call the henhouse a palace out of gratitude to it for keeping me dry. You laugh and say that in such circumstances a henhouse is as good as a mansion. Yes, I answer, if one had to live simply to keep out of the rain.

But what is to be done if I have taken it into my head that that is not the only object in life, and that if one must live one had better live in a mansion. That is my choice, my desire. You will only eradicate it when you have changed my preference. Well, do change it, allure me with something else, give me another ideal. But meanwhile I will not take a henhouse for a mansion. The palace of crystal may be an idle dream, it may be that it is inconsistent with the laws of nature and that I have invented it only through my own stupidity, through the old-fashioned irrational habits of my generation. But what does it matter to me that it is inconsistent? That makes no difference since it exists in my desires, or rather exists as long as my desires exist. Perhaps you are laughing again? Laugh away; I will put up with any mockery rather than pretend that I am satisfied when I am hungry. I know, anyway, that I will not be put off with a compromise, with a recurring zero, simply because it is consistent with the laws of nature and actually exists. I will not accept as the crown of my desires a block of buildings with tenements for the poor on a lease of a thousand years, and perhaps with the signboard of a dentist hanging out. Destroy my desires, eradicate my ideals, show me something better, and I will follow you. You will say, perhaps, that it is not worth your trouble; but in that case I can give you the answer. We are discussing things seriously; but if you won't deign to give me your attention, I will drop your acquaintance. I can retreat into my underground hole.

But while I am alive and have desires I would rather my hand were withered away than bring one brick to such a building! Don't remind me that I have just rejected the crystal palace for the sole reason that one cannot put out one's tongue at it. I did not say that, because I am so fond of putting my tongue out. Perhaps the only thing I resented was that of all your edifices there has not been one at which one could not put out one's tongue. On the contrary, I would let my tongue be cut off out of gratitude if things could be so arranged that I should lose all desire to put it out. It is not my fault that things cannot be so arranged, and that one must be satisfied with model flats. Then why am I made with such desires? Can I have been constructed simply in order to come to the conclusion that my whole mechanism is a cheat? Can this be the whole purpose? I do not believe it.

But do you know what: I am convinced that we underground folk ought to be kept on a curb. Though we may sit forty years underground without speaking, when we do come out into the light of day and break out, we talk and talk and talk. . . .

XI

The long and the short of it is, gentlemen, that it is better to do nothing! Better conscious inertia! And so hurrah for ✻ the underground! Though I have said that I envy the normal man to the last drop of my bile, yet I should not care to be in his place such as he is now (though I shall not cease envying him). No, no; anyway the underground life is more advantageous. There, at any rate, one can. . . . Oh, but even now I am lying! I am lying because I know myself that it is not the underground that is better, but something different, quite different, for which I am thirsting, but which I cannot find! Damn the underground!

I will tell you another thing that would be better, and that is if I myself believed in any part of what I have just written. I swear to you, gentlemen, there is not one thing, not one word of what I have written that I really believe. That is, I believe it, perhaps, but at the same time I feel and suspect that I am lying like a cobbler.

"Then why have you written all this?" you will say to me.

"I ought to put you underground for forty years without anything to do and then come to you in your cellar, to find out what stage you have reached! How can a man be left with nothing to do for forty years?"

"Isn't that shameful, isn't that humiliating?" you will say, perhaps, wagging your heads contemptuously. "You thirst for life and try to settle the problems of life by a logical tangle. And how persistent, how insolent are your sallies, and at the same time what a funk you are in! You talk nonsense and are pleased with it; you say impudent things and are in continual alarm and apologizing for them. You declare that you are afraid of nothing and at the same time try to ingratiate yourself with us. You declare that you are gnashing your teeth and at the same time you try to be witty so as to amuse us. You know that your witticisms are not witty, but you are evidently well satisfied with their literary value. You may, perhaps, have really suffered, but you have no respect for your own suffering. You may have sincerity, but you have no modesty; out of the pettiest vanity you expose your sincerity to publicity and ignominy. You doubtlessly mean to say something, but hide your last word through fear, because you have not the resolution to utter it, and only have a cowardly impudence. You boast of consciousness, but you are not sure of your ground, for though your mind works, yet your heart is darkened and corrupt, and you cannot have a full, genuine consciousness without a pure heart. And how intrusive you are, how you insist and grimace! Lies, lies, lies!"

Of course I have myself made up all the things you say. That, too, is from underground. I have been for forty years listening to you through a crack in the wall. I have invented them myself, there was nothing else I could invent. It is no wonder that I have learned this by heart and it has taken a literary form. . . .

But can you really be so credulous as to think that I will print all this and give it to you to read too? And another problem: why do I call you "gentlemen," why do I address you as though you really were my readers? Such confessions as I intend to make are never printed or given to other people to read. Anyway, I am not strong-minded enough for that, and I don't see why I should be. But you see a fancy has occurred to me and I want to realize it at all costs. Let me explain.

Every man has reminiscences which he would not tell to everyone, but only to his friends. He has other matters in his mind which he would not reveal even to his friends, but only to himself, and that in secret. But there are other things which a man is afraid to tell even to himself, and every decent man has a number of such things stored away in his mind. The more decent he is, the greater the number of such things in his mind. Anyway, I have only lately determined to remember some of my early adventures. Till now I have always avoided them, even with a certain uneasiness. Now, when I am not only recalling them, but have actually decided to write an account of them, I want to try the experiment whether one can, even with oneself, be perfectly open and not take fright at the whole truth. I will observe, in parenthesis, that Heine says that a true autobiography is almost an impossibility, and that man is bound to lie about himself. He considers that Rousseau certainly told lies about himself in his confessions, and even intentionally lied, out of vanity. I am convinced that Heine is right; I quite understand how sometimes one may, out of sheer vanity, attribute regular crimes to oneself, and indeed

I can very well conceive that kind of vanity. But Heine judged of people who made their confessions to the public. I write only for myself, and I wish to declare once and for all that if I write as though I were addressing readers, that is simply because it is easier for me to write in that form. It is a form, an empty form—I shall never have readers. I have made this plain already. . . .

I don't wish to be hampered by any restrictions in the compilation of my notes. I shall not attempt any system or method. I shall jot things down as I remember them.

But here, perhaps, someone will catch at the word and ask me: if you really don't reckon on readers, why do you make such compacts with yourself—and on paper too—that is, that you won't attempt any system or method, that you jot things down as you remember them, and so on, and so on? Why are you explaining? Why do you apologize?

Well there it is, I answer.

There is a whole psychology in all this, though. Perhaps it is simply that I am a coward. And perhaps I purposely imagine an audience before me in order to be more dignified while I write. There may be thousands of reasons. Again, what precisely is my object in writing? If it is not for the benefit of the public, why should I not simply recall these incidents in my own mind without putting them on paper?

Quite so; but yet it is more imposing on paper. There is something more impressive in it; I shall be better able to criticize myself and improve my style. Besides, I shall perhaps obtain actual relief from writing. Today, for instance, I am particularly oppressed by one memory of a distant past. It came back vividly to my mind a few days ago, and has remained haunting me like an annoying tune that one cannot get rid of. And yet I must get rid of it somehow. I have hundreds of such reminiscences; but at times some one stands out from the hundreds and oppresses me. For some reason I believe that if I write it down I shall get rid of it. Why not try?

Besides, I am bored, and I never have anything to do. Writing will be a sort of work. They say work makes man kind-hearted and honest. Well, here is a chance for me, anyway.

Snow is falling today, yellow and dingy. It fell yesterday, too, and a few days ago. I fancy it is the wet snow that has reminded me of that incident which I cannot shake off now. And so, let it be a story apropos of the wet snow.

Part II: Apropos of the Wet Snow

When from dark error's subjugation
My words of passionate exhortation
  Had wrenched thy fainting spirit free;
And writhing prone in thine affliction
Thou didst recall with malediction
  The vice that had encompassed thee:
And when thy slumbering conscience, fretting
  By recollection's torturing flame,
Thou didst reveal the hideous setting
  Of thy life's current ere I came:
When suddenly I saw thee sicken,
  And weeping, hide thine anguished face,
Revolted, maddened, horror-stricken,
  At memories of foul disgrace.
              NEKRASOV (*translated by Juliet Soskice*)

I

At that time I was only twenty-four. My life was even then gloomy, ill-regulated, and as solitary as that of a savage. I made friends with no one and positively avoided talking, and buried myself more and more in my hole. At work in the office I never looked at anyone, and I was perfectly well aware that my companions not only regarded me as a queer fellow, but even looked upon me—I always fancied this—with a sort of loathing. I sometimes wondered why it was that nobody except me fancied that he was looked upon with aversion? One of the clerks had a most repulsive, pockmarked face, which was positively villainous. I believe I should not have dared to look at anyone if I had such an unsightly countenance. Another wore such a very dirty old uniform that there was an unpleasant odor in his proximity. Yet not one of these gentlemen showed the slightest self-consciousness—either about their clothes or their countenance or their character in any way. Neither of them ever imagined that they were regarded with repulsion; if they had imagined it, they would not have minded—so long as their superiors did not look at them in that way. It is clear to me now that, owing to my unbounded vanity and to the high standard I set for myself, I often looked at myself with furious discontent, which verged on loathing, and so I inwardly attributed the same feeling to everyone. I hated my face, for instance: I thought it disgusting, and even suspected that there was something base in my expression, and so every day when I turned up at the office I tried to behave as independently as possible, and to assume a lofty expression, so that I might not be suspected of being abject. "My face may be ugly," I thought, "but let it be lofty, expressive, and, above all, *extremely* intelligent." But I was positively and painfully certain that it was impossible for my countenance ever to express those qualities. And what was worst of all, I thought it actually stupid looking, and I would have been quite satisfied if I could have looked intelligent. In fact, I would even have put up with looking base if, at the same time, my face could have been thought strikingly intelligent.

Of course, I hated my fellow-clerks one and all, and I despised them all, yet at the same time I was, as it were, afraid of them. In fact, it happened at times that I thought more highly of them than of myself. It somehow happened quite suddenly that I alternated between despising them and thinking them superior to myself. A cultivated and decent man cannot be vain without setting a fearfully high standard for himself, and without despising and almost hating himself at certain moments. But whether I despised them or thought them superior I dropped my eyes almost every time I met anyone. I even made experiments whether I could face So-and-so's looking at me, and I was always the first to drop my eyes. This worried me to distraction. I had a sickly dread, too, of being ridiculous, and so had a slavish passion for the conventional in everything external. I loved to fall into the common rut, and had a wholehearted terror of any kind of eccentricity in myself. But how could I live up to it? I was morbidly sensitive, as a man of our age should be. They were all stupid, and as like one another as so many sheep. Perhaps I was the only one in the office who fancied that I was a coward and a slave, and I fancied it just because I was more highly developed. But it was not only that I fancied it, it really was so. I was a coward and a slave. I say this without the slightest embarrassment. Every decent man of our age must be a coward and a slave. That is his normal condition. Of that I am firmly persuaded. He is made and constructed to that very end. And not only at the present time owing to some casual circumstances, but always, at all times, a decent man is bound to be a coward and a slave. It is the law of nature for all decent people all over the earth. If any one of them happens to be valiant about something, he need not be comforted or carried away by that; he would show the white feather just the same before something else. That is how it invariably and inevitably ends. Only donkeys and mules are valiant, and they only till they are pushed up to the wall. It is not worth while to pay attention to them, for they really are of no consequence.

Another circumstance, too, worried me in those days: that there was no one like me and I was unlike anyone else. "I am alone and they are *all*," I thought—and pondered.

From that it is evident that I was still a youngster.

The very opposite sometimes happened. It was loathsome sometimes to go to the office; things reached such a point that I often came home ill. But all at once, apropos of nothing, there would come a phase of skepticism and indifference (everything happened to me in phases), and I myself would laugh at my intolerance and fastidiousness, I would reproach myself with being *romantic*. At one time I was unwilling to speak to anyone, while at other times I would not only talk, but go to the length of contemplating making friends with them. All my fastidiousness would suddenly, without rhyme or reason, vanish. Who knows, perhaps I never had really had it, and it had simply been affected and got out of books. I have not decided that question even now. Once I quite made friends with them, visited their homes, played preference, drank vodka, talked of promotions. . . . But here let me make a digression.

We Russians, speaking generally, have never had those foolish transcendental "romantics"—German, and still more French—on whom nothing produces any effect; if there were an earthquake, if all France perished at the barricades, they would still be the same, they would not even have the decency to affect a change, but would still go on singing their transcendental songs to the hour of their death, because they are fools. We, in Russia, have no fools; that is well known. That is what distinguishes us from foreign lands. Consequently these transcendental natures are not found amongst us in their pure form. The idea that they are is due to our "realistic" journalists and critics of that day, always on the lookout for Kostanzhoglos[10] and Uncle Pyotr Ivanoviches[11] and foolishly accepting them as our ideal; they have slandered our romantics, taking them for the same transcendental sort as in Germany or France. On the contrary, the characteristics of our romantics are absolutely and directly opposed to the transcendental European type, and no European standard can be applied to them. (Allow me to make use of this word "romantic"—an old-fashioned and much respected word which has done good service and is familiar to all.) The characteristics of our romantics are to understand everything, to *see everything, and to see it often*

[10] Kostanzhoglo is a character in Gogol's *Dead Souls.*—A.Y.
[11] Uncle Pyotr Ivanovich is the hero of Goncharov's novel, *An Ordinary Story.*—A.Y.

incomparably more clearly than our most realistic minds see it; to refuse to accept anyone or anything, but at the same time not to despise anything; to give way, to yield, from policy; never to lose sight of a useful practical object (such as rent-free quarters at the government expense, pensions, decorations), to keep their eye on that object through all the enthusiasms and volumes of lyrical poems, and at the same time to preserve "the good and the beautiful" inviolate within them to the hour of their death, and to preserve themselves also, incidentally, like some precious jewel wrapped in cotton wool if only for the benefit of "the good and the beautiful." Our romantic is a man of great breadth and the greatest rogue of all our rogues, I assure you. . . . I can assure you from experience, indeed. Of course, that is, if he is intelligent. But what am I saying! The romantic is always intelligent, and I only meant to observe that although we have had foolish romantics they don't count, and they were only so because in the flower of their youth they degenerated into Germans, and, to preserve their precious jewel more comfortably, settled somewhere out there—by preference in Weimar or the Black Forest.

I, for instance, genuinely despised my official work and did not openly abuse it simply because I was in it myself and got a salary for it. Anyway, take note, I did not openly abuse it. Our romantic would rather go out of his mind—a thing, however, which very rarely happens—than take to open abuse, unless he had some other career in view; and he is never kicked out. At most, they would take him to the lunatic asylum as "the King of Spain" if he should go very mad. But it is only the thin, fair people who go out of their minds in Russia. Innumerable romantics attain later in life to considerable rank in the service. Their many-sidedness is remarkable! And what a faculty they have for the most contradictory sensations! I was comforted by this thought even in those days, and I am of the same opinion now. That is why there are so many "broad natures" among us who never lose their ideal even in the depths of degradation;

[handwritten margin note: contradiction]

and though they never stir a finger for their ideal, though they are arrant thieves and knaves, yet they tearfully cherish their first ideal and are extraordinarily honest at heart. Yes, it is only among us that the most incorrigible rogue can be absolutely and loftily honest at heart without in the least ceasing to be a rogue. I repeat, our romantics, frequently, become such accomplished rascals (I use the term "rascals" affectionately), suddenly display such a sense of reality and practical knowledge, that their bewildered superiors and the public generally can only ejaculate in amazement.

Their many-sidedness is really amazing, and goodness knows what it may develop into later on, and what the future has in store for us. It is not poor materiall I do not say this from any foolish or boastful patriotism. But I feel sure that you are again imagining that I am joking. Or perhaps it's just the contrary, and you are convinced that I really think so. Anyway, gentlemen, I shall welcome both views as an honor and a special favor. And do forgive my digression.

I did not, of course, maintain friendly relations with my comrades and soon was at loggerheads with them, and in my youth and inexperience I even gave up bowing to them, abruptly. That, however, only happened to me once. As a rule, I was always alone.

In the first place, I spent most of my time at home, reading. I tried to stifle all that was continually seething within me by means of external impressions. And the only external means I had was reading. Reading, of course, was a great help—exciting me, giving me pleasure and pain. But at times it bored me fearfully. One longed for movement in spite of everything, and I plunged all at once into dark, underground, loathsome vice of the pettiest kind. My wretched passions were acute, smarting, from my continual, sickly irritability. I had hysterical impulses, with tears and convulsions. I had no resource except reading, that is, there was nothing in my surroundings which I could respect and which attracted me. I was overwhelmed with depression, too; I had an hysterical craving for incongruity and for contrast, and so I took to vice. I have not said all this to justify myself. . . . But, no! I am lying. I did want to justify myself. I make that little observation for my own benefit, gentlemen. I don't want to lie. I vowed to myself I would not.

And so, furtively, timidly, in solitude, at night, I indulged in filthy vice, with a feeling of shame which never deserted me, even at the most loathsome moments, and which at such moments nearly made me curse. Already even then I had my underground world in my soul. I was fearfully afraid of being seen, of being met, of being recognized. I visited various obscure haunts.

One night as I was passing a tavern I saw through a lighted window some gentlemen fighting with billiard cues, and saw one of them thrown out of the window. At other times I should have felt very much disgusted, but I was in such a mood at the time that I actually envied the gentleman thrown out of the window—and I envied him so much that I even went into the tavern and into the billiard room. "Perhaps," I thought, "I'll have a fight, too, and they'll throw me out of the window."

I was not drunk—but what is one to do—the blues will drive a man to such a pitch of hysteria. But nothing happened. It seemed that I was not even equal to being thrown out of the window and I went away without having my fight.

An officer put me in my place from the first moment.

I was standing by the billiard table and in my ignorance blocking up the way, and he wanted to pass; he took me by the shoulders and without a word—without a warning or explanation—moved me from where I was standing to another spot and passed by as though he had not noticed me. I could have forgiven blows, but I could not forgive his having moved me without noticing me.

Devil knows what I would have given for a real regular quarrel—a more decent, a more *literary* one, so to speak. I had been treated like a fly. This officer was over six foot, while I was a spindly little fellow. But the quarrel was in my hands. I had only to protest and I certainly would have been thrown out of the window. But I changed my mind and preferred to beat an embittered retreat.

From the tavern I went straight home, confused and troubled, and the next night I went on with my petty debauch, still more furtively, abjectly, and miserably than before, as it were, with tears in my eyes—but still I did go out again. Don't imagine, though, it was cowardice made me slink away from the officer: I never have been a coward at heart, though I have always been a coward in action. Don't be in a hurry to laugh—I assure you I can explain it all.

Oh, if only that officer had been one of the sort who would consent to fight a duel! But no, he was one of those gentlemen (alas, long extinct!) who preferred fighting with cues or, like Gogol's Lieutenant Pirogov,[12] appealing to the police. They did not fight duels and would have thought a duel with a civilian like me an utterly unseemly procedure in any case—and they looked upon the duel altogether as something impossible, something freethinking and French. But they were quite ready to bully, especially when they were over six foot.

I did not slink away through cowardice, but through an unbounded vanity. I was afraid not of his six foot, nor of getting a sound thrashing and being thrown out of the window; I should have had physical courage enough, I assure you; but I had not the moral courage. What I was afraid of was that everyone present, from the insolent marker down to the lowest little stinking, pimply clerk in a greasy collar, would jeer at me and fail to understand when I began to protest and to address them in literary language. For of the point of honor—not of honor, but of the point of honor (*point d'honneur*)—one cannot speak among us except in literary language. You can't allude to the "point of honor" in ordinary language. I was fully convinced (the

12 Hero of Gogol's story, "Nevsky Prospect."—A.Y.

sense of reality, in spite of all my romanticism!) that they would all simply split their sides with laughter, and that the officer would not simply beat me, that is, without insulting me, but would certainly prod me in the back with his knees, kick me around the billiard table, and only then perhaps have pity and drop me out of the window.

Of course, this trivial incident could not end for me in that alone. I often met that officer afterward in the street and noticed him very carefully. I am not quite sure whether he recognized me, I imagine not; I judge from certain signs. But I—I stared at him with spite and hatred and so it went on . . . for several years! My resentment grew even deeper with years. At first I began making stealthy inquiries about this officer. It was difficult for me to do so, for I knew no one. But one day I heard someone shout his surname in the street as I was following him at a distance, as though I were tied to him—and so I learned his surname. Another time I followed him to his flat, and for ten copecks learned from the porter where he lived, on which story, whether he lived alone or with others, and so on—in fact, everything one could learn from a porter. One morning, though I had never tried my hand with the pen, it suddenly occurred to me to write a satire on this officer in the form of a novel which would unmask his villainy. I wrote the novel with relish. I did unmask his villainy, I even exaggerated it; at first I so altered his surname that it could easily be recognized, but on second thoughts I changed it, and sent the story to *Otechestvennye zapiski*. But at that time such attacks were not the fashion and my story was not printed. That was a great vexation to me.

Sometimes I was positively choked with resentment. At last I determined to challenge my enemy to a duel. I composed a splendid, charming letter to him, imploring him to apologize to me, and hinting rather plainly at a duel in case of refusal. The letter was so composed that if the officer had had the least understanding of the good and the beautiful he would certainly have flung himself on my neck and have offered me his friendship. And how fine that

would have been! How we should have got on together!
"He could have shielded me with his higher rank, while I
could have improved his mind with my culture, and, well
. . . my ideas, and all sorts of things might have happened." Only fancy, this was two years after his insult to
me, and my challenge would have been a ridiculous anachronism, in spite of all the ingenuity of my letter in disguising and explaining away the anachronism. But, thank
God (to this day I thank the Almighty with tears in my
eyes), I did not send the letter to him. Cold shivers run
down my back when I think of what might have happened
if I had sent it.

And all at once I revenged myself in the simplest way,
by a stroke of genius! A brilliant thought suddenly dawned
upon me. Sometimes on holidays I used to stroll along
the sunny side of the Nevsky about four o'clock in the
afternoon. Though it was hardly a stroll so much as a
series of innumerable miseries, humiliations, and resent-
ments; but no doubt that was just what I wanted. I used to
wriggle along in a most unseemly fashion, like an eel, continually moving aside to make way for generals, for officers
of the guards and the hussars, or for ladies. At such minutes
there used to be a convulsive twinge at my heart, and I
used to feel hot all down my back at the mere thought of
the wretchedness of my attire, of the wretchedness and abjectness of my little scurrying figure. This was a regular
martyrdom, a continual, intolerable humiliation at the
thought, which passed into an incessant and direct sensation, that I was a mere fly in the eyes of all this world, a
nasty, disgusting fly—more intelligent, more highly developed, more refined in feeling than any of them, of course—
but a fly that was continually making way for everyone,
insulted and injured by everyone. Why I inflicted this torture upon myself, why I went to the Nevsky, I don't know.
I felt simply drawn there at every possible opportunity.

Already then I began to experience a rush of the enjoyment of which I spoke in the first chapter. After my affair
with the officer I felt even more drawn there than before:

it was on the Nevsky that I met him most frequently, there I could admire him. He, too, went there chiefly on holidays. He, too, turned out of his path for generals and persons of high rank, and he, too, wriggled between them like an eel; but people like me, or even the better dressed ones, he simply walked over; he made straight for them as though there was nothing but empty space before him, and never, under any circumstances, turned aside. I gloated over my resentment watching him and . . . always resentfully made way for him. It exasperated me that even in the street I could not be on an even footing with him.

"Why must you invariably be the first to move aside?" I kept asking myself in hysterical rage, waking up sometimes at three o'clock in the morning. "Why it is you and not he? There's no regulation about it; there's no written law. Let the making way be equal as it usually is when refined people meet: he moves halfway and you move halfway; you pass with mutual respect."

But that never happened, and I always moved aside, while he did not even notice my making way for him. And lo and behold a bright idea dawned upon me! "What," I thought, "if I meet him and don't move to one side? What if I don't move aside on purpose, if I even knock up against him? How would that be?" This audacious idea took such a hold on me that it gave me no peace. I was dreaming of it continually, horribly, and I purposely went more frequently to the Nevsky in order to picture more vividly how I should do it when I did do it. I was delighted. This intention seemed to me more and more practical and possible.

"Of course I shall not really push him," I thought, already more good-natured in my joy. "I will simply not turn aside, will run up against him, not very violently, but just so that we shoulder each other—just as much as decency permits. I will push against him just as much as he pushes against me." At last I made up my mind completely. But my preparations took a great deal of time. To begin with, when I carried out my plan I should need to be looking rather more decent, and so I had to think of my get-up.

"In case of emergency, if, for instance, there were any sort of public scandal (and the public there is of the most recherché: the Countess walks there; Prince D. walks there; all the literary world is there), I must be well dressed; that inspires respect and of itself puts us on an equal footing in the eyes of society."

With this object I asked for some of my salary in advance, and bought at Churkin's a pair of black gloves and a decent hat. Black gloves seemed to me both more dignified and bon ton than the lemon-colored ones which I had contemplated at first. "The color is too gaudy, it looks as though one were trying to be conspicuous," and I did not take the lemon-colored ones. I had got ready long beforehand a good shirt, with white bone studs; my overcoat was the only thing that held me back. The coat in itself was a very good one, it kept me warm; but it was wadded and it had a raccoon collar which was the height of vulgarity. I had to change the collar at any sacrifice, and to have a beaver one like an officer's. For this purpose I began visiting the shops and after several attempts I pitched upon a piece of cheap German beaver. Though these German beavers soon grow shabby and look wretched, yet at first they look exceedingly well, and I only needed it for one occasion. I asked the price; even so, it was too expensive. After thinking it over thoroughly I decided to sell my raccoon collar. The rest of the money—a considerable sum for me, I decided to borrow from Anton Antonych Setochkin, my immediate superior, an unassuming person, though grave and judicious. He never lent money to anyone, but I had, on entering the service, been specially recommended to him by an important personage who had got me my berth. I was horribly worried. To borrow from Anton Antonych seemed to me monstrous and shameful. I did not sleep for two or three nights. Indeed, I did not sleep well at that time, I was in a fever; I had a vague sinking at my heart or else a sudden throbbing, throbbing, throbbing! Anton Antonych was surprised at first, then he frowned, then he reflected, and did after all lend me the money, receiving from me a written authorization to take from my salary a fortnight later the sum that he had lent me.

In this way everything was at last ready. The handsome beaver replaced the mean-looking raccoon, and I began by degrees to get to work. It would never have done to act offhand, at random; the plan had to be carried out skillfully, by degrees. But I must confess that after many efforts I began to despair: we simply could not run into each other. I made every preparation, I was quite determined—it seemed as though we should run into one another directly—and before I knew what I was doing I had stepped aside for him again and he had passed without noticing me. I even prayed as I approached him that God would grant me determination. One time I had made up my mind thoroughly, but it ended in my stumbling and falling at his feet because at the very last instant when I was six inches from him my courage failed me. He very calmly stepped over me, while I flew to one side like a ball. That night I was ill again, feverish and delirious.

And suddenly it ended most happily. The night before I had made up my mind not to carry out my fatal plan and to abandon it all, and with that object I went to the Nevsky for the last time, just to see how I would abandon it all. Suddenly, three paces from my enemy, I unexpectedly made up my mind—I closed my eyes, and we ran full tilt, shoulder to shoulder, against one another! I did not budge an inch and passed him on a perfectly equal footing! He did not even look around and pretended not to notice it; but he was only pretending, I am convinced of that. I am convinced of that to this day! Of course, I got the worst of it—he was stronger, but that was not the point. The point was that I had attained my object, I had kept up my dignity, I had not yielded a step, and had put myself publicly on an equal social footing with him. I returned home feeling that I was fully avenged for everything. I was delighted. I was triumphant and sang Italian arias. Of course, I will not describe to you what happened to me three days later; if you have read my first chapter you can guess that for yourself. The officer was afterward transferred; I have not seen him now for fourteen years. What is the dear fellow doing now? Whom is he walking over?

II

But the period of my dissipation would end and I always felt very sick afterward. It was followed by remorse—I tried to drive it away: I felt too disgusted. By degrees, however, I grew used to that too. I grew used to everything, or rather I voluntarily resigned myself to enduring it. But I had a means of escape that reconciled everything—that was to find refuge in "the good and the beautiful," in dreams, of course. I was a terrible dreamer, I would dream for three months on end, tucked away in my corner, and you may believe me that at those moments I had no resemblance to the gentleman who, in the perturbation of his chicken heart, put a collar of German beaver on his overcoat. I suddenly became a hero. I would not have admitted my six-foot lieutenant even if he had called on me. I could not even picture him before me then. What my dreams were and how I could satisfy myself with them—it is hard to say now, but at the time I was satisfied with them. Though, indeed, even now, I am to some extent satisfied with them. Dreams were particularly sweet and vivid after a spell of dissipation; they came with remorse and with tears, with curses and transports. There were moments of such positive intoxication, of such happiness, that there was not the faintest trace of irony within me, on my honor. I had faith, hope, love. I believed blindly at such times that by some miracle, by some external circumstance, all this would suddenly open out, expand; that suddenly a vista of suitable activity—beneficent, good, and, above all, *ready-made* (what sort of activity I had no idea, but the great thing was that it should be all ready for me)—would rise up before me—and I should come out into the light of day, almost riding a white horse and crowned with laurel. Anything but the foremost place I could not conceive for myself, and for that very reason I quite contentedly occupied the lowest in reality. Either to be a hero or to grovel in the mud—there was nothing between. That was my ruin, for when I was in the mud I comforted myself with the thought that at other times I was a hero, and the hero was a cloak for the mud: for an ordinary man it was shameful to defile himself, but a hero was too lofty to be utterly defiled, and so he might defile himself. It is worth noting that these attacks of the "good and the beautiful" visited me even during the period of dissipation and just at the times when I was touching bottom. They came in separate spurts, as though reminding me of themselves, but did not banish the dissipation by their appearance. On the contrary, they seemed to add a zest to it by contrast, and were only sufficiently present to serve as an appetizing sauce. That sauce was made up of contradictions and sufferings, of agonizing inward analysis, and all these pangs and pinpricks gave a certain piquancy, even a significance to my dissipation—in fact, completely answered the purpose of an appetizing sauce. There was a certain depth of meaning in it. And I could hardly have resigned myself to the simple, vulgar, direct debauchery of a clerk and have endured all the filthiness of it. What could have allured me about it then and have drawn me at night into the street? No, I had a lofty way of getting out of it all.

And what loving-kindness, oh Lord, what loving-kindness I felt at times in those dreams of mine, in those "escapes into the good and the beautiful"; though it was fantastic love, though it was never applied to anything human in reality, yet there was so much of this love that one did not feel afterward even the impulse to apply it in reality; that would have been superfluous. Everything, however, passed satisfactorily by a lazy and fascinating transition into the sphere of art, that is, into the beautiful forms of life, lying ready, largely stolen from the poets and novelists and adapted to all sorts of needs and uses. I, for instance, was triumphant over everyone; everyone, of course, was in dust and ashes, and was forced spontaneously to recognize my superiority, and I forgave them all. I was a poet and a grand gentleman, I fell in love; I came in for countless millions and immediately devoted them to humanity, and at the same time I confessed before all the people my shameful deeds, which, of course, were not merely shameful, but had in them much that was "good and beautiful," something in the Manfred style. Everyone would kiss me and weep (what idiots they would be if they did not), while I should go barefoot and hungry preaching new ideas and fighting a victorious Austerlitz against the obscurantists. Then the band would play a march, an amnesty would be declared, the Pope would agree to retire from Rome to Brazil; then there would be a ball for the whole of Italy at the Villa Borghese on the shores of Lake Como, Lake Como being for that purpose transferred to the neighborhood of Rome; then would come a scene in the bushes, and so on, and so on—as though you did not know all about it! You will say that it is vulgar and contemptible to drag all this into the market place after all the tears and transports which I have myself confessed. But why is it contemptible? Can you imagine that I am ashamed of it all, and that it was stupider than anything in your life, gentlemen? And I can assure you that some of these fancies were by no means badly composed. . . . It did not all happen on the shores of Lake Como. And yet you are right—it really is vulgar and contemptible. And most contemptible of all is that now I am attempting to justify myself to you. And even more contemptible than that is my making this remark now. But that's enough, or there will be no end to it: each step will be more contemptible than the last. . . .

I could never stand more than three months of dreaming at a time without feeling an irresistible desire to plunge into society. To plunge into society meant to visit my superior at the office, Anton Antonych Setochkin. He was the only steady acquaintance I have had in my life, and I wonder at the fact myself now. But I only went to see him when that phase came over me, and when my dreams had reached such a point of bliss that it became essential at once to embrace my fellows and all mankind; and for that purpose I needed, at least, one human being, actually existing. I had to call on Anton Antonych, however, on Tuesday—his day at home; so I had always to time my passionate desire to embrace humanity so that it might fall on a Tuesday.

This Anton Antonych lived on the fourth story in a house at Five Corners, in four low-pitched rooms, one smaller than the other, of a particularly mean and sallow appearance. His two daughters and their aunt used to pour out the tea. Of the daughters one was thirteen and the other fourteen, they both had snub noses, and I was awfully shy of them because they were always whispering and giggling together. The master of the house usually sat in his study on a leather couch in front of the table with some gray-headed gentleman, usually a colleague from our office or some other department. I never saw more than two or three visitors there, always the same. They talked about the excise duty, about business in the senate, about salaries, about promotions, about his Excellency, and the best means of pleasing him, and so on. I had the patience to sit like a fool beside these people for four hours at a stretch, listening to them without knowing what to say to them or venturing to say a word. I became stupefied, several times I felt myself perspiring, I was overcome by a sort of paralysis; but this was pleasant and good for me. On returning home I deferred for a time my desire to embrace all mankind.

I had, however, one other acquaintance of a sort, Simonov, who was an old schoolfellow. Indeed I had a number of schoolfellows in Petersburg, but I did not associate with them and had even given up nodding to them in the street. I believe I had transferred to the department I was in simply to avoid their company and to cut off all connection with my hateful childhood. Curses on that school and all those terrible years of penal servitude! In short, I parted from my schoolfellows as soon as I got out into the world. There were two or three left to whom I nodded in the street. One of them, Simonov, who had been in no way distinguished at school, was of a quiet and equable disposition; but I discovered in him a certain independence of character and even honesty. I don't even suppose that he was particularly stupid. I had at one time spent some rather soulful moments with him, but these had not lasted long and had somehow been suddenly clouded over. He was evidently uncomfortable at these reminiscences, and was, I fancy, always afraid that I might take up the same tone again. I suspected that he had an aversion for me, but still I went on going to see him, not being quite certain of it.

And so on one occasion, unable to endure my solitude and knowing that, as it was Thursday, Anton Antonych's door would be closed, I thought of Simonov. Climbing up to his fourth story, I was thinking that the man disliked me and that it was a mistake to go and see him. But as it always happened that such reflections impelled me, as though purposely, to put myself into a false position, I went in. It was almost a year since I had last seen Simonov.

III

I found two of my old schoolfellows with him. They seemed to be discussing an important matter. All of them took scarcely any notice of my entrance, which was strange, for I had not met them for years. Evidently they looked upon me as something on the level of a common fly. I had not been treated like that even at school, though they all hated me. I knew, of course, that they must despise me now for my lack of success in the service, and for having let myself sink so low, going about badly dressed and so on—which seemed to them a sign of my incapacity and insignificance. But I had not expected such contempt. Simonov was positively surprised at my turning up. Even in former days he had always seemed surprised at my coming. All this disconcerted me: I sat down, feeling rather miserable, and began listening to what they were saying.

They were engaged in warm and earnest conversation about a farewell dinner which they wanted to arrange for the next day to a comrade of theirs called Zverkov, an officer in the army, who was going away to a distant province. This Zverkov had been at school with me too. I had begun to hate him, particularly in the upper forms. In the lower forms he had simply been a pretty, playful boy whom everybody liked. I had hated him, however, even in the lower forms, just because he was a pretty and playful boy. He was always bad at his lessons and got worse and worse as he went on; however, he left with a good certificate, as he had powerful friends. During his last year at school he came in for an estate of two hundred serfs, and, as almost all of us were poor, he took up a swaggering tone among us. He was vulgar in the extreme, but at the same time he was a good-natured fellow, even in his swaggering. In spite of superficial, fantastic, and sham notions of honor and dignity, all but very few of us positively groveled before Zverkov, and the more so the more he swaggered. And it was not from any interested motive that they groveled, but simply because he had been favored by the gifts of nature. Moreover, it was, as it were, an accepted idea among us that Zverkov was a specialist in regard to tact and the social graces. This last fact particularly infuriated me. I hated the abrupt self-confident tone of his voice, his admiration of his own witticisms, which were often frightfully stupid, though he was bold in his language; I hated his handsome, but stupid face (for which I would, however, have gladly exchanged my intelligent one), and the free and easy military manners in fashion in the forties. I hated the way in which he used to talk of his future conquests of women (he did not venture to begin his attack upon women until he had the epaulettes of an officer, and was looking forward to them with impatience), and boasted of the duels he would constantly be fighting. I remember how I, invariably so taciturn, suddenly fastened upon Zverkov, when one day talking at a moment of leisure with his schoolfellows of his future relations with the fair sex, and growing as sportive as a puppy in the sun, he all at once declared that he would not leave a single village girl on his estate unnoticed, that that was his *droit du seigneur*, and that if the peasants dared to protest he would have them all flogged and double the tax on them, the bearded rascals. Our servile rabble applauded, but I attacked him, not from compassion for the girls and their fathers, but simply because they were applauding such an insect.

I got the better of him on that occasion, but, though Zverkov was stupid, he was lively and impudent, and so laughed it off, and in such a way that my victory was not really complete: the laugh was on his side. He got the better of me on several occasions afterward, but without malice, jestingly, casually. I remained angrily and contemptuously silent and would not answer him. When we left school he made advances to me; I did not rebuff them, for I was flattered, but we soon parted and quite naturally. Afterward I heard of his barrack-room success as a lieutenant, and of the fast life he was leading. Then there came other rumors—of his successes in the service. By then he had taken to cutting me in the street, and I suspected that he was afraid of compromising himself by greeting a personage as insignificant as me. I saw him once in the theater, in the third tier of boxes. By then he was wearing shoulder straps. He was twisting and twirling about, ingratiating himself with the daughters of an ancient general. In three years he had gone off considerably, though he was still rather handsome and adroit. One could see that by the time he was thirty he would be corpulent. So it was for this Zverkov that my schoolfellows were going to give a dinner on his departure. They had kept up with him for those three years, though privately they did not consider themselves on an equal footing with him, I am convinced of that.

Of Simonov's two visitors, one was Ferfichkin, a Russianized German—a little fellow with the face of a monkey, a blockhead who was always deriding everyone, a very bitter enemy of mine from our days in the lower forms—a vulgar, impudent, swaggering fellow, who affected a most sensitive feeling of personal honor, though, of course, he was a wretched little coward at heart. He was one of those worshipers of Zverkov who made up to the latter from interested motives, and often borrowed money from him. Simonov's other visitor, Trudolyubov, was a person in no way remarkable—a tall young fellow, in the army, with a cold face, fairly honest, though he worshiped success of every sort, and was only capable of thinking of promotion. He was some sort of distant relation of Zverkov's, and this, foolish as it seems, gave him a certain importance among us. He always thought me of no consequence whatever; his behavior to me, though not quite courteous, was tolerable.

"Well, with seven roubles each," said Trudolyubov, "twenty-one roubles between the three of us, we ought to be able to get a good dinner. Zverkov, of course, won't pay."

"Of course not, since we are inviting him," Simonov decided.

"Can you imagine," Ferfichkin interrupted hotly and conceitedly, like some insolent flunky boasting of his master the general's decorations, "can you imagine that Zverkov will let us pay alone? He will accept from delicacy, but he will order half a dozen bottles of champagne."

"Do we want half a dozen for the four of us?" observed Trudolyubov, taking notice only of the half-dozen.

"So the three of us, with Zverkov for the fourth, twenty-one roubles, at the Hôtel de Paris at five o'clock tomorrow," Simonov, who had been asked to make the arrangements, concluded finally.

"How twenty-one roubles?" I asked in some agitation, with a show of being offended; "if you count me, it will not be twenty-one, but twenty-eight roubles."

It seemed to me that to invite myself so suddenly and unexpectedly would be positively graceful, and that they would all be conquered at once and would look at me with respect.

"Do you want to join, too?" Simonov observed, with no

appearance of pleasure, seeming to avoid looking at me. He knew me through and through.

It infuriated me that he knew me so thoroughly.

"Why not? I am an old schoolfellow of his, too, I believe, and I must own I feel hurt that you have left me out," I said, boiling over again.

"And where were we to find you?" Ferfichkin put in roughly.

"You never were on good terms with Zverkov," Trudolyubov added, frowning.

But I had already clutched at the idea and would not give it up.

"It seems to me that no one has a right to form an opinion upon that," I retorted in a shaking voice, as though something tremendous had happened. "Perhaps that is just my reason for wishing it now, that I have not always been on good terms with him."

"Oh, there's no making you out . . . with these refinements," Trudolyubov jeered.

"We'll put your name down," Simonov decided, addressing me. "Tomorrow at five o'clock at the Hôtel de Paris."

"What about the money?" Ferfichkin began in an undertone, indicating me to Simonov, but he broke off, for even Simonov was embarrassed.

"That will do," said Trudolyubov, getting up. "If he wants to come so much, let him."

"But it's a private thing, among us friends," Ferfichkin said crossly, as he, too, picked up his hat. "It's not an official gathering."

"We do not want at all, perhaps . . ."

They went away. Ferfichkin did not greet me in any way as he went out, Trudolyubov barely nodded. Simonov, with whom I was left tête-à-tête, was in a state of vexation and perplexity, and looked at me queerly. He did not sit down and did not ask me to.

"H'm . . . yes . . . tomorrow, then. Will you pay your share now? I just ask so as to know," he muttered in embarrassment.

I flushed crimson, and as I did so I remembered that I had owed Simonov fifteen roubles for ages—which I had, indeed, never forgotten, though I had not paid it.

"You will understand, Simonov, that I could have no idea when I came here. . . . I am very much vexed that I have forgotten. . . ."

"All right, all right, that doesn't matter. You can pay tomorrow after the dinner. I simply wanted to know. . . . Please don't . . ."

He broke off and began pacing the room, still more vexed. As he walked he began to stamp with his heels.

"Am I keeping you?" I asked, after two minutes of silence.

"Oh!" he said, starting, "that is—to be truthful—yes. I have to go and see someone . . . not far from here," he added in an apologetic voice, somewhat abashed.

"My goodness, why didn't you say so?" I cried, seizing my cap, with an astonishingly free and easy air, which was the last thing I should have expected of myself.

"It's close by . . . not two paces away," Simonov repeated, accompanying me to the front door with a fussy air which did not suit him at all. "So five o'clock, punctually, tomorrow," he called down the stairs after me. He was very glad to get rid of me. I was in a fury.

"What possessed me, what possessed me to force myself upon them?" I wondered, grinding my teeth as I strode along the street, "for a scoundrel, a pig like that Zverkov! Of course, I had better not go; of course, I must just snap my fingers at them. I am not bound in any way. I'll send Simonov a note by tomorrow's post. . . ."

But what made me furious was that I knew for certain that I should go, that I should make a point of going; and the more tactless, the more unseemly my going would be, the more certainly I would go.

And there was a positive obstacle to my going: I had no money. All I had was nine roubles, I had to give seven of that to my servant, Apollon, for his monthly wages. That was all I paid him—he had to keep himself.

Not to pay him was impossible, considering his character. But I will talk about that fellow, about that plague of mine, another time.

However, I knew I should go and should not pay him his wages.

That night I had the most hideous dreams. No wonder; all the evening I had been oppressed by memories of my miserable days at school, and I could not shake them off. I was sent to the school by distant relations, upon whom I was dependent and of whom I have heard nothing since—they sent me there, a forlorn, silent boy, already crushed by their reproaches, already troubled by doubt, and looking with savage distrust at everyone. My schoolfellows met me with spiteful and merciless gibes because I was not like any of them. But I could not endure their taunts; I could not give in to them with the ignoble readiness with which they gave in to one another. I hated them from the first, and shut myself away from everyone in timid, wounded, and disproportionate pride. Their coarseness revolted me. They laughed cynically at my face, at my clumsy figure; and yet what stupid faces they had themselves. In our school the boys' faces seemed in a special way to degenerate and grow stupider. How many fine-looking boys came to us! In a few years they became repulsive. Even at sixteen I wondered at them morosely; even then I was struck by the pettiness of their thoughts, the stupidity of their pursuits, their games, their conversations. They had no understanding of such essential things, they took no interest in such striking, impressive subjects, that I could not help considering them inferior to myself. It was not wounded vanity that drove me to it, and for God's sake do not thrust upon me your hackneyed remarks, repeated to nausea, that "I was only a dreamer," while they even then had an understanding of life. They understood nothing, they had no idea of real life, and I swear that that was what made me most indignant with them. On the contrary, the most obvious, striking reality they accepted with fantastic stupidity and even at that time were accustomed to respect success.

Everything that was just, but despised and looked down upon, they laughed at heartlessly and shamefully. They took rank for intelligence; even at sixteen they were already talking about a snug berth. Of course, a great deal of it was due to their stupidity, to the bad examples with which they had always been surrounded in their childhood and boyhood. They were monstrously depraved. Of course, a great deal of that, too, was superficial and an assumption of cynicism; of course, there were glimpses of youth and freshness even in their depravity; but even that freshness was not attractive, and showed itself in a certain rakishness.

I hated them horribly, though perhaps I was worse than any of them. They repaid me in the same way, and did not conceal their aversion for me. But by then I did not desire their affection: on the contrary I continually longed for their humiliation. To escape from their derision I purposely began to make all the progress I could with my studies and forced my way to the very top. This impressed them. Moreover, they all began by degrees to grasp that I had already read books none of them could read, and understood things (not forming part of our school curriculum) of which they had not even heard. They took a savage and sarcastic view of it, but were morally impressed, especially as the teachers began to notice me on those grounds. The mockery ceased, but the hostility remained, and cold and strained relations became permanent between us.

In the end I could not put up with it: with the years a craving for society, for friends, developed in me. I attempted to get on friendly terms with some of my schoolfellows; but somehow or other my intimacy with them was always strained and soon ended of itself. Once, indeed, I did have a friend. But I was already a tyrant at heart; I wanted to exercise unbounded sway over him; I tried to instill into him a contempt for his surroundings; I required of him a disdainful and complete break with those surroundings. I frightened him with my passionate affection; I reduced him to tears, to hysterics. He was a simple and devoted soul; but when he devoted himself to me entirely

I began to hate him immediately and repulsed him—as though all I needed him for was to win a victory over him, to subjugate him and nothing else. But I could not subjugate all of them; my friend was not at all like them either, he was, in fact, a rare exception. The first thing I did on leaving school was to give up the special job for which I had been destined so as to break all ties, to curse my past and shake the dust from off my feet. . . . And goodness knows why, after all that, I should go trudging off to Simonov's!

Early next morning I roused myself and jumped out of bed with excitement, as though it were all about to happen at once. But I believed that some radical change in my life was coming, and would inevitably come that day. Owing to its rarity, perhaps, any external event, however trivial, always made me feel as though some radical change in my life were at hand. I went to the office, however, as usual, but sneaked away home two hours earlier to get ready. The great thing, I thought, is not to be the first to arrive, or they will think I am overjoyed at coming. But there were thousands of such great points to consider, and they all agitated and overwhelmed me. I polished my boots a second time with my own hands; nothing in the world would have induced Apollon to clean them twice a day, as he considered that it was more than his duties required of him. I stole the brushes to clean them from the passage, being careful he should not detect it, for fear of his contempt. Then I minutely examined my clothes and thought that everything looked old, worn, and threadbare. I had let myself get too slovenly. My uniform, perhaps, was tidy, but I could not go out to dinner in my uniform. The worst of it was that on the knee of my trousers was a big yellow stain. I had a foreboding that that stain would deprive me of nine-tenths of my personal dignity. I knew, too, that it was very abject to think so. "But this is no time for thinking: now I am in for the real thing," I thought, and my heart sank. I knew, too, perfectly well even then, that I was monstrously exaggerating the facts. But how could I help it? I could not control myself and was already shaking with fever. With despair I pictured to myself how coldly and disdainfully that "scoundrel" Zverkov would meet me; with what dull-witted, invincible contempt the blockhead Trudolyubov would look at me; with what impudent rudeness the insect Ferfichkin would snigger at me in order to curry favor with Zverkov; how completely Simonov would take it all in, and how he would despise me for the abjectness of my vanity and lack of spirit—and, worst of all, how paltry, *unliterary*, commonplace it would all be.

Of course, the best thing would be not to go at all. But that was altogether impossible; if I feel impelled to do anything, I seem to be pitchforked into it. I should have jeered at myself ever afterward: "So you funked it, you funked it, you funked the *real thing!*" On the contrary, I passionately longed to show all that "rabble" that I was by no means such a spiritless creature as I seemed to myself. What is more, even in the acutest paroxysm of this cowardly fever, I dreamed of getting the upper hand, of dominating them, carrying them away, making them like me—if only for my "elevation of thought and unmistakable wit." They would abandon Zverkov, he would sit on one side, silent and ashamed, while I should crush him. Then, perhaps, we would be reconciled and drink to our everlasting friendship; but what was most bitter and most humiliating for me was that I knew even then, knew fully and for certain, that I needed nothing of all this really, that I did not really want to crush, to subdue, to attract them, and that I did not care a straw really for the result, even if I did achieve it. Oh, how I prayed for the day to pass quickly! In unutterable anguish I went to the window, opened the movable pane, and looked out into the troubled darkness of the thickly falling wet snow.

At last my wretched little clock hissed out five. I seized my hat and, trying not to look at Apollon, who had been all day expecting his month's wages, but in his foolishness was unwilling to be the first to speak about it, I slipped between him and the door and, jumping into a high-class sledge, on which I spent my last half-rouble, I drove up in grand style to the Hôtel de Paris.

IV

I had been certain the day before that I should be the first to arrive. But it was not a question of being the first to arrive. Not only were they not there, but I had difficulty in finding our room. The table was not even laid. What did it mean? After a good many questions I elicited from the waiters that the dinner had been ordered not for five, but for six o'clock. This was confirmed at the buffet too. I felt really ashamed to go on questioning them. It was only twenty-five minutes past five. If they changed the dinner hour they ought at least to have let me know—that is what the post is for, and not to have put me in an absurd position in my own eyes and . . . and even before the waiters. I sat down; the servant began laying the table; I felt even more humiliated when he was present. Toward six o'clock they brought in candles, though there were lamps burning in the room. It had not occurred to the waiter, however, to bring them in at once when I arrived. In the next room two gloomy, angry-looking persons were eating their dinners in silence at two different tables. There was a great deal of noise, even shouting, in a room further away; one could hear the laughter of a crowd of people, and nasty little shrieks in French: there were ladies at the dinner. It was sickening, in fact. I have rarely passed more wretched moments, so much so that when they did arrive all together punctually at six I was overjoyed to see them, as though they were my deliverers, and even forgot that it was incumbent upon me to show resentment.

Zverkov walked in at the head of them; evidently he was the leading spirit. He and all of them were laughing; but, seeing me, Zverkov drew himself up a little, and walked up to me slowly with a slight, rather jaunty bend from the waist. He shook hands with me in a friendly, but not overfriendly, fashion, with a sort of circumspect courtesy like that of a general, as though in giving me his hand he were warding off something. I had imagined, on the contrary, that on coming in he would at once break into his habitual thin, shrill laugh and fall to making his insipid jokes and witticisms. I had been preparing for them ever since the previous day, but I had not expected such condescension, such high-official courtesy. So, then, he felt himself ineffably superior to me in every respect! If he only meant to insult me by that high-official tone, it would not matter, I thought—I could pay him back for it one way or another. But what if, in reality, without the least desire to be offensive, that sheepshead had a notion in earnest that he was superior to me and could only look at me in a patronizing way? The very supposition made me gasp.

"I was surprised to hear of your desire to join us," he began, lisping and drawling, which was something new. "You and I seem to have seen nothing of one another. You fight shy of us. You shouldn't. We are not such terrible people as you think. Well, anyway, I am glad to renew our acquaintance."

And he turned carelessly to put his hat down on the window sill.

"Have you been waiting long?" Trudolyubov inquired.

"I arrived at five o'clock as you told me yesterday," I answered aloud, with an irritability that threatened an explosion.

"Didn't you let him know that we had changed the hour?" said Trudolyubov to Simonov.

"No, I didn't. I forgot," the latter replied, with no sign of regret, and without even apologizing to me he went off to order the hors d'oeuvres.

"So you've been here a whole hour? Oh, poor fellow!" Zverkov cried ironically, for to his notions this was bound to be extremely funny. That rascal Ferfichkin followed with his nasty little snigger like a puppy yapping. My position struck him, too, as exquisitely ludicrous and embarrassing.

"It isn't funny at all!" I cried to Ferfichkin, more and more irritated. "It wasn't my fault, but other people's. They neglected to let me know. It was . . . it was . . . it was simply absurd."

"It's not only absurd, but something else as well," muttered Trudolyubov, naïvely taking my part. "You are not hard enough upon it. It was simply rudeness—unintentional, of course. And how could Simonov . . . h'm!"

"If a trick like that had been played on me," observed Ferfichkin, "I should . . ."

"But you should have ordered something for yourself," Zverkov interrupted, "or simply asked for dinner without waiting for us."

"You will allow that I might have done that without your permission," I rapped out. "If I waited, it was . . ."

"Let us sit down, gentlemen," cried Simonov, coming in. "Everything is ready; I can answer for the champagne; it is capitally frozen. . . . You see, I did not know your address, where was I to look for you?" he suddenly turned to me, but again he seemed to avoid looking at me. Evidently he had something against me. It must have been what happened yesterday.

All sat down; I did the same. It was a round table. Trudolyubov was on my left, Simonov on my right. Zverkov was sitting opposite, Ferfichkin next to him, between him and Trudolyubov.

"Tell me, are you . . . in a government office?" Zverkov went on making a show of an interest in me. Seeing that I was embarrassed, he seriously thought that he ought to be friendly to me, and, so to speak, cheer me up.

"Does he want me to throw a bottle at his head?" I thought, in a fury. In my novel surroundings I was unnaturally ready to be irritated.

"In the N—— office," I answered jerkily, with my eyes on my plate.

"And ha-ave you a go-od berth? I say, what ma-ade you leave your original job?"

"What ma-ade me was that I wanted to leave my original job," I drawled more than he, hardly able to control myself. Ferfichkin went off into a guffaw. Simonov looked at me ironically. Trudolyubov left off eating and began looking at me with curiosity.

Zverkov winced, but he tried not to notice it.

"And the remuneration?"

"What remuneration?"

"I mean, your sa-alary?"

"Why are you cross-examining me?" However, I told him at once what my salary was. I turned horribly red.

"It is not very handsome," Zverkov observed majestically.

"Yes, you can't afford to dine at cafés on that," Ferfichkin added insolently.

"To my thinking it's very poor," Trudolyubov observed gravely.

"And how thin you have grown! How you have changed!" added Zverkov, with a shade of venom in his voice, scanning me and my attire with a sort of insolent compassion.

"Oh, spare his blushes," cried Ferfichkin, sniggering.

"My dear sir, allow me to tell you I am not blushing," I broke out at last; "do you hear? I am dining here, at this café, at my own expense, not at other people's—note that, Mr. Ferfichkin."

"What-at? Isn't everyone here dining at his own expense? You would seem to be . . ." Ferfichkin flew out at me, turning as red as a lobster, and looking me in the eye with fury.

"Yes," I answered, feeling I had gone too far, "and I imagine it would be better to talk of something more intelligent."

"You intend to show off your intelligence, I suppose?"

"Don't disturb yourself, that would be quite out of place here."

"Why are you clacking away like that, my good sir, eh? Have you gone out of your wits in your government office?"

"Enough, gentlemen, enough!" Zverkov cried authoritatively.

"How stupid it is!" muttered Simonov.

"It really is stupid. We have met here, a company of friends, for a farewell dinner to a comrade, and you carry on an altercation," said Trudolyubov, rudely addressing himself to me alone. "You invited yourself to join us, so don't disturb the general harmony."

"Enough, enough!" cried Zverkov. "Give over, gentlemen, it's out of place. Better let me tell you how I nearly got married the day before yesterday. . . ."

And then followed a burlesque narrative of how this gentleman had almost been married two days before. There was not a word about the marriage, however, but the story was adorned with generals, colonels, and kammer-junkers, while Zverkov almost took the lead among them. It was greeted with approving laughter; Ferfichkin positively squealed.

No one paid any attention to me, and I sat crushed and humiliated.

"Good Heavens, these are not the people for me!" I thought. "And what a fool I have made of myself before them! I let Ferfichkin go too far, though. The brutes imagine they are doing me an honor in letting me sit down with them. They don't understand that it's an honor to them and not to me! I've grown thinner! My clothes! Oh, damn my trousers! Zverkov noticed the yellow stain on the knee as soon as he came in. . . . But what's the use! I must get up at once, this very minute, take my hat, and simply go without a word . . . with contempt! And tomorrow I can send a challenge. The scoundrels! As though I cared about the seven roubles. They may think. . . . Damn it! I don't care about the seven roubles. I'll go this minute!"

Of course I remained.

I drank sherry and Lafite by the glassful in my discomfiture. Being unaccustomed to it, I was quickly affected. My annoyance increased as the wine went to my head. I longed all at once to insult them all in a most flagrant manner and then go away. To seize the moment and show what I could do, so that they would say, "He's clever, though he is absurd," and . . . and . . . in fact, damn them all!

I scanned them all insolently with my drowsy eyes. But they seemed to have forgotten me altogether. They were noisy, vociferous, cheerful. Zverkov was talking all the time. I began listening. Zverkov was talking of some sumptuous lady whom he had at last led on to declaring her love (of course, he was lying like a horse), and how he had been helped in this affair by an intimate friend of his, a Prince Kolya, an officer in the hussars, who had three thousand serfs.

"And yet this Kolya, who has three thousand serfs, has not put in an appearance here tonight to see you off," I cut in suddenly.

For a minute everyone was silent. "You are drunk already." Trudolyubov deigned to notice me at last, glancing contemptuously in my direction. Zverkov, without a word, examined me as though I were an insect. I dropped my eyes. Simonov made haste to fill up the glasses with champagne.

Trudolyubov raised his glass, as did everyone else but me.

"Your health and good luck on the journey!" he cried to Zverkov. "To old times, to our future, hurrah!"

They all tossed off their glasses, and crowded around Zverkov to kiss him. I did not move; my full glass stood untouched before me.

"Why, aren't you going to drink it?" roared Trudolyubov, losing patience and turning menacingly to me.

"I want to make a speech separately, on my own account . . . and then I'll drink it, Mr. Trudolyubov."

"Spiteful brute!" muttered Simonov. I drew myself up in my chair and feverishly seized my glass, prepared for something extraordinary, though I did not know myself precisely what I was going to say.

"*Silence!*" cried Ferfichkin. "Now for a display of wit!"

Zverkov waited very gravely, knowing what was coming.

"Mr. Lieutenant Zverkov," I began, "let me tell you that I hate phrases, phrasemongers, and men in corsets . . . that's the first point, and there is a second one to follow it."

There was a general stir.

"The second point is: I hate ribaldry and ribald talkers.

Especially ribald talkers! The third point: I love justice, truth, and honesty," I went on almost mechanically, for I was beginning to shiver with horror myself and had no idea how I came to be talking like this. "I love thought, Monsieur Zverkov; I love true comradeship, on an equal footing and not . . . H'm . . . I love. . . . But, however, why not? I will drink your health, too, Mr. Zverkov. Seduce the Circassian girls, shoot the enemies of the fatherland, and . . . and . . . to your health, Monsieur Zverkov!"

Zverkov got up from his seat, bowed to me, and said: "I am very much obliged to you." He was frightfully offended and turned pale.

"Damn the fellow!" roared Trudolyubov, bringing his fist down on the table.

"Well, he wants a punch in the face for that," squealed Ferfichkin.

"We ought to turn him out," muttered Simonov.

"Not a word, gentlemen, not a movement!" cried Zverkov solemnly, checking the general indignation. "I thank you all, but I can show him for myself how much value I attach to his words."

"Mr. Ferfichkin, you will give me satisfaction tomorrow for your words just now!" I said aloud, turning with dignity to Ferfichkin.

"A duel, you mean? Certainly," he answered. But probably I was so ridiculous as I challenged him and it was so out of keeping with my appearance that everyone, including Ferfichkin, was prostrate with laughter.

"Yes, let him alone, of course! He is quite drunk," Trudolyubov said with disgust.

"I shall never forgive myself for letting him join us," Simonov muttered again.

"Now is the time to throw a bottle at their heads," I thought to myself. I picked up the bottle . . . and filled my glass. . . . "No, I'd better sit on to the end," I went on thinking; "you would be pleased, my friends, if I went away. Nothing will induce me to go. I'll go on sitting here and drinking to the end, on purpose, as a sign that I don't think you of the slightest consequence. I will go on sitting and drinking, because this is a public house and I paid my entrance money. I'll sit here and drink, for I look upon you as so many pawns, as inanimate pawns. I'll sit here and drink and sing if I want to, yes, sing, for I have the right to . . . to sing. . . . H'm!"

But I did not sing. I simply tried not to look at any of them. I assumed most unconcerned attitudes and waited with impatience for them to speak *first*. But alas, they did not address me! And, oh, how I wished, how I wished at that moment to be reconciled to them! It struck eight, at last nine. They moved from the table to the sofa. Zverkov stretched himself on a lounge and put one foot on a round table. Wine was brought there. He did, as a fact, order three bottles on his own account. I, of course, was not invited to join them. They all sat around him on the sofa. They listened to him, almost with reverence. It was evident that they were fond of him. "What for? What for?" I wondered. From time to time they were moved to drunken enthusiasm and kissed each other. They talked of the Caucasus, of the nature of true passion, of a certain card game, of snug berths in the service, of the income of an hussar called Podharzhevsky, whom none of them knew personally, and rejoiced in the largeness of it, of the extraordinary grace and beauty of a Princess D., whom none of them had ever seen; then it came to Shakespeare's being immortal.

I smiled contemptuously and walked up and down the other side of the room, opposite the sofa, from the table to the stove and back again. I tried my very utmost to show them that I could do without them, and yet I purposely made a noise with my boots, thumping with my heels. But it was all in vain. They paid no attention. I had the patience to walk up and down in front of them from eight o'clock till eleven, in the same place, from the table to the stove and back again. "I walk up and down to please myself and no one can prevent me." The waiter who came into the room stopped, from time to time, to look at me. I was somewhat giddy from turning around so often; at moments it seemed to me that I was in delirium. During those three hours I was three times soaked with sweat and dry again. At times, with an intense, acute pang I was stabbed to the heart by the thought that ten years, twenty years, forty years would pass, and that even in forty years I would remember with loathing and humiliation those filthiest, most ludicrous, and most awful moments of my life. No one could have gone out of his way to degrade himself more shamelessly, and I fully realized it, fully, and yet I went on pacing up and down from the table to the stove. "Oh, if you only knew what thoughts and feelings I am capable of, how cultured I am!" I thought at moments, mentally addressing the sofa on which my enemies were sitting. But my enemies behaved as though I were not in the room. Once—only once—they turned toward me, just when Zverkov was talking about Shakespeare, and I suddenly gave a contemptuous laugh. I laughed in such an affected and disgusting way that they all at once broke off their conversation, and silently and gravely for two minutes watched me walking up and down from the table to the stove, *taking no notice of them*. But nothing came of it: they said nothing, and two minutes later they ceased to notice me again. It struck eleven.

"Friends," cried Zverkov, getting up from the sofa, "let us all be off now, *there!*"

"Of course, of course," the others assented. I turned sharply to Zverkov. I was so harassed, so exhausted, that I would have cut my throat to put an end to it. I was in a fever; my hair, soaked with perspiration, stuck to my forehead and temples.

"Zverkov, I beg your pardon," I said abruptly and resolutely. "Ferfichkin, yours too, and everyone's, everyone's: I have insulted you all!"

"Aha! A duel is not in your line, old man," Ferfichkin hissed venomously.

It sent a sharp pang to my heart.

"No, it's not the duel I am afraid of, Ferfichkin! I am ready to fight you tomorrow, after we are reconciled. I insist upon it, in fact, and you cannot refuse. I want to show you that I am not afraid of a duel. You shall fire first and I shall fire into the air."

"He is comforting himself," said Simonov.

"He's simply raving," said Trudolyubov.

"But let us pass. Why are you barring our way? What do you want?" Zverkov answered disdainfully.

They were all flushed; their eyes were bright: they had been drinking heavily.

"I ask for your friendship, Zverkov; I insulted you, but——"

"Insulted? *You* insulted *me?* Understand, sir, that you never, under any circumstances, could possibly insult *me.*"

"And that's enough for you. Out of the way!" concluded Trudolyubov.

"Olympia is mine, friends, that's agreed!" cried Zverkov.

"We won't dispute your right, we won't dispute your right," the others answered, laughing.

I stood as though spat upon. The party went noisily out of the room. Trudolyubov struck up some stupid song. Simonov remained behind for a moment to tip the waiters. I suddenly went up to him.

"Simonov! give me six roubles!" I said, with desperate resolution.

He looked at me in extreme amazement, with vacant eyes. He, too, was drunk.

"You don't mean you are coming with us?"

"Yes."

"I've no money," he snapped out, and with a scornful laugh he went out of the room.

I clutched at his overcoat. It was a nightmare.

"Simonov, I saw you had money. Why do you refuse me? Am I a scoundrel? Beware of refusing me: if you knew, if you knew why I am asking! My whole future, my whole plans depend upon it!"

Simonov pulled out the money and almost flung it at me.

"Take it, if you have no sense of shame!" he pronounced pitilessly, and ran to overtake them.

I was left for a moment alone. Disorder, the remains of dinner, a broken wineglass on the floor, spilled wine, cigarette ends, fumes of drink and delirium in my brain, an agonizing misery in my heart and finally the waiter, who had seen and heard all and was looking inquisitively into my face.

"I am going there!" I cried. "Either they shall all go down on their knees to beg for my friendship, or I will give Zverkov a slap in the face!"

V

"So this is it, this is it at last—contact with real life," I muttered as I ran headlong downstairs. "This is very different from the Pope's leaving Rome and going to Brazil, very different from the ball on Lake Como!"

"You are a scoundrel," a thought flashed through my mind, "if you laugh at this now."

"No matter!" I cried, answering myself. "Now everything is lost!"

There was no trace of them to be seen, but that made no difference—I knew where they had gone.

At the steps was standing a solitary night sledge-driver in a rough peasant coat, powdered over with the still falling, wet, and as it were warm, snow. It was hot and steamy. The little shaggy piebald horse was also covered with snow and coughing, I remember that very well. I made a rush for the roughly made sledge; but as soon as I raised my foot to get into it, the recollection of how Simonov had just given me six roubles seemed to double me up and I tumbled into the sledge like a sack.

"No, I must do a great deal to make up for all that," I cried. "But I will make up for it or perish on the spot this very night. Start!"

We set off. There was a perfect whirl in my head.

"They won't go down on their knees to beg for my friendship. That is a mirage, a cheap mirage, revolting, romantic, and fantastical—that's another ball on Lake Como. And so I am bound to slap Zverkov's face! It is my duty to. And so it is settled; I am flying to give him a slap in the face. Hurry up!"

The driver tugged at the reins.

"As soon as I go in I'll give it him. Ought I before giving him the slap to say a few words by way of preface? No. I'll simply go in and give it him. They will all be sitting in the drawing room, and he with Olympia on the sofa. That damned Olympia! She laughed at my looks on one occasion and refused me. I'll pull Olympia's hair, pull Zverkov's ears! No, better one ear, and pull him by it around the room. Maybe they will all begin beating me and will kick me out. That's most likely, indeed. No matter! Anyway, I shall first slap him; the initiative will be mine; and by the laws of honor that is everything: he will be branded and cannot wipe off the slap by any blows, by nothing but a duel. He will be forced to fight. And let them beat me now. Let them, the ungrateful wretches! Trudolyubov will beat me hardest, he is so strong; Ferfichkin will be sure to catch hold sideways and tug at my hair. But no matter, no matter! That's what I am going for. The blockheads will be forced at last to see the tragedy of it all! When they drag me to the door I shall call out to them that in reality they are not worth my little finger. Get on, driver, get on!" I cried to the driver. He started and flicked his whip, I shouted so savagely.

"We shall fight at daybreak, that's a settled thing. I've done with the office. Ferfichkin made a joke about it just now. But where can I get pistols? Nonsense! I'll get my salary in advance and buy them. And powder, and bullets? That's the second's business. And how can it all be done by daybreak? And where am I to get a second? I have no friends. Nonsense!" I cried, lashing myself up more and more. "It's of no consequence! the first person I meet in the street is bound to be my second, just as he would be bound to pull a drowning man out of water. The most eccentric things may happen. Even if I were to ask the director himself to be my second tomorrow, he would be bound to consent, if only from a feeling of chivalry, and to keep the secret! Anton Antonych. . . ."

The fact is that at that very minute the disgusting absurdity of my plan and the other side of the question was clearer and more vivid to my imagination than it could be to anyone on earth. But . . .

"Get on, driver, get on, you rascal, get on!"

"Ugh, sir!" said the son of toil.

Cold shivers suddenly ran down me. Wouldn't it be better . . . to go straight home? My God, my God! Why had I invited myself to this dinner yesterday? But no, it's impossible. And my walking up and down for three hours from the table to the stove? No, they, they and no one else must pay for my walking up and down! They must wipe out this dishonor! Drive on!

And what if they give me into custody? They won't dare! They'll be afraid of the scandal. And what if Zverkov is so contemptuous that he refuses to fight a duel? He is sure to; but in that case I'll show them. . . . I will turn up at the posting station when he is setting off tomorrow, I'll catch him by the leg, I'll pull off his coat when he gets into the carriage. I'll get my teeth into his hand, I'll bite him. "See what lengths you can drive a desperate man to!" He may hit me on the head and they may belabor me from behind. I will shout to the assembled multitude, "Look at this young puppy who is driving off to captivate Circassian girls after letting me spit in his face!"

Of course, after that everything will be over! The office will have vanished off the face of the earth. I shall be arrested, I shall be tried, I shall be dismissed from the service, thrown into jail, sent to Siberia. Never mind! In fifteen years when they let me out of prison I will trudge off to him, a beggar, in rags. I shall find him in some provincial town. He will be married and happy. He will have a grown-up daughter. . . . I shall say to him, "Look, monster, at my hollow cheeks and my rags! I've lost everything

—my career, my happiness, art, science, *the woman I loved*, and all through you. Here are pistols. I have come to discharge my pistol and . . . and I . . . forgive you." Then I shall fire into the air and he will hear nothing more of me. . . .

I was actually on the point of tears, though I knew perfectly well at that moment that all this was out of Sylvio[13] and Lermontov's *Masquerade*. And all at once I felt horribly ashamed, so ashamed that I stopped the horse, got out of the sledge, and stood still in the snow in the middle of the street. The driver gazed at me, sighing and astonished.

What was I to do? I could not go on there—it was evidently stupid, and I could not leave things as they were, because that would seem as though . . . Heavens, how could I leave things! And after such insults! "No!" I cried, throwing myself into the sledge again. "It is ordained! It is fate! Drive on, drive on!"

And in my impatience I punched the sledge-driver on the back of the neck.

"What are you up to? What are you hitting me for?" the peasant shouted, but he whipped up his nag so that it began kicking.

The wet snow was falling in big flakes; regardless of it, I unbuttoned my coat. I forgot everything else, for I had finally decided on the slap, and felt with horror that it was going to happen *now*, *at once*, and that *no force could stop it*. The deserted street lamps gleamed sullenly in the snowy darkness like torches at a funeral. The snow drifted under my greatcoat, under my coat, under my cravat, and melted there. I did not wrap myself up—all was lost, anyway.

At last we arrived. I jumped out, almost unconscious, ran up the steps, and began knocking and kicking at the door. I felt fearfully weak, particularly in my legs and my knees. The door was opened quickly as though they knew I was coming. As a fact, Simonov had warned them that perhaps another gentleman would arrive, and this was a place in

[13] Character in Pushkin's story, "The Shot."—A.Y.

which one had to give notice and to observe certain precautions. It was one of those "millinery establishments" which were abolished by the police a good time ago. By day it really was a shop; but at night, if one had an introduction, one might visit it for other purposes.

I walked rapidly through the dark shop into the familiar drawing room, where there was only one candle burning, and stood still in amazement: there was no one there. "Where are they?" I asked somebody. But by now, of course, they had separated. Before me was standing a person with a stupid smile, the "madam" herself, who had seen me before. A minute later a door opened and another person came in.

Taking no notice of anything, I strode about the room, and, I believe, I talked to myself. I felt as though I had been saved from death and was conscious of this, joyfully, all over: I should have given that slap, I should certainly, certainly have given it! But now they were not here and . . . everything had vanished and changed! I looked around. I could not realize my condition yet. I looked mechanically at the girl who had come in: and had a glimpse of a fresh, young, rather pale face, with straight, dark eyebrows, and with grave, as it were wondering, eyes that attracted me at once; I should have hated her if she had been smiling. I began looking at her more intently and, as it were, with effort. I had not fully collected my thoughts. There was something simple and good-natured in her face, but something strangely grave. I am sure that this stood in her way here, and no one of those fools had noticed her. She could not, however, have been called a beauty, though she was tall, strong-looking, and well built. She was very simply dressed. Something loathsome stirred within me. I went straight up to her.

I chanced to look into the glass. My harassed face struck me as revolting in the extreme, pale, angry, abject, with disheveled hair. "No matter, I am glad of it," I thought; "I am glad that I shall seem repulsive to her; I like that."

VI

. . . Somewhere behind a partition a clock began gasping, as though squeezed hard, as though someone were strangling it. After an unnaturally prolonged wheezing there followed a shrill, nasty, and as it were unexpectedly rapid, chime—as though someone were suddenly jumping forward. It struck two. I woke up, though I had indeed not been asleep but lying half-dozing.

It was almost completely dark in the narrow, cramped, low-pitched room, cumbered up with an enormous wardrobe and piles of cardboard boxes and all sorts of frippery and litter. The candle end that had been burning on the table was going out and gave a faint flicker from time to time. In a few minutes there would be complete darkness.

I was not long in coming to myself; everything came back to my mind at once, without an effort, as though it had been in ambush to pounce upon me again. And, indeed, even while I was unconscious a point seemed continually to remain in my memory unforgotten, and around it my dreams moved drearily. But, strange to say, everything that had happened to me on that day seemed to me now, on waking, to be in the far, far away past, as though I had long, long ago lived all that down.

My head was full of fumes. Something seemed to be hovering over me, rousing me, exciting me, and making me restless. Misery and spite seemed surging up in me again and seeking an outlet. Suddenly I saw beside me two wide-open eyes scrutinizing me curiously and persistently. The look in those eyes was coldly detached, sullen, as it were utterly remote; it weighed upon me.

A grim idea came into my brain and passed all over my body, as a horrible sensation, such as one feels when one goes into a damp and moldy cellar. There was something unnatural in those two eyes, beginning to look at me only now. I recalled, too, that during those two hours I had not said a single word to this creature, and had, in fact, considered it utterly superfluous; in fact, the silence had for some reason gratified me. Now I suddenly realized vividly the hideous idea—revolting as a spider—of vice, which, without love, grossly and shamelessly begins with that in which true love finds its consummation. For a long time we gazed at each other like that, but she did not drop her eyes before mine and her expression did not change, so that at last I felt uncomfortable.

"What is your name?" I asked abruptly, to put an end to it.

"Liza," she answered almost in a whisper, but somehow far from graciously, and she turned her eyes away.

I was silent.

"What weather! The snow . . . it's disgusting!" I said, almost to myself, putting my arm under my head despondently, and gazing at the ceiling.

She made no answer. This was horrible.

"Have you always lived in Petersburg?" I asked a minute later, almost angrily, turning my head slightly toward her.

"No."

"Where do you come from?"

"From Riga," she answered reluctantly.

"Are you a German?"

"No, Russian."

"Have you been here long?"

"Where?"

"In this house?"

"A fortnight."

She spoke more and more jerkily. The candle went out; I could no longer distinguish her face.

"Have you a father and mother?"

"Yes . . . no . . . I have."

"Where are they?"

"There . . . in Riga."

"Who are they?"

"Oh, nobody."

"How's that? Who are they? What kind of people?"

"Tradespeople."

"Have you always lived with them?"

"Yes."

"How old are you?"

"Twenty."

"Why did you leave them?"

"Oh, for no reason."

That answer meant, "Let me alone; I feel sick, sad."

We were silent.

God knows why I did not go away. I felt myself more and more sick and dreary. The images of the previous day began of themselves, apart from my will, flitting through my memory in confusion. I suddenly recalled something I had seen that morning when, full of anxious thoughts, I was hurrying to the office.

"I saw them carrying a coffin out yesterday and they nearly dropped it," I suddenly said aloud, not that I desired to open the conversation, but as it were by accident.

"A coffin?"

"Yes, in the Haymarket; they were bringing it up out of a cellar."

"From a cellar?"

"Not from a cellar, but from a basement. Oh, you know —down below—from a house of ill-fame. It was filthy all around. . . . Eggshells, litter—a stench. It was loathsome."

Silence.

"A nasty day to be buried," I began, simply to avoid being silent.

"Nasty, in what way?"

"The snow, the wet." (I yawned.)

"It makes no difference," she said suddenly, after a brief silence.

"No, it's horrid." (I yawned again.) "The gravediggers must have sworn at getting drenched by the snow. And there must have been water in the grave."

"Why water in the grave?" she asked, with a sort of curiosity, but speaking even more harshly and abruptly than before.

I suddenly began to feel provoked.

"Why, there must have been water at the bottom a foot deep. You can't dig a dry grave in Volkovo Cemetery."

"Why?"

"Why? Why, the place is waterlogged. It's a regular marsh. So they bury them in water. I've seen it myself—many times."

(I had never seen it once, indeed I had never been in Volkovo, and had only heard stories of it.)

"Do you mean to say, you don't mind how you die?"

"But why should I die?" she answered, as though defending herself.

"Why, some day you will die, and you will die just the same as that dead woman. She was—a girl like you. She died of consumption."

"A wench would have died in hospital. . . ." (She knows all about it already: she said "wench," not "girl.")

"She was in debt to her madam," I retorted, more and more provoked by the discussion; "and went on earning money for her up to the end, though she was in consumption. Some sledge-drivers standing by were talking about her to some soldiers and telling them so. No doubt they knew her. They were laughing. They were going to meet in a pothouse to drink to her memory."

A great deal of this was my invention. Silence followed, profound silence. She did not stir.

"And is it better to die in a hospital?"

"Isn't it just the same? Besides, why should I die?" she added irritably.

"If not now, a little later."

"Well, then, later."

"Soon enough! Now you are young, pretty, fresh, you fetch a high price. But after another year of this life you will be very different—you will go off."

"In a year?"

"Anyway, in a year you will be worth less," I continued malignantly. "You will go from here to something lower, another house; a year later—to a third, lower and lower, and in seven years you will come to a basement in the Haymarket. That is, if you are lucky. But it would be much worse if you got some disease, consumption, say . . . and caught a chill, or something or other. It's not easy to get over an illness in your way of life. If you catch anything you may not get rid of it. And so you will die."

"Oh, well, then I shall die," she answered, quite viciously, and she made a quick movement.

"Aren't you sorry?"

"Sorry for what?"

"Sorry that life's over."

Silence.

"Have you been engaged to be married? Eh?"

"What's that to you?"

"Oh, I am not cross-examining you. It's nothing to me. Why are you so cross? Of course you may have had your own troubles. What is it to me? It's simply that I felt sorry."

"Sorry for whom?"

"Sorry for you."

"No need," she whispered hardly audibly, and again made a faint movement.

That incensed me at once. What! I was so gentle with her, and she . . .

"Why, do you think that you are on the right path?"

"I don't think anything."

"That's what's wrong, that you don't think. Realize it while there is still time. There still is time. You are still young, good-looking; you might love, be married, be happy. . . ."

"Not all married women are happy," she snapped out in the rude abrupt tone she had used at first.

"Not all, of course, but anyway it is much better than the life here. Infinitely better. Besides, with love one can live even without happiness. Even in sorrow life is sweet; life is sweet, however one lives. But here what is there but . . . foulness. Phew!"

I turned away with disgust; I was no longer reasoning coldly. I began myself to feel what I was saying and warmed to the subject. I was already longing to expound the cherished ideas I had brooded over in my corner. Something suddenly flared up in me. An object had appeared before me.

"Never mind my being here, I am not an example for you. I am, perhaps, worse than you are. I was drunk when I came here, though," I hastened, however, to say in self-defense. "Besides, a man is no example for a woman. It's a different thing. I may degrade and defile myself, but I am not anyone's slave. I come and go, and that's an end of it. I shake it off, and I am a different man. But you are a slave from the start. Yes, a slave! You give up everything, your whole freedom. If you want to break your chains afterward, you won't be able to: you will be more and more tightly ensnared. It is an accursed bondage. I know it. I won't speak of anything else, maybe you won't understand, but tell me: no doubt you are in debt to your madam? There, you see," I added, though she made no answer, but only listened in silence, entirely absorbed, "that's a bondage for you! You will never buy your freedom. They will see to that. It's like selling your soul to the devil. . . . And besides . . . perhaps I, too, am just as unlucky—how do you know—and wallow in the mud on purpose, out of misery? You know, men take to drink from grief; well, maybe I am here from grief. Come, tell me, what is there good here? Here you and I—came together—just now and did not say one word to one another all the time, and it was only afterward you began staring at me like a wild creature, and I at you. Is that loving? Is that how one human being should meet another? It's hideous, that's what it is!"

"Yes!" she assented sharply and hurriedly.

I was positively astounded by the promptitude of this "Yes." So the same thought may have been straying through her mind when she was staring at me just before. So she, too, was capable of certain thoughts? "Damn it all, this is interesting, this is kinship!" I thought, almost rubbing my hands. And indeed it's easy to master a young soul like that!

It was the game that attracted me most.

She turned her head nearer to me, and it seemed to me in the darkness that she propped herself on her arm. Perhaps she was scrutinizing me. How I regretted that I could not see her eyes. I heard her deep breathing.

"Why have you come here?" I asked her, with a note of authority already in my voice.

"Oh, I don't know."

"But how nice it would be to be living in your father's house! It's warm and free; you have a home of your own."

"But what if it's worse than this?"

"I must take the right tone," flashed through my mind. "I may not get far with sentimentality." But it was only a momentary thought. I swear she really did interest me. Besides, I was exhausted and moody. And cunning so easily goes hand in hand with feeling.

"Who denies it!" I hastened to answer. "Anything may happen. I am convinced that someone has wronged you, and that you are more sinned against than sinning. Of course, I know nothing of your story, but it's not likely a girl like you has come here of her own inclination. . . ."

"A girl like me?" she whispered, hardly audibly; but I heard it.

Damn it all, I was flattering her. That was horrid. But perhaps it was a good thing. . . . She was silent.

"See, Liza, I will tell you about myself. If I had had a home from childhood, I shouldn't be what I am now. I often think that. However bad it may be at home, anyway they are your father and mother, and not enemies, strangers. Once a year at least, they'll show their love of you. Anyway, you know you are at home. I grew up without a home; and perhaps that's why I've turned so—unfeeling."

I waited again. "Perhaps she doesn't understand," I thought, "and, indeed, it is absurd—it's moralizing."

"If I were a father and had a daughter, I believe I should love my daughter more than my sons, really," I began indirectly, as though talking of something else, to distract her attention. I must confess I blushed.

"Why so?" she asked.

Ah! so she was listening!

"I don't know, Liza. I knew a father who was a stern, austere man, but used to go down on his knees to his daughter, used to kiss her hands, her feet, he couldn't make enough of her, really. When she danced at parties he used to stand for five hours at a stretch, gazing at her. He was mad over her: I understand that! She would fall asleep tired at night, and he would wake to kiss her in her sleep and make the sign of the cross over her. He would go about in a dirty old coat, he was stingy to everyone else, but would spend his last groat for her, giving her expensive presents, and it was his greatest delight when she was pleased with what he gave her. Fathers always love their daughters more than the mothers do. Some girls live happily at home! And I believe I should never let my daughters marry."

"What next?" she said, with a faint smile.

"I should be jealous, I really should. To think that she should kiss anyone else! That she should love a stranger more than her father! It's painful to imagine it. Of course, that's all nonsense, of course every father would be reasonable at last. But I believe before I should let her marry, I should worry myself to death; I should find fault with all her suitors. But I should end by letting her marry whom she herself loved. The one whom the daughter loves always seems the worst to the father, you know. That is always so. So many family troubles come from that."

"Some are glad to sell their daughters, rather than marrying them honorably."

Ah, so that was it!

"Such a thing, Liza, happens in those accursed families in which there is neither love nor God," I retorted warmly, "and where there is no love, there is no sense either. There are such families, it's true, but I am not speaking of them. You must have seen wickedness in your own family, if you talk like that. Truly, you must have been unlucky. M'h! . . . that sort of thing mostly comes about through poverty."

"And is it any better with the gentry? Even among the poor, honest people live happily."

"H'm . . . yes. Perhaps. Another thing, Liza, man is fond of reckoning up his troubles, but does not count his joys. If he counted them up as he ought, he would see that every lot has enough happiness provided for it. And what if all goes well with the family, if the blessing of God is upon it, if the husband is a good one, loves you, cherishes you, never leaves you! There is happiness in such a family! Sometimes there is even happiness in the midst of sorrow; and indeed sorrow is everywhere. If you marry *you will find out for yourself*. But think of the first years of married life with one you love: what happiness, what happiness there sometimes is in it! And indeed it's the ordinary thing. In those early days even quarrels with one's husband end happily. Some women get up quarrels with their husbands just because they love them. Indeed, I knew a woman like that: she seemed to say that, because she loved him, she would torment him and make him feel it. You know that you may torment a man on purpose through love. Women are particularly given to that, thinking to themselves, 'I will love him so, I will make so much of him afterward, that it's no sin to torment him a little now.' And all in the house rejoice in the sight of you, and you are happy and gay and peaceful and honorable. . . . Then there are some women who are jealous. If he went off anywhere—I knew one such woman, she couldn't restrain herself, but would jump up at night and run off on the sly to find out where he was, whether he was with some other woman. That's a pity. And the woman herself knows it's wrong, and her heart fails her and she suffers, but she loves—it's all through love. And how sweet it is to make it up after quarrels, to own herself in the wrong or to forgive him! And they are both so happy all at once—as though they had met anew, been married over again; as though their love had begun afresh. And no one, no one should know what passes between husband and wife if they love one another. And whatever quarrels there may be between them they ought not to call in their own mother to judge between them and tell tales of one another. They are their own judges. Love is a holy mystery and ought to be hidden from all other eyes, whatever happens. That makes it holier and better. They respect one another more, and much is built on respect. And if once there has been love, if they have married for love, why should love pass away? Surely one can keep it! It is rare that one cannot keep it. And if the husband is kind and straightforward, why should not love last? The first phase of married love will pass, it is true, but then there will come a love that is better still. Then there will be the union of souls, they will have everything in common, there will be no secrets between them. And once they have children, the most difficult times will seem happy to them, so long as there is love and courage. Even toil will be a joy, you may deny yourself bread for your children and even that will be a joy. They will love you for it afterward; so you are laying by for your future. As the children grow up you feel that you are an example, a support for them; that even after you die your children will always keep your thoughts and feelings, because they have received them from you, they will take on your semblance and likeness. So you see this is a great duty. How can it fail to draw the father and mother nearer? People say it's a trial to have children. Who says that? It is heavenly happiness! Are you fond of little children, Liza? I am awfully fond of them. You know—a little rosy baby boy at your bosom, and what husband's heart is not touched, seeing his wife nursing his child! A plump little rosy baby, sprawling and snuggling, chubby little hands and feet, clean tiny little nails, so tiny that it makes one laugh to look at them; eyes that look as if they understand everything. And while it sucks, it clutches at your bosom with its little hand, plays. When its father comes up, the child tears itself away from the bosom, flings itself back, looks at its father, laughs, as though it were fearfully funny, and falls to sucking again. Or it will bite its mother's breast when its little teeth are coming, while it looks sideways at her with its little eyes as though to say, 'Look, I am biting!'

Is not all that happiness when the three are together, husband, wife, and child? One can forgive a great deal for the sake of such moments. Yes, Liza, one must first learn to live oneself before one blames others!"

"It's with pictures, pictures like that one must get at you," I thought to myself, though I did speak with real feeling, and all at once I flushed crimson. "What if she were suddenly to burst out laughing, what should I do then?" That idea drove me to fury. Toward the end of my speech I really was excited, and now my vanity was somehow wounded. The silence continued. I almost nudged her.

"Why are you——" she began and stopped.

But I understood: there was a quiver of something different in her voice, not abrupt, harsh, and unyielding as before, but something soft and shamefaced, so shamefaced that I suddenly felt ashamed and guilty.

"What?" I asked, with tender curiosity.

"Why, you . . ."

"What?"

"Why, you—speak somehow like a book," she said, and again there was a note of irony in her voice.

That remark sent a pang to my heart. It was not what I was expecting.

I did not understand that she was hiding her feelings under irony, that this is usually the last refuge of modest and chaste-souled people when the privacy of their souls is coarsely and intrusively invaded, and that their pride makes them refuse to surrender till the last moment and shrink from giving expression to their feelings before you. I ought to have guessed the truth from the timidity with which she had repeatedly approached her sarcasm, only bringing herself to utter it at last with an effort. But I did not guess, and an evil feeling took possession of me.

"Wait a bit!" I thought.

"Oh, hush, Liza! How can you talk about being like a book, when it makes even me, an outsider, feel sick? Though I don't look at it as an outsider, for, indeed, it touches me to the heart. . . . Is it possible, is it possible that you do not feel sick at being here yourself? Evidently habit does wonders! God knows what habit can do to one. Can you seriously think that you will never grow old, that you will always be good-looking, and that they will keep you here forever and ever? I say nothing of the loathsomeness of the life here. . . . Though let me tell you this about it—about your present life, I mean; though you are young now, attractive, nice, with soul and feeling, yet you know as soon as I came to myself just now I felt at once sick at being here with you! One can only come here when one is drunk. But if you were anywhere else, living as good people live, I should perhaps be more than attracted by you, should fall in love with you, should be glad of a look from you, let alone a word; I should hang about your door, should go down on my knees to you, should look upon you as my betrothed, and think it an honor to be allowed to. I should not dare to have an impure thought about you. But here, you see, I know that I have only to whistle and you have to come with me whether you like it or not. I don't consult your wishes, but you mine. The lowest laborer hires himself as a workman but he doesn't make a slave of himself altogether; besides, he knows that he will be free again presently. But when are you free? Only think what you are giving up here! What is it you are making a slave of? It is your soul, together with your body; you are selling your soul, which you have no right to dispose of! You give your love to be outraged by every drunkard! Love! But that's everything, you know, it's a priceless diamond, it's a maiden's treasure, love—why, a man would be ready to give his soul, to face death to gain that love. But how much is your love worth now? You are sold, all of you, body and soul, and there is no need to strive for love when you can have everything without love. And you know there is no greater insult to a girl than that, do you understand? To be sure, I have heard that they comfort you, poor fools, they let you have lovers of your own here. But you know that's simply a farce, that's simply a sham, it's just laughing at you, and you are taken in by it! Why, do you suppose he really loves you, that lover of yours? I don't believe it. How can he love you when he knows you may be called away from him any minute? He would be a low fellow if he did! Will he have a grain of respect for you? What have you in common with him? He laughs at you and robs you—that is all his love amounts to! You are lucky if he does not beat you. Very likely he does beat you, too. Ask him, if you have got one, whether he will marry you. He will laugh in your face, if he doesn't spit in it or give you a blow—though maybe all he is worth himself is two bad groats. And for what have you ruined your life, if you come to think of it? For the coffee they give you to drink and the plentiful meals? But with what object are they feeding you up? An honest girl couldn't swallow the food, for she would know what she was being fed for. You are in debt here, and, of course, you will always be in debt, and you will go on in debt to the end, till the visitors here begin to scorn you. And that will soon happen, don't rely upon your youth—all that flies by express train here, you know. You will be kicked out. And not simply kicked out; long before that she'll begin nagging at you, scolding you, abusing you, as though you had not sacrificed your health for her, had not thrown away your youth and your soul for her benefit, but as though you had ruined her, beggared her, robbed her. And don't expect anyone to take your part: the others, your companions, will attack you, too, to win her favor, for all are in slavery here, and have lost all conscience and pity here long ago. They have become utterly vile, and nothing on earth is viler, more loathsome, and more insulting than their abuse. And you are laying down everything here, unconditionally, youth and health and beauty and hope, and at twenty-two you will look like a woman of five and thirty, and you will be lucky if you are not diseased, pray to God to keep you from it! No doubt you are thinking now that you have a gay time and no work to do! Yet there is no work harder or more dreadful in the world or ever has been. One would think that the heart alone would be worn out with tears. And you won't dare to say a word, not half a word when they drive you away from here; you will go away as though you were to blame. You will change to another house, then to a third, then somewhere else, till you come down at last to the Haymarket. There you will be beaten at every turn; that is good manners there, the visitors don't know how to be friendly without beating you. You don't believe that it is so hateful there? Go and look for yourself some time, you can see with your own eyes. Once, one New Year's Day, I saw a woman at a door. They had turned her out as a joke, to give her a taste of the frost because she had been crying so much, and they shut the door behind her. At nine o'clock in the morning she was already quite drunk, disheveled, half-naked, covered with bruises, her face was powdered, but she had a black eye, blood was trickling from her nose and her teeth; some cabman had just given her a drubbing. She was sitting on the stone steps, a salt fish of some sort was in her hand; she was crying, wailing something about her luck and beating with the fish on the steps, and cabmen and drunken soldiers were crowding in the doorway taunting her. You don't believe that you will ever be like that? I should be sorry to believe it, too, but how do you know? Maybe ten years, eight years ago that very woman with the salt fish came here fresh as a cherub, innocent, pure, knowing no evil, blushing at every word. Perhaps she was like you, proud, ready to take offense, not like the others; perhaps she looked like a queen, and knew what happiness was in store for the man who would love her and whom she would love. Do you see how it ended? And what if at that very minute when she was beating on the filthy steps with that fish, drunken and disheveled—what if at that very minute she recalled the pure early days in her father's house, when she used to go to school and the neighbor's son watched for her on the way, declaring that he would love her as long as he lived, that he would devote his life to her, and when they vowed to love one another forever and be married as soon as they were grown up! No, Liza, it would be happy for you if you were to die soon of consumption in some corner, in some cellar like that woman just now. In the hospital, do you say? You will be lucky if they take you, but what if you are still of use to the madam here? Consumption is a queer disease, it is not like fever. The patient goes on hoping till the last minute and says he is all right. He deludes himself. And that just suits your madam. Don't doubt it, that's how it is; you have sold your soul, and what is more you owe money, so you daren't say a word. But when you are dying, all will abandon you, all will turn away from you, for then there will be nothing to get from you. What's more, they will reproach you for cumbering the place, for being so long over dying. However you beg, you won't get a drink of water without abuse: 'Whenever are you going off, you nasty hussy, you won't let us sleep with your moaning, you make the gentlemen sick.' That's true, I have heard such things said myself. They will thrust you dying into the filthiest corner in the cellar—in the damp and darkness; what will your thoughts be, lying there alone? When you die, strange hands will lay you out, with grumbling and impatience; no one will bless you, no one will sigh for you, they will only want to get rid of you as soon as may be; they will buy a coffin, take you to the grave as they did that poor woman today, and celebrate your memory at the tavern. In the grave, sleet, filth, wet snow—no need to put themselves out for you—'Let her down, Vanyuha; it's just like her luck—even here, she is head-foremost, the hussy. Shorten the cord, you rascal.' 'It's all right as it is.' 'All right, is it? Why, she's on her side! She was a fellow-creature, after all! But, never mind, throw the earth on her.' And they won't care to waste much time quarreling over you. They will scatter the wet blue clay as quick as they can and go off to the tavern . . . and there your memory on earth will end; other women have children to go to their graves, fathers, husbands. While for you neither tear, nor sigh, nor remembrance; no one in the whole world will ever come to you, your name will vanish from the face of the earth—as though you had never existed, never been born at all! Nothing but filth and mud, however you knock at your coffin lid at night, when the dead arise, however you cry, 'Let me out, kind people, to live in the light of day! My life was no life at all; my life has been thrown away like a dishclout; it was drunk away in the tavern at the Haymarket; let me out, kind people, to live in the world again.'"

And I worked myself up to such a pitch that I began to have a lump in my throat myself, and—and all at once I stopped, sat up in dismay, and, bending over apprehensively, began to listen with a beating heart. I had reason to be troubled.

I had felt for some time that I was turning her soul upside down and rending her heart, and—and the more I was convinced of it, the more eagerly I desired to gain my object as quickly and as effectually as possible. It was the exercise of my skill that carried me away; yet it was not merely sport. . . .

I knew I was speaking stiffly, artificially, even bookishly, in fact, I could not speak except "like a book." But that did not trouble me: I knew, I felt that I should be understood and that this very bookishness might be an assistance. But now, having attained my effect, I was suddenly panic-stricken. Never before had I witnessed such despair! She was lying on her face, thrusting her face into the pillow and clutching it in both hands. Her heart was being torn. Her youthful body was shuddering all over as though in convulsions. Suppressed sobs rent her bosom and suddenly burst out in weeping and wailing, then she pressed closer into the pillow: she did not want anyone here, not a living soul, to know of her anguish and her tears. She bit the pillow, bit her hand till it bled (I saw that afterward), or, thrusting her fingers into her disheveled hair, seemed rigid with the effort of restraint, holding her breath and clenching her teeth. I began saying something, begging her to calm herself, but felt that I did not dare; and all at once, in a sort of cold shiver, almost in terror, began fumbling in the dark, trying hurriedly to get dressed to go. It was dark: though I tried my best I could not finish dressing quickly. Suddenly I felt a box of matches and a candlestick with a whole candle in it. As soon as the room was lighted up, Liza sprang up, sat up in bed, and, with a contorted face, with a half-insane smile, looked at me almost senselessly. I sat down beside her and took her hands; she came to herself, made an impulsive movement toward me, would have caught hold of me, but did not dare, and slowly bowed her head before me.

"Liza, my dear, I was wrong. . . . Forgive me, my dear," I began, but she squeezed my hand in her fingers so tightly that I felt I was saying the wrong thing and stopped.

"This is my address, Liza, come to me."

"I will come," she answered resolutely, her head still bowed.

"But now I am going, good-by . . . till we meet again."

I got up; she, too, stood up and suddenly flushed all over, gave a shudder, snatched up a shawl that was lying on a chair, and muffled herself in it to her chin. As she did this she gave another sickly smile, blushed, and looked at me strangely. I felt wretched; I was in haste to get away— to disappear.

"Wait a minute," she said suddenly, in the passage just at the doorway, stopping me with her hand on my overcoat. She put down the candle in hot haste and ran off; evidently she had thought of something or wanted to show me something. As she ran away she flushed, her eyes shone, and there was a smile on her lips—what was the meaning of it? Against my will I waited: she came back a minute later with an expression that seemed to ask forgiveness for something. In fact, it was not the same face, not the same look as the evening before: sullen, mistrustful, and obstinate. Her eyes now were imploring, soft, and at the same time trustful, caressing, timid. The expression with which children look at people they are very fond of, of whom they are asking a favor. Her eyes were a light hazel, they were lovely eyes, full of life, and capable of expressing love as well as sullen hatred.

Making no explanation, as though I, as a sort of higher being, must understand everything without explanations, she held out a piece of paper to me. Her whole face was positively beaming at that instant with naïve, almost childish triumph. I unfolded it. It was a letter to her from a medical student or someone of that sort—a very high-flown and flowery, but extremely respectful, love letter. I don't recall the words now, but I remember well that through the high-flown phrases there was apparent a genuine feeling, which cannot be feigned. When I had finished reading it I met her glowing, questioning, and childishly impatient eyes fixed upon me. She fastened her eyes upon my face and waited impatiently for what I should say. In a few words, hurriedly, but with a sort of joy and pride, she explained to me that she had been to a dance somewhere in a private house, a family of "very nice people, *who knew nothing*, absolutely nothing, for she had only come here so lately and it had all happened . . . and she hadn't made up her mind to stay and was certainly going away as soon as she had paid her debt . . ." and at that party there had been the student who had danced with her all the evening. He had talked to her, and it turned out that he had known her in former days in Riga when he was a child, they had played together, but a very long time ago—and he knew her parents, but *about this* he knew nothing, nothing whatever, and had no suspicion! And the day after the dance (three days ago) he had sent her that letter through the friend with whom she had gone to the party . . . and . . . well, that was all.

She dropped her shining eyes with a sort of bashfulness as she finished.

The poor girl was keeping that student's letter as a precious treasure, and had run to fetch it, her only treasure, because she did not want me to go away without knowing that she, too, was honestly and genuinely loved; that she, too, was addressed respectfully. No doubt that letter was destined to lie in her box and lead to nothing. But none the less, I am certain that she would keep it all her life as a precious treasure, as her pride and justification, and now at such a minute she had thought of that letter and brought it with naïve pride to raise herself in my eyes that I might see, that I, too, might think well of her. I said nothing, pressed her hand, and went out. I so longed to get away. . . . I walked all the way home, in spite of the fact that the melting snow was still falling in heavy flakes. I was exhausted, shattered, in bewilderment. But behind the bewilderment the truth was already gleaming. The loathsome truth!

VIII

It was some time, however, before I consented to recognize that truth. Waking up in the morning after some hours of heavy, leaden sleep, and immediately realizing all that had happened on the previous day, I was positively amazed at my last night's *sentimentality* with Liza, at all those "outcries of horror and pity . . . To think of having such an attack of womanish hysteria, pah!" I concluded. And what did I thrust my address upon her for? What if she comes? Let her come, though; it doesn't matter. . . . But *obviously,* that was not now the chief and the most important matter: I had to make haste and at all costs save my reputation in the eyes of Zverkov and Simonov as quickly as possible; that was the chief business. And I was so taken up that morning that I actually forgot all about Liza.

First of all I had at once to repay what I had borrowed the day before from Simonov. I resolved on a desperate measure: to borrow fifteen roubles straight off from Anton Antonych. As luck would have it, he was in the best of humors that morning, and gave it to me at once, on the first asking. I was so delighted at this that, as I signed the

IOU with a swaggering air, I told him casually that the night before "I had been keeping it up with some friends at the Hôtel de Paris; we were giving a farewell party to a comrade, in fact, I might say a friend of my childhood, and you know—a desperate rake, fearfully spoiled—of course, he belongs to a good family, and has considerable means, a brilliant career; he is witty, charming, a regular Lovelace, you understand; we drank an extra 'half-dozen' and . . ."

And it went off all right; all this was uttered very easily, unconstrainedly, and complacently.

On reaching home I promptly wrote to Simonov.

To this hour I am lost in admiration when I recall the truly gentlemanly, good-humored, candid tone of my letter. With tact and good breeding, and, above all, entirely without superfluous words, I blamed myself for all that had happened. I defended myself, "if I really may be allowed to defend myself," by alleging that, being utterly unaccustomed to wine, I had been intoxicated with the first glass, which, I said, I had drunk before they arrived, while I was waiting for them at the Hôtel de Paris between five and six o'clock. I begged Simonov's pardon especially; I asked him to convey my explanations to all the others, especially to Zverkov, whom "I seemed to remember as though in a dream" I had insulted. I added that I would have called upon all of them myself, but my head ached, and besides I had not the face to. I was particularly pleased with a certain lightness, almost carelessness (strictly within the bounds of politeness, however), which was apparent in my style, and better than any possible arguments, gave them at once to understand that I took rather an independent view of "all that unpleasantness last night"; that I was by no means so utterly crushed as you, my friends, probably imagine; but, on the contrary, looked upon it as a gentleman serenely respecting himself should look upon it. "On a young hero's past no censure is cast!"

"There is actually an aristocratic playfulness about it!" I thought admiringly, as I read over the letter. And it's all because I am an intellectual and cultivated man! Another man in my place would not have known how to extricate himself, but here I have got out of it and am as jolly as ever again, and all because I am "a cultivated and educated man of our day." And, indeed, perhaps, everything was due to the wine yesterday. H'm! . . . no, it was not the wine. I did not drink anything at all between five and six when I was waiting for them. I had lied to Simonov; I had lied shamelessly; and indeed I wasn't ashamed now. . . . Hang it all, though, the great thing was that I was rid of it.

I put six roubles in the letter, sealed it up, and asked Apollon to take it to Simonov. When he learned that there was money in the letter, Apollon became more respectful and agreed to take it. Toward evening I went out for a walk. My head was still aching and giddy after yesterday. But as evening came on and the twilight grew denser, my impressions and, following them, my thoughts grew more and more different and confused. Something was not dead within me, in the depths of my heart and conscience it would not die, and it showed itself in acute depression. For the most part I jostled my way through the most crowded business streets, along Meshchansky Street, along Sadovy Street and in Yusupov Garden. I always particularly liked sauntering along these streets in the dusk, just when there were crowds of working people of all sorts going home from their daily work, with faces looking cross with anxiety. What I liked was just that cheap bustle, that bare prose. On this occasion the jostling of the streets irritated me more than ever. I could not make out what was wrong with me, I could not find the clue, something seemed rising up continually in my soul, painfully, and refusing to be appeased. I returned home completely upset, it was just as though some crime were lying on my conscience.

The thought that Liza was coming worried me continually. It seemed queer to me that of all my recollections of yesterday this tormented me, as it were, especially, as it were, quite separately. Everything else I had quite succeeded in forgetting by the evening; I dismissed it all and was still perfectly satisfied with my letter to Simonov. But on this point I was not satisfied at all. It was as though I were worried only by Liza. "What if she comes," I thought incessantly. "Well, it doesn't matter, let her come! H'm! it's horrid that she should see, for instance, how I live. Yesterday I seemed such a hero to her, while now, h'm! It's horrid, though, that I have let myself go so, the room looks like a beggar's. And I brought myself to go out to dinner in such a suit! And my American leather sofa with the stuffing sticking out. And my dressing gown, which will not cover me, such tatters, and she will see all this and she will see Apollon. That beast is certain to insult her. He will fasten upon her in order to be rude to me. And I, of course, shall be panic-stricken as usual, I shall begin bowing and scraping before her and pulling my dressing gown around me, I shall begin smiling, telling lies. Oh, the beastliness! And it isn't the beastliness of it that matters most! There is something more important, more loathsome, viler! Yes, viler! And to put on that dishonest lying mask again!" . . .

When I reached that thought I fired up all at once.

"Why dishonest? How dishonest? I was speaking sincerely last night. I remember there was real feeling in me, too. What I wanted was to excite an honorable feeling in her. . . . Her crying was a good thing, it will have a good effect."

Yet I could not feel at ease. All that evening, even when I had come back home, even after nine o'clock, when I calculated that Liza could not possibly come, she still haunted me, and what was worse, she came back to my mind always in the same position. One moment out of all that had happened last night stood vividly before my imagination; the moment when I struck a match and saw her pale, distorted face, with its look of torture. And what a pitiful, what an unnatural, what a distorted smile she had at that moment! But I did not know then that fifteen years later I should still in my imagination see Liza, always with the pitiful, distorted, inappropriate smile which was on her face at that minute.

Next day I was ready again to look upon it all as nonsense, due to overexcited nerves, and, above all, as *exaggerated*. I was always conscious of that weak point of mine, and sometimes very much afraid of it. "I exaggerate everything, that is where I go wrong," I repeated to myself every hour. But, however, "Liza will very likely come all the same," was the refrain with which all my reflections ended. I was so uneasy that I sometimes flew into a fury. "She'll come, she is certain to come!" I cried, running about the room, "if not today, she will come tomorrow; she'll find me out! The damnable romanticism of these pure hearts! Oh, the vileness—oh, the silliness—oh, the stupidity of these 'wretched sentimental souls!' Why, how fail to understand? How could one fail to understand? . . ."

But at this point I stopped short, and in great confusion, indeed.

And how few, how few words, I thought, in passing, were needed; how little of the idyllic (and affectedly, bookishly, artificially idyllic too) had sufficed to turn a whole human life at once according to my will. That's virginity, to be sure! Freshness of soil!

At times a thought occurred to me, to go to her, "to tell her all," and beg her not to come to me. But this thought stirred such wrath in me that I believed I should have crushed that "damned" Liza if she had chanced to be near me at the time. I should have insulted her, have spat at her, have turned her out, have struck her!

One day passed, however, another and another; she did not come and I began to grow calmer. I felt particularly bold and cheerful after nine o'clock, I even sometimes began dreaming, and rather sweetly; I, for instance, become the salvation of Liza, simply through her coming to me and my talking to her. . . . I develop her, educate her. Finally, I notice that she loves me, loves me passionately. I pretend not to understand (I don't know, however, why I pretend, just for effect, perhaps). At last all confusion, transfigured, trembling and sobbing, she flings herself at my feet and says that I am her savior, and that she loves me better than anything in the world. I am amazed, but . . . "Liza," I say, "can you imagine that I have not noticed your love, I saw it all, I divined it, but I did not dare to approach you first, because I had an influence over you and was afraid that you would force yourself, from gratitude, to respond to my love, would try to rouse in your heart a feeling which was perhaps absent, and I did not wish that . . . because it would be tyranny . . . it would be indelicate (in short, I launch off at that point into European, inexplicably lofty subtleties à la George Sand), but now, now you are mine, you are my creation, you are pure, you are good, you are my noble wife.

> Into my house come bold and free,
> Its rightful mistress there to be."

Then we begin living together, go abroad and so on, and so on. In fact, in the end it seemed vulgar to me myself, and I began putting out my tongue at myself.

Besides, they won't let her out, "the strumpet!" I thought. They don't let them go out very readily, especially in the evening (for some reason I fancied she would come in the evening, and at seven o'clock precisely). Though she did say she was not altogether a slave there yet, and had certain rights; so, h'm! Damn it all, she will come, she is sure to come!

It was a good thing, in fact, that Apollon distracted my attention at that time by his rudeness. He drove me beyond all patience! He was the bane of my life, the curse laid upon me by Providence. We had been squabbling continually for years, and I hated him. My God, how I hated him! I believe I had never hated anyone in my life as I hated him, especially at some moments. He was an elderly, dignified man, who worked part of his time as a tailor. But for some unknown reason he despised me beyond all measure, and looked down upon me insufferably. Though, indeed, he looked down upon everyone. Simply to glance at that flaxen, smoothly brushed head, at the tuft of hair he combed up on his forehead and oiled with sunflower oil, at that dignified mouth, compressed into the shape of the letter V, made one feel one was confronting a man who never doubted himself. He was a pedant, to the most extreme point, the greatest pedant I had met on earth, and with that had a vanity only befitting Alexander of Macedon. He was in love with every button on his coat, every nail on his fingers—absolutely in love with them, and he looked it! In his behavior to me he was a perfect tyrant, he spoke very little to me, and if he chanced to glance at me he gave me a firm, majestically self-confident, and invariably ironical look that drove me sometimes to fury. He did his work with the air of doing me the greatest favor. Though he did scarcely anything for me, and did not, indeed, consider himself bound to do anything. There could be no doubt that he looked upon me as the greatest fool on earth, and that if he "did not get rid of me" it was because he could get wages from me every month. He consented to do nothing for me for seven roubles a month. Many sins should be forgiven me for what I suffered from him. My hatred reached such a point that sometimes his very step almost threw me into convulsions. What I loathed particularly was his lisp. His tongue must have been a little too long or something of that sort, for he continually lisped, and seemed to be very proud of it, imagining that it greatly added to his dignity. He spoke in a slow, measured tone, with his hands behind his back and his eyes fixed on the ground. He maddened me particularly when he read aloud the psalms to himself behind his partition. Many a battle I waged over that reading! But he was awfully fond of reading aloud in the evening, in a slow, even singsong voice, as though over the dead. It is interesting that that is how he has ended: he hires himself out to read the psalms over the dead, and at the same time he kills rats and makes blacking. But at that time I could not get rid of him, it was as though he were chemically combined with my existence. Besides, nothing would have induced him to consent to leave me. I could not live in furnished lodgings: my lodging was my private solitude, my shell, my cave, in which I concealed myself from all mankind, and Apollon seemed to me, for some reason, an integral part of that flat, and for seven years I could not turn him away.

To be two or three days behind with his wages, for instance, was impossible. He would have made such a fuss, I should not have known where to hide my head. But I was so exasperated with everyone during those days that I made up my mind for some reason and with some object to *punish* Apollon and not to pay him for a fortnight the wages that were owing him. I had for a long time—for the last two years—been intending to do this, simply in order to teach him not to give himself airs with me, and to show him that if I liked I could withhold his wages. I purposed to say nothing to him about it, and was purposely silent indeed, in order to score off his pride and force him to be the first to speak of his wages. Then I would take the seven roubles out of a drawer, show him I had the money put aside on purpose, but that I wouldn't, I wouldn't, I simply wouldn't pay him his wages, I wouldn't just because that is "what I wish," because "I am master, and it is for me to decide," because he had been disrespectful, because he had been rude; but if he were to ask respectfully I might be softened and give it to him, otherwise he might wait another fortnight, another three weeks, a whole month. . . .

But, angry as I was, yet he got the better of me. I could not hold out for four days. He began as he always did begin in such cases, for there had been such cases already, there had been attempts (and it may be observed I knew all this beforehand, I knew his nasty tactics by heart). He would begin by fixing upon me an exceedingly severe stare, keeping it up for several minutes at a time, particularly on meeting me or seeing me out of the house. If I held out and pretended not to notice these stares, he would, still in silence, proceed to further tortures. All at once, apropos of nothing, he would walk softly and smoothly into my room, when I was pacing up and down or reading, stand at the door, one hand behind his back and one foot behind the other, and fix upon me a stare more than severe, utterly contemptuous. If I suddenly asked him what he wanted, he would make me no answer, but continue staring at me persistently for some seconds, then, with a peculiar compression of his lips and a most significant air, deliberately turn around and deliberately go back to his room. Two hours later he would come out again and again present himself before me in the same way. It had happened that in my fury I did not even ask him what he wanted, but simply raised my head sharply and imperiously and began staring back at him. So we stared at one another for two minutes; at last he turned with deliberation and dignity and went back again for two hours.

If I were still not brought to reason by all this, but persisted in my revolt, he would suddenly begin sighing while he looked at me, long, deep sighs as though measuring by them the depths of my moral degradation, and, of course, it ended at last by his triumphing completely: I raged and shouted, but still was forced to do what he wanted.

This time the usual staring maneuvers had scarcely begun when I lost my temper and flew at him in a fury. I was irritated beyond endurance apart from him.

"Stay," I cried, in a frenzy, as he was slowly and silently turning, with one hand behind his back, to go to his room, "stay! Come back, come back, I tell you!" and I must have bawled so unnaturally that he turned around and even looked at me with some wonder. However, he persisted in saying nothing, and that infuriated me.

"How dare you come and look at me like that without being sent for? Answer!"

After looking at me calmly for half a minute, he began turning around again.

"Stay!" I roared, running up to him, "don't stir! There. Answer, now: what did you come in to look at?"

"If you have any order to give me it's my duty to carry it out," he answered, after another silent pause, with a slow, measured lisp, raising his eyebrows and calmly twisting his head from one side to another, all this with exasperating composure.

"That's not what I am asking you about, you executioner!" I cried, turning crimson with anger. "I'll tell you why you came here myself; you see, I don't give you your wages, you are so proud you don't want to bow down and ask for them, and so you come to punish me with your stupid stares, to worry me and you have no sus-pi-cion how stupid it is—stupid, stupid, stupid, stupid!" . . .

He would have turned around again without a word, but I seized him.

"Listen," I shouted to him. "Here's the money, do you see, here it is" (I took it out of the table drawer); "here's the seven roubles complete, but you are not going to have it, you—are—not—going—to—have it until you come respectfully with bowed head to beg my pardon. Do you hear?"

"That cannot be," he answered, with the most unnatural self-confidence.

"It shall be so," I said, "I give you my word of honor, it shall be!"

"And there's nothing for me to beg your pardon for," he went on, as though he had not noticed my exclamations at all. "Why, besides, you called me 'executioner,' for which I can summon you to the police station at any time for insulting behavior."

"Go, summon me," I roared, "go at once, this very minute, this very second! You are an executioner all the same! an executioner!"

But he merely looked at me, then turned, and, regardless of my loud calls to him, he walked to his room with an even step and without looking around.

"If it had not been for Liza, nothing of this would have happened," I decided inwardly. Then, after waiting a minute, I myself went behind his screen with a dignified and solemn air, though my heart was beating slowly and violently.

"Apollon," I said quietly and emphatically, though I was breathless, "go at once without a minute's delay and fetch the police officer."

He had meanwhile settled himself at his table, put on his

spectacles, and taken up some sewing. But, hearing my order, he burst into a guffaw.

"At once, go this minute! Go on, or else you can't imagine what will happen."

"You are certainly out of your mind," he observed, without even raising his head, lisping as deliberately as ever and threading his needle. "Whoever heard of a man sending for the police against himself? And as for being frightened—you are upsetting yourself about nothing, for nothing will come of it."

"Go!" I shrieked, clutching him by the shoulder. I felt I should strike him in a minute.

But I did not notice the door from the passage softly and slowly open at that instant and a figure come in, stop short, and begin staring at us in perplexity. I glanced, nearly swooned with shame, and rushed back to my room. There, clutching at my hair with both hands, I leaned my head against the wall and stood motionless in that position.

Two minutes later I heard Apollon's deliberate footsteps. "There is some woman asking for you," he said, looking at me with peculiar severity. Then he stood aside and let in Liza. He would not go away, but stared at us sarcastically.

"Go away, go away," I commanded in desperation. At that moment my clock began whirring and wheezing and struck seven.

IX

Into my house come bold and free,
Its rightful mistress there to be.
—*From the same poem*

I stood before her crushed, crestfallen, revoltingly confused, and I believe I smiled as I did my utmost to wrap myself in the skirts of my ragged wadded dressing gown—exactly as I had imagined the scene not long before in a fit of depression. After standing over us for a couple of minutes Apollon went away, but that did not make me more at ease.

What made it worse was that she, too, was overwhelmed with confusion, more so, in fact, than I should have expected. At the sight of me, of course.

"Sit down," I said mechanically, moving a chair up to the table, and I sat down on the sofa. She obediently sat down at once and gazed at me open-eyed, evidently expecting something from me at once. This naïveté of expectation drove me to fury, but I restrained myself.

She ought to have tried not to notice, as though everything had been as usual, while instead of that, she . . . and I dimly felt that I should make her pay dearly for *all this*.

"You have found me in a strange position, Liza," I began, stammering and knowing that this was the wrong way to begin. "No, no, don't imagine anything," I cried, seeing that she had suddenly flushed. "I am not ashamed of my poverty. . . . On the contrary, I look with pride on my poverty. I am poor but honorable. . . . One can be poor and honorable," I muttered. "However—would you like tea?"

"No," she was beginning.

"Wait a minute."

I leaped up and ran to Apollon. I had to get out of the room somehow.

"Apollon," I whispered in feverish haste, flinging down before him the seven roubles which had remained all the time in my clenched fist, "here are your wages, you see I give them to you; but for that you must come to my rescue: bring me tea and a dozen rusks from the restaurant. If you won't go, you'll make me a miserable man! You don't know what this woman is. . . . This is—everything! You may be imagining something. . . . But you don't know what this woman is!" . . .

Apollon, who had already sat down to his work and put on his spectacles again, at first glanced askance at the money without speaking or putting down his needle; then, without paying the slightest attention to me or making any answer, he went on busying himself with his needle, which he had not yet threaded. I waited, standing before him for three minutes with my arms crossed à la Napoleon. My temples were moist with sweat. I was pale, I felt it. But, thank God, he must have been moved to pity, looking at me. Having threaded his needle he deliberately got up from his seat, deliberately moved back his chair, deliberately took off his spectacles, deliberately counted the money, and finally, asking me over his shoulder, "Shall I get a whole portion?" deliberately walked out of the room. As I was going back to Liza, the thought occurred to me on the way: shouldn't I run away just as I was in my dressing gown, no matter where, and then let happen what would?

I sat down again. She looked at me uneasily. For some minutes we were silent.

"I will kill him," I shouted suddenly, striking the table with my fist so that the ink spurted out of the inkstand.

"What are you saying!" she cried, starting.

"I will kill him! kill him!" I shrieked, suddenly striking the table in absolute frenzy, and at the same time fully understanding how stupid it was to be in such a frenzy. "You don't know, Liza, what that torturer is to me. He is my torturer. . . . He has gone now to fetch some rusks; he——"

And suddenly I burst into tears. It was an hysterical attack. How ashamed I felt in the midst of my sobs; but still I could not restrain them.

She was frightened.

"What is the matter? What is wrong?" she cried, fussing about me.

"Water, give me water, over there!" I muttered in a faint voice, though I was inwardly conscious that I could have got on very well without water and without muttering in a faint voice. But I was what is called *putting it on*, to save appearances, though the attack was a genuine one.

She gave me water, looking at me in bewilderment. At that moment Apollon brought in the tea. It suddenly seemed to me that this commonplace, prosaic tea was horribly undignified and paltry after all that had happened, and I blushed crimson. Liza looked at Apollon with positive alarm. He went out without a glance at either of us.

"Liza, do you despise me?" I asked, looking at her fixedly, trembling with impatience to know what she was thinking.

She was confused, and did not know what to answer.

"Drink your tea," I said to her angrily. I was angry with myself, but, of course, it was she who would have to pay for it. A horrible spite against her suddenly surged up in my heart; I believe I could have killed her. To revenge myself on her I swore inwardly not to say a word to her all the time. "She is the cause of it all," I thought.

Our silence lasted for five minutes. The tea stood on the table; we did not touch it. I had got to the point of purposely refraining from beginning in order to embarrass her further; it was awkward for her to begin alone. Several times she glanced at me with mournful perplexity. I was obstinately silent. I was, of course, myself the chief sufferer, because I was fully conscious of the disgusting meanness of my spiteful stupidity, and yet at the same time I could not restrain myself.

"I want to . . . get away . . . from there altogether," she began, to break the silence in some way, but, poor girl, that was just what she ought not to have spoken about at such a stupid moment to a man so stupid as I was. My heart positively ached with pity for her tactless and unnecessary straightforwardness. But something hideous at once stifled all compassion in me; it even provoked me to greater venom. I did not care what happened. Another five minutes passed.

"Perhaps I am in your way," she began timidly, hardly audibly, and was getting up.

But as soon as I saw this first impulse of wounded dignity I positively trembled with spite, and at once burst out.

"Why have you come to me, tell me that, please?" I began, gasping for breath and regardless of logical connection in my words. I longed to have it all out at once, at one burst; I did not even trouble how to begin. "Why have you come? Answer, answer," I cried, hardly knowing what I was doing.

"I'll tell you, my good girl, why you have come. You've come because I talked sentimental stuff to you then. So now you are soft as butter and longing for fine sentiments again. So you may as well know that I was laughing at you then. And I am laughing at you now. Why are you shuddering? Yes, I was laughing at you! I had been insulted just before, at dinner, by the fellows who came that evening before me. I came to you, meaning to thrash one of them, an officer; but I didn't succeed, I didn't find him; I had to avenge the insult on someone to get back my own again; you turned up, I vented my spleen on you and laughed at you. I had been humiliated, so I wanted to humiliate; I had been treated like a rag, so I wanted to show my power. . . . That's what it was, and you imagined I had come there on purpose to save you. Yes? You imagined that? You imagined that?"

I knew that she would perhaps be muddled and not take it all in exactly, but I knew, too, that she would grasp the gist of it very well indeed. And so, indeed, she did. She turned white as a handkerchief, tried to say something, and her lips worked painfully; but she sank on a chair as though she had been felled by an ax. And all the time afterward she listened to me with her lips parted and her eyes wide open, shuddering with awful terror. The cynicism, the cynicism of my words overwhelmed her. . . .

"Save you!" I went on, jumping up from my chair and running up and down the room before her. "Save you from what? But perhaps I am worse than you myself. Why didn't you throw it in my teeth when I was giving you that sermon: 'But what did you come here yourself for? was it to read us a sermon?' Power, power was what I wanted then, sport was what I wanted, I wanted to wring out your tears, your humiliation, your hysteria—that was what I wanted then! Of course, I couldn't keep it up then, because I am a wretched creature, I was frightened, and, the devil knows why, gave you my address in my folly. Afterward, before I got home, I was cursing and swearing at you because of that address, I hated you already because of the lies I had told you. Because I only like playing with words, only dreaming, but, do you know, what I really want is that you should all go to hell. That is what I want. I want peace; yes, I'd sell the whole world for a copeck, straight off, so long as I was left in peace. Is the world to go to pot, or am I to go without my tea? I say that the world may go to pot for me so long as I always get my tea. Did you know that, or not? Well, anyway, I know that I am a blackguard, a scoundrel, an egoist, a sluggard. Here I have been shuddering for the last three days at the thought of your coming. And do you know what has worried me particularly for these three days? That I posed as such a hero to you, and now you would see me in a wretched torn dressing gown, beggarly, loathsome. I told you just now that I was not ashamed of my poverty; so you may as well know that I am ashamed of it; I am more ashamed of it than of anything, more afraid of it than of being found out if I were a thief, because I am as vain as though I had been skinned and the very air blowing on me hurt. Surely by now you must realize that I shall never forgive you for having found me in this wretched dressing gown, just as I was flying at Apollon like a spiteful cur. The savior, the former hero, was flying like a mangy, unkempt sheepdog at his lackey, and the lackey was jeering at him! And I shall never forgive you for the tears I could not help shedding before you just now, like some silly woman put to shame! And for what I am confessing to you now, I shall never forgive *you* either! Yes —you must answer for it all because you turned up like this, because I am a blackguard, because I am the nastiest, stupidest, absurdest, and most envious of all the worms on earth, who are not a bit better than I am, but, the devil knows why, are never put to confusion; while I shall always be insulted by every louse, that is my doom! And what is it to me that you don't understand a word of this! And what do I care, what do I care about you, and whether you go to ruin there or not? Do you understand? How I shall hate you now after saying this, for having been here and listening. Why, it's not once in a lifetime a man speaks out like this, and then it is in hysterics! . . . What more do you want? Why do you still stand confronting me, after all this? Why are you worrying me? Why don't you go?"

But at this point a strange thing happened. I was so accustomed to think and imagine everything from books, and to picture everything in the world to myself just as I had made it up in my dreams beforehand, that I could not all at once take in this strange circumstance. What happened was this: Liza, insulted and crushed by me, understood a great deal more than I imagined. She understood from all this what a woman understands first of all, if she feels genuine love, that is, that I was myself unhappy.

The frightened and wounded expression on her face was followed first by a look of sorrowful perplexity. When I began calling myself a scoundrel and a blackguard and my tears flowed (the tirade was accompanied throughout by tears) her whole face worked convulsively. She was on the point of getting up and stopping me; when I finished she took no notice of my shouting, "Why are you here, why don't you go away?" but realized only that it must have been very bitter to me to say all this. Besides, she was so crushed, poor girl; she considered herself infinitely beneath me; how could she feel anger or resentment? She suddenly leaped up from her chair with an irresistible impulse and held out her hands, yearning toward me, though still timid and not daring to stir. . . . At this point there was a revulsion in my heart, too. Then she suddenly rushed to me, threw her arms around me, and burst into tears. I, too, could not restrain myself, and sobbed as I never had before.

"They won't let me . . . I can't be good!" I managed to articulate; then I went to the sofa, fell on it face downward, and sobbed on it for a quarter of an hour in genuine hysterics. She came close to me, put her arms around me, and stayed motionless in that position.

But the trouble was that the hysterics could not go on forever, and (I am writing the loathsome truth) lying face downward on the sofa with my face thrust into my nasty leather pillow, I began by degrees to be aware of a faraway, involuntary but irresistible feeling that it would be awkward now for me to raise my head and look Liza straight in the face. Why was I ashamed? I don't know, but I was ashamed. The thought, too, came into my overwrought brain that our parts now were completely changed, that she was now the heroine, while I was just such a crushed and humiliated creature as she had been before me that night —four days ago. . . . And all this came into my mind during the minutes I was lying on my face on the sofa.

My God! can it be that I was envious of her then?

I don't know, to this day I cannot decide, and at the time, of course, I was still less able to understand what I was feeling than now. I cannot get on without domineering and tyrannizing over someone, but . . . there is no explaining anything by reasoning and so it is useless to reason.

I conquered myself, however, and raised my head; I had to do so sooner or later . . . and I am convinced to this day that it was just because I was ashamed to look at her that another feeling was suddenly kindled and flamed up in my heart . . . a feeling of mastery and possession. My eyes gleamed with passion, and I gripped her hands tightly. How I hated her and how I was drawn to her at that minute! The one feeling intensified the other. It was almost like an act of vengeance. At first there was a look of amazement, even of terror on her face, but only for one instant. She warmly and rapturously embraced me.

x

A quarter of an hour later I was rushing up and down the room in frenzied impatience, from minute to minute I went up to the screen and peeped through the crack at Liza. She was sitting on the ground with her head leaning against the bed, and must have been crying. But she did not go away, and that irritated me. This time she understood it all. I had insulted her finally, but . . . there's no need to describe it. She realized that my outburst of passion had been simply revenge, a fresh humiliation, and that to my earlier, almost causeless hatred was added now a *personal hatred,* born of envy. . . . Though I do not maintain positively that she understood all this distinctly; but she certainly did fully understand that I was a despicable man, and, what was worse, incapable of loving her.

I know I shall be told that this is incredible—but it is incredible to be as spiteful and stupid as I was; it may be added that it was strange I should not love her, or at any rate, appreciate her love. Why is it strange? In the first place, by then I was incapable of love, for I repeat, with me loving meant tyrannizing and showing my moral superiority. I have never in my life been able to imagine any other sort of love, and have nowadays come to the point of sometimes thinking that love really consists in the right—freely given by the beloved object—to tyrannize over her.

Even in my underground dreams I did not imagine love except as a struggle. I began it always with hatred and ended it with moral subjugation, and afterward I never knew what to do with the subjugated object. And what is there to wonder at in that, since I had succeeded in so corrupting myself, since I was so out of touch with "real life," as to have actually thought of reproaching her, and putting her to shame for having come to me to hear "fine sentiments"; and did not even guess that she had come not to hear fine sentiments, but to love me, because to a woman all reformation, all salvation from any sort of ruin, and all moral renewal is included in love and can only show itself in that form.

I did not hate her so much, however, when I was running about the room and peeping through the crack in the screen. I was only insufferably oppressed by her being here. I wanted her to disappear. I wanted "peace," to be left alone in my underground world. Real life oppressed me with its novelty so much that I could hardly breathe.

But several minutes passed and she still remained, without stirring, as though she were unconscious. I had the shamelessness to tap softly at the screen as though to remind her. . . . She started, sprang up, and flew to seek her kerchief, her hat, her coat, as though making her escape from me. . . . Two minutes later she came from behind the screen and looked with heavy eyes at me. I gave a spiteful grin, which was forced, however, to *keep up appearances,* and I turned away from her eyes.

"Good-by," she said, going toward the door.

I ran up to her, seized her hand, opened it, thrust something in it, and closed it again. Then I turned at once and dashed away in haste to the other corner of the room to avoid seeing, anyway. . . .

I did mean a moment since to tell a lie—to write that I did this accidentally, not knowing what I was doing, through foolishness, through losing my head. But I don't want to lie, and so I will say straight out that I opened her hand and put the money in it . . . from spite. It came into my head to do this while I was running up and down the room and she was sitting behind the screen. But this I can say for certain: though I did that cruel thing purposely, it was not an impulse from the heart, but came from my evil brain. This cruelty was so affected, so purposely made up, so completely a product of the brain, of books, that I could not even keep it up a minute—first I dashed away to avoid seeing her, and then in shame and despair rushed after Liza. I opened the door in the passage and began listening.

"Liza! Liza!" I cried on the stairs, but in a low voice, not boldly.

There was no answer, but I fancied I heard her footsteps, lower down on the stairs.

"Liza!" I cried, more loudly.

No answer. But at that minute I heard the stiff outer glass door open heavily with a creak and slam violently, the sound echoed up the stairs.

She had gone. I went back to my room in hesitation. I felt horribly oppressed.

I stood still at the table, beside the chair on which she had sat and looked aimlessly before me. A minute passed, suddenly I started; straight before me on the table I saw . . . In short, I saw a crumpled blue five-rouble note, the one I had thrust into her hand a minute before. It was the same note; it could be no other, there was no other in the flat. So she had managed to fling it from her hand on the table at the moment when I had dashed into the farther corner.

Well! I might have expected that she would do that. Might I have expected it? No, I was such an egoist, I was so lacking in respect for my fellow-creatures that I could not even imagine she would do so. I could not endure it. A minute later I flew like a madman to dress, flinging on what I could at random, and ran headlong after her. She could not have got two hundred paces away when I ran out into the street.

It was still night and the snow was coming down in masses and falling almost perpendicularly, covering the pavement and the empty street as though with a pillow. There was no one in the street, no sound was to be heard. The street lamps shed a disconsolate and useless glimmer. I ran two hundred paces to the crossroads and stopped short.

Where had she gone? And why was I running after her? Why? To fall down before her, to sob with remorse, to kiss her feet, to entreat her forgiveness! I longed for that, my whole breast was being rent to pieces, and never, never shall I recall that minute with indifference. But—what for, I thought. Should I not begin to hate her, perhaps, even tomorrow, just because I had kissed her feet today? Should I give her happiness? Had I not recognized that day, for the hundredth time, what I was worth? Should I not torture her?

I stood in the snow, gazing into the troubled darkness and pondered this.

"And will it not be better?" I mused fantastically, afterward, at home, stifling the living pang of my heart with fantastic dreams. "Will it not be better that she should keep the resentment of the insult forever? Resentment—why, it is purification; it is a most stinging and painful consciousness! Tomorrow I should have defiled her soul and have exhausted her heart, while now the feeling of insult will never die in her heart, and however loathsome the filth awaiting her—the feeling of insult will elevate and purify her . . . by hatred . . . h'm! . . . perhaps, too, by forgiveness. . . . Will all that make things easier for her though?" . . .

And, indeed, I will ask on my own account here an idle question: which is better—cheap happiness or exalted suffering? Well, which is better?

So I dreamed as I sat at home that evening, almost dead with the pain in my soul. Never have I endured such suffering and remorse, yet could there have been the faintest doubt when I ran out from my lodging that I should turn back halfway? I never met Liza again and I have heard nothing of her. I will add, too, that I remained for a long time afterward pleased with the phrase about the benefit from resentment and hatred in spite of the fact that I almost fell ill from misery.

Even now, so many years later, all this is somehow a very evil memory. I have many evil memories now, but . . . hadn't I better end my "Notes" here? I believe I made a mistake in beginning to write them, anyway I have felt ashamed all the time I've been writing this story; so it's not so much literature as a corrective punishment. Why, to tell long stories, showing how I have spoiled my life through morally rotting in my corner, through lack of fitting environment, through divorce from real life, and rankling spite in my underground world, would certainly not be interesting; a novel needs a hero, and all the traits for an anti-hero are *expressly* gathered together here, and, what matters most, it all produces a most unpleasant impression, for we are all divorced from life, we are all cripples, every one of us, more or less. We are so divorced from it that we feel at times a sort of loathing for real "living life," and so cannot bear to be reminded of it. Why, we have come almost to looking upon real "living life" as an effort, almost as hard work, and we are all privately agreed that it is better in books. And why do we fuss and fume sometimes? Why are we perverse, and why do we ask for something else? We don't know what ourselves. It would be the worse for us if our petulant prayers were answered. Come, try, give any one of us, for instance, a little more independence, untie our hands, widen the spheres of our activity, relax the control, and we . . . yes, I assure you . . . we should be begging to be under control again at once. I know that you will very likely be angry with me for that, and will begin shouting and stamping. "Speak for yourself," you say, "and for your miseries in your underground hole, and don't dare to say 'all of us.'" Excuse me, gentlemen, I am not justifying myself with that "all of us." As for what concerns me in particular I have only carried to an extreme in my life what you have not dared to carry halfway, and, what's more, you have taken your cowardice for good sense, and have found comfort in deceiving yourselves. So that perhaps, after all, there is more life in me than in you. Look into it more carefully! Why, we don't even know what living means now, what it is, and what it is called! Leave us alone without books and we shall be lost and in confusion at once. We shall not know what to join onto, what to cling to, what to love and what to hate, what to respect and what to despise. It's a burden to us even to be human beings—men with our own real body and blood; we are ashamed of it, we think it a disgrace and try to contrive to be some sort of impossible generalized man. We are stillborn, and for generations past have not been begotten by living fathers, and that suits us better and better. We are developing a taste for it. Soon we shall contrive to be born somehow of an idea. But enough; I don't want to write more "from the Underground."

[*The "notes" of this paradoxalist do not end here, however. He could not refrain from going on with them, but it seems to us that we may as well stop here.*]

THE ETERNAL
HUSBAND
A Story

Chapter I: Velchaninov

THE summer had come, and, contrary to expectation, Velchaninov remained in Petersburg. The trip he had planned to the south of Russia had fallen through, and the end of his case was not in sight. This case—a lawsuit concerning an estate—was taking a very unfortunate turn. Three months earlier it had appeared to be quite straightforward, almost incontestable; but somehow suddenly everything was changed. "And, in general, everything started changing for the worse!" Velchaninov began repeating that phrase to himself often and gloatingly. He was employing an adroit, expensive, well-known lawyer, and was not sparing money; but through impatience and lack of trust he took to meddling in the case himself, too. He read documents and wrote statements which the lawyer rejected point-blank, ran from one government office to another, made inquiries, and probably hindered everything; the lawyer complained, at any rate, and tried to pack him off to the country. But Velchaninov could not even make up his mind to go away. The dust, the stifling heat, the white nights of Petersburg that always fret the nerves were what he was enjoying in town. His flat was somewhere near the Bolshoy Theatre; he had only recently taken it, and it, too, was a failure. "Everything is a failure!" he thought. His hypochondria increased every day; but he had long been subject to hypochondria.

A man who had lived fully and in grand style, he was by no means young, thirty-eight or even thirty-nine, and all this "old age," as he expressed it himself, had come upon him "quite unexpectedly"; but he realized himself that he had grown older less by the number than by the quality, so to say, of his years, and that if his infirmities had already set in, the change was rather from within than from without. In appearance he was still hale and hearty. He was a tall, sturdily built fellow, with thick flaxen hair without a single silver thread and a long fair beard almost halfway down his chest; at first sight he seemed somewhat slack and clumsy, but if you looked more closely, you would detect at once that he was a man who had command of himself and who had formerly received the education of an aristocrat. Velchaninov's manners were still free, assured, and even graceful, in spite of his acquired grumpiness and awkwardness. And he was still, even now, full of the most unshakable, the most snobbishly insolent self-confidence, the depth of which he did not perhaps himself suspect, although he was a man not merely intelligent, but even sometimes sensible, almost a person of culture and unmistakable gifts. His open and ruddy face had been in old days marked by a feminine softness of complexion which attracted the notice of women; and even now some people, looking at him, would say, "What a strapping fellow! What a complexion!" And yet this strapping fellow was cruelly racked by hypochondria. Ten years earlier his large, blue eyes had possessed much that was winsome, had possessed great fascination; they were so bright, so gay, so careless that they could not but attract everyone who came in contact with him. Now that he was verging on the forties, the brightness and good nature were almost extinguished in those eyes, which were already surrounded by tiny wrinkles. On the contrary, they had begun to betray slyness, most often mockery, the cynicism of a worn-out man of doubtful morals, and also a new feeling that had not been there before: a shade of sadness and of pain—a sort of absent-minded sadness as though about nothing in particular and yet acute. This sadness was especially marked when he was alone. And, strange to say, this man who only a couple of years before had been boisterous, jolly, and carefree, who had been so capital a teller of funny stories, liked nothing now so well as being absolutely alone. He purposely gave up a great number of acquaintances whom he need not have given up even now, in spite of his serious financial difficulties. It is true that his vanity counted for something in this. With his vanity and mistrustfulness he could not have endured the society of his former acquaintances. But, by degrees, his vanity too began to change its character in solitude. It grew no less, quite the contrary; but it began to degenerate into a peculiar sort of vanity which was new in him; it began at times to suffer from causes entirely unlike the former ones—from unexpected causes which would have formerly been quite inconceivable, from causes of a "higher order" than ever before— "if one may use such an expression, if there really are higher or lower causes. . . ." This he added on his own account.

Yes, he had even come to that; he was worrying about some sort of *higher* causes of which he would never have thought twice in earlier days. In his own mind and in all conscience he called "higher" all "causes" at which (he found to his surprise) he could not laugh in his heart— there had never been such hitherto—in his heart only, of course; oh, in company it was a different matter! He knew very well, indeed, that—if only the occasion were to arise —he would the very next day, in spite of all the mysterious and reverent resolutions of his conscience, with perfect composure disavow all these "higher causes" and be the first to hold them up to ridicule, without, of course, admitting anything. And this was really the case, in spite of a certain and, indeed, considerable independence of thought, which he had of late gained at the expense of the "lower causes" that had mastered him till then. And how often, when he got up in the morning, he began to be ashamed of the thoughts and feelings he had had during a sleepless night! And he had suffered continually of late from sleeplessness. He had noticed for a long time past that he was becoming overanxious about everything, trifles as well as matters of importance, and so he made up his mind to trust himself as little as possible. But he could not overlook some facts, the reality of which he was forced to admit. Of late his thoughts and sensations were sometimes at night completely transformed, and for the most part became utterly unlike those which came to him in the early part of the day. This struck him—and he even consulted a well-known doctor who was, however, an acquaintance; he spoke to him about it jocosely, of course. The answer he received was that the transformation of thoughts and sensations was a universal fact among persons "who think strongly and feel strongly," that the convictions of a whole lifetime were sometimes transformed under the melancholy influences of night and insomnia; that without rhyme or reason most momentous decisions were made; but, of course, everything has its limits, and if finally the individual is too keenly aware of the double nature of his thoughts, so that it causes him suffering, it is certainly a sign that we are dealing with an illness, and that steps must be taken at once. The best thing of all is to make a radical change in the mode of life, to alter one's diet, or even to travel. A laxative is, of course, beneficial.

Velchaninov did not care to hear more; but the presence of disease was conclusively proved to him.

"And so all this is only illness, all these 'higher things' are mere illness and nothing more!" he sometimes exclaimed to himself caustically. He was very loath to admit this.

Soon, however, what had happened exclusively in the hours of the night began to be repeated in the morning, only with more rancor than at night, with malice instead of remorse, with mockery instead of tender emotion. What really happened was that certain incidents in his past, even in his distant past, began "suddenly, and God knows why," to come more and more frequently back to his mind, but they came back in a peculiar way. Velchaninov had, for instance, complained for a long time past of loss of memory: he would forget the faces of acquaintances so that they were offended by his cutting them when they met; he sometimes completely forgot a book he had read months before. And yet, in spite of this loss of memory, evident every day (and a source of great uneasiness to him), everything concerning the remote past, things that had been quite forgotten for ten or fifteen years, would sometimes come suddenly into his mind now with such amazing exactitude of details and impressions that he felt as though he were experiencing them again. Some of the facts he remembered had been so completely forgotten that it seemed to him a miracle that they could be recalled. But this was not all, and, indeed, what man who has lived in grand style has not some memory of a peculiar sort? But the fact was that all that was recalled presented itself to him from a point of view that was entirely new, surprising, until then inconceivable and prearranged by someone, as it were. Why did some things he remembered strike him now as positive crimes? And it was not a question of the judgments of his mind only: he would have put little faith in his gloomy, solitary and sick mind; but it reached the point of curses and almost of tears, of inward tears. Why, two years before, he would not have believed it if he had been told that he would ever shed tears! At first, however, what he remembered was of a rather sentimental character: he recalled certain failures and humiliations in society; he remembered, for instance, how he "had been slandered by an intriguing fellow," and in consequence refused admittance to a certain house; how, for instance, and not so long ago, he had been publicly and unmistakably insulted, and had not challenged the offender to a duel; how in a circle of very pretty women he had been made the subject of an extremely witty epigram and had found no suitable answer. He even recollected one or two unpaid debts—trifling ones, it is true, but debts of honor—owing to people with whom he had given up associating and even spoke ill of. He was also worried (but only in his worst moments) by the thought of the two fortunes, both considerable ones, which he had squandered in the stupidest way possible. But soon he began to remember things of a "higher order."

Suddenly, for instance, "apropos of nothing," he remembered the forgotten, utterly forgotten, figure of a harmless, gray-headed, and absurd old clerk, whom he had once, long, long ago, and with absolute impunity, insulted in public simply to gratify his own conceit, simply to make use of an amusing and successful pun, which people afterward repeated and which added to his renown. The incident had been so completely forgotten that he could not even recall the old man's surname, though the entire setting of the incident rose before his mind at once with incredible clearness. He distinctly remembered that the old man was defending his daughter, a spinster, who lived with him and had become the subject of gossip in the town. The old man had begun to answer angrily, but he suddenly burst out crying before the whole company, which made an impression. They had ended by making him drunk with champagne as a joke and getting a hearty laugh out of it. And now when, "apropos of nothing," Velchaninov remembered how the poor old man was sobbing and hiding his face in his hands like a child, it suddenly seemed to him as though he had never forgotten it. And, strange to say, it had all seemed to him very amusing at the time, especially some of the details, such as the way he had covered his face with his hands; but now it was quite the contrary.

Then he recalled how, simply as a joke, he had slandered the very pretty wife of a schoolmaster, and how the slander had reached the husband's ears. Velchaninov had left the town soon after and never knew what the final consequences of his slander had been, but now he began to imagine how all might have ended—and there is no knowing to what lengths his imagination might have gone, if this memory had not suddenly been supplanted by a much more recent reminiscence of a young girl of the working class, to whom he had not even felt attracted, and of whom, it must be admitted, he was actually ashamed. Yet, though he could not have said what had induced him, he had got her with child and had simply abandoned her and his child without even saying good-by (it was true, he had no time to spare), when he left Petersburg. He had tried to find that girl for a whole year afterward, but he had not succeeded in tracing her. He had, it seemed, hundreds of such reminiscences—and each one of them seemed to bring dozens of others in its train. By degrees his vanity, too, began to suffer.

We have said already that his vanity had degenerated into something peculiar. That was true. At moments (rare moments, however), he even forgot himself to such a degree that he ceased to be ashamed of not keeping his own carriage, that he trudged on foot from one government office to another, that he began to be somewhat negligent in his dress. And if some one of his old acquaintance had scanned him with a sarcastic stare in the street or had simply refused to recognize him, he might really have had pride enough to pass him by without a frown. And indifference would have been genuine, not assumed for effect. Of course, this was only at times: these were only the moments of self-forgetfulness and irritation, yet his vanity had by degrees grown less concerned with the matter that had once affected it, and was becoming concentrated on one question, which haunted him continually.

"Why, one would think," he would sometimes begin to reflect satirically (and he almost always began by being satirical when he thought about himself), "why, one would think someone up there troubled about reforming my morals, and was sending me these cursed reminiscences and 'tears of repentance'! So be it, but it's all useless! It is all shooting with blank cartridges! As though I did not know for sure, for surer than sure that, in spite of these fits of tearful remorse and self-condemnation, I haven't a grain of independence for all my foolish forty years! Why, if the same temptation were to turn up tomorrow, if, for instance, circumstances were to make it advantageous for me to spread a rumor that the schoolmaster's wife had taken presents from me, I should certainly spread it, I shouldn't hesitate—and it would be even worse, more loathsome than the first time, just because it would be the second time and not the first time. Yes, if I were insulted again this minute by that little prince whose leg I shot off eleven years ago, though he was his mother's only son, I should challenge him at once and give him a wooden leg again. So they are no better than blank cartridges, and there's no sense in them! And what's the good of remembering the past when I've not the slightest power of escaping from myself?"

And though the adventure with the schoolmaster's wife was not repeated, though he did not condemn anyone else to a wooden leg, the very idea that it would inevitably happen if the same circumstances arose, almost killed him . . . at times. One cannot, really, suffer from memories all the time; one can rest and enjoy oneself in the intervals.

So, indeed, Velchaninov did: he was ready to enjoy himself in the intervals; yet his stay in Petersburg grew more and more unpleasant as time went on. July was approaching. Sometimes he had a flash of determination to give up everything, the lawsuit itself, and to go away somewhere without looking back, to go suddenly, on the spur of the moment, to the Crimea, for instance. But, as a rule, an hour later he scorned the idea and laughed at it: "These nasty thoughts won't stop short in the south, if once they've begun and I've any sense of decency, and so it's useless to run away from them, and, indeed, there's no reason to.

"And what's the object of running away?" he went on brooding in his despondency; "it's so dusty here, so stifling, everything in the house is so messy. In those offices where I loiter, among those busy people, there is such a scurrying to and fro as of mice, such a mass of sordid cares! All these people left in town, all the faces that flit by from morning till night so naïvely and openly betray all their self-love, all their guileless insolence, the cowardice of their petty souls, all their chicken-heartedness—that, why, it's a paradise for a hypochondriac, seriously speaking! Everything is open, everything is clear, no one thinks it necessary to hide anything as they do among our gentry in our summer villas or at watering places abroad—and so it's more deserving of respect, if only for its openness and simplicity! . . . I won't go away! I'll stay here, even if I burst!"

Chapter II
The Gentleman with Crape on His Hat

It was the third of July. The heat and stuffiness were insufferable. The day had been a very busy one for Velchaninov; he had had to spend the whole morning walking and driving from place to place, and he had before him the prospect of an unavoidable visit that evening to a gentleman —a man of affairs and a councilor of state—whom he hoped to catch unawares in his summer cottage somewhere in the vicinity of Black River. At six o'clock Velchaninov went at last into a restaurant (the fare was not beyond criticism, though the cooking was French), on the Nevsky Prospect, near the Police Bridge. He sat down at the little table in his usual corner and asked for his daily dinner.

Every day he ate a dinner that was provided for a rouble and paid extra for the wine, and he regarded this as a sacrifice to the unsettled state of his finances and an act of prudence on his part. Though he wondered how he could possibly eat such stuff, he nevertheless used to consume it to the last crumb—and every time with as much appetite as though he had not eaten for three days before. "There's something morbid about it," he would mutter to himself sometimes, noticing his appetite. But this time he took his seat at his little table in a very bad humor, tossed his hat down irritably, put his elbows on the table, and sank into thought. Though he could be polite and, on occasion, loftily imperturbable, he would probably now have blustered like a cadet and would perhaps have made a scene, if someone dining near him had not been quiet or if the boy waiting on him had failed to understand him at the first word.

The soup was put before him. He took up the spoon, but, before he had time to help himself, he dropped it and almost jumped up from the table. A surprising idea suddenly dawned upon him: at that instant—and God knows by what process—he suddenly realized the cause of his depression, of the special depression which had tormented him of late for several days together; in some unknown way it had fastened upon him and for some unknown reason refused to be shaken off; now he suddenly saw it all and it was as plain as a pikestaff.

"It's all that hat," he muttered as though inspired. "It's nothing but that damned bowler hat with that beastly mourning crape that is the cause of it *all!*"

He began pondering—and the more he pondered the more morose he grew, and the more extraordinary "the whole incident" seemed to him.

"But . . . it is not an adventure, though," he protested, distrustful of himself. "As though there were anything in the least like an adventure about it!"

All that had happened was this. Nearly a fortnight before (he did not really remember, but he fancied it was about a fortnight), he had first met somewhere in the street, at the corner of Podyatchesky Street and Myestchansky Street, a gentleman with crape on his hat. The gentleman was like anyone else, there was nothing peculiar about him, he passed quickly, but he stared somewhat too fixedly at Velchaninov, and for some reason at once attracted his attention in a marked degree. At least his countenance struck Velchaninov as familiar. He had evidently at some time met it somewhere. "But I must have seen thousands of faces in my life, I can't remember them all!"

Before he had gone twenty paces farther he seemed to have forgotten the encounter, in spite of the impression it had made at first. But the impression persisted the whole day—and it was somewhat singular, it took the form of a peculiar undefined animosity. Now, a fortnight later, he remembered all that distinctly; he remembered, too, what he had failed to grasp at the time—that is, what his animosity was due to; and he had so utterly failed to grasp it that he had not even connected his ill-humor all that evening with the meeting that morning.

But the gentleman had lost no time in recalling himself to Velchaninov's mind, and the next day had run into the latter in the Nevsky Prospect again, and again stared at him rather strangely. Velchaninov spat and immediately afterward wondered why he had done so. It is true that there are faces that at once arouse an undefined and pointless aversion.

"Yes, I certainly have met him somewhere," he muttered pensively half an hour after the meeting. And he again remained in a very bad humor the whole evening afterward; he even had a bad dream at night, and yet it never entered his head that the whole cause of this new fit of despondency was nothing but that gentleman in mourning, although he did think of him that evening more than once! He had even got angry at himself in passing that "such trash" could occupy his attention as long as it did, and would certainly have thought it degrading to ascribe his agitation to him, if it had ever occurred to his mind to do so. Two days later they met again in a crowd coming off one of the Neva steamers. On this third occasion Velchaninov was ready to swear that the gentleman with the crape on his hat had recognized him and made a dash for him, but was pressed back in the crush; that he had even had the "effrontery" to hold out his hand to him; perhaps he had even cried out and hailed him by name. That, however, Velchaninov had not heard distinctly, but . . . "Who is the low fellow, though, and why does he not come up to me, if he really does recognize me, and if he is so anxious to accost me?" he thought angrily, as he got into a cab and drove toward Smolny monastery. Half an hour later he was noisily arguing with his lawyer, but in the evening and at night he was suffering again from the most abominable and most fantastic attack of acute depression. "Am I in for a bilious attack?" he wondered uneasily, looking at himself in the mirror.

This was the third encounter. Afterward, for five days in succession, he met "no one," and not a sign was seen of the "low fellow." And yet he would now and then recall the gentleman with the crape on his hat. With some surprise Velchaninov caught himself wondering, "What's the matter with me—and I pining for him, or what? H'm! . . . And he must have a lot to do in Petersburg, too—and for whom is he wearing crape? He evidently recognized me, but I don't recognize him. And why do these people put on crape? It somehow does not become them. . . . I fancy if I look at him closer, I shall recognize him. . . ."

And something seemed to begin stirring in his memory, like some familiar but momentarily forgotten word, which you try with all your might to recall; you know it very well and know that you know it; you know exactly what it means; you circle about it and yet it refuses to be recalled, in spite of all your efforts.

"It was . . . it was long ago . . . and it was somewhere. . . . There was . . . there was something . . . but, damn the fellow, whatever there was or wasn't . . ." he cried angrily all at once; "it is not worth while to soil and degrade myself over that wretched fellow. . . ."

He flew into a rage, but in the evening, when he suddenly remembered that he had got angry that morning, and "horribly" angry, it was extremely disagreeable to him; he felt as though someone had caught him red-handed. He was confused and surprised.

"Then there must be reasons for my being so angry . . . without rhyme or reason . . . at a mere reminiscence. . . ." He left the thought unfinished.

And next day he felt angrier than ever, but this time he

fancied he had grounds for it, and that he was quite right in feeling so; "it was unheard-of insolence," he thought. The fact is that the fourth encounter had taken place. The gentleman with crape on his hat had suddenly made his appearance again, as though he had sprung out of the ground. Velchaninov had just caught in the street the aforementioned indispensable councilor of state, of whom he was still in pursuit, meaning to pounce on him unawares at his summer villa, for the official, whom Velchaninov scarcely knew and whom he found it necessary to see about his business, on that occasion as on this eluded him, and was evidently keeping out of sight and extremely reluctant to meet him. Delighted at coming across him at last, Velchaninov walked hurriedly beside him, glancing into his face and straining every effort to steer the conversation to a certain subject, in the discussion of which the wily old fellow might be indiscreet enough to let slip a long sought-for word; but the old man was sly, and kept putting him off with laughter or silence—and it was just at this extremely absorbing moment that Velchaninov descried on the opposite pavement the gentleman with crape on his hat. He stood staring at them both—he was watching them, that was evident, and seemed to be sneering at them.

"Damnation!" cried Velchaninov in a fury, as he saw the councilor off and ascribed his failure with him to the sudden appearance of that "impudent fellow." "Damnation! Is he spying on me? He's evidently following me. Hired by someone, perhaps, is he? And . . . and . . . and, I swear, he was sneering at me! I swear, I'll thrash him. . . . I'm sorry I've no stick with me! I'll buy a stick! I won't let it pass. Who is he? I insist on knowing who he is."

It was three days after this fourth encounter that Velchaninov was at his restaurant, as stated above, agitated in earnest and even distraught. He could not help being conscious of it himself, in spite of his pride. He was forced at last, putting all the circumstances together, to suspect that all his depression, all his *peculiar* despondency, and the agitation that had persisted for the last fortnight was caused by none other than this gentleman in mourning, "nonentity as he was."

"I may be a hypochondriac," thought Velchaninov, "and so I am ready to make a mountain out of a molehill, but does it make it any the better for me that all this is *perhaps* only a fantasy! Why, if every rogue like that is going to be able to upset one in this way, why . . . it's . . . it's . . ."

Certainly in the encounter of that day (the fifth), which had so agitated Velchaninov, the mountain had proved to be little more than a molehill: the gentleman had as before darted by him, but this time without scrutinizing Velchaninov, and without, as before, pretending that he recognized him; on the contrary, he dropped his eyes and seemed to be very anxious to escape being noticed. Velchaninov turned around and shouted at the top of his voice:

"Look here! You with the crape on your hat! Now you're hiding! Stop: who are you?"

The question (and his shouting) was very stupid, but Velchaninov only realized that after he had uttered it. The gentleman turned around at the shout, stood still for a minute, became flustered, smiled, seemed on the point of doing or saying something, was obviously for a minute in a state of terrible indecision, then suddenly turned and ran away without turning his head. Velchaninov looked after him with astonishment.

"And what if it's a case of my pestering him, not his pestering me?" he thought, "and that's all it amounts to?"

When he had finished dinner he made haste to set off to the summer cottage to see the councilor. He did not find the official in; he was informed that his honor had not returned that day, and probably would not come back till three or four o'clock in the morning, as he was attending a birthday party in town. This was so mortifying that, in his first fury, Velchaninov decided to go to the birthday party, and even set off to do so; but, reflecting on the road that this was to go too far, he dismissed the cab and trudged home on foot to his flat near the Bolshoy Theatre. He felt that he needed exercise. To soothe his excited nerves he had to get a good night's sleep at all costs in spite of his insomnia; and in order to sleep he must at least get tired. And, as it was a long walk, it was half-past ten before he reached home, and he certainly was very tired.

Though he so criticized the flat that he had taken in March, and abused it so gloatingly, excusing himself to himself on the ground that he was only "camping there temporarily," and that he was stranded in Petersburg through that "damned lawsuit"—the flat was by no means so bad and indecent as he made out. The approach was really rather dark and "grubby" and through the gateway, but the flat itself, on the second story, consisted of two big, high-ceilinged and bright rooms, separated from one another by a dark entry, and looking one on the street, the other on the courtyard. Adjoining the room the windows of which looked on the courtyard was a small study, which had been designed to serve as a bedroom; but Velchaninov kept it littered with books and papers; he slept in one of the larger rooms, the one that looked on the street. He had a bed made up on the sofa. The furniture was quite decent, though secondhand, and he had besides a few articles of value—the relics of his former prosperity: bronze and china bric-a-brac, and big, genuine Bokhara rugs; even two fairly good pictures had been preserved; but everything had been unmistakably in disorder, out of place, and even dusty ever since his servant, Pelagea, had gone home to Novgorod for a stay and left him alone. The oddity of having an unmarried female acting as a servant for a bachelor and man of the world who was still anxious to keep up the style of a gentleman almost made Velchaninov blush, though he was very well satisfied with his Pelagea. The girl had come to him when he took the flat in the spring, from a family of his acquaintance who were going abroad, and she had put the flat to rights. But when she went away he could not bring himself to engage another woman; to engage a manservant was not worth while for a short time; besides, he did not like menservants. And so it was arranged that the sister of the porter's wife should come in every morning to clear up and that Velchaninov should leave the key at the porter's lodge when he went out. She did absolutely nothing, merely pocketed her wages; and he suspected her of pilfering. Yet he dismissed everything with a shrug and was positively glad that he was left quite alone in the flat. But there are limits to everything; and at some jaundiced moments the "filth" was absolutely insufferable to his nerves, and he almost always went into his rooms with a feeling of repugnance.

But this time he barely gave himself time to undress; flinging himself on the bed, he irritably resolved to think of nothing, but to go to sleep "this minute," whatever might happen; and, strange to say, he did fall asleep as soon as his head touched the pillow; such a thing had not happened to him for almost a month.

He slept for nearly three hours, but his sleep was uneasy, and he had strange dreams such as one has in fever. He dreamed of some crime which he had committed and concealed and of which he was accused unanimously by people who kept coming up to him. An immense crowd collected, but more people still came, so that the door was not shut but remained wide open. But his whole interest was centered on a strange person, once an intimate friend of his, who was dead, but had now somehow suddenly also come to see him. What tormented Velchaninov most was that he did not know who the man was, had forgotten his name, and could nowise recall it. All he knew was that he had once liked him very much. All the other people who had come in seemed to expect from this man a final word that would decide Velchaninov's guilt or innocence, and all were waiting impatiently. But he sat at the table without moving, kept silent, and would not speak. The noise did not cease for a moment, the general irritation grew more intense, and suddenly in a fury Velchaninov struck the man for refusing to speak, and felt a strange enjoyment in doing it. His heart stood stock-still with misery and horror at what he had done, but there was enjoyment in that. Utterly en-

raged, he struck him a second time and a third, and, drunk
with rage and terror, which reached the pitch of madness,
but in which there was infinite delight, he lost count of his
blows, and went on beating him without stopping. He
wanted to demolish all, all this. Suddenly something happened; they all shrieked horribly and turned around to the
door, as though expecting something, and at that instant
there came the sound of a ring at the bell, repeated three
times, with violence enough to pull the bell off. Velchaninov
woke up and was wide awake in an instant. He leaped
headlong out of bed and rushed to the door; he was absolutely convinced that the ring at the bell was not a dream
and that someone really had rung his bell that moment.
"It would be too unnatural for such a distinct, such a real,
palpable ring to be part of a dream!"

But to his surprise the ring at the bell turned out to be a
dream, too. He opened the door, went out into the passage, even peeped down the stairs—there was absolutely
no one there. The bell hung motionless. Surprised, but relieved, he went back into his room. When he had lighted a
candle he remembered that he had left the door closed but
not locked. He had often in the past forgotten when he
came home to lock the door for the night, not thinking it
of much importance.

Several times Pelagea had given him a talking to about it.
He went back into the passage to lock the door, opened it
once more, and looked out on the landing, but only fastened the door on the inside with the hook, without taking
the trouble to turn the key. The clock struck half-past two;
so he must have slept three hours.

His dream had so disturbed him that he did not want to
go to bed again at once, and made up his mind to walk up
and down his room for half an hour—"time enough to smoke
a cigar." Hastily dressing, he went to the window and lifted
the thick damask curtain and the white blind behind it. It
was already daylight out of doors. The light summer nights
of Petersburg always worked on his nerves and of late had
intensified his insomnia, so that it was expressly on this ac-

count that he had, a fortnight previously, put up thick damask curtains which completely excluded the light when they were fully drawn. Letting in the daylight and forgetting the lighted candle on the table, he fell to pacing up and down the room, still oppressed by a sort of morbid and heavy feeling. The impression of the dream was still upon him. A feeling of distress that he should have been capable of raising his hand against that man and beating him persisted.

"That man doesn't exist, and never has existed; it's all a dream. So why am I worrying about it?"

He fell to thinking with exasperation, as though all his troubles were concentrated on this, that he was certainly beginning to be ill—"a sick man."

It was always painful to him to think that he was getting old and sickly, and in his bad moments he exaggerated his aging and sickening on purpose to irritate himself.

"Old age," he muttered; "I'm getting quite old, I'm losing my memory, I see apparitions, I have dreams, bells ring. . . . Damn it all, I know from experience that such dreams are always a sign of fever with me. . . . I am convinced that all this business with the crape is a dream too. I was certainly right yesterday: it's I, I, who am pestering him, not he me. I've woven a romance about him, and I have crawled under the table in fright. And why do I call him a low fellow? He may be a very decent person. His face is not attractive, certainly, though there is nothing particularly ugly about it; he's dressed like anyone else. Only in his eyes there's something. . . . Here I'm at it again! I'm thinking about him again! What the devil does the look in his eyes matter to me? Can't I get on without that gallows bird?"

Among the thoughts that kept starting up in his mind, one rankled painfully: he felt suddenly convinced that this gentleman with the crape on his hat had once been an acquaintance on friendly terms with him, and that he now sneered at him when he met him because he knew some former great secret of his, and saw him now in such a humiliating position. He went mechanically over to the window, meaning to open it and get a breath of the night air, and—and he suddenly shuddered all over: it seemed to him that something incredible and unheard of had suddenly happened before his eyes.

He had not yet opened the window but he quickly slipped to one side of it and hid himself: on the deserted pavement opposite he suddenly saw directly facing the house the man with the crape on his hat. The gentleman was standing on the pavement looking toward his windows, but evidently not noticing him, staring inquisitively at the house as though considering something. He seemed to be deliberating and unable to decide: he lifted his hand and seemed to put his finger to his forehead. At last he made up his mind; took a cursory glance around, and began, stealthily, on tiptoe, crossing the street. Yes, he went in at the gateway by the wicket (which sometimes in summer was left unbolted till three o'clock). "He's coming to me," flashed on Velchaninov's mind, and, also on tiptoe, he ran headlong to the door and stood before it silent and numb with suspense, softly laying his trembling right hand on the hook of the door he had just fastened, listening intently for the sound of footsteps on the stairs.

His heart beat so violently that he was afraid he might not hear the stranger come up on tiptoe. He did not understand the situation, but he felt it all with tenfold intensity. His dream seemed to have merged with reality. Velchaninov was by nature bold. He sometimes liked to flaunt fearlessness in the face of danger, even if there was only himself to admire it. But now there was something else as well. The man who had so lately been given to morbid depression and complaining was completely transformed; he was not the same man. A nervous, noiseless laugh broke from him. Behind the closed door he divined every movement of the stranger.

"Ah, now he's going up the stairs, he has gone up, he's looking about him; he's listening; he's holding his breath, moving stealthily. . . . Ah! He has taken hold of the handle, he's pulling it, trying it! He reckoned on the door not being locked! So he knows I sometimes forget to lock it! He's pulling at the handle again; why, does he imagine that the hook will come off? He's sorry to leave! Is he sorry to leave with no results?"

And indeed everything must have happened just as he pictured it; someone really was standing on the other side of the door, and was softly and noiselessly trying the lock, pulling at the handle and—"of course, had his object in doing all this." But by now Velchaninov had resolved to settle the matter, and with a sort of rapture he got ready for the moment. He had an irresistible longing suddenly to unfasten the hook, suddenly to fling open the door, to confront the "bugbear" face to face and say, "What may you be doing here, honored sir?"

And so he did: seizing the moment, he suddenly lifted the hook, pushed the door, and—almost fell over the gentleman with crape on his hat.

Chapter III: Pavel Pavlovich Trusotzky

The latter stood speechless, rooted to the spot. They stood facing one another in the doorway, and stared fixedly into each other's faces. Some moments passed and suddenly—Velchaninov recognized his visitor!

At the same time the visitor evidently realized that Velchaninov recognized him fully. There was a gleam in his eye that betrayed it. In one instant his white face melted into a sugary smile.

"I have the pleasure, I believe, of addressing Alexey Ivanovich?" he almost chanted in a voice of deep feeling, ludicrously incongruous with the circumstances.

"Surely you are not Pavel Pavlovich Trusotzky?" Velchaninov brought out with an air of perplexity.

"We were acquainted nine years ago at T——, and if

you will allow me to remind you—we were intimately acquainted."

"Yes . . . to be sure, but now it's three o'clock, and for the last ten minutes you've been trying to see whether my door was locked or not."

"Three o'clock!" cried the visitor, taking out his watch and showing grievous surprise; "why, so it is. Three! I beg your pardon, Alexey Ivanovich, I ought to have considered that before coming up: I'm quite ashamed. I'll come again and explain, in a day or two, but now . . ."

"Oh, no! If there's to be an explanation, will you kindly give it me this minute!" Velchaninov interposed. "This way, please, across the threshold, into my flat. No doubt you intended to come inside yourself, and have not turned up in the middle of the night simply to try locks."

He was excited and at the same time taken aback, and felt that he could not grasp the situation. He was even somewhat ashamed—there was neither mystery nor danger, the whole phantasmagoria had proved to be nothing, all that had turned up was the foolish figure of some Pavel Pavlovich. And yet he did not believe that it was all so simple; he had a vague presentiment and dread of something. Having made his visitor sit down in an armchair, he seated himself impatiently on his bed, not a yard away, bent forward with his hands on his knees, and waited irritably for him to speak. He scanned him greedily and tried to recall him. But, strange to say, the man was silent, quite silent, and seemed not to realize that he was "obliged" to speak at once; on the contrary, he, too, gazed at Velchaninov with a look of expectation. It was possible that he was simply timid, feeling at first a certain awkwardness like a mouse in a trap; but Velchaninov flew into a rage.

"Well, now!" he cried; "you are not a phantom or a dream, I suppose! You've not come to play at being dead, surely? Explain yourself, my good man!"

The visitor fidgeted, smiled, and began warily:

"So far as I see, what strikes you most of all, sir, is my coming at such an hour and under such peculiar circumstances. . . . So that, remembering all the past, and how we parted, sir, I really find it strange now. . . . I had no intention of calling, though, and it has only happened by accident, sir. . . ."

"How by accident? Why, I saw you through the window run across the street on tiptoe!"

"Ah, you saw me! So perhaps you know more about it all than I do! But I'm only irritating you. . . . You see, sir, I arrived here some three weeks ago on business of my own. . . . I am Pavel Pavlovich Trusotzky, you know; you recognized me yourself, sir. I am trying to get transferred to another province and to a considerably superior post in another department. . . . But all that's neither here nor there, though . . . The point is, if you must know, that I have been hanging about here for the last three weeks, and I seem to be dragging out my business on purpose—that is, the business of my transfer—and really, if it comes off I do believe I shan't notice that it has come off and shall stay on in your Petersburg, sir, what with my mood. I hang about as though I had lost sight of my object and, as it were, pleased to have lost sight of it, sir, what with my mood. . . ."

"What mood?" Velchaninov asked, frowning.

The visitor raised his eyes to him, lifted his hat, and pointed to the crape on it with firm dignity.

"Yes, that's my mood."

Velchaninov gazed blankly first at the crape and then at the countenance of his visitor. Suddenly the blood rushed into his cheeks and he grew terribly agitated.

"Surely not Natalya Vassilyevna?"

"Yes! Natalya Vassilyevna! Last March . . . consumption, and almost suddenly, after two or three months! And I am left—as you see!"

As he said this, the visitor, in deep emotion, spread out his hand. The hat with the crape on it was in his left one, and for ten seconds at least his bald head remained bowed low.

His air and this gesture seemed to revive Velchaninov; a

sneering and even provocative smile hovered on his lips—
but only for a moment: the news of the death of this lady
(whom he had known so long ago and had long ago succeeded in forgetting) gave him a shock which was a complete surprise to him.

"Is it possible?" he muttered the first words that came to
his tongue; "and why didn't you come straight and tell
me?"

"I thank you for your sympathy. I see it and appreciate
it, in spite of . . ."

"In spite of?"

"In spite of so many years of separation, you have just
shown such sympathy for my sorrow and even for me that
I am, of course, sensible of gratitude. That was all I wanted
to express, sir. It's not that I had doubts of my friends:
even here I can find sincerest friends—Stepan Mihailovich
Bagautov, for instance. But you know, Alexey Ivanovich,
our acquaintance with you—friendship rather, as I gratefully recall it—dates as far back as nine years ago, you
never came back to us, there was no interchange of
letters. . . ."

The visitor chanted his phrases as though following a
score, but all the while that he was holding forth he looked
at the floor, though, no doubt, all the time he saw everything. But Velchaninov, too, had by now regained his composure to a degree.

With a very strange feeling, which grew stronger and
stronger, he listened to Pavel Pavlovich and watched him,
and when the latter suddenly paused, the most incongruous
and surprising ideas rushed into his mind.

"But how was it I didn't recognize you till now?" he
cried, growing more animated. "Why, we've stumbled
across each other five times in the street!"

"Yes; I remember that, too; you were constantly crossing my path—twice, or perhaps three times. . . ."

"That is, *you* were constantly running into me, not I into
you."

Velchaninov stood up and suddenly, quite unexpectedly,

burst into laughter. Pavel Pavlovich paused, looked at him attentively, but at once continued:

"And as for your not recognizing me, you might well have forgotten me, and, besides, I've had smallpox and it has left some traces on my face."

"Smallpox? To be sure, he has had smallpox! How——"

"How the devil did I manage that? Anything may happen. One never can tell, Alexey Ivanovich; one does have such misfortunes."

"Only it's awfully funny, all the same. But continue, continue, my dear friend!"

"Though I too did meet you, sir . . ."

"Stay! Why did you say 'how the devil did I manage that' just now? I meant to use a much more polite expression. But go on, go on!"

For some reason he felt more and more cheerful. The feeling of shock was completely effaced by another emotion. He walked up and down the room with rapid steps.

"Even though I too did meet you, sir, and though when I set out for Petersburg I intended to seek you out, yet now, I repeat, I have been in such a frame of mind . . . and so mentally shattered ever since March. . . ."

"Oh, yes! shattered since March . . . Wait a minute, do you smoke?"

"As you know, when Natalya Vassilyevna was living I . . ."

"To be sure, to be sure; and since March?"

"A cigarette, perhaps."

"Here is a cigarette. Light it—and go on! Go on. It's awfully——"

And, lighting a cigar, Velchaninov quickly settled himself on the bed again.

Pavel Pavlovich paused.

"But how excited you are yourself. Are you quite in good health?"

"Oh, damn my health!" Velchaninov suddenly grew angry. "Continue!"

The visitor, for his part, seeing his companion's agitation, was becoming better pleased and more self-confident.

"But what is there to continue?" he began again. "Imagine, Alexey Ivanovich, in the first place, a man destroyed —that is, not simply destroyed, but radically, so to say; a man whose existence is transformed after twenty years of married life, who wanders about the dusty streets with no proper object, as though in a steppe, almost in a state of self-forgetfulness, and finding a certain fascination in that self-forgetfulness. It is natural that sometimes, when I meet an acquaintance, even a real friend, I purposely go out of my way to avoid approaching him, at such a moment of self-forgetfulness, I mean. And at another moment you remember everything, and so long to see anyone who witnessed and participated in that recent but irrevocable past, and your heart beats so violently that you are ready to risk throwing yourself into the arms of a friend not only by day but by night as well, even if you may have to wake him up at three o'clock in the morning. . . . I have made a mistake about the time only, not about our friendship; for at this moment I am rewarded more than enough. And as for the time, I really thought it was only twelve, feeling as I do. You drink the cup of your sorrow till you are drunk with it. And it's not sorrow, indeed, but the novelty of my state that crushes me. . . ."

"How strangely you express yourself!" Velchaninov observed gloomily, becoming extremely grave again.

"Yes, I do express myself strangely. . . ."

"And you're . . . not joking?"

"Joking!" exclaimed Pavel Pavlovich in pained surprise, "and at the moment when I am announcing . . ."

"Oh, don't speak of that, I entreat you!"

Velchaninov got up and began pacing the room again. So passed five minutes. The visitor seemed about to get up too, but Velchaninov shouted, "Sit still, sit still!" and Pavel Pavlovich obediently sank back into his armchair at once.

"But how you have changed, though," Velchaninov began again, suddenly stopping before him as if all at once struck by the thought. "You've dreadfully changed! Extraordinarily! Quite a different person."

"That's not strange: nine years, sir."

"No, no, no, it's not a question of years! It's not that you've changed so much in appearance; you've changed in another respect!"

"That, too, may well be due to nine years, sir."

"Or is it since March!"

"He—he!" Pavel Pavlovich sniggered slyly. "That's a playful idea of yours. . . . But if I may venture—what is the change exactly?"

"Why, the Pavel Pavlovich I used to know was such a solid, proper person, that Pavel Pavlovich was such a clever chap, and now—this Pavel Pavlovich is a regular *vaurien!*"

He was at that stage of irritability in which even reserved people say more than they ought to.

"*Vaurien!* you think so? And not a clever chap now—not clever?" Pavel Pavlovich chuckled with delight.

"Clever chap be damned! Now I daresay you really are *clever.*"

"I'm insolent, but this low fellow's more so and . . . and what is his object?" Velchaninov was thinking all the while.

"Oh, dearest, most precious friend!" cried the visitor suddenly, growing extremely agitated and turning around in his chair. "What are we saying? We are not in society now, we're not in the brilliant company of the great and the worldly! We're two former old friends, very sincere friends! And we've come together in the fullest sincerity and we recall to one another the priceless bond of friendship of which the dear departed was the most precious link!"

And he was so carried away, as it were, by the ecstasy of his feeling that he bowed his head as before, and hid his face in his hat. Velchaninov watched him with aversion and uneasiness.

"What if he's simply a buffoon?" flashed through his mind; "but, n-no, n-no! I don't think he's drunk—he may be drunk, though: his face is red. Even if he were drunk—it comes to the same thing. What's he driving at? What does the low fellow want?"

"Do you remember, do you remember," cried Pavel Pavlovich, removing the hat by degrees and seeming more and more carried away by his reminiscences, "do you remember our trips into the country, our evenings and little parties with dancing and innocent games at the house of his Excellency, our most hospitable Semyon Semyonovich? And how we used to read together, the three of us, in the evening! And our first acquaintance with you, sir, when you called on me that morning to make inquiries about your business, and even raised your voice, and suddenly Natalya Vassilyevna came in, and within ten minutes you had become a real friend of the family and so you were for a whole year, exactly as in Mr. Turgenev's play, *A Provincial Lady*."[1]

Velchaninov paced slowly up and down, looked at the floor, listened with impatience and loathing, but—listened intently.

"The thought of *A Provincial Lady* never entered my head," he interrupted, somewhat confused, "and you never used to talk in such a squeaky voice and such . . . unnatural language. What is that for?"

"I certainly used to be more silent, sir—that is, I was more reserved, sir," Pavel Pavlovich interposed hurriedly. "You know I used to prefer listening while the dear departed talked. You remember how she used to talk, how wittily. . . . And as for *A Provincial Lady* and Stupendyev particularly, you are quite right, for I remember it was afterward we ourselves, the precious departed and I, used to speak of that at quiet moments after you'd gone away—comparing our first meeting with that drama, for there really was a resemblance. In regard to Stupendyev especially."

"What Stupendyev? Damn him!" cried Velchaninov, and

[1] In the play the young wife of an elderly official by the name of Stupendyev makes a visiting count fall in love with her.

he actually stamped his foot, utterly put out at the mention of "Stupendyev," owing to a disturbing recollection evoked by the name.

"Stupendyev is a character, sir, a character in a play, the husband in *A Provincial Lady*," Pavel Pavlovich piped in a voice of honeyed sweetness; "but that belongs to another class of our precious and happy memories, when after your departure Stepan Mihailovich Bagautov bestowed his friendship on us, exactly as you did, for five whole years."

"Bagautov? What do you mean? What Bagautov?" Velchaninov stood still as though petrified.

"Bagautov, Stepan Mihailovich, who bestowed his friendship on us, a year after you and . . . and exactly as you did, sir."

"Good heavens, yes! I know that!" cried Velchaninov, recovering himself at last. "Bagautov! Why, of course, he had a berth in your town. . . ."

"He had, he had! At the governor's! From Petersburg, a very elegant young man, belonging to the best society!" Pavel Pavlovich exclaimed in a positive ecstasy.

"Yes, yes, yes! What was I thinking of? Why, he, too——"

"He too, he too," Pavel Pavlovich repeated in the same ecstasy, catching up the incautious word his companion had dropped. "He too! Well, we acted *A Provincial Lady* at his Excellency's, our most hospitable Semyon Semyonovich's private theater—Stepan Mihailovich was the 'count,' I was the 'husband,' and the dear departed was 'the Provincial Lady'—only they took away the 'husband's' part from me. Natalya Vassilyevna insisted on it, so that I did not act the 'husband,' allegedly because I was not fitted for the part. . . ."

"How the devil could you be Stupendyev? You're pre-eminently Pavel Pavlovich Trusotzky and not Stupendyev," said Velchaninov, speaking with coarse rudeness and almost trembling with irritation. "Only, excuse me; Bagautov's in Petersburg, I saw him myself in the spring! Why don't you go and see him too?"

"I have called on him every blessed day, for the last fortnight. I'm not admitted! He's ill, he can't see me! And, only fancy, I've found out from firsthand sources that he really is very dangerously ill! The friend of six years! Oh, Alexey Ivanovich, I tell you, and I repeat it, that sometimes you're in such a mood that you wish the earth would open beneath your feet; yes, really; at another moment you feel like embracing any one of those who, so to say, witnessed and participated in the past, and solely that you may weep, absolutely for no other purpose than to be able to weep!"

"Well, anyway, I've had enough of you for today, haven't I?" Velchaninov brought out abruptly.

"More than enough, more!" Pavel Pavlovich got up from his seat at once. "It's four o'clock and, what's worse, I have so selfishly disturbed you. . . ."

"Listen, I will be sure to come and see you myself, and then, I hope . . . Tell me straight out, tell me frankly, you are not drunk today?"

"Drunk! Not a bit of it. . . ."

"Hadn't you been drinking, just before you came, or earlier?"

"Do you know, Alexey Ivanovich, you're in a regular fever."

"I'll come and see you tomorrow morning before one o'clock."

"And I've been noticing for a long time that you seem, as it were, delirious," Pavel Pavlovich interrupted with relish, still harping on the same subject. "I feel conscience-stricken, really, that by my awkwardness . . . but I'm going, I'm going! And you lie down and get some sleep!"

"Why, you haven't told me where you're living," Velchaninov called hastily after him.

"Didn't I tell you? At the Pokrovsky Hotel."

"What Pokrovsky Hotel?"

"Why, close to the Pokrovsky Church, close by, in the side street. I've forgotten the name of the street and I've forgotten the number, only it's close by the Pokrovsky Church."

"I shall find it!"

"You'll be very welcome."

He was by now on his way downstairs.

"Wait!" Velchaninov shouted after him again; "you are not going to give me the slip?"

"How do you mean, give you the slip?" cried Pavel Pavlovich, staring at him and turning around to smile on the third step.

Instead of answering, Velchaninov shut the door with a loud slam, carefully locked it, and fastened the hook. Returning to the room, he spat as though he had been in contact with something unclean.

After standing for some five minutes in the middle of the room, he flung himself on the bed without undressing and in one minute fell asleep. The forgotten candle burned itself out on the table.

Chapter IV: Wife, Husband, and Lover

He slept very soundly and woke up at half-past nine sharp; he immediately raised himself, sat up in bed, and began at once thinking of "that woman's death." The shock of the sudden news of that death the night before had left a certain agitation and even pain. That pain and agitation had only for a time been smothered by a strange idea while Pavel Pavlovich was with him. But now, on waking up, all that had happened nine years before rose before his mind with extraordinary vividness.

This woman, this Natalya Vassilyevna, the wife of "that Trusotzky," he had once loved, and he had been her lover for the whole year that he had spent at T——, ostensibly on business of his own (that, too, was a lawsuit over a disputed inheritance), although his presence had not really been necessary for so long. The real cause of his remaining was this liaison. The liaison and his love had such complete possession of him that it was as though he were in bondage to Natalya Vassilyevna, and he would probably have been ready on the spot to do anything, however monstrous and senseless, to satisfy that woman's slightest caprice.

Nothing like it had happened to him before or was to happen to him since. At the end of the year, when separation was inevitable, although it was expected to be only a brief one, Velchaninov was in such despair, as the fatal time drew near, that he proposed to Natalya Vassilyevna that she should elope with him, that he should carry her off from her husband, that they should throw up everything and settle abroad forever. Nothing but the gibes and firm determination of the lady (who had quite approved of the project at first, probably from boredom or to amuse herself) could have dissuaded him and forced him to go alone. And actually, before two months had passed, he was asking himself in Petersburg the question which had always remained unanswered: had he really loved that woman or had it been nothing but an "infatuation"? And it was not levity or the influence of some new passion that had given rise to this question; for those first two months in Petersburg he had been rather deranged and had scarcely noticed any woman, although he had at once joined his former circle of acquaintances and had seen a hundred women. At the same time he knew that if he found himself that moment in T—— he would promptly fall under the oppressive influence of that woman's fascination again, in spite of any questions. Even five years later his conviction was unchanged. But five years later he admitted this to himself with indignation and he even thought of "that woman" herself with hatred. He was ashamed of that year at T——; he could not even understand how such a "stupid" passion could have been possible for him, Velchaninov. All his memories of that passion had become a disgrace to him; and he blushed to the point of tears and was tormented by remorse. It is true that a few years later he had become somewhat calmer; he tried to forget it all—and almost succeeded. And now, all at once, nine years afterward, all this had so suddenly and strangely risen up before him again, after he heard that night of the death of Natalya Vassilyevna.

Now, sitting in his bed, with confused thoughts crowding his mind in disorder, he felt and realized clearly one thing only—that, in spite of the "shock" he had experienced at the news, he was nevertheless quite undisturbed by her death. "Can it be that I am not even sorry for her?" he asked himself. It is true that he had now no feeling of hatred for her, and that he could judge her more impartially, more fairly. In the course of those nine years of separation he had long since formulated the view that Natalya Vassilyevna belonged to the class of most ordinary provincial ladies moving in good provincial society, "and, who knows? perhaps she really was such, and it was only I who formed so fantastic an idea about her." He had always suspected, however, that there might be an error in that view; and he felt it even now. And, indeed, the facts were opposed to it; this Bagautov, too, had had for several years a liaison with her and apparently he, too, had been "under the influence of her fascination." Bagautov really was a young man belonging to the best Petersburg society and, as he was an "empty-headed fellow" (Velchaninov used to say of him), he could only have had a successful career in Petersburg. Yet he had neglected Petersburg— that is, sacrificed his most important advantage—and remained for five years in T—— solely on account of that woman! Yes, and he had finally returned to Petersburg, perhaps only because he, too, had been cast off like "an old, worn-out shoe." So there must have been in that woman something exceptional—a power of attracting, of enslaving, of dominating.

And yet one would have thought that she had not the means with which to attract and to enslave. She was not exactly pretty; perhaps she was actually plain. She was twenty-eight when Velchaninov first knew her. Though not altogether beautiful, her face was sometimes charmingly animated, but her eyes were not pretty: there was something too hard in their gaze. She was very thin. On the intellectual side she had not been well educated; her keen intelligence was unmistakable, but one-sided. Her manners were those of a provincial lady and at the same time, it is true, she had a great deal of tact; she had taste, but showed it principally in knowing how to dress. In character she was resolute and domineering; she could never compromise in anything: it was all, or nothing. In difficult situations her firmness and determination were amazing. She was capable of generosity and at the same time utterly unjust. To argue with that lady was impossible: "twice two makes four" meant nothing to her. She never thought herself wrong or to blame in anything. Her continual unfaithfulness to her husband did not weigh on her conscience in the least. But, to quote Velchaninov's own comparison, she was like a Blessed Virgin of the Khlysty,[2] who believes implicitly that she is the Mother of God—so Natalya Vassilyevna believed implicitly in everything she did. She was faithful to her lover, but only as long as he did not bore her. She was fond of tormenting her lover, but she liked making up for it too. She was of a passionate, cruel, and sensual type. She hated depravity and condemned it with exaggerated severity and—was herself depraved. No sort of factual evidence could have made her aware of her own depravity. "Most likely she *genuinely* does not know it," Velchaninov thought about her even before he left T——. (We may remark, by the way, that he was the accomplice of her depravity.) "She is one of those women who are born to be unfaithful wives. Such women never surrender their chastity while unwed; it's a law of their nature to be married to the end of committing adultery. The husband is the first lover but never till after the wedding. No one gets married more adroitly and easily than this type of woman. For her first infidelity the husband is always to blame. And it is all accomplished in a spirit of perfect sin-

[2] A Russian sect; according to its doctrine, each community of the faithful has its *bogaraditza* (Mother of God), as also its Christ.

cerity: to the end they feel themselves absolutely right, and, of course, entirely innocent."

Velchaninov was convinced that there really was such a type of woman; but, on the other hand, he was also convinced that there was a type of husband corresponding to that woman, whose sole vocation was to correspond to that feminine type. To his mind, the essence of such a husband lay in his being, so to say, "the eternal husband," or rather in being, all his life, a husband and nothing more. "Such a man is born and grows up only to be a husband, and, having married, is promptly transformed into a supplement of his wife, even when he happens to have an unmistakable character of his own. The chief sign of such a husband is a well-known decoration. He can no more escape wearing horns than the sun can help shining; he is not only unaware of the fact, but is bound by the very laws of his nature to be unaware of it." Velchaninov firmly believed in the existence of these two types and in Pavel Pavlovich Trusotzky's being a perfect representative of one of them. The Pavel Pavlovich of the previous night was, of course, very different from the Pavel Pavlovich he had known at T——. He found him incredibly changed, but Velchaninov knew that he was bound to have changed and that all that was perfectly natural; only as long as his wife was alive could Mr. Trusotzky have remained all that he used to be, but, as it was, he was only a fraction of a whole, suddenly cut off and set free—that is, something astonishing and unique.

As for the Pavel Pavlovich as he had been at T——, this is what Velchaninov remembered of him.

"Of course, at T——, Pavel Pavlovich had been simply a husband," and nothing more. If he was in addition an official, for instance, it was solely because his post, too, was one of the obligations of his married life; he was in the service for the sake of his wife and her social position in T——, though he was for his own part a zealous functionary. He was thirty-five then and was possessed of a considerable fortune. In the execution of his official duties he showed no special ability or special lack of it either. He used to mix with all the best people in the province and was said to be on an excellent footing with them. Natalya Vassilyevna was deeply respected in T——; she did not, however, greatly appreciate that, accepting it as simply her due, but in her own house she was superb at entertaining guests, and Pavel Pavlovich had been so well trained by her that he was able to behave with nobility of manner even when entertaining the highest dignitaries of the province. Perhaps (it seemed to Velchaninov) he had intelligence, too, but, as Natalya Vassilyevna did not like her spouse to talk too much, his intelligence was not very noticeable. Perhaps he had many natural good qualities, as well as bad ones. But his good qualities were kept under a slip-cover, as it were, and his evil propensities were almost completely stifled. Velchaninov remembered, for instance, that Pavel Pavlovich sometimes betrayed a disposition to laugh at his neighbors, but this was sternly forbidden him. He was fond, too, at times of telling anecdotes; but a watch was kept on that weakness too: and he was only allowed to tell such as were brief and of little importance. He was inclined to spend some time with a circle of friends outside of the house and even have a drop with a crony; but this failing had been torn up by the roots. And it is noteworthy that no outside observer would have said that Pavel Pavlovich was a hen-pecked husband; Natalya Vassilyevna seemed an absolutely obedient wife, and most likely believed herself to be one. It was possible that Pavel Pavlovich loved Natalya Vassilyevna passionately; but no one noticed it, and, indeed, it was impossible to notice it, and this reserve was probably due to her domestic discipline.

Several times during his stay at T——, Velchaninov had asked himself whether the husband had any suspicion at all about his wife. Several times he questioned Natalya Vassilyevna seriously about it, and always received the answer, uttered with a certain annoyance, that her husband knew nothing and never could know anything about it and that it was "no concern of his." Another characteristic of hers was that she never laughed at Pavel Pavlovich and did not consider him ridiculous or very homely and would, indeed, have taken his part very warmly if anyone had dared to be uncivil to him. Having no children, she was naturally bound to become a society woman, but her home life, too, was essential to her. Social pleasures had never completely dominated her, and at home she was very fond of needlework and looking after the house. Pavel Pavlovich had recalled, that night, the evenings they had spent in reading; it happened that sometimes Velchaninov read aloud and sometimes Pavel Pavlovich: to Velchaninov's surprise, he read aloud excellently. Meanwhile, Natalya Vassilyevna did sewing as she listened, always calmly and serenely. They read Dickens' novels, something from a Russian magazine, at times even something "serious." Natalya Vassilyevna highly appreciated Velchaninov's culture, but appreciated it in silence, as something final and established, of which there was no need to talk. Altogether, her attitude to everything intellectual and literary was rather one of indifference, as to something extraneous though perhaps useful. On the other hand, Pavel Pavlovich's attitude was at times rather warm.

The liaison at T—— was broken suddenly when on Velchaninov's part it had reached its zenith—that is, almost the point of madness. He was suddenly and abruptly dismissed, though it was all so arranged that he went away without grasping that he had been cast off "like a worthless old shoe." Six weeks before his departure, a young artillery officer, fresh out of military school, arrived in T—— and took to visiting the Trusotzkys. Instead of three, they were now a party of four. Natalya Vassilyevna welcomed the boy graciously but treated him as a boy. No suspicion crossed Velchaninov's mind and indeed he had no thought to spare for it, for he had just been told that separation was inevitable. One of the hundreds of reasons urged by Natalya Vassilyevna for his leaving her as soon as possible was that she believed herself to be with child; and, therefore, naturally, he must disappear at once for three or four months at least, so that it would not be so easy for her husband to feel any doubt, if there were any kind of malicious gossip afterward. It was rather a farfetched argument. After a stormy proposition on the part of Velchaninov that she should flee with him to Paris or America, he departed alone to Petersburg, "only for a brief moment, of course," that is, for no more than three months, or nothing would have induced him to go, in spite of any reasons or arguments. Exactly two months later he received in Petersburg a letter from Natalya Vassilyevna asking him never to return, as she already loved another; she informed him that she had been mistaken about her condition. This information was superfluous. It was all clear to him now: he remembered the young officer. With that it was all over for good. He chanced to hear afterward, some years later, that Bagautov had appeared on the scene and spent five whole years there. He explained the disproportionate duration of that affair partly by the fact that Natalya Vassilyevna, by now, was a good deal older, and so more constant in her attachments.

He remained sitting up in bed for nearly an hour; at last he roused himself, rang for Mavra to bring his coffee, drank it hastily, and at eleven o'clock set out to look for the Pokrovsky Hotel. In going there he had a special idea which had only come to him in the morning. He felt somewhat ashamed of his treatment of Pavel Pavlovich the night before and now he wanted to efface the impression.

The whole fantastic business with the door handle the night before, he now put down to chance, to the tipsy condition of Pavel Pavlovich, and perhaps to something else, but he did not really know, exactly, why he was going now to form a new relation with the former husband, when everything had so naturally and by itself ended between them. Something attracted him. He had received a peculiar impression and he was attracted in consequence of it.

Chapter V: Liza

Pavel Pavlovich had no idea of "taking to his heels," and goodness knows why Velchaninov had asked him the question the night before; he must really have been confused. At his first inquiry in a grocery near the Pokrovsky Church, he was directed to the hotel in the side street a couple of paces away. At the hotel, he was told that Mr. Trusotzky was now staying in Marya Sysoevna's furnished rooms, situated in an outbuilding in the same courtyard. Going up the narrow, wet, and very dirty stone stairs, to the second story, where these rooms were, he suddenly heard the sound of crying. It seemed like the crying of a child of seven or eight; the sound was distressing; he heard smothered sobs which would break out, and with them the stamping of feet and shouts of fury, which were smothered, too, in a hoarse falsetto voice, evidently that of a grown-up man. This man seemed to be trying to quiet the child and was apparently very anxious that the crying should not be heard, but was making more noise than it did. The shouts sounded pitiless, and the child seemed to be begging the man's forgiveness. In a small passage at the top, with two doors on both sides of it, Velchaninov met a tall, stout, slovenly-looking peasant woman of forty and asked for Pavel Pavlovich. She pointed toward the door from which the crying was coming. There was a look of some indignation on the fat, purple face of this woman.

"That's how he gets his fun!" she said gruffly and went downstairs.

Velchaninov was just about to knock at the door, but changed his mind and walked straight in. In a small room, roughly though amply furnished with common painted furniture, stood Pavel Pavlovich without his coat and waistcoat. Flushed and irritated, he was trying, by means of shouts, gestures, and perhaps (Velchaninov fancied)

338

kicks, to silence a little girl of eight, dressed in a short black woolen frock, shabby, but befitting a gentleman's daughter. She seemed to be genuinely in hysterics, she gasped hysterically and reached out for Pavel Pavlovich as though she wanted to embrace him, to hug him, to beseech and implore him about something. In one instant the whole scene was transformed: seeing the visitor, the child cried out and dashed away into a tiny room adjoining, and Pavel Pavlovich, for a moment disconcerted, instantly melted into smiles, exactly as he had done the night before, when Velchaninov flung open the door upon him on the stairs.

"Alexey Ivanovich!" he cried, in genuine surprise. "I could never have expected . . . but come in, come in! Here, on the sofa, or here in the armchair, while I . . ."

And he rushed to put on his coat, forgetting to put on his waistcoat.

"Stay as you are, don't stand on ceremony."

Velchaninov sat down on the chair.

"No, allow me to stand on ceremony, sir; here, now I am more respectable. But why are you sitting in the corner? Sit here in the armchair, by the table. . . . Well, I didn't expect you, I didn't expect you!"

He, too, sat down on the edge of a rush-bottomed chair, not beside his "unexpected" visitor, but setting his chair at an angle so as to sit more nearly facing him.

"Why didn't you expect me? Didn't I tell you last night that I would come at this time?"

"I thought you wouldn't come, sir; and when, waking this morning, I reflected on all that happened yesterday, I despaired of ever seeing you again."

Meanwhile Velchaninov was looking about him. The room was in disorder, the bed was not made, clothes were scattered about, on the table were glasses with dregs of coffee in them, crumbs and a bottle of champagne, half full, with the cork out and a glass beside it. He stole a glance toward the next room, but there all was quiet; the child was in hiding and perfectly still.

"Surely you are not drinking that now," said Velchaninov, indicating the champagne.

"The remains . . ." said Pavel Pavlovich in confusion.

"Well, you have changed!"

"It's a bad habit, come upon me all at once, sir; yes, really, since that date. I'm not lying! I can't restrain myself. Don't be uneasy, Alexey Ivanovich, I'm not drunk now, and I'm not going to talk nonsense now as I did at your flat yesterday; but I'm telling the truth, it's all since then, sir! And if anyone had told me six months ago that I should break down like this, if anyone had shown me to myself in the looking glass—I shouldn't have believed it."

"You were drunk last night, then?"

"I was, sir," Pavel Pavlovich admitted in a low voice, looking down in embarrassment. "And you see I wasn't exactly drunk then, but I had been a little before. I want to explain, because I'm always worse a little while after. When there is little left of the drunkenness, a kind of brutality and foolishness remain, and I feel my grief more intensely too. It's because of my grief, perhaps, I drink. Then I'm capable of playing all sorts of pranks quite stupidly and insulting people for nothing. I must have presented myself very strangely to you yesterday."

"Do you mean to say you don't remember?"

"Not remember! I remember it all. . . ."

"You see, Pavel Pavlovich, that's just what I thought," Velchaninov said in a conciliatory voice. "What's more, I was myself rather irritable with you last night and . . . too impatient, I readily admit it. I don't feel quite well at times, and then your unexpected arrival last night . . ."

"Yes, at night, at night!" Pavel Pavlovich shook his head, as though surprised and disapproving. "And what possessed me! Nothing would have induced me to come in to you if you had not opened the door yourself; I should have gone away from the door, sir. I came to you about a week ago, Alexey Ivanovich, and did not find you in, but perhaps I should never have come again. I have some pride, too, Alexey Ivanovich, although I do recognize the position I am in. We met in the street, too, and I kept thinking, 'What if he doesn't recognize me? What if he turns away? Nine years are no joke,' and I couldn't make up my mind to approach you. And last night I was making my way from the Petersburg Side and I forgot the time. It all came from that"—he pointed to the bottle—"and from my feelings, sir. It was stupid! Very! And if it had been anyone but you—for you've come to see me even after what happened yesterday, for the sake of old times—I should have given up all hope of renewing our acquaintance!"

Velchaninov listened attentively. The man seemed to him to be speaking sincerely and even with a certain dignity; and yet he did not believe one word he had heard since he came into the room.

"Tell me, Pavel Pavlovich, you are not alone here, then? Whose little girl is that I found with you just now?"

Pavel Pavlovich was positively amazed and raised his eyebrows, but looked frankly and pleasantly at Velchaninov.

"Whose little girl? Why, it's Liza!" he said, with an affable smile.

"What Liza?" muttered Velchaninov, with a sort of inward tremor. The effect was too sudden. When he came in and saw Liza, just before, he was surprised, but had absolutely no presentiment, and thought nothing particular about her.

"Why, our Liza, our daughter Liza!" Pavel Pavlovich smiled.

"Your daughter? Do you mean that you and Natalya . . . Natalya Vassilyevna had children?" Velchaninov asked timidly and mistrustfully, in an oddly low voice.

"Why, of course! But there, upon my word, how should you have heard of it? What am I thinking about! It was after you went away, God blessed us with her!"

Pavel Pavlovich positively jumped up from his chair in some agitation, though of a seemingly agreeable kind.

"I heard nothing about it," said Velchaninov, and he turned pale.

"To be sure, to be sure; from whom could you have

heard it, sir?" said Pavel Pavlovich, in a voice weak with emotion. "My poor wife and I had lost all hope, as no doubt you remember, and suddenly God sent us this blessing, and what it meant to me—He only knows! Just a year after you went away, I believe. No, not a year, not nearly a year. Wait a bit; why, you left us, if my memory does not deceive me, in October or November, I believe."

"I left T—— at the beginning of September, the twelfth of September; I remember it very well."

"In September, was it? H'm! . . . what was I thinking about?" cried Pavel Pavlovich, much surprised. "Well, if that's so, let me see: you went away on the twelfth of September, and Liza was born on the eighth of May, so —September—October—November—December—January—February—March—April—a little over eight months! And if you only knew how my poor wife . . ."

"Show me . . . call her . . ." Velchaninov faltered in a breaking voice.

"Certainly, sir!" said Pavel Pavlovich fussily, at once breaking off what he was saying, as though it were of no consequence. "Directly, directly, I'll introduce her!" And he went hurriedly into the other room to Liza.

Fully three or perhaps four minutes passed; there was a hurried, rapid whispering in the room, and he just caught the sound of Liza's voice. "She's begging not to be brought in," thought Velchaninov. At last they came out.

"You see, she's so bashful," said Pavel Pavlovich; "she's so shy, so proud . . . the image of my poor wife!"

Liza came in, looking down and no longer tearful; her father led her by the hand. She was a tall, slim, very pretty little girl. She quickly raised her big blue eyes to glance with curiosity at the visitor, looked at him sullenly, and dropped them again at once. Her eyes were full of that gravity one sees in children, when they are left alone with a stranger and, retreating into a corner, look gravely and mistrustfully at the unfamiliar visitor; but there may have been some other thought, by no means childish, in her mind—so Velchaninov fancied.

Her father led her straight up to him.

"This nice man Mummy used to know long ago; he was our friend. Don't be shy, hold out your hand."

The child bent forward a little, and timidly held out her hand.

"Natalya Vassilyevna would not have her curtsy, but taught her to make a little bow, and hold out her hand in the English fashion," he added by way of explanation to Velchaninov, watching him intently.

Velchaninov knew that he was being watched, but had quite ceased to trouble himself to conceal his emotion; he sat perfectly still in his chair, held Liza's hand in his, and fixedly gazed at the child. But Liza was in great anxiety about something, and, forgetting her hand in the visitor's hand, kept her eyes fixed on her father. She listened apprehensively to all that he was saying. Velchaninov recognized those big blue eyes at once, but what struck him most of all was the wonderful soft whiteness of her face and the color of her hair; these characteristics were all too significant for him. On the other hand, the molding of her face and the lines of the lips reminded him vividly of Natalya Vassilyevna. Meanwhile, Pavel Pavlovich had for some time been telling him something, speaking, it seemed, with very great warmth and feeling, but Velchaninov did not hear him. He only caught the last sentence:

". . . so that you can't imagine our joy at this gift from the Lord, Alexey Ivanovich! She became everything to me as soon as she came to us, so that I used to think that even if my tranquil happiness should, by God's will, cease to be, Liza would always be left me; that at least I reckoned upon for certain, sir!"

"And Natalya Vassilyevna?" Velchaninov queried.

"Natalya Vassilyevna?" said Pavel Pavlovich affectedly. "You know her way, you remember that she never cared to say a great deal, but when she said good-by to her on her deathbed . . . everything came out then! I said just now 'on her deathbed,' but yet only a day before her death she was upset and angry, said that they were trying to kill her by too much doctoring, that there was nothing wrong with her but an ordinary fever, and that both our doctors were nincompoops, and that as soon as Koch came back (do you remember the old man, our army doctor?) she would be up again in a fortnight! What's more, five hours before her end she remembered that in three weeks' time we must visit her aunt, Liza's godmother, on her name day at her estate. . . ."

Velchaninov suddenly got up from his chair, still holding the child's hand. Among other things it struck him that there was something reproachful in the intense look the child kept fixed upon her father.

"She's not ill?" he asked hurriedly and somewhat oddly.

"I don't think so, sir, but . . . our circumstances here are such . . ." said Pavel Pavlovich, with mournful solicitude. "She's a strange child and nervous at all times; after her mother's death she was ill for a fortnight, hysterical. Why, what a weeping and wailing we had just before you came in . . . do you hear, Liza, do you hear? And what was it all about? All because I go out and leave her; she says it shows I don't love her any more as I used to when Mother was alive—that's her complaint against me. And to think that a fantastic notion like that would get into the head of a child who ought to be playing with her toys. Though here she has no one to play with."

"Why, you . . . you're surely not alone here?"

"Quite alone; the servant only comes in once a day."

"And you go out and leave her like this alone?"

"What else could I do? And when I went out yesterday I locked her in, into that little room there, that's what the tears have been about today. But what else could I do? Judge for yourself: the day before yesterday she went down when I was out, and a boy threw a stone at her in the yard and hit her on the head. Or else she begins crying and runs around to all the lodgers in the yard, asking where I've gone. And that's not right, you know. And I'm a nice one, too; I go out for an hour and come back next morning; that's what happened yesterday. It was a good thing, too, that while I was away the landlady let her out, sent for a locksmith to break the lock—such a disgrace—I literally feel myself a monster. It's all my disturbed state, sir. . . ."

"Papa!" the child said timidly and uneasily.

"There you are, at it again! You're at the same thing again. What did I tell you just now?"

"I won't, I won't!" Liza repeated in terror, hurriedly clasping her hands before him.

"You can't go on like this in these surroundings," Velchaninov all of a sudden said impatiently, in a voice of authority. "Why, you . . . why, you're a man of property; how is it you're living like this—in this outbuilding and in such surroundings?"

"In the outbuilding? But, you see, we may be going away in a week's time, and we've wasted a great deal of money already, even though I have means. . . ."

"Come, that's enough, that's enough." Velchaninov cut him short with increasing impatience, as though meaning plainly, "There's no need to talk, I know all that you will say, and I know with what purpose you are speaking."

"Listen, I'll make you an offer: you said just now that you'll be staying a week, maybe possibly even a fortnight. I know a household here, that is, a family where I'm quite at home—have known them twenty years. The father, Alexander Pavlovich Pogoreltzev, is a privy councilor; he might be of use to you in your business. They are at their summer villa now. They've got a splendid villa. Klavdia Petrovna is like a sister to me or a mother. They have eight children. Let me take Liza to them at once . . . that we may lose no time. They will be delighted to take her in for the whole time you are here, and will treat her like their own child, their own child!"

He was terribly impatient and did not conceal it.

"That's scarcely possible, sir," said Pavel Pavlovich, with a grimace, looking, so Velchaninov fancied, slyly in his face.

"Why, why impossible?"

"Why, how can I let the child go so suddenly, sir—with such a real friend as you, it is true—but into a house of strangers, and of such high rank, where I don't know how she'd be received either?"

"But I've told you that I'm like one of the family!" cried Velchaninov, almost wrathfully. "Klavdia Petrovna will be delighted to take her at a word from me—as though it were my child. Damn it all! Why, you know yourself that you only say all this for the sake of wagging your tongue. . . . There's nothing to discuss!"

He positively stamped his foot.

"I only mean, won't it seem strange, sir! I should have to go and see her once or twice anyway, or she would be left without a father! He—he! . . . And in such a grand household."

"But it's the simplest household, not 'grand' at all!" shouted Velchaninov. "I tell you there are a lot of children there. She'll revive there, that's the whole object. . . . And I'll introduce you myself tomorrow, if you like. And of course you would have to call on them to thank them; we'll drive over every day, if you like."

"It's all so——"

"Nonsense! And, what's more, you know that yourself! Listen, come to me this evening, and stay the night, perhaps, and we'll set off early in the morning so as to get there at twelve."

"My benefactor! And even to stay the night with you . . ." Pavel Pavlovich agreed suddenly with a show of fervent feeling. "That's truly a good deed . . . and where is their villa, sir?"

"Their villa is in Lesnoe."

"Only, I say, what about her dress, sir? For, you know, in such a distinguished household and in their summer villa, too, you know yourself . . . A father's heart, sir. . . ."

"What about her dress? She's in mourning. She couldn't be dressed differently, could she? It's the most suitable dress you could possibly imagine! The only thing is she ought to have clean linen . . . a clean little kerchief. . . ."

Her tucker and what showed of her underlinen were, in fact, very dirty.

"She must change her things at once," said Pavel Pavlovich fussily, "and we'll get together the rest of what she needs in the way of underclothes; Marya Sysoevna has got them in the wash."

"Then you should tell them to fetch a carriage," Velchaninov interposed; "and make haste if you can."

But a difficulty presented itself: Liza resolutely opposed the plan; she had been listening all the time in terror, and, if Velchaninov had had time to look at her attentively while he was persuading Pavel Pavlovich, he would have seen an expression of utter despair upon her little face.

"I am not going," she said firmly, in a low voice.

"There, there! You see, she's her mama over again, sir."

"I'm not Mama over again, I'm not Mama over again!" cried Liza in despair, wringing her little hands, and, as it were, trying to defend herself before her father from the awful reproach of being like her mother. "Papa, Papa, if you leave me . . ."

She suddenly turned on Velchaninov, who was startled, and said, "If you take me, I'll . . ."

But before she had time to say more, Pavel Pavlovich clutched her by the arm and with undisguised anger dragged her almost by the collar into the little room. Whispering followed for some minutes; there was the sound of suppressed crying. Velchaninov was on the point of going in himself, but Pavel Pavlovich came out and with a wry smile announced that she was coming directly. Velchaninov tried not to look at him and kept his eyes turned away.

Marya Sysoevna too appeared, the same peasant woman that he had met just before in the passage; she began packing the linen she had brought with her in a pretty little bag belonging to Liza.

"Is it you, sir, who are taking the little girl away?" she asked, addressing Velchaninov. "Have you a family, then?

It's a good deed, sir: she's a quiet child, you are saving her from a Sodom."

"Come, come, Marya Sysoevna!" muttered Pavel Pavlovich.

"Marya Sysoevna, indeed! That's my name, right enough. It is a Sodom here, isn't it? Is it the proper thing for a child that can understand to see such wicked goings on? They've fetched you a carriage, sir—to Lesnoe, is it?"

"Yes, yes."

"Good luck, then!"

Liza came out pale and, looking down, took her bag. Not one glance in Velchaninov's direction; she restrained herself and did not, as before, rush to embrace her father, even at parting; she was apparently even unwilling to look at him. Her father kissed her decorously on the head and patted it; her lips twitched as he did so and her little chin quivered, but still she did not raise her eyes to her father. Pavel Pavlovich looked pale, and his hands were trembling —Velchaninov noticed that distinctly, though he was doing his utmost not to look at him. The one thing he longed for was to get away as quickly as possible. "After all, it's not my fault," he thought. "It was bound to be so."

They went downstairs; there Marya Sysoevna kissed Liza good-by, and only when she was sitting in the carriage Liza lifted her eyes to her father, flung up her hands, and screamed; another minute and she would have flung herself out of the carriage to him, but the horses had started.

Chapter VI: A New Fantasy of an Idle Man

"Are you feeling ill?" asked Velchaninov in alarm. "I will tell the driver to stop, I'll get you some water. . . ."

She turned her eyes upon him and looked at him angrily, reproachfully.

"Where are you taking me?" she asked sharply and abruptly.

"It's a wonderful family, Liza. They're in a delightful summer villa now; there are a lot of children; they'll love you; they are kind. Don't be angry with me, Liza; I only wish you well."

How strange it would have seemed to all who knew him if anyone could have seen him at that moment.

"How—how—how . . . how horrid you are!" said Liza, choking with stifled tears and glaring at him with her beautiful eyes full of resentment.

"Liza, I . . ."

"You are wicked, wicked, wicked, wicked!"

She wrung her hands. Velchaninov was completely at a loss.

"Liza, darling, if you knew how you drive me to despair!"

"Is it true that he will come tomorrow? Is it true?" she asked peremptorily.

"Yes, yes, I'll bring him myself; I'll take him with me and bring him."

"He'll cheat," she whispered, looking down.

"Doesn't he love you, Liza?"

"He doesn't love me."

"Did he treat you badly? Did he?"

Liza looked at him gloomily and said nothing. She turned away from him again and sat with her eyes obstinately cast down. He began to coax her; he spoke to her with heat, he was in a perfect fever. Liza listened with mistrust and hostility, but she did listen. Her attention gladdened him extremely; he even began explaining to her what was meant by a man's drinking. He told her that he loved her himself and would look after her father. Liza lifted her eyes at last and looked at him intently. He began telling her how he used to know her mama, and he saw that what he told her interested her. Little by little she began answering his questions, though cautiously, stubbornly, and in monosyllables. She still refused to answer his most important questions; she remained obstinately silent about everything to do with her relations with her father in the past. As he talked to her, Velchaninov took her hand in his as before and held it; she did not pull it away. The child was not silent all the time, however; she let out in her vague answers that she loved her father more than her mama, because he had always been fonder of her, and her mama had not cared so much for her, but that when her mama was dying she had kissed her and cried a great deal when everyone had gone out of the room and they were left alone . . . and that now she loved her more than anyone, more than anyone, more than anyone in the world, and every night she loved her more than anyone. But the child was certainly proud. Realizing that she had spoken too freely, she suddenly shrank into herself again and indeed glanced with positive hatred at Velchaninov, who had led her into saying so much. Toward the end of the ride her hysterical condition was almost over, but she sank into brooding and had the look of a wild creature, sullen and gloomily, resolutely stubborn. The fact that she was being taken to a strange house, in which she had never been before, seemed for the time being not to trouble her much. What tormented her was something else. Velchaninov saw that; he guessed that she was ashamed of *him*, that she was ashamed of her father's having so easily let her go with him, of his having, as it were, flung her into his keeping.

"She is ill," he thought, "perhaps very ill; she's been horribly tormented to death. . . . Oh, the drunken, vile beast! I understand him now!"

He urged on the driver; he rested his hopes on the country, the fresh air, the garden, the children, and the new, unfamiliar life, and then, later on . . . But of what would come afterward he had no doubts at all; of the future he had the fullest, brightest hopes. One thing only he knew for certain: that he had never before felt what he was experiencing now and that it would not leave him all his life. "Here is an object, here is life!" he thought rapturously.

A great many thoughts flashed across his mind, but he

did not dwell upon them and obstinately avoided details; without details everything seemed clear and unassailable. His plan of action took shape of itself.

"It will be possible to work upon that wretch," he mused, "by our joint efforts, and he will leave Liza in Petersburg at the Pogoreltzevs', though at first only temporarily, for a certain time, and will go away alone, and Liza will be left to me; that's the whole thing. What more do I want? And . . . of course, he wants that himself; or else why does he torment her?"

At last they arrived. The Pogoreltzevs' country home really was a charming place; they were met first of all by a noisy crowd of children, who thronged the porch. Velchaninov had not been there for a long time, and the children were in a frenzy of delight; they were fond of him. The elder ones shouted to him at once, before he got out of the carriage:

"And how about the case, how is your case getting on?"

The cry was caught up even by the smallest, and they shrieked it mirthfully in imitation of their elders. They were in the habit of teasing him about the lawsuit. But, seeing Liza, they surrounded her at once and began scrutinizing her with intent, silent, childish curiosity. Klavdia Petrovna came out, followed by her husband. She and her husband, too, began with a laughing question about the lawsuit.

Klavdia Petrovna was a lady of about thirty-seven, a plump and still good-looking brunette, with a fresh, rosy face. Her husband was fifty-five, a shrewd and clever man, but above everything good-natured. Their house was in the fullest sense of the word "a home" to Velchaninov, as he had said himself. But underlying this was the special circumstance that, twenty years before, Klavdia Petrovna had been on the point of marrying Velchaninov, then a student, hardly more than a boy. It was a case of first love, ardent, ridiculous, and splendid. It had ended, however, in her marrying Pogoreltzev. Five years later they had met again, and it had all ended in a quiet, serene friendship. A certain warmth, a peculiar glow suffusing their relations, had remained forever. All was pure and irreproachable in Velchaninov's memories of this friendship, and it was the dearer to him for being perhaps the solitary case in which this was so. Here in this family he was simple, unaffected, and kind; he fussed over the children, admitted all his failings, confessed his shortcomings, and never gave himself airs. He swore more than once to the Pogoreltzevs that he should before long give up society, come and live with them, and never leave them again. In his heart he thought of this project seriously.

He told them all that was necessary about Liza in some detail; but a mere request from him was enough, without any special explanations. Klavdia Petrovna kissed the "orphan" and promised for her part to do everything. The children took possession of Liza and carried her off to play in the garden.

After half an hour of lively conversation Velchaninov got up and began saying good-by. He was so impatient that everyone noticed it. They were all astonished; he had not been to see them for three weeks and now he was going after half an hour's stay. He laughed and pledged himself to come next day. They remarked that he seemed to be in a state of great excitement; he suddenly took Klavdia Petrovna's hand and, on the pretext of having forgotten to tell her something important, drew her aside into another room.

"Do you remember what I told you—you alone—what even your husband does not know—of my year at T——?"

"I remember perfectly; you often talked of it."

"It was not talking, it was a confession to you alone, to you alone! I never told you the surname of that woman; she was the wife of this Trusotzky. She is dead, and Liza, her daughter—is my daughter!"

"Is it certain? You are not mistaken?" Klavdia Petrovna asked with some excitement.

"It's perfectly certain, perfectly certain; I am not mistaken!" Velchaninov said ecstatically.

And as briefly as he could, in haste and great agitation,

he told her everything. Klavdia Petrovna already knew the whole story, but not the lady's name. Velchaninov had always been so alarmed at the very idea that anyone who knew him might ever meet Madame Trusotzky and think that *he* could *so* have loved that woman, that he had not till that day dared to reveal her name even to Klavdia Petrovna, his one friend.

"And the father knows nothing?" asked Klavdia Petrovna, when she had heard his story.

"Y-yes, he does know. . . . It worries me that I've not got to the bottom of it yet!" Velchaninov went on eagerly. "He knows, he knows; I noticed it today and yesterday. But I must know how much he knows. That's why I'm in a hurry now. He is coming to me this evening. I can't imagine, though, how he can have found out—found out *everything*, I mean. He knows about Bagautov, there's no doubt of that. But about me? You know how clever women are in reassuring their husbands in such cases! If an angel came down from heaven—the husband would not believe him, but he would believe his wife! Don't shake your head and don't condemn me; I blame and condemned myself, for the whole affair, long ago, long ago! . . . You see, I was so certain he knew when I was there this morning that I compromised myself before him. Would you believe it, I felt so wretched and ashamed of having met him so rudely yesterday (I will tell you all about it fully afterward). He came to me yesterday because of an irresistible malicious desire to let me know that he knew of the wrong done him, and that he knew who had done it; that was the whole reason of his stupid visit in a drunken state. But that was so natural on his part! He simply came to reproach me! I was altogether too impetuous with him this morning and yesterday! Careless—stupid! I betrayed myself to him. Why did he turn up at a moment when I was upset? I tell you he's even been tormenting Liza, tormenting the child, and probably that, too, was to work off his resentment—to vent his spite if only on the child! Yes, he is spiteful—insignificant as he is, yet he is spiteful; very much so, indeed. In himself, he is no more than a buffoon, though, God knows, in the old days he seemed to be a very decent fellow within his limits —it's so natural that he should be indulging in debauchery! One must look at it from a Christian point of view! And you know, my dear, my best of friends, I want to be utterly different to him; I want to show him much kindness. That would be really a 'good deed' on my part. For, you know, after all, I am guilty toward him! Listen, you know there's something else I must tell you. On one occasion in T—— I was in want of four thousand roubles, and he lent me the money on the spot, with no security, and showed genuine pleasure at being of use to me; and, do you know, I took it then, I took it from his hands, I borrowed money from him, do you understand, as from a friend!"

"Only be more careful," Klavdia Petrovna anxiously observed, in response to all this. "And what a state of exaltation you're in! I feel uneasy about you! Of course, Liza will be like a child of my own now. But there's so much, so much still to be settled! The great thing is that you must now be more circumspect; you absolutely must be more circumspect when you are happy or so ecstatic; you're too generous when you are happy," she added, with a smile.

They all came out to see Velchaninov off. The children, who had been playing with Liza in the garden, brought her with them. They seemed to be even more puzzled about her now than at first. Liza was overcome with shyness when, at parting, Velchaninov kissed her before them all, and warmly repeated his promise to come next day with her father. Till the last minute she was silent and did not look at him, but then suddenly she clutched at his arm and drew him aside, fixing an imploring look on him; she wanted to tell him something. He promptly led her away into another room.

"What is it, Liza?" he asked her tenderly and reassuringly; but she, still looking about her apprehensively, drew him into the farthest corner; she wanted to hide from them all.

"What is it, Liza? What's the matter?"

She was silent, she could not bring herself to speak; she gazed fixedly with her blue eyes into his face, and every feature of her little face expressed nothing but frantic terror.

"He'll . . . hang himself!" she whispered, as though in delirium.

"Who will hang himself?" asked Velchaninov in dismay.

"He, he! He tried to hang himself with a noose at night!" the child said hurriedly and breathlessly. "I saw him! He has recently tried to hang himself with a noose, he told me so, he told me so! He meant to before, he always meant to . . . I saw him at night. . . ."

"Impossible," whispered Velchaninov, perplexed.

She suddenly fell to kissing his hands; she cried, almost choking with sobs, begged and implored him, but he could make nothing of her hysterical babble. And the tortured face of that terror-stricken child who looked to him as her last hope remained printed on his memory forever, haunting him awake and visiting his dreams.

"And can she, can she really love him so much?" he thought, jealously and enviously, as with feverish impatience he returned to town. "She had said herself in the morning that she loved her mother more . . . perhaps she hated him and did not love him at all! . . . And what did that mean: he will hang himself? What did she mean by that? Would the fool hang himself? . . . I must find out, I must certainly find out! It is necessary to get to the bottom of it all as soon as possible—to settle the matter once and for all."

Chapter VII: Husband and Lover Kiss

He was in terrible haste "to find out." "This morning I was overwhelmed. This morning I hadn't the time to think," he reflected, recalling his first sight of Liza, "but now I must find out." To find out more quickly he was on the point of telling the driver to take him to Trusotzky's lodging directly, but on second thought decided: "No, better let him come to me, and meanwhile I'll make haste and get this accursed legal business off my hands."

He set to work feverishly; but this time he was conscious himself that he was very absent-minded and that he was hardly capable that day of attending to business. At five o'clock, when he went out to dinner, he was struck for the first time by a droll idea that perhaps he really was only hindering the progress of his case by meddling in the lawsuit himself, fussing about in the government offices and pursuing his lawyer, who was beginning to hide from him. He laughed gaily at his supposition. "And to think that if this idea had occurred to me yesterday, I should have been dreadfully distressed," he added, even more gaily. In spite of his gaiety, he grew more and more absent-minded and more and more impatient. He fell to musing at last; and, though his restless mind clutched at one thing after another, he could arrive at nothing that would satisfy him.

"I must have that man!" he decided finally. "I must solve the riddle of that man, and then make up my mind. It's—a duel!"

Returning home at seven o'clock, he did not find Pavel Pavlovich and was extremely surprised, then became angry, and still later depressed; finally he began to be actually frightened. "God knows, God knows how it will end!" he repeated, as he walked about the room or stretched himself on the sofa, continually looking at his watch. At last, about nine o'clock, Pavel Pavlovich appeared. "If the fellow were trying to be crafty with me, he couldn't have caught me at a more favorable time—I feel so unhinged at this moment," he thought, his confidence all of a sudden completely restored and his spirits rising again.

In response to his brisk and cheerful inquiry why he was so late coming, Pavel Pavlovich smiled wryly, seated himself with a free and easy air, very different from his manner the night before, and carelessly threw his hat with the crape on it on another chair close by. Velchaninov at once noticed this free and easy manner and took it into consideration.

Calmly, without wasting words, with none of the excitement he had shown in the morning, he told him, as though giving a report, how he had taken Liza, how kindly she had been received, how good it would be for her, and little by little, as though forgetting Liza, he imperceptibly turned the conversation entirely on the Pogoreltzevs—what charming people they were, how long he had known them, what a splendid and influential man Pogoreltzev was, and so on. Pavel Pavlovich listened absent-mindedly and from time to time glanced up sullenly at the speaker with an ill-humored and crafty sneer.

"You're an impulsive person," he muttered, with a particularly nasty smile.

"You're rather ill-humored today, though," Velchaninov observed with vexation.

"And why shouldn't I be ill-humored, sir, like everyone else?" Pavel Pavlovich snapped suddenly, just as though he had only been waiting for that to bounce out from behind a corner.

"As you please," laughed Velchaninov. "I wondered if anything had happened to you."

"So it has!" the other exclaimed, as though boasting that something had happened.

"What is it?"

Pavel Pavlovich delayed answering for a little.

"Well, sir, our Stepan Mihailovich has played me a trick. . . . Bagautov, that elegant young Petersburg gentleman of the best society."

"Did he again fail to receive you?"

"No, this time he didn't. For the first time I was admitted, and I gazed upon his face . . . only he was dead!"

"Wha—at! Bagautov is dead?" Velchaninov was awfully surprised, though there was no apparent reason for his being so surprised.

"Yes, sir! For six years our devoted friend! He died yesterday, almost at midday, and I knew nothing of it! That very minute I may have been inquiring after his health. The funeral will take place tomorrow, he's already in his coffin.

The coffin is faced with crimson velvet trimmed with gold . . . he died of brain fever. I was admitted—I was admitted and I gazed upon his countenance! I told them at the door that I was an intimate friend, that was why I was admitted. What's one to think of the way he's treated me now, my intimate friend for six long years—I ask you? Perhaps it was only on his account I came to Petersburg!"

"But what are you angry with him for?" laughed Velchaninov. "He didn't die on purpose, you know!"

"But I speak with regret; he was a precious friend; this is, sir, what he meant to me, you know."

And all at once, quite unexpectedly, Pavel Pavlovich put up his two fingers like two horns over his bald forehead and went off into a low, prolonged chuckle. He sat like that, chuckling, for a full half-minute, staring into Velchaninov's face in a rapture of spiteful insolence. The latter was petrified as though at the sight of some ghost. But his stupefaction lasted but one brief instant; a sarcastic and insolently composed smile came slowly to his lips.

"What's the meaning of that?" he asked, carelessly, drawling the words.

"The meaning of it is—horns!" Pavel Pavlovich rapped out, taking away his fingers from his forehead at last.

"That is . . . your horns?"

"My own, honestly acquired!" Pavel Pavlovich said with a very nasty grimace. Both were silent.

"You're a plucky fellow, I must say!" Velchaninov pronounced.

"Because I showed you my horns? Do you know, Alexey Ivanovich, you'd better offer me something! You know I entertained you every blessed day for a whole year at T——. Send for a bottle, my throat is dry."

"With pleasure; you should have said so long before. What will you have?"

"Why you? Say we; we'll drink together, won't we?" said Pavel Pavlovich, gazing into his face with a challenging, but at the same time strangely uneasy look.

"Champagne?"

"What else? It's not the time for vodka yet. . . ."

Velchaninov got up deliberately, rang for Mavra, and gave instructions.

"To the joy of our merry reunion after nine years' separation," said Pavel Pavlovich, with a quite superfluous and inappropriate snigger. "Now you, and you only, are the one true friend left me! Stepan Mihailovich Bagautov is no more! As the poet says:

> Great Patroclus is no more,
> Vile Thersites still lives on![3]

And at the word "Thersites" he poked himself in the chest.

"You'd better hurry up and speak out, you swine; I don't like hints," Velchaninov thought to himself. His anger was rising and for a long time he had hardly been able to restrain himself.

"Tell me," he said in a tone of vexation, "since you accuse Stepan Mihailovich"—he did not call him simply Bagautov now—"I should have thought you would have been glad that the man who has wronged you is dead; why are you angry about it?"

"Glad? Why glad?"

"I imagine those must be your feelings."

"He—he! You are quite mistaken about my feelings on that score; as some wise man has said, 'A dead enemy is good, but a living one is better,' he—he!"

"But you saw him alive every day for five years, I believe; you had time to get tired of the sight of him," Velchaninov observed with spiteful impertinence.

"But you don't suppose I knew then . . . you don't suppose I knew?" Pavel Pavlovich blurted out suddenly, just as though he had bounced out from behind a corner again, and as though he were delighted to be asked a question he had long been waiting for. "Who do you take me for, then, Alexey Ivanovich?"

And there was a gleam in his face of something quite

---

[3] Lines from Zhukovsky's translation of a ballad by Schiller.

new and unexpected, which seemed to transform his countenance, till then full of spite and vile grimacing.

"Is it possible you didn't know, then?" said Velchaninov, perplexed and completely taken by surprise.

"Is it possible I knew? Is it possible I knew? Oh, you race of Jupiters! For you a man's no more than a dog, and you judge all according to your own petty nature. Here, sir! You can swallow that!" And he banged frantically on the table with his fist, but was at once frightened by his banging and glanced about him apprehensively.

Velchaninov assumed an air of dignity.

"Listen, Pavel Pavlovich, it's all the same to me, you will agree, whether you knew, or whether you didn't. If you didn't know, it's to your credit in any case, though . . . I can't understand, though, why you've chosen me as your confidant."

"I didn't mean you . . . don't be angry. I didn't mean you . . ." muttered Pavel Pavlovich, looking down.

Mavra came in with the champagne.

"Here it is!" cried Pavel Pavlovich, evidently relieved at her entrance. "Glasses, my good woman, glasses; splendid! We ask for nothing more, my dear. And uncorked already! Honor and glory to you, sweet creature! Now make yourself scarce!"

And, taking heart again, he looked impudently at Velchaninov again.

"Confess," he chuckled suddenly, "that all this interests you terribly and is by no means 'all the same to you,' as you were pleased to declare; so much so that you would be disappointed if I were to get up this minute and go away without explaining myself."

"I really shouldn't be disappointed."

"Oh, that's a lie!" was what Pavel Pavlovich's smile expressed.

"Well, let's get down to business!" And he filled two glasses. "Let's drink a toast," he said, raising his glass, "to the health of our departed friend, Stepan Mihailovich."

He raised his glass, and drank it.

"I'm not going to drink such a toast," said Velchaninov, putting down his glass.

"Why not? It's a pleasant toast."

"I say, were you drunk when you came in just now?"

"I had had a drop. But why?"

"Nothing in particular, but I thought last night, and this morning still more, that you were genuinely grieved at the loss of Natalya Vassilyevna."

"And who told you that I'm not genuinely grieved at the loss of her now?" Pavel Pavlovich bounced out again, exactly as though he were worked by a spring.

"And I didn't mean that; but you must admit that you may be mistaken about Stepan Mihailovich, and it is—a grave matter."

Pavel Pavlovich smiled craftily and winked.

"And wouldn't you like to know how I found out about Stepan Mihailovich?"

Velchaninov flushed.

"I tell you again that it's nothing to me."

"Hadn't I better chuck him out this minute, bottle and all?" he thought furiously, and he flushed a deeper crimson.

"It doesn't matter!" said Pavel Pavlovich, as though trying to encourage him, and he poured himself out another glass.

"I will explain at once how I found out all about it, and so gratify your ardent desire . . . for you are an ardent man, Alexey Ivanovich, a terribly ardent man! He—he! Only give me a cigarette, for ever since March . . . !"

"Here's a cigarette for you."

"I have gone to the bad since March, Alexey Ivanovich, and I'll tell you, sir, how it's all happened—listen. Consumption, as you know yourself, my best of friends," he grew more and more familiar, "is a curious disease, sir. Consumptives have scarcely a suspicion they may be dying tomorrow. I tell you that only five hours before her death, Natalya Vassilyevna was planning a visit a fortnight later to her aunt, thirty miles away. You are aware, too, probably, of the practice, or rather bad habit—common to many ladies and very likely their admirers as well—of preserving all sorts of rubbish in the way of love letters. . . . It would be much safer to put them in the stove, wouldn't it, sir? No, every scrap of paper is carefully stored away in a box or toilet can; even numbered and arranged by date and content. Whether it's a comfort to them—I don't know; but, no doubt, it's for the sake of pleasant memories. Since only five hours before her end she was arranging to go to visit her aunt, Natalya Vassilyevna naturally had no thought of death to the very last hour, and was still waiting for Koch. So it happened that Natalya Vassilyevna died, and an ebony box inlaid with mother-of-pearl and silver was left standing on her bureau. And it was a pretty little box, with a lock and key, an heirloom that had come to her from her grandmother. In that box everything lay revealed, sir, absolutely everything; all, without exception, with the year and the day, everything for the last twenty years. And as Stepan Mihailovich had a distinct literary bent (he actually sent a passionate love story to a journal), his contributions ran into the hundreds—to be sure they were spread out over five years. Some items had been annotated in Natalya Vassilyevna's own handwriting. A pleasant surprise for a husband. What do you think of it, sir?"

Velchaninov reflected hurriedly and felt sure that he had never sent Natalya Vassilyevna a single letter, not a note of any kind. Though he had written twice from Petersburg, his letters, in accordance with a compact between them, had been addressed to the husband as well as the wife. Natalya Vassilyevna's last letter, in which she had decreed his banishment, he had not answered.

When he had ended his story, Pavel Pavlovich paused for a full minute with an importunate and expectant smile.

"Why haven't you answered my little question?" he brought out at last in evident torment.

"What little question?"

"Why, about the pleasant surprise for a husband on opening that box."

"Oh! What has it to do with me!" exclaimed Velchaninov, with a caustic gesture, and he got up and walked about the room.

"And I bet you're thinking now, 'What a swine you are to have shown me your horns yourself.' He—he! You're a very fastidious man . . . you are, sir."

"I am not thinking anything about it. On the contrary, you are exasperated by the death of the man who wronged you and you've drunk much wine, too. I see nothing extraordinary in all this; I quite understand why you wanted Bagautov alive, and I am ready to respect your vexation, but——"

"And what did I want Bagautov for, do you suppose, sir?"

"That's your affair."

"I bet you meant a duel!"

"Damn it all!" cried Velchaninov, growing less and less able to control himself. "I imagine that a decent man . . . in such cases does not stoop to ridiculous babble, to stupid antics, to ludicrous complaints, and disgusting insinuations, by which he only degrades himself more, but acts openly, directly, straightforwardly—like a decent man."

"He—he! But perhaps I'm not a decent man?"

"That's your affair again . . . but in that case, what the devil did you want Bagautov alive for?"

"Why, if only to see a friend. We'd have had a bottle and drunk together."

"He wouldn't have drunk with you."

"Why not? *Noblesse oblige!* Here, you're drinking with me; in what way is he better than you?"

"I haven't drunk with you."

"Why such pride all of a sudden?"

Velchaninov suddenly broke into a nervous and irritated laugh.

"Damnation! Why, you are really a 'predatory type'! I thought you were only 'the eternal husband,' and nothing more!"

"What do you mean by 'the eternal husband,' what's that?" Pavel Pavlovich suddenly pricked up his ears.

"Oh, it's one type of husband . . . it would be a long story. You'd better clear out, it's time you were gone; I'm sick of you."

"And predatory? You said 'predatory'!"

"I said you were a 'predatory type'; I said it sarcastically."

"What do you mean by a 'predatory type,' sir? Tell me, please, Alexey Ivanovich, for God's sake, or for Christ's sake!"

"Come, that's enough, that's enough!" cried Velchaninov, all of a sudden growing horribly angry again. "It's time you were off. Get along."

"No, it's not enough!" Pavel Pavlovich too flared up; "even though you are sick of me it's not enough, for we must drink together and clink glasses! Let us drink together, and then I'll go, but now it's not enough!"

"Pavel Pavlovich! Will you go to the devil now or will you not?"

"I can go to the devil, but first we'll drink! You said that you would not drink just *with me;* but I *want* you to drink just with me!"

There was no grimacing, no sniggering about him now. He seemed all at once entirely transformed, and to have become in his whole tone and appearance so completely the opposite of the Pavel Pavlovich of the moment before that Velchaninov was completely taken aback.

"Do let us drink, Alexey Ivanovich! Don't refuse me," Pavel Pavlovich persisted, gripping his hand tightly and looking strangely into his eyes. Clearly there was more at stake than merely drinking.

"Yes, if you like," muttered Velchaninov; "but how can we? . . . This is hogwash. . . ."

"There are just two glasses left, hogwash it is, sir, but we'll drink it and clink glasses! Here, take your glass."

They clinked their glasses and emptied them.

"Since that's so—since that's so . . . Ach!"

Pavel Pavlovich suddenly clutched his forehead with his hand and remained for some moments in that position. Velchaninov fancied that he was on the point of uttering the very *last* word. But Pavel Pavlovich uttered nothing; he simply gazed at Velchaninov and smiled again the same sly, meaningful smile.

"What do you want of me, you drunken fellow! You're making a fool of me!" Velchaninov shouted furiously, stamping his feet.

"Don't shout, don't shout; why shout?" cried Pavel Pavlovich, gesticulating hurriedly. "I'm not making a fool of you. I'm not! Do you know what you are to me now?"

And he suddenly seized his hand and kissed it. Velchaninov was utterly taken aback.

"That's what you mean to me now, sir! And now—and now I'll go to the devil!"

"Wait a minute, stay!" cried Velchaninov, recovering himself. "I forgot to tell you . . ."

Pavel Pavlovich turned back from the door.

"You see," muttered Velchaninov, very quickly, flushing crimson and looking away, "you must be at the Pogoreltzevs' tomorrow . . . to make their acquaintance and thank them; you must. . . ."

"Certainly, I must. I understand that, of course, sir!" Pavel Pavlovich acquiesced with the utmost readiness, waving his hand quickly as though to protest that there was no need to remind him.

"And besides, Liza is very anxious to see you. I promised her——"

"Liza!" Pavel Pavlovich suddenly returned. "Liza? Do you know what Liza has meant to me? What she meant and still means to me!" he suddenly cried, almost frantic. "But . . . he! of that later, sir; all that can be later. . . . But now it's not enough that we've drunk together, Alexey Ivanovich, I must have something else for my satisfaction, sir!"

He laid his hat on a chair and gazed at him, gasping for breath a little as he had done just before.

"Kiss me, Alexey Ivanovich!" he proposed suddenly.

"You're drunk!" Velchaninov cried, stepping back.

"Yes, but kiss me all the same, Alexey Ivanovich. Oh, kiss me! Why, I kissed your hand just now."

For some minutes Velchaninov was silent, as though hit by a cudgel on the head. But suddenly he bent down to Pavel Pavlovich, who was shorter by a head than he, and kissed him on the lips, which smelled very strongly of spirits. He was not perfectly certain that he had kissed him, though!

"Well, now, now . . ." Pavel Pavlovich cried again in a drunken frenzy, his eyes flashing; "now I'll tell you: at the time, I thought, 'What if he too? What if that one, I thought, what if he too . . . whom can I trust after that!'"

Pavel Pavlovich suddenly burst into tears.

"So you understand, you're the one friend left me now!"

And he ran out of the room with his hat. Velchaninov again stood still for some minutes, just as he had done after Pavel Pavlovich's first visit.

"Ah! A drunken clown and nothing more!" He waved his hand, dismissing the subject.

"Absolutely nothing more," he repeated energetically, as he undressed and got into bed.

Chapter VIII: Liza Ill

Next morning Velchaninov walked about his room expecting Pavel Pavlovich, who had promised to arrive in good time to go to the Pogoreltzevs'. As he smoked and sipped his coffee he confessed to himself at every moment that he was like a man who, on waking up in the morning, cannot forget for one instant that he has received a slap in the face the previous day. "H'm! . . . he clearly understands the situation and will take his revenge on me through Liza!" he thought with fear.

The sweet image of the poor child rose mournfully before him for a moment. His heart beat faster at the thought that he would soon, within two hours, see *his* Liza again. "Ah! It's no use talking about it!" he decided hotly. "It's my whole life and my whole object now! What do slaps in the face or memories of the past matter? What have I lived for till now? Disorder and sadness . . . but now—it's all different, everything's changed!"

But, in spite of his rapture, he grew more and more pensive.

"He will torment me to death by means of Liza—that's clear! And he will torment Liza too. In that way he will do me in for everything. H'm! . . . Of course, I can't allow him to go on as he did yesterday"—he flushed crimson all at once—"and . . . here it's already past eleven, though, and he hasn't arrived."

He waited a long time, till half-past twelve, and his anguish grew more and more acute. Pavel Pavlovich did not appear. At last the thought, which had long been stirring in his mind, that Pavel Pavlovich was not going to come on purpose, simply in order to get up another prank like that of the night before, put the finishing touch to his irritation. "He knows that I depend on him, and what a state Liza will be in now. And how can I appear before her without him?"

At last he could stand it no longer, and at one o'clock he rushed off to the Pokrovsky Hotel. At the lodging he was told that Pavel Pavlovich had not slept at home, but had only turned up at nine o'clock in the morning, had stayed no more than a quarter of an hour, and then gone out again. Velchaninov stood at the door of Pavel Pavlovich's rooms listening to what the servant said, and mechanically turned and jiggled the handle of the locked door. Realizing what he was doing, he spat and asked the servant to take him to Marya Sysoevna. But the landlady, hearing he was there, came out readily herself.

She was a good-natured woman. "A woman with noble feelings," as Velchaninov said of her when he was afterward reporting his conversation with her to Klavdia Petrovna.

Having inquired briefly about his trip with the child the day before, Marya Sysoevna launched into accounts of Pavel Pavlovich's doings. In her words: "If it had not been for the child, I would have got rid of him long ago. He was turned out of the hotel because of his disorderly conduct. Wasn't it a sin to bring home with him a wench at night when there was a child here old enough to understand? He was shouting, 'She will be your mother, if I choose!' And would you believe it? A street wench! But even she spat in his ugly mug. 'You're not my daughter, but a bastard!' he cried."

"Really?" Velchaninov was horrified.

"I heard it myself. Sure the man is dead drunk. All the same, it ain't right to carry on like that in front of a child. She's only a tot, but she can figure things out. The little girl cries; I see she's all wore out. And the other day a terrible thing happened in our building: a clerk, so folks say, took a room in the hotel overnight, and in the morning hanged himself. They say he had squandered away his money. People flocked to see. Pavel Pavlovich was not at home, and no one to take care of the child; I looked, and there she was in the passage among the people, and peeping out from behind the others: she was looking so queerly at the body. I took her away as quickly as I could. And what do you think—she was all atremble, she looked quite black in the face, and as soon as I brought her in she flopped on the floor in a fit. She struggled and writhed, and only with difficulty came to. Must have been convulsions, and she's been poorly ever since that hour. He heard of it, came home, and pinched her all over—for he's not one for beating, he's more given to pinching her, and afterward, when he'd come home dead drunk he'd frighten her. 'I'll hang myself too,' he'd say; 'because of you; I'll hang myself with this cord here on the blind,' he'd say; and he'd make a noose before her eyes. And she'd be beside herself—she'd scream and throw her little arms around him. 'I won't!' she'd cry, 'I never will again.' It was pitiful."

Though Velchaninov had expected something strange,

this story amazed him so much that he could not believe it.

Marya Sysoevna told him a great deal more; on one occasion, for instance, had it not been for her, Liza might have thrown herself out of the window.

Velchaninov went out of the house reeling as though he were drunk.

"I'll kill him like a dog by knocking him on the head with a stick!" was the thought that floated before his mind. And for a long time he kept repeating this to himself.

He took a cab and drove to the Pogoreltzevs'. On the way the carriage was obliged to stop at the crossroads, near the bridge spanning a canal, over which a long funeral procession was passing. On both sides of the bridge there were several carriages waiting; people on foot were stopped too. It was a grand funeral and there was a very long string of vehicles with mourners in them. In the window of one of these carriages Velchaninov suddenly caught a glimpse of the face of Pavel Pavlovich. He would not have believed his eyes if Pavel Pavlovich had not thrust his head out and nodded to him with a smile. Evidently he was delighted at recognizing Velchaninov; he even began beckoning to him from the carriage. Velchaninov jumped out of his cab and, in spite of the crush, in spite of the police, and in spite of the fact that Pavel Pavlovich's carriage was driving onto the bridge, he ran right up to the window. Pavel Pavlovich was alone.

"What's the matter with you?" cried Velchaninov; "why didn't you come? How is it you are here?"

"I'm paying a debt, sir. Don't shout, don't shout, I am paying a debt," sniggered Pavel Pavlovich, screwing up his eyes gaily. "I'm following the mortal remains of my faithful friend, Stepan Mihailovich."

"That's all nonsense, you drunken madman," Velchaninov shouted louder than ever, though he was taken aback for an instant. "Get out this minute and come into the cab with me."

"I can't, it's a duty. . . ."

"I'll drag you out!" Velchaninov yelled.

"And I'll scream! I'll scream!" said Pavel Pavlovich, sniggering as gaily as before, as though it were a game, though he did huddle into the farthest corner of the carriage. . . .

"Look out, look out! You'll be run over!" shouted a policeman.

At the farther end of the bridge a carriage cutting across the procession did, in fact, cause a commotion. Velchaninov was forced to jump back; the stream of carriages and the crowd of people immediately carried him farther away. He spat, and he made his way back to the cab.

"No matter, I couldn't have taken a fellow like that with me, in any event!" he thought, with a feeling of anxious amazement that persisted.

When he told Klavdia Petrovna Marya Sysoevna's story and described the strange meeting in the funeral procession, she grew very thoughtful.

"I fear for you," she said. "You ought to break off all relations with him, and the sooner the better."

"He's a drunken clown and nothing more!" Velchaninov cried passionately; "as though I could be afraid of him! And how can I break off relations with him when there's Liza to be considered. Think of Liza!"

Liza meanwhile was lying ill; she had begun to be feverish the evening before and they were expecting a celebrated doctor, for whom they had sent a messenger to the town in the morning. This completed Velchaninov's distress.

Klavdia Petrovna took him to the patient.

"I watched her very carefully yesterday," she observed, stopping outside Liza's room. "She's a proud and sullen child; she is ashamed that she is here, and that her father has abandoned her; that's the whole cause of her illness, to my thinking."

"Abandoned her? Why do you think that he's abandoned her?"

"The very fact that he let her come here, among complete strangers and with a man . . . who's almost a stranger, too, or on such terms. . . ."

"But it was I took her, I took her by force; I don't see . . ."

"Oh, my God, and even Liza, a child, sees it! It's my belief that he simply won't come at all."

Liza was not astonished when she saw Velchaninov alone; she only smiled mournfully and turned her feverishly hot little head to the wall. She made no response to Velchaninov's timid efforts to comfort her and to his fervent promises to bring her father next day without fail. On coming away from her, he suddenly burst into tears.

It was evening before the doctor came. After examining the patient, he alarmed them all at first, by observing that they had done wrong not to have sent for him earlier. When it was explained to him that the child had been taken ill only the evening before, he was at first incredulous.

"It all depends how things go tonight," he said in conclusion. After giving various instructions, he went away, promising to come again next day as early as possible. Velchaninov would have insisted on staying the night, but Klavdia Petrovna begged him once more "to try and bring that monster."

"Try once more?" Velchaninov retorted in a frenzy. "Why, this time I'll tie him hand and foot and bring him here in my arms!" The idea of tying Pavel Pavlovich hand and foot and taking him there suddenly possessed him and made him violently impatient. "I don't feel in the least guilty toward him now, not in the least!" he said to Klavdia Petrovna, as he took leave. "I take back all the abject, snivcling things I said here yesterday," he added indignantly.

Liza was lying with her eyes shut, apparently asleep; she seemed to be better. When Velchaninov cautiously bent over her head, to say good-by and to kiss if only the edge of her garment, she suddenly opened her eyes, as though she had been expecting him, and whispered to him:

"Take me away!"

It was a gentle, sorrowful appeal, without a shade in it of the irritability of the previous day, but at the same time he could hear in it the conviction that her request would not be granted. As soon as Velchaninov, in complete despair, began trying to persuade her that this was impossible, she closed her eyes in silence and did not utter another word, as though she did not see or hear him.

On reaching the city he told the driver to take him straight to Pokrovsky Hotel. It was ten o'clock; Pavel Pavlovich was not in his lodging. Velchaninov spent a full half-hour waiting for him and walking up and down the passage with sickening impatience. Marya Sysoevna assured him at last that Pavel Pavlovich would not be back till daybreak. "Then I will come early in the morning," Velchaninov decided, and, beside himself, set off for home.

But what was his astonishment when, at the door of his flat, he learned from Mavra that his visitor of yesterday had been waiting for him since ten o'clock.

"And has been pleased to take tea here, and has again sent out for that wine, and has given me a five-rouble note to get it."

Chapter IX: An Apparition

Pavel Pavlovich had made himself exceedingly comfortable. He was sitting in the same chair as the day before, smoking a cigarette, and had just poured himself out the fourth and last glass from a bottle. The teapot and an unfinished glass of tea were standing on a table close by. His flushed face was beaming with good humor. He had even taken off his coat, as it was warm, and was sitting in his waistcoat.

"Excuse me, most faithful of friends!" he cried, seeing Velchaninov and jumping up to put on his coat. "I took it off for the greater enjoyment of the moment. . . ."

Velchaninov went up to him menacingly.

"You are not quite drunk yet? Is it still possible to talk to you?"

Pavel Pavlovich was a little flustered.

"No, not quite. . . . I've been commemorating the deceased, but—not quite——"

"Will you understand me?"

"That's what I've come for, to understand you."

"Well, then; I begin by telling you straight out that you are a worthless scoundrel!" cried Velchaninov.

"If you begin like that, how will you end?" Pavel Pavlovich protested, evidently cowed, but Velchaninov went on shouting without heeding him.

"Your daughter is dying, she is ill; have you abandoned her or not?"

"Can she really be dying?"

"She is ill, ill, exceedingly, dangerously ill!"

"Possibly some little fits. . . ."

"Don't talk nonsense! She is ex—ceed—ing—ly, dangerously ill! You ought to have gone if only to . . ."

"To express my gratitude, my gratitude for their hospitality! I quite understand that! Alexey Ivanovich, my precious, perfect friend." He suddenly clutched Velchaninov's hand in both of his, and with drunken sentimentality, almost with tears, as though imploring forgiveness, he kept crying out, "Alexey Ivanovich, don't shout, don't shout! Whether I die or fall drunk into the Neva—what does it matter in the present condition of affairs? The visit to Mr. Pogoreltzev can wait, sir. . . ."

Velchaninov recollected himself and restrained himself a little.

"You're drunk, and so I don't understand what you are driving at," he observed sternly. "I am always ready to have things out with you, shall be glad to, in fact, as soon as possible. . . . In fact, I've come to . . . But first of all I warn you that I am taking measures: you must stay the night here! Tomorrow morning I'll take you and we'll go together. I won't let go of you," he yelled again. "I'll tie you up and take you there in my arms! . . . Does this sofa suit you?" he said breathlessly, pointing to a wide, soft sofa, which stood opposite the one against the other wall on which he used to sleep himself.

"By all means, I can sleep anywhere. . . ."

"Not anywhere, but on that sofa! Here, take your sheets, your quilt, your pillow." All these Velchaninov took out of the closet and hurriedly flung them to Pavel Pavlovich, who held out his arms submissively. "Make the bed at once, make it at once!"

Pavel Pavlovich, loaded with his burden, stood in the middle of the room as though hesitating, with a broad drunken grin on his drunken face. But at a second menacing shout from Velchaninov he suddenly began bustling about at full speed; he pushed back the table and, panting, began to unfold the sheets and make the bed. Velchaninov went over to assist him; he was, to some extent, pleased with his visitor's alarm and submissiveness.

"Finish your glass and go to bed," he commanded again; he felt as though he could not help giving orders. "You sent for that wine yourself, didn't you?"

"Yes. . . . I knew you wouldn't send for any more, Alexey Ivanovich."

"It was well you knew it, and there is something more you must know too. I tell you once more I've taken measures now, I won't put up with any more of your antics, I won't put up with your drunken kisses as I did yesterday."

"I understand myself, Alexey Ivanovich, that that was only possible once," sniggered Pavel Pavlovich.

Hearing his answer, Velchaninov, who had been striding up and down the room, stopped almost solemnly before Pavel Pavlovich.

"Pavel Pavlovich, speak frankly! You're a sensible man, I admit that again, but I assure you, you are on the wrong tack! Speak straightforwardly, act straightforwardly, and I give you my word of honor I will answer any question you like."

Pavel Pavlovich grinned his broad grin again, which was enough in itself to drive Velchaninov to fury.

"Stop!" Velchaninov shouted again. "Don't sham, I see

through you! I repeat: I give you my word of honor that I am ready to answer *any* question of yours and you shall receive every satisfaction possible, that is every, even the impossible kind! Oh, how I wish you could understand me! . . ."

"Since you are so good, sir"—Pavel Pavlovich moved cautiously toward him—"I was much interested in what you said last night about a 'predatory type'!"

Velchaninov spat and fell to pacing about the room more rapidly than ever.

"No, Alexey Ivanovich, don't spit, because I'm very much interested, and have come on purpose to check. . . . I can't manage my tongue, but you must forgive me, sir, I myself, you know, have read in a magazine,[4] in the department of criticism, about that 'predatory type,' and the 'meek type.' I remembered it this morning . . . only I have forgotten what the article said, and to tell the truth I did not understand it at the time, sir. This is what I wanted you to explain: the deceased, Stepan Mihailovich Bagautov —was he 'predatory' or 'meek'? How would you classify him, sir?"

Velchaninov remained silent, and did not cease pacing the floor.

"The predatory type," he began, stopping suddenly in a rage, "is the man who would rather have put poison in Bagautov's glass when drinking champagne with him in honor of their delightful meeting, as you drank with me yesterday; and he would not have followed Bagautov's coffin to the cemetery, as you have today, the devil only knows from what secret, underground, loathsome impulse and distorted affectation that only degrades you! Yes, degrades you!"

"It's true that I shouldn't have gone," Pavel Pavlovich assented; "but you do pitch into me. . . ."

"It's not the man," Velchaninov went on shouting ex-

---

[4] The issue of the monthly *Zarya*, for February, 1869, carried an essay on Tolstoy's *War and Peace*, which discussed the treatment of the two types in Russian literature.

citedly without heeding him; "it's not the man who imagines goodness knows what, who reckons up the score of what is just and what is lawful, learns his grievance like a lesson, whines, grimaces, gives himself airs, hangs on people's necks—and spends all his time at it too! Is it true that you wanted to hang yourself—is it?"

"When I was drunk I may have talked wildly—I don't remember. It isn't quite seemly, Alexey Ivanovich, for me to put poison in wine. Apart from the fact that I am a civil servant in good repute, I am a man of means, sir, and, what's more, I may want to get married again."

"Besides, you'll be condemned to hard labor."

"To be sure, sir, there is that unpleasantness also, though nowadays they admit many extenuating circumstances in the law courts. I want to tell you a killing little anecdote, Alexey Ivanovich, sir—I recalled it in the carriage. You said just now 'hangs on people's necks.' You remember, perhaps, Semyon Petrovich Livtzov, he used to come and see us when you were in T——; well, his younger brother, who was also a Petersburg swell, was on the staff of the governor at V——, and he, too, was conspicuous for various qualities. One day he had a quarrel with Golubenko, a colonel, in the presence of ladies and the lady of his heart, and considered himself insulted, but he swallowed the affront and concealed it; and, meanwhile, Golubenko cut him out with the lady of his heart and made her an offer. And what do you think? This Livtzov formed a genuine friendship with Golubenko, he quite made it up with him, and, what's more, insisted on being his best man, he held the wedding crown, and when they came from the wedding, he went up to kiss and congratulate Golubenko; and right there, in the presence of the governor and all the noble company, himself in swallowtails, and his hair in curls, he stuck a knife into the bridegroom's stomach—so that Golubenko rolled over! His own best man! What a disgrace, sir! And, what's more, when he'd stabbed him like that, he rushed about crying, 'Oh, what have I done! Oh, what is it I've done!' His tears were streaming, he trembled all over, flung himself on people's necks, even ladies'! 'Ah, what have I done!' he kept saying. 'What have I done now!' He—he—he! He was killing. One felt sorry for Golubenko, though, but, after all, he recovered."

"I don't see why you have told me the story," observed Velchaninov, frowning sternly.

"Why, all because Livtzov did stick the knife in him, you know," Pavel Pavlovich tittered; "it is clear that he wasn't that type, sir, but a sniveling fellow, since he forgot all good manners in his fright and flung himself on the ladies' necks in the presence of the governor—but you see he did stab him, he got his own back! That was all I meant."

"Go to hell!" Velchaninov yelled suddenly, in a voice not his own, as though something had exploded in him. "Go to hell with your underground trash; you are nothing but underground trash yourself. You thought you'd scare me—you base man, you child torturer, you scoundrel, scoundrel, scoundrel!" he shouted, beside himself, gasping for breath at every word.

Pavel Pavlovich was convulsed, and even sobered up; his lips quivered.

"Is it you, Alexey Ivanovich, who are calling me a scoundrel, *you* are calling *me?*"

But Velchaninov had already come to himself.

"I am ready to apologize," he answered, after a pause of gloomy hesitation; "but only if you will act openly yourself from now on."

"In your place I would apologize without any ifs, Alexey Ivanovich."

"Very good, so be it," said Velchaninov, after another slight pause. "I apologize to you; but you'll admit yourself, Pavel Pavlovich, that, after all this, I need not consider that I owe you anything. I'm speaking with reference to the *whole* matter and not only to the present incident."

"That's all right, why cast up accounts?" Pavel Pavlovich sniggered, without, however, raising his eyes.

"So much the better, then, so much the better! Finish

your wine and go to bed, for I won't let you go, anyway. . . ."

"Oh, the wine . . ." Pavel Pavlovich seemed, as it were, a little disconcerted. He went to the table, however, and finished the last glass of wine he had poured out long before. Perhaps he had drunk a great deal before, for his hand trembled and he spilled part of the wine on the floor, and on his shirt and waistcoat. He finished it all, however, as though he could not bear to leave a drop, and, respectfully replacing the empty glass on the table, he went submissively to his bed to undress.

"But wouldn't it be better for me not to stay the night!" he brought out for some reason, though he had taken off one boot and was holding it in his hand.

"No, it wouldn't," Velchaninov answered angrily, still pacing up and down the room without looking at him.

Pavel Pavlovich undressed and got into bed. A quarter of an hour later Velchaninov went to bed, too, and put out the candle.

He was falling asleep uneasily. The new element that had turned up unexpectedly and complicated the whole business more than ever worried him now, and at the same time he felt that he was for some reason ashamed of his uneasiness. He was just dozing off, when he was waked up all at once by a rustling sound. He looked around at once toward Pavel Pavlovich's bed. The room was dark (the curtains were drawn), but Velchaninov fancied that Pavel Pavlovich was not lying down, but was sitting up in bed.

"What's the matter?" Velchaninov called to him.

"A ghost, sir," Pavel Pavlovich said, almost inaudibly, after a brief pause.

"What do you mean, what sort of ghost?"

"There in that room, I seem to see a ghost in the doorway."

"Whose ghost?" Velchaninov asked again, after a pause.

"Natalya Vassilyevna's, sir."

Velchaninov stood up on the rug, and looked across the passage, into the other room, the door of which always stood open. There were only blinds, instead of curtains on the window, and so it was much lighter there.

"There's nothing in that room and you are drunk. Go to bed!" said Velchaninov. He got into bed and wrapped himself in the quilt. Pavel Pavlovich got into bed, too, without saying a word.

"And have you ever seen ghosts before?" Velchaninov asked suddenly, ten minutes afterward.

Pavel Pavlovich, too, was silent for a while.

"I thought I saw one once," he responded faintly. Then silence fell again. Velchaninov could not have said for certain whether he had been asleep or not, but about an hour had passed—when he suddenly turned around again: whether he was roused again by a rustle—he was not sure, but felt as though in the pitch dark something white was standing over him, not quite close, but in the middle of the room. He sat up in bed and for a full minute gazed into the darkness.

"Is that you, Pavel Pavlovich?" he said, in a slackened voice. His voice ringing out suddenly in the stillness and the dark seemed to him somehow strange.

No answer followed, but there could be no doubt that someone was standing there.

"Is that you . . . Pavel Pavlovich?" he repeated, more loudly—so loudly, in fact, that if Pavel Pavlovich had been quietly asleep in his bed, he would certainly have waked up and answered.

But again no answer came, yet he fancied that the white, hardly distinguishable figure moved nearer to him. Then something strange happened: something seemed to explode within him, exactly as it had that evening, and he shouted at the top of his voice, in a most absurd, frantic voice, gasping for breath at each word:

"If you, drunken clown that you are, dare to imagine that you can frighten me, I'll turn to the wall, I'll put the blanket over my head, and won't turn around again all night to show you how much I care even if you were to stand there till morning like a clown and I spit upon you!"

And he spat furiously in the direction, as he supposed, of Pavel Pavlovich, turned to the wall, drew the blanket over his head as he had said, and grew rigid in that position, not stirring a muscle. A dead silence followed. Whether the shadow was moving nearer or standing still he could not tell, but his heart was beating, beating violently. Fully five minutes passed, and suddenly, two steps from him, he heard the weak, plaintive voice of Pavel Pavlovich.

"I got up, Alexey Ivanovich, to look for the . . ." (and he mentioned an indispensable domestic article). "I didn't find one there. . . . I meant to look quietly under your bed, sir."

"Why didn't you speak when I shouted?" Velchaninov asked with a catch in his voice, after a pause of about half a minute.

"I was frightened, you shouted so. . . . I was frightened, sir."

"There in the corner on the left, in the little cupboard. Light the candle. . . ."

"I can do without the candle, sir," Pavel Pavlovich brought out meekly, making for the corner. "Forgive me, Alexey Ivanovich, for disturbing you so. . . . I got so tipsy all of a sudden, sir. . . ."

But Velchaninov made no reply. He still lay with his face to the wall, and lay so all night, without once turning around. Was it that he wanted to do as he had said and so show his contempt? He did not know himself what was the matter with him. His nervous irritability turned at last almost into delirium, and it was a long time before he fell asleep. Waking next morning between nine and ten, he jumped up and sat up in bed, as though someone had given him a shove—but Pavel Pavlovich was no longer in the room! The unmade bed stood there empty; he had slipped away at dawn.

"I knew it would be so," cried Velchaninov, slapping himself on the forehead.

Chapter X: In the Cemetery

The doctor's fears turned out to be justified; Liza was suddenly worse—worse than Velchaninov and Klavdia Petrovna had imagined possible the evening before. Velchaninov found the patient conscious in the morning, though she was in a high fever; afterward he declared that she had smiled and even held out her hot little hand to him. Whether this was really so, or whether he had imagined it involuntarily in an effort to comfort himself, he had no time to verify; by nightfall the sick child was unconscious, and she remained so till the end. Ten days after her coming to the Pogoreltzevs' she died.

It was a sorrowful time for Velchaninov; in fact, the Pogoreltzevs were very anxious about him. He stayed those bitter days for the most part with them. During the last days of Liza's illness he would sit for whole hours together alone in a corner apparently thinking of nothing; Klavdia Petrovna attempted to divert him, but he made little response, and seemed to find it a burden to talk to her. Klavdia Petrovna had not expected that "all this would have such an effect upon him." The children succeeded best in diverting him; in their company he sometimes even laughed, but almost every hour he would get up from his chair and go on tiptoe to look at the patient. He sometimes fancied that she recognized him. He had no hope of her recovery, nor had anyone, but he could not tear himself away from the room in which she lay dying, and usually sat in the next room.

On two occasions in the course of those days, however, he showed great activity; he roused himself and rushed off to Petersburg to the doctors, called on all the most distinguished of them, and arranged for consultations. The second and last consultation took place the evening before Liza's death. Three days before that Klavdia Petrovna urged upon Velchaninov the necessity of seeking out Mr. Trusotzky at last, pointing out that "if the worst happened, the funeral would be impossible without him." Velchaninov mumbled in reply that he would write to him. Thereupon Pogoreltzev declared that he would undertake to find him through the police. Velchaninov did finally write a note of two lines and took it to the Pokrovsky Hotel. Pavel Pavlovich, as usual, was not at home, and he left the letter for him with Marya Sysoevna.

At last Liza died, on a beautiful summer evening at sunset, and only then Velchaninov seemed to come to himself. When they dressed the dead child in a white frock that belonged to one of Klavdia Petrovna's daughters and was kept for festivals, and laid her on the table in the drawing room with flowers in her folded hands, he went up to Klavdia Petrovna with glittering eyes, and told her that he would bring the "murderer" at once. Refusing to listen to their advice to put off going till next day, he set off for Petersburg at once.

He knew where to find Pavel Pavlovich; he had not only been to fetch the doctors when he would go to Petersburg. He had sometimes fancied during those days that if he brought her father to Liza, and she heard his voice, she might come to herself, then he would go hunting for him like one possessed. Pavel Pavlovich was in the same lodging as before, but it was useless for him to inquire there. "Sometimes he doesn't sleep here for three nights on end, and isn't near the place," Marya Sysoevna reported; "and if he does come, by chance, he's bound to be drunk, and before he's been here an hour he's off again; he's going to rack and ruin." The waiter at the Pokrovsky Hotel told Velchaninov, among other things, that Pavel Pavlovich used to visit some young women in Voznesensky Prospect. Velchaninov promptly looked up these young women. Entertained and loaded with presents, they readily remembered their visitor, chiefly from the crape on his hat, and, of course, they abused him roundly for not having been to see them again. One of them, Katya, undertook "to find

Pavel Pavlovich any time, because nowadays he was all the time with Mashka Prostakov, and he had heaps of money, and she ought to have been Mashka Prohvostov instead of Prostakov[5] and she'd been in hospital, and if she, Katya, liked, she could pack the wench off to Siberia in a minute—she had only to say the word." Katya did not, however, find Pavel Pavlovich on that occasion, but she promised faithfully to do so another time. It was on her help that Velchaninov was reckoning now.

On reaching Petersburg at ten o'clock, he at once asked for her, paid the proper person to let her go, and set off with her to search for Pavel Pavlovich. He did not know himself what he was going to do with him: whether he would kill him, or whether he was looking for him simply to tell him of his daughter's death and the necessity of his help in connection with the funeral. At first they were unsuccessful. It turned out that this Mashka had had a fight with Pavel Pavlovich two days before, and that some cashier "had broken his head with a stool." In a word, for a long time the search was in vain, and it was only at two o'clock in the afternoon that Velchaninov, coming out of an establishment to which he had been sent, suddenly and unexpectedly ran into him.

Pavel Pavlovich, hopelessly drunk, was being conducted to this establishment by two ladies, one of whom was supporting him by the arm. They were followed by a tall, bold claimant, who was shouting at the top of his voice and threatening Pavel Pavlovich with all sorts of horrors. He bawled among other things that Pavel Pavlovich "was exploiting him and poisoning his existence." There seemed to have been some dispute about money; the women were much frightened and in a great hurry. Seeing Velchaninov, Pavel Pavlovich rushed to him with outstretched arms and screamed as though he were being murdered:

"My own brother, defend me!"

At the sight of Velchaninov's athletic figure the claimant

[5] Pun: *prohvost* and *prostun* mean respectively "scoundrel" and "simpleton."—A.Y.

promptly disappeared; Pavel Pavlovich in triumph shook
his fist after him with a yell of victory; at that point Velchaninov seized him by the shoulder in a fury, and, without
knowing why he did it, shook him until his teeth chattered.
Pavel Pavlovich instantly ceased shouting and stared at
his tormentor in stupid, drunken terror. Probably not knowing what to do with him next, Velchaninov firmly bent him
and sat him down on the sidewalk post.

"Liza is dead!" he said to him.

Pavel Pavlovich, still staring at Velchaninov, sat on the
post, supported by one of the ladies. He understood at last,
and his face suddenly looked somehow pinched.

"Dead . . ." he whispered strangely. Whether in his
drunken state his face broke into his loathsome, extended
grin, or whether it was otherwise contorted, Velchaninov
could not make out, but a moment later Pavel Pavlovich,
with an effort, lifted his trembling hand to make the sign
of the cross; his trembling hand dropped again, however,
without completing it. A little while after he slowly got up
from the post, clutched at his lady, and, leaning upon her,
went on his way, like a man in a daze, as if Velchaninov
had not been there. But the latter seized him by the shoulder again.

"Do you understand, you drunken monster, that without
you she can't be buried?" he shouted breathlessly.

Pavel Pavlovich turned his head toward him.

"The artillery . . . lieutenant . . . do you remember
him?" he stammered.

"Wha—at!" yelled Velchaninov, with a sickening pang.

"There's her father for you! Seek him out for the burial."

"You're lying," Velchaninov yelled like one distraught.
"You say that from spite. . . . I knew you were preparing
that for me."

Beside himself, he raised his terrible fist over Pavel Pavlovich's head. In another moment he might have killed him
at one blow; the ladies squealed and beat a retreat, but
Pavel Pavlovich did not turn a hair. His face was contorted
by a frenzy of ferocious hatred.

"Do you know," he said, much more steadily, almost as though he were sober, "our Russian . . . ?" (and he uttered an absolutely unprintable term of abuse) "Well, you go to it!" Then with a violent effort he tore himself out of Velchaninov's hands, stumbled, and almost fell down. The ladies caught him and this time ran, squealing and almost dragging Pavel Pavlovich after them. Velchaninov did not follow them.

On the afternoon of the next day a very presentable-looking, middle-aged government clerk in uniform arrived at the Pogoreltzevs' villa and politely handed Klavdia Petrovna an envelope addressed to her by Pavel Pavlovich Trusotzky. In it was a letter enclosing three hundred roubles and the legal papers necessary for the burial. Pavel Pavlovich wrote briefly, respectfully, and most properly. He warmly thanked her Excellency for the beneficent interest she had taken in the little motherless girl, for which God alone could repay her. He indicated vaguely that extreme ill-health would prevent him from coming to bury his beloved and unhappy daughter, and that in this matter he could only count upon the angelic kindness of her Excellency's heart. The three hundred roubles were, as he explained later in the letter, to pay for the funeral, and the expenses caused by the child's illness. And should any of this money be left over, he most humbly and respectfully begged that it might be spent on a perpetual mass for the rest of the soul of the departed.

The clerk who brought the letter could add nothing in explanation; it appeared, indeed, from what he said that it was only at Pavel Pavlovich's earnest entreaty that he had undertaken personally to deliver the letter to her Excellency. Pogoreltzev was almost offended at the expression "the expenses caused by the child's illness," and after setting aside fifty roubles for the funeral—since it was impossible to prevent the father from paying for his child's burial—he proposed to send the remaining two hundred and fifty roubles back to Mr. Trusotzky at once. Klavdia Petrovna finally decided not to send back the two hundred and fifty roubles, but only a receipt from the cemetery church for that sum in payment for a perpetual mass for the repose of the soul of the deceased maiden Elizaveta. This receipt was afterward given to Velchaninov to be dispatched forthwith to Pavel Pavlovich. Velchaninov posted it to his lodging.

After the funeral he disappeared from the villa. For a whole fortnight he wandered about the town aimlessly and alone, so lost in thought that he stumbled against people in the street. Sometimes he would lie stretched out on his sofa for days together, forgetting the commonest things of every-day life. Several times the Pogoreltzevs sent for him; he promised to come, but immediately forgot. Klavdia Petrovna even went herself to see him, but did not find him at home. The same thing happened to his lawyer; the lawyer had, indeed, something to tell him: his lawsuit had been very adroitly settled, and his opponents had come to an amicable arrangement, agreeing to accept an insignificant portion of the disputed inheritance. All that remained was to obtain Velchaninov's own consent. When at last he did find him at home, the lawyer was surprised at the apathy and indifference with which Velchaninov, once such a troublesome client, listened to his explanation.

The very hottest days of July had come, but Velchaninov was oblivious of time. His grief ached in his heart like a ripe abscess, and he was constantly conscious of it with agonizing acuteness. His chief suffering was the thought that Liza had had no time to know him, and that she had died unaware of how poignantly he loved her! The object in life, of which he had had such a joyful glimpse, had suddenly vanished into everlasting darkness. That object— he thought of it every moment now—had been that Liza should be incessantly conscious of his love every day, every hour, all her life. "No one has or can have a higher aim," he thought sometimes, in gloomy rapture. "If there are other goals, none can be holier than that! My love for Liza," he mused, "would purify and redeem my former disreputable and useless life; to make up for my own idle, vicious, and wasted life I would cherish and bring up a pure and exquisite creature, and for her sake everything would be forgiven me and I could forgive myself everything."

All these *conscious* thoughts always rose before his mind, together with the vivid, ever-present and ever-poignant memory of the dead child. He re-created for himself her little pale face, recalled every expression on it; he recalled her in the coffin decked with flowers, and as she had lain unconscious in fever, with fixed and open eyes. He suddenly remembered that when she was lying on the table he had noticed one of her fingers, which had somehow turned black during her illness; this had struck him so much at the time, and he had felt so sorry for that poor little finger, that for the first time he thought of seeking out Pavel Pavlovich and killing him; until that time he had been "as it were, unfeeling." Was it wounded pride that had tortured her childish heart to death, or was it those three months of suffering at the hands of her father, whose love had suddenly changed to hatred, who had insulted her with shameful words, laughed at her terror, and abandoned her at last to strangers? All this he dwelt upon incessantly in a thousand variations. "Do you know what Liza has been to me?" —he suddenly recalled the drunkard's exclamation and felt that that exclamation was sincere, not a pose, and that there was love in it. "How, then, could that monster be so cruel to a child whom he had loved so much, and is it credible?" But every time he made haste to dismiss that question, as it were, brush it aside; there was something awful in that question, something he could not bear and could not solve.

One day, scarcely conscious where he was going, he wandered into the cemetery where Liza was buried and found her little grave. He had not been to the cemetery since the funeral; he had always fancied it would be too great an agony, and had not dared to go. But, strange to say, when he had pressed against her little grave and kissed it, he grew easier in his mind. It was a fine evening, the sun was setting; all around the graves the grass was lush and green; the bees were humming in a rosebush close by; the flowers and wreaths left by the children and Klavdia Petrovna on

Liza's grave were lying there with half of the petals on the ground. After many days something like hope refreshed his heart. "How serene!" he thought, feeling the stillness of the cemetery, and looking at the clear, tranquil sky. A rush of pure, calm faith flooded his soul. "Liza has sent me this, it's Liza speaking to me," he thought.

It was quite dark when he left the cemetery and went home. Not far from the cemetery gates, in a low-pitched wooden house on the road, there was some sort of eating house or tavern; through the windows he could see people sitting at the tables. It suddenly seemed to him that one of them, placed close to the window, was Pavel Pavlovich, and that he saw him, too, and was staring at him inquisitively. He walked on, and soon heard someone following him; Pavel Pavlovich was, in fact, running after him; probably he had been attracted and encouraged by Velchaninov's conciliatory expression as he watched him from the window. On overtaking him he smiled timidly, but it was not his old drunken smile; he was actually sober.

"Good evening," he said.

"Good evening," answered Velchaninov.

Chapter XI: Pavel Pavlovich Means to Marry

As he responded with this "good evening," he was surprised at himself. It struck him as extremely strange that he met this man now without a trace of spite, and that in his feeling for him at that moment there was something quite different, and, indeed, a sort of impulse toward something new.

"What a pleasant evening," observed Pavel Pavlovich, looking him in the eye.

"You've not gone away yet?" said Velchaninov, not by way of a question, but simply thinking aloud as he walked on.

"My case has dragged on, but I have been promoted to a

higher post, sir. I shall be going away the day after to-morrow for certain."

"You've got a post?" he said this time, asking a question.

"Why shouldn't I?" said Pavel Pavlovich, making a wry face.

"Oh, I only asked . . ." Velchaninov said apologetically, and with a frown looked askance at Pavel Pavlovich. To his surprise, the attire, the hat with the crape band, and the whole appearance of Mr. Trusotzky were incomparably more presentable than they had been a fortnight before. What was he sitting in that tavern for, he kept wondering.

"I was intending, Alexey Ivanovich, to apprise you of another joyful event in my life," Pavel Pavlovich began again.

"Joyful?"

"I'm going to get married."

"What?"

"After sorrow comes joy, so it is always in life; I should have liked very much, Alexey Ivanovich, to . . . but—I don't know, perhaps you're in a hurry now, for you appear to be. . . ."

"Yes, I am in a hurry . . . and I'm unwell too."

He felt a sudden and intense desire to get rid of him; his readiness for some new feeling had vanished in a flash.

"I should have liked, sir . . ."

Pavel Pavlovich did not say what he would have liked; Velchaninov was silent.

"In that case it must be later on, if only we meet again, sir. . . ."

"Yes, yes, later on," Velchaninov muttered rapidly, without stopping or looking at him. They were both silent again for a minute; Pavel Pavlovich went on walking beside him.

"In that case, good-by till we meet again," Pavel Pavlovich brought out at last.

"Good-by; I wish . . ."

Velchaninov returned home thoroughly upset again. Contact with "that man" was too much for him. As he got into bed he asked himself again, "Why was he at the cemetery?"

Next morning he made up his mind to visit the Pogo-reltzevs, but he made up his mind reluctantly; sympathy from anyone, even from the Pogoreltzevs, was too painful for him now. But they were so anxious about him that he felt absolutely obliged to go. He suddenly had a foreboding that he would feel horribly ashamed at their first meeting again. Should he go or not, he thought, as he made haste to finish his breakfast, when, to his intense amazement, Pavel Pavlovich walked in.

In spite of their meeting the day before Velchaninov could never have conceived that the man would come to see him again, and was so taken aback that he stared at him and did not know what to say. But Pavel Pavlovich was equal to the occasion. He greeted his host and sat down on the very same chair on which he had sat on his last visit three weeks earlier. Velchaninov had a sudden and pecu-liarly vivid memory of that visit, and looked uneasily and with disgust at his visitor.

"You're surprised, sir?" began Pavel Pavlovich, interpret-ing Velchaninov's gaze correctly.

He seemed altogether much more free and easy than on the previous day, and at the same time it could be detected that he was more timid than he had been then. His ap-pearance was particularly curious. Mr. Trusotzky was not only presentably but quite foppishly dressed—in a light-weight summer jacket, light trousers of a smart, close-fitting cut, a light waistcoat; gloves, a gold lorgnette, which he had suddenly adopted for some reason; his linen was ir-reproachable; he even smelled of scent. About his whole getup there was something ridiculous, and at the same time suggestive of something strange and unpleasant.

"Of course, Alexey Ivanovich," he went on, wriggling, "I'm surprising you by coming, and I'm sensible of it, sir. But something higher is, I imagine, and, to my mind, should be preserved, between people, isn't that so? Higher, I mean, than all the conditions and even unpleasantnesses that may come to pass. . . . Isn't that so?"

"Pavel Pavlovich, come to the point quickly, and without ceremony," said Velchaninov, frowning.

"In two words," Pavel Pavlovich began hastily, "I'm going to get married and I am just setting off to see my future bride. They are in a summer cottage, too. I should like to have the great honor to make bold to introduce you, sir, to the family, and I have come to ask an unusual favor"— Pavel Pavlovich bent his head humbly—"to beg you, sir, to accompany me. . . ."

"Accompany you, where?" Velchaninov stared at him.

"To them, that is, to their cottage. Forgive me, I am talking as though in a fever, and perhaps I've not been clear; but I'm so afraid of your declining, sir."

And he looked mournfully at Velchaninov.

"Do you want me to go with you now to see your future bride?" Velchaninov repeated, scrutinizing him rapidly, unable to believe his eyes or ears.

"Yes," said Pavel Pavlovich, all of a sudden extremely abashed. "Don't be angry, Alexey Ivanovich. It's not impertinence; I only beg you most humbly as a great favor. I had imagined that you wouldn't perhaps refuse. . . ."

"To begin with, it's utterly out of the question." Velchaninov writhed uneasily.

"It is merely an extraordinary desire on my part and nothing more," Pavel Pavlovich went on, imploring him. "I will not conceal, either, that there is a reason for it, but I should prefer not to reveal it till later, and for the present to confine myself to the very earnest request, sir. . . ."

And he even got up from his seat in an access of deference.

"But in any case it is quite impossible, you must admit that yourself. . . ." Velchaninov, too, stood up.

"It is quite possible, Alexey Ivanovich. I had intended to present you as a friend, sir; and besides, you are an acquaintance of theirs already; you see, it's to Zahlebinin's, to his villa that I am going. The councilor of state, Zahlebinin."

"What?" cried Velchaninov.

It was the councilor for whom he had been constantly

looking a month before, and whom he had never found at home. As it turned out, the man had been acting in the interests of the other party.

"Yes, yes!" said Pavel Pavlovich, smiling and seeming to be encouraged by Velchaninov's great astonishment; "the very man, you remember, beside whom you were walking and to whom you were talking, while I stood opposite watching you; I was waiting to go up to him when you had finished. Twenty years ago we were in the same office, sir, and that day, when I meant to go up to him after you had finished, I had as yet no such idea. It occurred to me suddenly, only a week ago, sir."

"But, look here, aren't they apparently quite a decent family?" said Velchaninov, in naïve surprise.

"Well, what then, if they are?" Pavel Pavlovich made a wry face.

"No, of course, I didn't mean . . . only as far as I've observed when I was there . . ."

"They remember, they remember your being there, sir," Pavel Pavlovich put in joyfully; "only you couldn't have seen the family then, sir; but he remembers you and has great esteem for you. I respectfully told them about you."

"But you've only been a widower three months!"

"But you see the wedding will not be at once, sir; the wedding will be in nine or ten months, so that the year of mourning will be over. I assure you that everything is all right. To begin with, Fedosey Petrovich has known me from a boy; he knew my late wife, he knows my style of living, and what people think of me, and what's more, I have property, and just now I've been officially promoted—so all that has weight."

"Is it a daughter of his?"

"I will tell you all about it." Pavel Pavlovich huddled up ingratiatingly. "Allow me to light a cigarette. Besides, you'll see her yourself today. To begin with, such capable men as Fedosey Petrovich are sometimes very highly valued here in Petersburg, if they succeed in attracting notice. But you know, apart from his salary and the additional and supplementary fees, bonuses, his expense account, and grants-in-aid, he has nothing—that is, nothing substantial that could be called capital. They are comfortably off, but there is no possibility of saving, what with a family, sir. Judge for yourself: Fedosey Petrovich has eight girls and only one son, still a child. If he were to die tomorrow, there would be nothing left but a niggardly pension, sir. And eight girls! Just imagine—only imagine—what it must run into simply for their shoes! Of these eight girls five are grown up, the eldest is four and twenty (a most charming young lady, as you will see) and the sixth, a girl of fifteen, is still in high school. Of course, husbands must be found for the five elder ones, and that ought to be done in good time, as far as possible, so their father ought to bring them out, sir, and what do you suppose that will cost? And then I turn up, the first suitor they have had in the house, and one they know all about, that I really have property, I mean. Well, that's all."

Pavel Pavlovich was holding forth rapturously.

"You've the eldest in marriage?"

"N-no, I . . . no, not the eldest; you see, I'm proposing to the sixth, the one who is still in high school."

"What?" said Velchaninov, with an involuntary smile. "Why, you say she's only fifteen!"

"Fifteen now, sir; but in nine months she'll be sixteen, she'll be sixteen and three months, so why not? But as it would be improper at present, there is now no open engagement but only an understanding with the parents. . . . I assure you, sir, that everything is all right!"

"Then it's not settled yet?"

"Yes, it is settled, it's all settled, sir, I assure you, everything is all right."

"And does she know?"

"Well, it's only in appearance, for the sake of propriety, that they are not telling her; of course she knows." Pavel Pavlovich screwed up his eyes pleasantly. "Well, will you make me happy, Alexey Ivanovich?" Pavel Pavlovich concluded very timidly.

"But what should I go there for? However," he added hurriedly, "since I'm not going in any case, don't try to persuade me."

"Alexey Ivanovich. . . ."

"But do you expect me to get in beside you and drive off there with you. Think of it!"

The feelings of disgust and hostility came back after the momentary distraction of Pavel Pavlovich's chatter about his future bride. In another minute he would have turned him out. He even felt angry with himself for some reason.

"Do come, Alexey Ivanovich, do, and you won't regret it!" Pavel Pavlovich implored him in a voice fraught with feeling. "No, you won't!" He waved his hands, noticing Velchaninov's impatient and determined gesture. "Alexey Ivanovich, Alexey Ivanovich, wait a bit before you decide! I see that you have perhaps misunderstood me. Of course, I know only too well that you cannot be to me, nor I to you . . . that we're not comrades, sir; I am not so absurd as not to understand it, and that the favor I'm asking of you will not pledge you to anything in the future. Besides, I'm going away the day after tomorrow altogether, absolutely; so it is just as though nothing had happened. Let this day be a single exception. I have come to you resting my hopes on the nobility of the special feelings of your heart, Alexey Ivanovich—precisely those feelings which might of late have been awakened in your heart, sir. . . . I think I'm speaking clearly, am I not?"

Pavel Pavlovich's agitation reached an extreme point. Velchaninov looked at him strangely.

"You ask for some service from me," he said hesitatingly, "and are very insistent about it. That strikes me as suspicious; I should like to know more about it."

"The only service is that you should come with me. And afterward, on our way back, I will unfold all to you as though at confession. Alexey Ivanovich, believe me!"

But Velchaninov still refused, and the more stubbornly because he was conscious of an oppressive and spiteful thought. This spiteful thought had been faintly stirring within him from the very beginning, ever since Pavel Pavlovich had mentioned his future bride: whether it was simply curiosity, or some other quite obscure inclination, he felt tempted to consent. And the more he felt tempted, the more he resisted. He sat with his elbow on one hand, hesitating.

Pavel Pavlovich beside him kept fawning on him and begging.

"Very good, I'll come," he consented all at once, uneasily and almost apprehensively, getting up from his seat.

Pavel Pavlovich was extremely delighted.

"But, Alexey Ivanovich, you must dress up now," Pavel Pavlovich delightedly cajoled Velchaninov, who was changing. "Put on your best suit."

"And why must he meddle in this, too, the strange fellow?" Velchaninov thought to himself.

"This is not the only service I'm expecting of you, Alexey Ivanovich. Since you have given your consent, please be my adviser."

"In what, for example?"

"The great question, for instance, is crape. What would be more proper: to remove the crape, or keep it on?"

"As you prefer."

"No, I want you to decide, sir; what would you do yourself in my place, that is, if you had crape on your hat? My own idea is that retaining it will point to the constancy of my feelings and so be a flattering recommendation."

"Take it off, of course."

"Do you really mean it?" Pavel Pavlovich hesitated. "No, I think I had better keep it. . . ."

"As you like."

"He doesn't trust me, that's a good thing," thought Velchaninov.

They went out; Pavel Pavlovich gazed with satisfaction at Velchaninov's smartened appearance; his countenance seemed to betray an even greater degree of deference and of dignity! Velchaninov wondered at him and even more at himself. An excellent carriage stood waiting for them at the gate.

"You had a carriage all ready too? So you felt sure I would come?"

"I engaged the carriage for myself, but I did feel confident that you would consent to accompany me," Pavel Pavlovich replied, with the air of a perfectly happy man.

"Ah, Pavel Pavlovich," Velchaninov said, laughing irritably when they were in the carriage and had set off; "aren't you too sure of me?"

"But it's not for you, Alexey Ivanovich, it's not for you to tell me because of it that I'm a fool," Pavel Pavlovich responded in a firm voice full of feeling.

"And Liza," thought Velchaninov, and at once hastened to dismiss the thought of her as though afraid of sacrilege. And it suddenly seemed to him that he was so petty, so insignificant at that moment; it struck him that the thought that had tempted him was so small and nasty. . . . And he longed again, at all costs, to throw everything aside and to get out of the carriage at once, even if he had to thrash Pavel Pavlovich. But the latter began talking and the temptation mastered his heart again.

"Alexey Ivanovich, are you a good judge of jewelry?"

"What sort of jewelry?"

"Diamonds."

"I am."

"I should like to make a little present. Advise me, should I or not?"

"I think you shouldn't."

"But I feel I should so like to," retorted Pavel Pavlovich, "only, what am I to buy? A whole set, that is, a brooch, earrings, a bracelet, or simply one article?"

"How much do you want to spend?"

"About four or five hundred roubles."

"Ugh!"

"Is it too much?" Pavel Pavlovich started.

"Buy a single bracelet for a hundred roubles."

Pavel Pavlovich was positively mortified; he was so eager

to spend more and buy a "whole set." He persisted. They drove to a shop. The upshot, however, was that he bought only a bracelet, and not the one that he wanted to, but the one that Velchaninov had pointed out. Pavel Pavlovich wanted to take both. When the merchant, who had asked a hundred and seventy-five roubles for the bracelet, consented to take a hundred and fifty for it, Pavel Pavlovich was positively vexed; he would have paid two hundred if that sum had been asked, he was so eager to spend more.

"It doesn't matter, my being in a hurry with presents," he gushed blissfully, when they had set off again. "They're not grand people, they are simple folk, sir. Innocence is fond of little presents," he said, with a sly and gay grin. "You smiled just now, Alexey Ivanovich, when you heard she was fifteen; but that's just what has bowled me over; that she is still going to school with the satchel on her arm full of copybooks and pens, he—he! That satchel has captivated me! It's innocence that charms me, Alexey Ivanovich; it's not so much beauty of face, it's that. She giggles in the corner with her school friend, and how they laugh, goodness me! And what at? It's all because the kitten jumped off the chest of drawers onto the bed and curled up like a little ball. . . . There's the scent of fresh apples here, you know, sir! Shall I take off the crape?"

"As you please."

"I will take it off."

He removed his hat, tore off the crape, and flung it on the road. Velchaninov saw that his face beamed with the brightest hopes, as he replaced his hat upon his bald head.

"Can it be that he is really like this?" Velchaninov thought, feeling genuinely angry; "can it be there isn't some trick in his inviting me? Can it be that really reckoning on my high-mindedness?" he went on, almost offended at the last supposition. "What is he—a buffoon, a fool, or the 'eternal husband'—but it's impossible!"

Chapter XII: At the Zahlebinins'

The Zahlebinins were really a "very decent family," as Velchaninov had put it, and Zahlebinin, himself, had an assured position in a government office and was well thought of by his superiors. All that Pavel Pavlovich had said about their income was true, too: "They live very comfortably, but if he dies there'll be nothing left."

Old Zahlebinin gave Velchaninov a warm and friendly welcome, and his former "foe" turned a friend.

"I congratulate you, it was better so," were his first words, uttered with a pleasant and dignified air. "I was in favor of settling it out of court myself, and Pyotr Karlovich [Velchaninov's lawyer] is priceless in such cases. Well, you get sixty thousand without any bother, without delays and disputes! And the case might have dragged on for three years!"

Velchaninov was at once presented to Madame Zahlebinin, an elderly lady of ample figure, with a very simple and tired-looking face. The young ladies, too, began to sail in one after another or in couples. Indeed, a great many young ladies made their appearance; by degrees ten or twelve of them gathered—Velchaninov lost count of them; some came in, others went out. Among them several were girl friends from the neighboring summer cottages. The Zahlebinins' villa, a large wooden house, built in a nondescript, whimsical style, with annexes added at different periods, had the advantage of a big garden; but this was shared by three or four other villas, an arrangement which naturally led to friendly relations among the girls of the different households. From the first, Velchaninov noticed that he was expected, and that his arrival in the capacity of a friend of Pavel Pavlovich, who was anxious to make their acquaintance, was announced almost solemnly.

His keen and experienced eye quickly detected something unusual in the atmosphere: the overcordial welcomes of the parents, a certain peculiar look about the girls and their getup (though, indeed, it was a holiday), all that aroused in his mind the suspicion that Pavel Pavlovich had, very possibly, cunningly suggested the idea, without, of course, spelling it out in so many words, here was a bored bachelor of the "best society" and a man of means and settled down, especially as he had just come into an inheritance. The manner of the eldest Mademoiselle Zahlebinin, Katerina Fedoseyevna, the one who was twenty-four and who had been described by Pavel Pavlovich as a charming person who might at last decide to put an end to his celibacy, was in keeping with that idea. She was distinguished from her sisters by her dress and the original way in which her luxuriant hair was done. Her sisters and the other girls all looked as though they were firmly convinced that Velchaninov was making their acquaintance "on Katya's account" and had come "to have a look at her." Their glances and even some words, dropped in the course of the day, confirmed him in this surmise. Katerina Fedoseyevna was a tall blonde of generous proportions, with an exceedingly sweet face, of a gentle, unenterprising, even torpid character. "Strange that a girl like that should still be available," Velchaninov could not help thinking, watching her with pleasure. "Of course, she has no dowry and she'll soon grow fat, but meantime lots of men would find her to their taste. . . ." All the other sisters, too, were by no means homely, and among their friends there were several amusing and even pretty faces. It began to divert him; he had come, moreover, with special ideas.

Nadezhda Fedoseyevna, the sixth, the schoolgirl and Pavel Pavlovich's alleged bride, did not appear till later. Velchaninov awaited her coming with an impatience which surprised him and made him smile at himself. At last she made her entrance, and not without effect, accompanied by a lively, keen-witted girl friend, a brunette with a comical face whose name was Marya Nikitishna, and of whom, as was at once apparent, Pavel Pavlovich stood in great dread. This Marya Nikitishna, a girl of twenty-three, sharp-tongued and clever, was a governess in a neighboring family with which the Zahlebinins were on friendly terms. She had long been accepted by them as one of themselves and was thought a great deal of by the girls. It was evident that Nadya found her indispensable now. Velchaninov discerned at once that all the girls were antagonistic to Pavel Pavlovich, even the friends, and two minutes after Nadya's arrival he had decided that she, too, *detested* him. He also observed that Pavel Pavlovich either failed or did not want to notice this.

Nadya was unquestionably the handsomest of the lot—a little brunette with a wild, untamed look and the boldness of a nihilist; a roguish imp with blazing eyes, a charming but often malicious smile, wonderful lips and teeth, a slender and graceful young thing, her face still childlike but glowing with incipient thought. Her age was evident in every step she took, in every word she uttered. It appeared afterward that Pavel Pavlovich did see her for the first time with an oilcloth satchel on her arm, but later she no longer carried it.

The presentation of the bracelet was a complete failure, and, indeed, made an unpleasant impression. As soon as Pavel Pavlovich saw his "future bride" come into the room, he went up to her with a smirk. He made the present under the pretense of gratitude for "the agreeable pleasure" he had experienced on his previous visit, "thanks to the charming romance sung by Nadezhda Fedoseyevna at the piano. . . ." He stumbled, could not finish, and stood helpless, holding out the case with the bracelet and thrusting it into the hand of Nadezhda Fedoseyevna, who did not want to take it, and, crimson with shame and anger, drew back her hands. She turned rudely to her mother, whose face betrayed embarrassment, and said aloud:

"I don't want to take it, *maman!*"

"Take it and say thank you," said her father, with calm severity: but he, too, was displeased. "Unnecessary, quite unnecessary!" he muttered reprovingly to Pavel Pavlovich.

Nadya, seeing there was no help for it, took the case and, dropping her eyes, curtsied, as tiny children curtsy—that is, suddenly bobbed down, and popped up again as though on springs. One of her sisters went up to look at it and Nadya handed her the case unopened, showing that, for her part, she did not care to look at it. The bracelet was taken out and passed from hand to hand; but they all looked at it in silence, and some even sarcastically. Only the mother murmured that the bracelet was very charming. Pavel Pavlovich was ready to sink into the ground.

Velchaninov came to the rescue.

He began talking, loudly and eagerly, about the first thing that occurred to him, and before five minutes were over he had gained the attention of everyone in the drawing room. He was a brilliant master of the art of small talk—that is, the art of seeming perfectly unsophisticated and at the same time appearing to consider his listeners as unsophisticated as himself. He could, with perfect naturalness, appear when necessary to be the most lighthearted and happy of men. He was very clever, too, in slipping in a witty remark, a gibe, a gay insinuation or amusing pun, always as it were accidentally and as though unconscious of doing it—though the witticism and pun and the whole conversation, perhaps, had been prepared and rehearsed long, long before and even used on more than one previous occasion. But at the present moment nature and art were at one, he felt that he was in good form and that something was drawing him on; he felt the most absolute confidence in himself and knew that in a few minutes all these eyes would be turned upon him, all these people would be listening only to him, talking to no one but him, and laughing only at what he said. And, in fact, laughter soon came, by degrees the others joined in the conversation—and he was exceedingly clever at drawing people into the conversation—three or four voices could be heard at once. The bored and weary face of Madame Zahlebinin was lighted up almost with joy; it was the same with Katerina Fedoseyevna, who gazed and listened as though enchanted.

Nadya watched him keenly and distrustfully; it was evident that she was already prejudiced against him. This spurred him on all the more. The "mischievous" Marya Nikitishna succeeded in getting in rather a good thrust at him; she asserted quite fictitiously that Pavel Pavlovich had spoken of Velchaninov as the friend of his boyhood, so putting with obvious intent at least seven years onto his age. But even the malicious Marya Nikitishna liked him. Pavel Pavlovich was completely nonplused. He had, of course, some idea of his friend's abilities and at first was delighted at his success; he tittered himself and joined in the conversation; but, by degrees, he began to sink into thoughtfulness, as it were, and finally into positive dejection, which was clearly apparent in his troubled countenance.

"Well, you're a guest who doesn't need entertaining," old Zahlebinin commented gaily, as he got up to go upstairs to his own room, where, in spite of the holiday, he had some business papers awaiting his attention; "and, only fancy, I thought of you as the gloomiest, most hypochondriac of young men. What mistakes one makes!"

They had a piano; Velchaninov asked who played, and suddenly turned to Nadya.

"I believe you sing?"

"Who told you?" Nadya snapped out.

"Pavel Pavlovich said so just now."

"It's not true. I only sing to get a laugh. I've no voice."

"And I've no voice either, but I sing."

"Then you'll sing to us? Well, then, I'll sing to you," said Nadya, her eyes gleaming; "only not now, but after dinner. I hate music," she added. "I'm sick of the piano—in our house they're all singing and playing from morning till night—what a clatter Katya alone makes!"

Velchaninov at once took this up, and it appeared that Katerina Fedoseyevna was the only one who played the piano seriously. He at once begged her to play. Everyone was evidently pleased at his addressing Katya, and *maman* positively flushed with gratification. Katerina Fedoseyevna got up, smiling, and went to the piano, and suddenly, to her own surprise, she too flushed and was horribly abashed that she, such a big girl, four and twenty and so plump, should be blushing like a child—and all this was written clearly on her face as she sat down to play. She played something from Haydn and played it carefully though without expression, but she was shy. When she had finished Velchaninov began warmly praising to her, not her playing but Haydn, and especially the little thing which she had played, and she was evidently so pleased and listened so gratefully and happily to his praises, not of herself but of Haydn, that he could not help looking at her with more friendliness and attention. "Ah, but you are a dear!" was reflected in the gleam of his eye—and everyone seemed instantly to understand that look, especially Katerina Fedoseyevna herself.

"You have a delightful garden," he said, suddenly addressing the company and looking toward the glass door that led onto the balcony. "You know, let us all go into the garden!"

"Let us, let us!" they shrieked joyfully, as though he had guessed the general wish.

They walked in the garden till dinnertime. Madame Zahlebinin, though she had been longing to have a nap, could not resist going out with them, but wisely sat down to rest on the balcony where she at once dozed off. In the garden Velchaninov and the girls got onto still more friendly terms. He noticed that two or three very young men from the summer cottages joined them; one was a student and another simply a high-school boy. They promptly made a dash each for *his* girl, and it was evident that they had come on their account; the third, a very morose and disheveled-looking youth of twenty, in huge blue spectacles, began, with a frown, whispering hurriedly with Marya Nikitishna and Nadya. He scanned Velchaninov sternly, and seemed to consider it incumbent upon himself to treat him with extraordinary contempt. Some of the girls suggested that they should play games. To Velchaninov's question, what games they played, they said all sorts of games, including catch, but in the evening they would play proverbs—that is, all would sit down and one would go out; then the others would choose a proverb—for instance: "More haste, less speed," and when the one outside is called in, each in turn has to say one sentence to him or her. For instance, the first person must say a sentence in which there is the word "more," the second, one in which there is the word "haste," and so on. And from their sentences whoever went out must guess the proverb.

"That must be very amusing," said Velchaninov.

"Oh, no, it's awfully boring," cried two or three voices at once.

"Or else we play at acting," Nadya observed, addressing him. "Do you see that thick tree, around which there's a seat: behind that tree are the wings, and there the actors sit, say a king, a queen, a princess, a young man—just as anyone likes; each one comes out when he chooses and says anything that comes into his head, and something turns out."

"But that's delightful!" Velchaninov was again complimentary.

"Oh, no, it's awfully dull! The beginning is always fun, but toward the end the game becomes nonsensical because no one knows how to bring it to conclusion; perhaps with you, though, it will be more amusing. We did think you were a friend of Pavel Pavlovich's, but it turns out that he was only bragging. I'm very glad you have come . . . for one thing. . . ." She looked very earnestly and impressively at Velchaninov and at once walked away to Marya Nikitishna.

"We're going to play proverbs in the evening," one of the girl friends whom Velchaninov had scarcely noticed before, and with whom he had not exchanged a word, whispered to him confidentially. "We're all going to make fun of Pavel Pavlovich, and you will too, of course."

"Ah, how nice it is that you've come, we were all so dull," observed another friendly young thing, who had sprung from goodness knows where and whom Velchaninov had completely failed to notice until then. She was a red-haired girl with freckles and a face absurdly flushed from walking and the heat.

Pavel Pavlovich's uneasiness grew more and more marked. In the garden Velchaninov had managed to become intimate with Nadya. She no longer looked at him distrustfully as she had at first; she seemed to have laid aside her critical attitude toward him, and laughed, skipped about, shrieked, and twice even seized him by the hand; she was extremely happy, she continued not to take the slightest notice of Pavel Pavlovich, and behaved as though she were not aware of his existence. Velchaninov discovered that there was an actual plot against Pavel Pavlovich. Nadya and the crowd of girls drew Velchaninov in one direction, while some of the other girl friends lured Pavel Pavlovich on various pretexts to go in another direction; but the latter would break away from them, and run full speed straight to Velchaninov and Nadya, and suddenly thrust his bald head in between them with uneasy curiosity. Toward the end he hardly attempted to restrain himself; the naïveté of his gestures and actions was sometimes amazing. Velchaninov could not but turn his attention once more to Katerina Fedoseyevna; it was clear to her now that he had not come on her account, and that he had become too much interested in Nadya, but her expression was just as sweet and good-humored as ever. She seemed to be happy simply at being beside them and listening to what their new visitor was saying; she, poor thing, could never join cleverly in a conversation.

"What a darling your sister Katerina Fedoseyevna is!" Velchaninov suddenly said to Nadya under his breath.

"Katya! Can there be a kinder heart than hers? She's an angel to all of us, I adore her," the girl responded enthusiastically.

At last dinner came at five o'clock; and it was evident that the dinner, too, was not an ordinary meal, but had been prepared expressly for a guest. There were two or three very elaborate dishes, which evidently were not part of their ordinary fare, and one of them so strange that no one could have found a name for it. In addition to ordinary table wine there was a bottle of Tokay, obviously for the benefit of the guest; at the end of dinner champagne was served for some reason. Old Zahlebinin took an extra glass, became extraordinarily good-humored, and was ready to laugh at anything Velchaninov said.

In the end Pavel Pavlovich could not restrain himself. Carried away by the spirit of competition, he suddenly attempted to make a pun too; at the end of the table, where he was sitting by Madame Zahlebinin, there was a sudden roar of loud laughter from the delighted girls.

"Papa, Papa! Pavel Pavlovich has made a pun too," the fourth and fifth Zahlebinin girls shouted in unison. "He says we're 'damsels who dazzle all. . . .'"

"Ah, so he too is punning! Well, what is his pun?" the old man responded sedately, turning patronizingly to Pavel Pavlovich and smiling beforehand at the expected pun.

"Why, he says we're 'damsels who dazzle all.'"

"Y-yes, well, and what then?" The old man did not understand and smiled more good-humoredly in expectation.

"Oh, Papa, how tiresome you are; you don't understand. Why, 'damsels' and then 'dazzle'; 'damsel' is like 'dazzle,' 'damsels who dazzle all. . . .'"

"A-a-ah," the old man drawled in a puzzled voice. "H'm, well, he'll make a better one next time!" And the old man laughed good-humoredly.

"Pavel Pavlovich, you can't have all the perfections at once," Marya Nikitishna teased him in a loud voice. "Oh, my goodness! He's choking on a bone," she exclaimed, jumping up from her chair.

There was a hubbub, but that was just what Marya Nikitishna wanted. Pavel Pavlovich had simply swallowed some wine the wrong way—he attacked it to cover his discomfiture—but Marya Nikitishna assured everyone and swore that it was a fishbone, that she had seen it herself, and that people sometimes died of it.

"Slap him on the back of the neck," someone shouted. "Yes, really that's the best thing to do!" Zahlebinin approved aloud.

There was no dearth of eager volunteers; Marya Nikitishna and the red-haired girl (who had also been invited to dinner), and, finally, the mother of the family herself, greatly alarmed—everyone wanted to slap Pavel Pavlovich on the back of the neck. Jumping up from the table, Pavel Pavlovich tried to evade them, for a full minute kept protesting that he had swallowed his wine the wrong way and that the cough would soon be over. In the end the company realized that it was all one of Marya Nikitishna's pranks.

"You certainly are a tease . . ." Madame Zahlebinin tried to say sternly to Marya Nikitishna; but she broke down and burst out laughing as she very rarely did, and that made quite a sensation of a sort.

After dinner they all went out on the veranda to have coffee.

"And what lovely days we're having!" the old man benevolently commended Nature, looking with pleasure into the garden. "If only we could have some rain. . . . Well, I'll go and have a nap. Enjoy yourselves and God bless you! And you enjoy yourself too," he added, patting Pavel Pavlovich on the shoulder as he went out.

When they had all gone out into the garden again, Pavel Pavlovich suddenly ran up to Velchaninov and pulled him by the sleeve.

"Just one minute," he whispered impatiently.

They turned into a lonely side path.

"No, in this case, excuse me, sir, no, I won't let you, sir . . ." he stuttered in a furious whisper, clutching Velchaninov's sleeve.

"What? What do you mean?" Velchaninov asked, opening his eyes in amazement.

Pavel Pavlovich stared at him mutely, his lips moved, and he smiled furiously.

"Where are you going? Where are you? Everything's ready," the impatient voices of the girls rang out.

Velchaninov shrugged his shoulders and returned to the rest of the party.

Pavel Pavlovich, too, ran after him.

"I'll bet he asked you for a handkerchief," said Marya Nikitishna; "he forgot one last time too."

"He'll always forget it!" the fifth Zahlebinin girl put in.

"He's forgotten his handkerchief, Pavel Pavlovich has forgotten his handkerchief, *maman*, Pavel Pavlovich has forgotten his pocket handkerchief, *maman*, Pavel Pavlovich has a cold!" cried voices.

"Then why doesn't he say so! You do stand on ceremony, Pavel Pavlovich!" Madame Zahlebinin drawled in a sing-song voice. "It's dangerous to trifle with a cold; I'll send you a handkerchief directly. And why does he always have a cold?" she added, as she moved away, glad of an excuse for returning home.

"I have two pocket handkerchiefs and I haven't a cold in my head!" Pavel Pavlovich called after her, but the lady apparently did not grasp what he said, and a minute later, when Pavel Pavlovich was ambling after the others, keeping near Velchaninov and Nadya, a breathless maidservant overtook him and brought him a handkerchief.

"Proverbs, a game of proverbs," the girls shouted on all sides, as though they expected something wonderful from "a game of proverbs."

They chose a place and sat down on benches; it fell to Marya Nikitishna's lot to guess; they insisted that she should go as far away as possible and not listen; in her absence they chose a proverb and distributed the words. Marya Nikitishna returned and guessed the proverb at once. The proverb was: "The dream is frightful, but God is merciful."

Marya Nikitishna was followed by the young man with disheveled hair and blue spectacles. They insisted on even greater precautions with him—he had to stand in the arbor and keep his face to the fence. The gloomy young man did what was required of him contemptuously, and seemed to feel morally degraded by it. When he was called he could guess nothing, he went the round of all of them and listened to what they said twice over, spent a long time in gloomy meditation, but nothing came of it. They put him to shame. The proverb was: "Praying to God and serving the Tsar ne'er fail of their reward."

"And the proverb's disgusting!" the exasperated young man exclaimed indignantly, as he retreated to his place.

"Oh, how dull it is!" cried voices.

Velchaninov went out; he was hidden even farther off; he, too, failed to guess.

"Oh, how dull it is!" more voices cried.

"Well, now, I'll go out," said Nadya.

"No, no, let Pavel Pavlovich go out now, it's Pavel Pavlovich's turn," they all shouted, growing more animated.

Pavel Pavlovich was led away, right up to the fence in the very corner, and made to stand facing it, and that he might not look around, the red-haired girl was sent to keep watch on him. Pavel Pavlovich, who had regained his self-confidence and almost cheered up again, intended to do his duty properly and stood stock-still, gazing at the fence and not daring to turn around. The red-haired girl stood on guard twenty paces behind him nearer to the party, close to the arbor, and excitedly exchanged signals with the girls; it was evident that all were uneasily expecting something; something was on foot. Suddenly the red-haired girl waved her arms from behind the arbor as a signal. Instantly they all jumped up and ran off at breakneck speed.

"Run, you run, too," a dozen voices whispered to Velchaninov, almost with horror at his not running.

"What's the matter? What has happened?" he asked, keeping in step with them all.

"Hush, don't shout! Let him stand there staring at the fence while we all run away. See, Nastya too is running."

The red-haired girl (Nastya) was running at breakneck speed, waving her arms as though something extraordinary had happened. They all ran at last to the other side of the pond, the very opposite end of the garden. When Velchaninov had got there he saw that Katerina Fedoseyevna was hotly disputing with the others, especially with Nadya and Marya Nikitishna.

"Katya, darling, don't be angry!" said Nadya, kissing her.

"Very well, I won't tell *maman,* but I shall go away myself, for it's very horrid. What must he be feeling at the fence there, poor man."

She went away—out of pity, but all the others were as implacable and ruthless as before. They all demanded sternly that when Pavel Pavlovich came back, Velchaninov should take no notice of him, as though nothing had happened. "And let us all play catch!" cried the red-haired girl ecstatically.

It was at least a quarter of an hour before Pavel Pavlovich rejoined the party. For two-thirds of that time he had certainly been standing at the fence. The game was in full swing, and was a great success—all were shouting and enjoying themselves. Frantic with rage, Pavel Pavlovich went straight up to Velchaninov and pulled at his sleeve again.

"Just a little minute, sir!"

"Good gracious, what does he want with his little minutes!"

"He's borrowing a handkerchief again," they shouted after him once more.

"Well, this time it was you; now it's all your doing. . . ."

Pavel Pavlovich's teeth positively chattered as he said this.

Velchaninov interrupted him, and mildly advised him to be more jovial or they would go on teasing him. "They tease you because you are cross, when all the rest are enjoying themselves." To his surprise, these words of advice made a great impression on Pavel Pavlovich; he quieted down at once—so much so, in fact, that he went back to the party with a penitent air and submissively took part in the games; after that, for some time they left him alone and played with him as with the rest—and before half an hour had passed he had almost regained his spirits. In all the games when he had to choose a partner he picked out by preference the red-haired traitress, or one of the Zahleb-inin sisters. But to his still greater surprise Velchaninov noticed that Pavel Pavlovich did not dare to speak to Nadya, although he continually hovered about her. At any rate, he accepted his position of one scorned and neglected by her, as though it were a fitting and natural thing. But toward the end they played a prank upon him again.

The game was hide-and-seek. The one who hid was allowed, however, to run anywhere in the part of the garden allotted him. Pavel Pavlovich, who had succeeded in concealing himself in a thick bush, conceived the idea of running out and making a bolt for the house. He was seen and shouts were raised; he crept hurriedly upstairs to the mezzanine, knowing of a place behind a chest of drawers, where he could hide. But the red-haired girl flew up after him, tiptoed to the door, and turned the key on him. All left off playing and ran just as they had done before to the other side of the pond, at the farther end of the garden. Ten minutes later, Pavel Pavlovich, becoming aware that no one was looking for him, peeped out of the window. There was no one to be seen. He did not dare to call out for fear of waking the parents; the maids had been sternly forbidden to answer Pavel Pavlovich's call or go to him. Katerina Fedoseyevna might have unlocked the door, but, returning to her room and sitting down to dream a little, she had unexpectedly fallen asleep. And so he stayed there about an hour. At last the girls appeared, as it were by chance, walking past the room, in twos or threes.

"Pavel Pavlovich, why don't you come out to us? Oh, it has been fun! We've been playing at acting. Alexey Ivano-vich had the part of a young man."

"Pavel Pavlovich, why don't you come, you will dazzle us!" others observed as they passed.

"Who will dazzle you?" they suddenly heard the voice of Madame Zahlebinin, who had only just waked up and decided to come out into the garden and watch the "chil-dren's" games while waiting for tea.

"But here's Pavel Pavlovich," they told her, pointing to

the window where Pavel Pavlovich, his face pale with anger, looked out with a wry smile.

"It's an odd fancy for a man to sit alone, when you're all enjoying yourselves!" said the mother of the family, shaking her head.

Meanwhile, Nadya had finally deigned to give Velchaninov an explanation of her words that there was a reason she was glad he had come. The explanation took place in a secluded avenue. Marya Nikitishna purposely summoned Velchaninov, who was taking part in some game and was horribly bored, and left him alone in the avenue with Nadya.

"I am absolutely convinced," she said boldly, in a rapid patter, "that you are not such a great friend of Pavel Pavlovich's as he boasted you were. I am reckoning on you as the one person who can do me a very great service. Here is his vile bracelet." She took the case out of her pocket and continued, "I humbly beg you to give this back to him at once, as I shall never speak to him again in my whole life. You can say so from me, and tell him in future not to dare butt in with presents. I'll let him know the rest through other people. Will you be so kind as to do me the pleasure of granting my desire?"

"Oh, for God's sake, spare me!" Velchaninov almost cried out, waving his arms.

"What? Spare you?" Nadya was extraordinarily surprised at his refusal, and she gazed at him round-eyed. The tone she had assumed for the occasion broke down immediately, and she was almost in tears. Velchaninov laughed.

"I don't mean that . . . I should be very glad . . . but I have my own account to settle with him. . . ."

"I knew that you were not his friend and that he was telling lies!" Nadya interrupted quickly and passionately. "I'll never marry him, I tell you! Never! I can't understand how he dared. . . . Only you must give him back his disgusting present or else what shall I do? I particularly, particularly want him to have it back today, the same day, so that his hopes may be crushed, and if the sneak tells Papa about it, he'll catch it, he may be sure."

From behind the bushes there suddenly emerged the young man in the blue spectacles.

"You must return the bracelet," he blurted out furiously, pouncing on Velchaninov. "If only out of respect for the rights of women, that is—if you are capable of rising to the full significance of the question."

But before he had time to finish Nadya tugged at his sleeve with all her might, and drew him away from Velchaninov.

"My goodness, how silly you are, Predposylov!" she cried. "Go away, go away, go away, and don't dare to eavesdrop; I ordered you to stand a long way off . . . !" She stamped her little foot at him, and when he had crept back into the bushes she still walked up and down across the path, with her eyes flashing and her arms folded before her, as though she were beside herself with anger.

"You wouldn't believe how silly they are!" She stopped suddenly before Velchaninov. "It amuses you, but think of how hard it is on me."

"That's not *he*, it's not *he*, is it?" laughed Velchaninov.

"Of course it isn't, and how could you imagine it?" cried Nadya, smiling and blushing. "That's only his friend. But I can't understand the friends he chooses; they all say that he's a 'future leader,' but I don't understand it. . . . Alexey Ivanovich, I've no one I can appeal to; I ask you for the last time, will you give it back?"

"Oh, very well, I will; give it me."

"Ah, you are kind, you are good!" she cried, delighted, handing him the case. "I'll sing for you the whole evening for that because I sing beautifully, you know. I told you a fib when I said I didn't like music. Oh, you must come again—once at any rate; how glad I should be. I would tell you everything, everything, everything, and a great deal more besides, because you're so kind—as kind, as kind, as—as Katya!"

And, indeed, when they went in to tea she did sing him

two songs, in a wholly untrained and hardly mature, but pleasant and powerful voice. When they came in from the garden Pavel Pavlovich was sedately sitting with the parents at the tea table, on which the big family samovar was already boiling, surrounded by cups of Sèvres china, an heirloom. He was probably discussing very grave matters with the old people, as two days later he was going away for nine whole months. He did not glance at the party as they came in from the garden, and particularly avoided looking at Velchaninov. It was evident, too, that he had not been bearing tales and that all was serene so far.

But when Nadya began singing he put himself forward at once. Nadya purposely ignored one direct question he addressed her, but this did not disconcert or shake Pavel Pavlovich. He stood behind her chair and his whole manner showed that this was his place and he was not going to give it up to anyone.

"Alexey Ivanovich's turn to sing, *maman;* Alexey Ivanovich wants to sing!" almost all the girls shouted at once, crowding around the piano at which Velchaninov confidently installed himself, intending to play his own accompaniment. The old people came in, and with them Katerina Fedoseyevna, who had been sitting with them and pouring out the tea.

Velchaninov chose a romance of Glinka's, now familiar to almost no one.

> In the glad hour when from thy lips
> Comes cooing tender as a dove's.[6]

He sang it, addressing himself entirely to Nadya, who was standing at his elbow nearer to him than anyone. His voice had passed its prime, but what was left of it showed that it had once been a fine one. Twenty years before Velchaninov as a student had the luck to hear that song for the first time sung by Glinka himself at the house of a friend of the composer's. It was at a literary-artistic stag

[6] From a lyric by the Polish poet Adam Mickiewicz translated into Russian.—A.Y.

party, and Glinka, letting himself go, played and sang his own favorite compositions, among them this song. By then little was left of his voice, too, but Velchaninov remembered the great impression made by that romance. A drawing-room singer, however skillful, would never have produced such an effect. In that song the intensity of passion rises, mounting higher and higher at every line, at every word; and because of this very intensity, the least trace of falsity, of exaggeration, or unreality, such as passes muster so easily at an opera, would distort and destroy its whole meaning. To sing that slight but extraordinary piece it was essential to have sincerity, genuine inspiration, real passion, or a complete poetical mastery of it. Otherwise the song would not only be a failure but might even appear hideous and all but shameless: it would be impossible to express such intensity of passion without arousing repulsion, but sincerity and simplicity saved everything. Velchaninov remembered that he himself had formerly made a success with this song. He had almost made his own Glinka's manner of singing, but now, with the first note, the first line, genuine inspiration, too, blazed up in his soul and quivered in his voice. With every word the emotion burst forth more boldly; in the last lines resounded the cry of passion, and when, with blazing eyes, Velchaninov addressed the final words of the song to Nadya:

> Grown bolder, in thine eyes I gaze;
> I bring nearer my lips, can no longer listen,
> I long to kiss thee, kiss thee, kiss thee!
> I long to kiss thee, kiss thee, kiss thee!

she started almost in fear, and even moved back a little; the color rushed into her cheeks, and at the same time Velchaninov seemed to catch a glimpse of something responsive in her abashed and almost dismayed little face. The faces of all those in the audience betrayed enchantment and also perplexity: all seemed to feel that it was impossible and shameful to sing like that, and yet at the same time all their faces were flushed and all their eyes glowed and seemed to be expecting something more. Among those faces Velchaninov caught a glimpse especially of the face of Katerina Fedoseyevna, which looked almost beautiful.

"What a song," old Zahlebinin muttered, a little taken aback; "but . . . isn't it too strong? Charming, but strong. . . ."

"Yes . . ." Madame Zahlebinin chimed in, but Pavel Pavlovich would not let her go on; he dashed forward suddenly like a madman, so far forgetting himself as to seize Nadya by the arm and pull her away from Velchaninov; he ran up to him and looked at him despairingly, moving his quivering lips.

"Just a minute, sir," he brought out faintly at last.

Velchaninov saw that in another minute the man might do something ten times as absurd; he made haste to take his arm and, disregarding the general bewilderment, drew him out into the veranda, and even took some steps into the garden with him, where it was now almost dark.

"Do you understand that you must go away with me right now, this very minute!" said Pavel Pavlovich.

"No, I don't understand. . . ."

"Do you remember," Pavel Pavlovich went on, in his frenzied whisper, "do you remember that you had demanded I should tell you everything, *everything* openly, the very last word . . . do you remember, sir? Well, the time has come to say that word . . . let us go, sir!"

Velchaninov thought awhile, looked at Pavel Pavlovich again, and agreed to go.

The sudden announcement of their departure upset the parents and made all the girls horribly indignant.

"At least have another cup of tea," groaned Madame Zahlebinin plaintively.

"Come, what's upset you?" old Zahlebinin said in a tone of severity and displeasure, addressing Pavel Pavlovich, who stood simpering and silent.

"Pavel Pavlovich, why are you taking Alexey Ivanovich away?" the girls cooed plaintively, looking daggers at him.

As for Nadya, she looked at him with so much hatred that he positively squirmed, but did not give way.

"You see, Pavel Pavlovich has reminded me—I thank him for it—of a very important engagement which I might have missed," Velchaninov said, smiling, as he shook hands with Zahlebinin, and bowed to the hostess and the girls, especially distinguishing Katerina Fedoseyevna in a manner that was again noted by all.

"We are very grateful for your visit and shall always be glad to see you," Zahlebinin said ponderously in conclusion.

"Oh, we are so delighted . . ." chimed in with feeling the mother of the family.

"Come again, Alexey Ivanovich, come again!" numerous voices were heard calling from the veranda, when he had already got into the carriage with Pavel Pavlovich; there was perhaps one voice that called more softly than the others, "Come again, dear, dear Alexey Ivanovich."

"That's the red-haired girl," thought Velchaninov.

Chapter XIII: On Whose Side Is There More?

He could think about the red-haired girl, but vexation and remorse had long been tormenting his soul. And, indeed, during the whole of that day, which seemed on the surface so amusingly spent, depression had scarcely left him. Just before singing the lyric he did not know how to escape from that feeling; perhaps that was why he had sung it with such fervor.

"And I could abase myself like that . . . tear myself away from everything," he began reproaching himself, but he hurriedly cut short his thoughts. Indeed, it seemed to him humiliating to lament; it was a great deal more pleasant to get angry.

"The fool!" he whispered spitefully, with a side glance at the silent figure of Pavel Pavlovich sitting beside him in the carriage.

Pavel Pavlovich remained obstinately silent, perhaps concentrating and getting himself in readiness. With an impatient gesture he sometimes took off his hat and wiped his brow with his handkerchief.

"Perspiring!" Velchaninov thought angrily.

On one occasion only Pavel Pavlovich addressed a question to the coachman. "Is there going to be a storm?" he asked.

"And what a storm! No doubt of it; it's been brewing all day."

The sky was indeed growing dark and there were flashes of lightning in the distance. They reached the town about half-past ten.

"I am coming in with you, of course," Pavel Pavlovich warned him, not far from Velchaninov's lodging.

"I understand, but I must tell you that I feel seriously ill."

"I won't stay long. I won't stay long."

When they reached the courtyard, Pavel Pavlovich ran into the porter's lodge to find Mavra.

"What did you run there for?" Velchaninov asked sternly, as the latter overtook him and they went into the flat.

"Oh . . . nothing, sir . . . the driver. . . ."

"I won't have you drink!"

No answer followed. Velchaninov lighted the candles, and Pavel Pavlovich at once sat down in the armchair. Velchaninov remained standing before him, with a frown on his face.

"I, too, promised to say my 'last' word," he began, with an inward, still suppressed irritation. "Here it is—that word: I consider in all conscience that everything between us is over, so that, in fact, there is nothing for us to talk about—do you hear?—nothing; and so wouldn't it be better for you to go away at once, and I'll lock the door after you?"

"Let us settle our account, Alexey Ivanovich," said Pavel Pavlovich, looking him in the eye, though with peculiar meekness.

"Settle our account?" repeated Velchaninov, greatly surprised. "That's a strange thing to say! Settle what account? Bah! Isn't that perhaps that 'last word' you promised . . . to reveal to me?"

"It is."

"We've no account to settle; we've long been quits!" said Velchaninov proudly.

"Can you really think so, sir?" Pavel Pavlovich brought out in a voice full of feeling, clasping his hands strangely and holding them before his breast. Velchaninov made no answer, and began to pace the floor. "Liza! Liza!" he was moaning in his heart.

"How did you want to settle our account, though?" He turned to him, frowning, after a rather prolonged silence.

Pavel Pavlovich had been following him about the room with his eyes all this time, still holding his hands clasped before him.

"Don't go there again, sir," he almost whispered in a pleading voice, and he suddenly got up from his chair.

"What! So that's all you mean?" Velchaninov laughed spitefully. "I've kept wondering at you all day, though!" he began maliciously, but suddenly his whole face changed. "Listen," he said mournfully, with deep and sincere feeling; "I consider that I have never lowered myself as I have today—to begin with, by consenting to go with you, and then—by what happened there. . . . It was so paltry, so pitiful . . . I've defiled and debased myself by mixing myself up in it . . . and forgetting . . . But what's the use?" he recollected suddenly. "Listen, you surprised me today at an unguarded moment when I was nervous and ill . . . but there's no need to justify myself! I shall not go there again, and I assure you I take no interest in them whatever," he concluded resolutely.

"Really, really?" cried Pavel Pavlovich, not concealing his joyous excitement.

Velchaninov looked at him contemptuously, and resumed pacing the floor again.

"You seem to have decided to be happy at all costs," he could not refrain from observing.

"Yes, sir," Pavel Pavlovich affirmed naïvely, in a low voice.

"What does it matter to me," Velchaninov reflected, "that he's a buffoon and only spiteful through stupidity? I can't help hating him, though he isn't worth it!"

"I am 'the eternal husband'!" said Pavel Pavlovich, with an abjectly submissive smile at his own expense. "I heard that expression from you, Alexey Ivanovich, long ago, when you were staying with us in those days. I remember a great many of your sayings. Last time, when you said here, 'the eternal husband,' I pondered over it."

Mavra came in with a bottle of champagne and two glasses.

"Forgive me, Alexey Ivanovich; you know that I can't get on without it! Don't set it down as impudence; look upon me, sir, as an outsider who is beneath you."

"Yes . . ." Velchaninov allowed with repugnance, "but I assure you I feel ill. . . ."

"Directly . . . directly . . . in a minute," said Pavel Pavlovich fussily; "just one little glass, because my throat . . ."

He greedily tossed off a glassful at a gulp and sat down, looking almost tenderly at Velchaninov. Mavra went out.

"How loathsome!" Velchaninov whispered.

"It's only those girl friends," Pavel Pavlovich said confidently, all of a sudden completely revived.

"What? Ah, yes, you are still at that. . . ."

"It's only those girl friends, sir! And then she's so young; we have our graces and we put on airs, that's what it is! Of course, it's all charming. But then—then, you know, I shall be her slave; when she's treated with deference, when she sees something of society . . . she'll be completely re-educated."

"I shall have to give him back that bracelet, though," thought Velchaninov, scowling, as he felt the case in the pocket of his coat.

"You say, sir, that I'm resolved to be happy. I must get

married, Alexey Ivanovich," Pavel Pavlovich went on confidentially and almost touchingly, "or what will become of me? You see for yourself!" He pointed to the bottle. "And that's only one-hundredth of my vices. I can't do without marriage and—without new faith, sir; I will come to believe and I will rise up again."

"But why on earth do you tell me all this?" Velchaninov asked, almost chuckling. It all struck him as preposterous. "But tell me," he cried, "what was your object in dragging me out there? What did you want me there for?"

"As a test, sir . . ." Pavel Pavlovich seemed suddenly embarrassed.

"A test of what?"

"The effect, sir . . . You see, Alexey Ivanovich, it's only a week altogether that I've been looking around there." Pavel Pavlovich grew more and more abashed. "Yesterday I met you and I thought, 'I've never yet seen her in society, that is, in the company of men other than myself. . . .' A stupid idea, sir; I feel that myself now; a superfluous one. I was too eager . . . it's my horrible character. . . ."

He suddenly raised his head and flushed crimson.

"Can he be telling the whole truth?" Velchaninov was stunned with surprise.

"Well, what happened?" he asked.

Pavel Pavlovich gave a sugary and, as it were, crafty smile.

"It's only charming childishness! It's all those girl friends! Only forgive me my stupid behavior before you today, Alexey Ivanovich; I will never do it again; and indeed it will never happen again."

"And I shan't be there again," said Velchaninov, with a smile.

"That's partly what I mean," Pavel Pavlovich remarked.

These words jarred upon Velchaninov somewhat.

"But I'm not the only man in the world, you know," he observed irritably.

Pavel Pavlovich flushed again.

"It's sad for me to hear that, Alexey Ivanovich, and,

believe me, I've such a respect for Nadezhda Fedoseyevna. . . ."

"Excuse me, excuse me, I didn't mean anything; it only
seems a little strange to me that you have such an exaggerated idea of my attractions . . . and . . . that you so
sincerely counted on me."

"I had such confidence just because it was after all . . .
that happened in the past."

"Then if so, you look upon me even now as a most
honorable man?" said Velchaninov, suddenly halting. At another time he would have been horrified by the naïveté of
his own question.

"I always have," said Pavel Pavlovich, dropping his eyes.

"Why, of course . . . I didn't mean that; that is, not in
that sense. I only meant to say that, in spite of any . . .
prejudices. . . ."

"Yes, in spite of prejudices, sir."

"And when you were on your way to Petersburg?" Velchaninov could not resist asking this question, though he
felt how utterly monstrous was his curiosity.

"When I was on my way to Petersburg, too, I looked
upon you as the most honorable of men. I always respected
you, Alexey Ivanovich."

Pavel Pavlovich raised his eyes and looked candidly,
without a trace of embarrassment, at his opponent. Velchaninov was suddenly panic-stricken; he was not at all
anxious that anything should happen, or that a certain line
should be overstepped, especially as he had provoked it.

"I loved you, Alexey Ivanovich," Pavel Pavlovich said as
though he had suddenly made up his mind to speak, "and
all that year at T—— I loved you, sir. You did not notice it,"
he went on, in a voice that quivered, to Velchaninov's
positive horror; "I was too insignificant, compared with you,
to let you see it. And there was perhaps no need. And I've
thought of you all these nine years, because there has never
been another year in my life like that one." A peculiar
sparkle came into Pavel Pavlovich's eyes. "I remembered

many of your phrases and sayings, sir, your thoughts. I always remembered you as a man with a passion for every noble feeling, an educated, a highly educated man and with ideas. 'Great ideas spring not so much from great intelligence as from great feeling.' You said that yourself; perhaps you've forgotten it, but I remembered it, sir. I have always looked on you, therefore, as a man of great feeling . . . and therefore counted on you and believed in you—in spite of anything, sir. . . ."

His chin suddenly began quivering. Velchaninov was in absolute terror; it was necessary to make him drop this unexpected tone at all costs.

"That's enough, Pavel Pavlovich, please," he muttered, flushing and irritably impatient. "And why," he exclaimed suddenly, "why do you pester a man who is irritated and ill, who is almost delirious, and drag him into this darkness . . . when it's all nothing but ghost and mirage, and a lie, and shameful, and unnatural, and excessive—yes, excessive! —that's what is worst, most shameful. And it's all nonsense; we are both vicious, underground, loathsome people. . . . And if you like I'll prove it to you that you don't like me at all, but hate me with all your heart, and that you're lying, though you don't know it; you took me there, not with the absurd object of testing your future bride (what an idea!); you saw me yesterday and you were seized with spite, and you took me there to show me and say to me, 'See what a prize! She will be mine; now try and do something here!' You challenged me! Perhaps you didn't know it yourself, but that's how it was, for that's what you were feeling. . . . And without hating me you couldn't have challenged me like that; and so you hate me!"

He rushed about the room as he shouted this. What harassed and mortified him most of all was the humiliating consciousness that he was lowering himself to the level of Pavel Pavlovich.

"I wanted to make it up with you, Alexey Ivanovich!" the latter brought out suddenly, in a rapid whisper, and his chin began twitching again. Velchaninov was overcome by furious rage, as though no one had ever insulted him so much.

"I tell you again," he yelled, "that you've fastened upon a man who's irritated and ill . . . that you've done it to extort some fantastic word from him in his delirium! We . . . we are men of different worlds, understand that, and . . . and . . . between us lies a grave!" he added in a furious whisper, and suddenly came to his senses.

"And how do you know"—Pavel Pavlovich's face was suddenly pale and distorted—"how do you know what that little grave means here . . . for me!" he cried, coming up to Velchaninov with a ridiculous but horrible gesture, beating his breast with his fist. "I know that little grave, sir, and we two stand at either side of that little grave, but on my side there is more than on yours, more, sir . . ." he whispered as though delirious, still beating his breast, "more, more, more, sir. . . ."

Suddenly an extraordinarily loud ring at the door brought both of them to their senses. The bell rang so violently that it seemed as though someone had vowed to break it with the first pull.

"People don't ring my bell like that," said Velchaninov, perplexed.

"Nor mine either, sir," Pavel Pavlovich whispered timidly, coming to himself too, and at once turning into the old Pavel Pavlovich again. Velchaninov scowled and went to open the door.

"M. Velchaninov, if I'm not mistaken?" a youthful, sonorous, and exceptionally self-confident voice rang out from the anteroom.

"What do you want?"

"I have accurate information," continued the ringing voice, "that a certain Trusotzky is with you at this moment. I must see him instantly, without fail."

It would certainly have pleased Velchaninov to have forthwith kicked the self-confident young gentleman onto the stairs; but he thought a moment, moved aside and let him in.

"Here is M. Trusotzky; come in. . . ."

Chapter XIV: Sashenka and Nadenka[7]

There walked into the room a very young man, of about nineteen, perhaps even less—to judge by the youthfulness of his handsome, self-confident, upturned face. He was fairly well dressed, or at any rate his clothes looked well on him; in height he was a little above the average; the thick locks of black hair, and the big, bold, dark eyes were his most conspicuous features. Were it not for his nose that was rather broad and turned up, he would have been a strikingly handsome fellow. He walked in with an air of importance.

"I believe I have the occasion of conversing with Mr. Trusotzky," he said in a measured tone, emphasizing with peculiar relish the word "occasion"—thereby making it clear that he could not consider it either an honor or a pleasure to converse with Mr. Trusotzky.

Velchaninov began to grasp the situation; something seemed to be dawning on Pavel Pavlovich too. There was a look of uneasiness in his face; but he stood his ground.

"Not having the honor of your acquaintance," he answered in a dignified tone, "I imagine that I can have no business of any sort with you, sir."

"You will first hear me out and then give your opinion," the young man announced self-confidently, and, taking out a tortoise-shell lorgnette hanging on a cord, he examined didactically through it the bottle of champagne standing on the table. When he had calmly completed his scrutiny of the bottle, he folded up the lorgnette and turned to Pavel Pavlovich again.

[7] Diminutives of "Alexander" and "Nadezhda (Nadya)," used as terms of endearment.—A.Y.

"Alexandr Lobov."

"What do you mean by Alexandr Lobov?"

"That's me. Haven't you heard of me?"

"No, sir."

"How should you, though? I've come on important business that, in fact, concerns you. Allow me to sit down; I'm tired."

"Sit down," Velchaninov urged him; but the young man succeeded in sitting down before he had been invited to do so.

In spite of the increasing pain in his chest Velchaninov was interested in this impudent youth. In his pretty, childlike, and rosy face, he fancied a remote resemblance to Nadya.

"You sit down too," the lad suggested to Pavel Pavlovich, motioning him with a careless nod of the head to a seat opposite.

"Never mind; I'll stand."

"You'll be tired. You needn't go away, Mr. Velchaninov."

"I've nowhere to go; I'm at home."

"As you please. I must confess I should prefer you to be present while I have an explanation with this gentleman. Nadezhda Fedoseyevna gave me rather a flattering account of you."

"Ah! When had she time to do that?"

"Why, just now after you left; I've just come from there, too. I've something to tell you, Mr. Trusotzky." He turned around to Pavel Pavlovich, who was standing. "We—that is, Nadezhda Fedoseyevna and I," he went on, speaking through his teeth as he lolled carelessly in the armchair, "have loved each other for a long time, and have pledged ourselves to each other. You are in our way now; I've come to propose that you should withdraw. Will it suit you to accept my proposal?"

Pavel Pavlovich positively reeled; he turned pale, but he at once forced a sarcastic smile upon his lips.

"No, it won't suit me at all, sir," he rapped out laconically.

"You don't say so!" The young man turned around in the armchair and crossed one leg over the other.

"I don't even know who it is I'm speaking to, sir," added Pavel Pavlovich. "I believe, indeed, that there's no object in continuing our conversation."

Having said this, he too thought fit to sit down.

"I told you you would get tired," the youth observed casually. "I told you just now that my name is Alexandr Lobov, and that Nadezhda and I are pledged to one another; consequently you can't say, as you did just now, that you don't know with whom you are dealing; you can't imagine, either, that I have nothing more to say to you; putting myself aside, it concerns Nadezhda Fedoseyevna, whom you persist in pestering so insolently. And that alone is sufficient reason for an explanation."

All this he said through his closed lips, with the air of a coxcomb, scarcely deigning to articulate his words; he even drew out his lorgnette again and turned it upon something while he was talking.

"Allow me, young man!" Pavel Pavlovich exclaimed irritably; but the young man instantly snubbed him.

"At any other time I should certainly have forbidden your calling me 'young man,' but now you will admit that my youth is my chief advantage over you, and that you would have been jolly glad, this morning, for instance, when you presented your bracelet, to be a tiny bit younger."

"Ah, you minnow!" murmured Velchaninov.

"In any case, sir," Pavel Pavlovich corrected himself with dignity, "I nevertheless do not consider the reasons you have advanced—most unseemly and dubious reasons—sufficient to continue discussing them. I see that all this is a foolish and childish business. Tomorrow I'll make inquiries of my highly respected friend, Fedosey Petrovich; and now I beg you to spare me, sir."

"Do you see the sort of man he is?" the youth cried at once, unable to sustain his previous tone, and turning hotly to Velchaninov. "It's not enough that they turn him out there and put out their tongues at him; he wants tomorrow to denounce us to the old man! Do you not prove by that, you obstinate man, that you want to take the girl by force, that you would buy her of people in their dotage, who in our barbarous state of society retain authority over her? Has she not shown you plainly enough that she despises you? She has given you back your indecent present today, your bracelet, hasn't she? What more do you want?"

"No one has returned me a bracelet, and it's utterly out of the question!" Pavel Pavlovich said, startled.

"Out of the question? Hasn't Mr. Velchaninov given it to you?"

"Damnation take you!" thought Velchaninov.

"Nadezhda Fedoseyevna did commission me," he said frowningly, "to give you this case, Pavel Pavlovich. I had refused to take it, but she begged me . . . here it is. . . . I'm sorry. . . ."

He took out the case and, much embarrassed, laid it before Pavel Pavlovich, who was struck dumb.

"Why didn't you give it to him before?" said the young man, addressing Velchaninov severely.

"Evidently, I hadn't time," the latter replied, frowning.

"That's queer."

"Wha-a-at?"

"It's queer, to say the least, you must admit. I am ready to allow, though, that there may be a misunderstanding here."

Velchaninov felt a strong desire to get up at once and pull the saucy urchin's ears, but he could not control himself and suddenly chuckled in his face; the boy promptly laughed too. It was very different with Pavel Pavlovich; if Velchaninov could have observed the terrible look the man turned upon him when he burst out laughing at Lobov, he would have realized that at that instant Pavel Pavlovich had crossed a fateful boundary. . . . But though Velchaninov did not see that glance, he felt that he must stand by Pavel Pavlovich.

"Listen, Mr. Lobov," he began in a friendly tone; "without entering into discussion of other reasons upon which I don't care to touch, I would only point out to you that, in wooing Nadezhda Fedoseyevna, Pavel Pavlovich has to his credit certain qualifications: in the first place, everything about him is known to that estimable family; in the second place, there is his excellent and highly respectable position; finally, his fortune. Consequently he must naturally be surprised at the sight of a rival like you—a man, perhaps, of great merit, but so exceedingly young that he can hardly take you for a serious rival . . . and so he is justified in asking you to finish."

"What do you mean by 'exceedingly young'? I was nineteen last month. According to the law, I could have been married long ago. That's all."

"But what father could bring himself to give you his daughter now—even if you were to be a multimillionaire in the future or some benefactor of mankind? At nineteen a man cannot answer even for himself, and you are ready to take the responsibility for another person's future, that is, the future of another child like yourself! Is that quite honorable, do you think? I have ventured to speak frankly, because you appealed to me just now as an intermediary between you and Pavel Pavlovich."

"Ah, to be sure, his name's Pavel Pavlovich!" observed the boy; "how is it I kept fancying that he was Vassily Petrovich? Well," he went on, addressing Velchaninov, "you haven't surprised me in the least; I knew you were all like that! It's odd, though, that they spoke to me of you as a man rather new. That's all nonsense, however; the fact is that not only is there nothing dishonorable on my part, as you allowed yourself to put it, but quite the opposite, as I hope to make you see: to begin with, we've pledged our word to each other, and, what's more, I've promised her, before two witnesses, that if she ever falls in love with someone else, or simply repents having married me and wants to divorce me, I will at once give her a formal declaration of my infidelity—and so will support her petition for divorce. What's more, in case I should later on go back upon my word and refuse to give her that declaration, I will give her as security on our wedding day an IOU for a hundred thousand roubles, so that if I should be stubborn about giving her the declaration she can at once protest my IOU and call me to account! In that way everything will be secured and I shouldn't be risking anybody's future. That's my first point."

"I bet that fellow-what's-his-name, Predposylov, invented that for you!" cried Velchaninov.

"He—he—he!" crackled Pavel Pavlovich venomously.

"What's that gentleman sniggering about? You guessed right, it was Predposylov's idea; and you must admit it was a shrewd one. The absurd law is completely paralyzed by it. Of course, I intend to love her forever, and she nearly dies with laughing at the scheme; at the same time it's ingenious, and you must admit that it's honorable, and that it's not every man who would consent to do it."

"To my thinking, so far from being honorable, it's positively disgusting."

The young man shrugged his shoulders.

"Again you don't surprise me," he observed, after a brief silence. "I gave up being surprised at that sort of thing long ago. Predposylov would tell you flatly that such lack of comprehension of the most natural things on your part is due to the perversion of your most ordinary feelings and ideas by a long life spent idly and absurdly. But possibly we still fail to understand one another; they spoke well of you, anyway . . . you're fifty, I suppose, aren't you?"

"Kindly come to the point."

"Excuse my indiscretion and don't be annoyed; it wasn't intentional. I continue: I'm by no means a future multimillionaire, as you put it (and what an idea of yours that was!); I am only what you see, but I have complete confidence in my future. I shan't be a hero or a benefactor of anyone either, but I shall provide for myself and my wife. Of course, I've nothing now; I was brought up in their house, you see, since childhood. . . ."

"How was that?"

"Well, you see, I'm the son of a distant relation of Zahlebinin's wife, and when all my people died and left me at the age of eight, the old man took me in and afterward sent me to high school. He's really a good-natured person, if you care to know. . . ."

"I know that, sir."

"Yes; all too antiquated in his ideas, but kind-hearted. Of course, I've long since ceased to be under his guardianship; I want to earn my own living, and to be under obligation to me alone."

"How long have you been independent?" Velchaninov inquired.

"Why, some four months."

"Oh, well, one can understand it then: you've been friends since childhood! Well, have you a situation, then?"

"Yes, a private situation, in a notary's office, at twenty-five roubles a month. Of course, only for the time being, but when I made my proposal I hadn't even that. I was working on the railway then for ten roubles a month, but only for the time being."

"Do you mean to say you've made an offer of marriage?"

"Yes, a formal proposal, and ever so long ago—some three weeks."

"Well, and what happened?"

"The old man laughed awfully at first, and then was awfully angry, and locked her up in the mezzanine. But Nadya held out heroically. But that was all because he had a grudge against me before, for throwing up the berth in his office which he got me into four months ago, before I had the railway job. He's a capital old chap, I tell you again, simple and jolly at home, but you can't imagine what he's like as soon as he's in his office! He thrones there like a Jove! I naturally let him know that his manners were beginning to displease me, but the chief trouble was through the head clerk's assistant: that gentleman took it into his head to complain that I had been 'rude' to him, and all that I said to him was that he was intellectually backward. I threw them all up, and now I'm at a notary's."

"And did you get much at the office?"

"Oh, I was not on the regular staff! It was the old man who used to give me an allowance; I tell you he's a good sort, but we shan't give in, all the same. Of course, twenty-five roubles is not enough to support a wife, but I hope soon to have a hand in the management of Count Zavileysky's neglected estates, and then get three thousand straight off, or else I'll become a lawyer. People are nowadays in demand . . . Dear me! What a thunderclap! There'll be a storm; it's a good thing I have managed to get here before it; I came on foot, I ran almost all the way."

"But excuse me, if so, when did you manage to talk things over with Nadezhda Fedoseyevna, especially if they refuse you admittance?"

"Why, one can talk over the fence! Did you notice that red-haired girl?" he laughed. "She's very active on our side, and Marya Nikitishna too; ah, she's a serpent, that Marya Nikitishna! . . . Why do you wince? Are you afraid of the thunder?"

"No, I'm ill, very ill. . . ."

Velchaninov, in positive agony from the pain in his chest, got up and tried to walk about the room.

"Oh, then, of course, I'm in your way. . . . Don't be uneasy, I'm just going!"

And the youth jumped up from his seat.

"You're not in the way; it doesn't matter," said Velchaninov, trying to be courteous.

"How can it help mattering 'when Kobylnikov has a stomach-ache' . . . do you remember in Shchedrin? Are you fond of Shchedrin?"

"Yes."

"So am I. Well, Vassily . . . oh, hang it, Pavel Pavlovich, let's finish, sir!" He turned, almost laughing, to Pavel Pavlovich. "I will once more formulate the question so that you may understand it: do you consent formally to withdraw tomorrow all claims to Nadezhda Fedoseyevna in my presence and in that of the old people?"

"I do not consent, not at all, sir." Pavel Pavlovich, too,

got up from his seat with an impatient and exasperated air. "And I beg you once more to spare me . . . for all this is childish and silly."

"Look out!" The youth shook his finger at him with a supercilious smile. "Don't make a mistake in your calculations! Do you know what such a mistake leads to? I warn you that in nine months' time, when you have had much expense and trouble, and you come back here, you'll be forced to give up Nadezhda Fedoseyevna, or if you don't give her up it will be the worst for you; that's what will be the end of it! I must warn you that you're like a dog in the manger—excuse me, it's only a comparison—getting nothing yourself and preventing others. In all humanity I repeat: reflect upon it, force yourself for once in your life to reflect seriously."

"I beg you to spare me your sermonizing!" cried Pavel Pavlovich furiously; "and as for your nasty insinuations, I shall take measures tomorrow without fail, severe measures, sir!"

"Nasty insinuations? What do you mean by that? You're nasty yourself, if that's what you've got in your head. However, I agree to wait till tomorrow, but if . . . Ah, thunder again! Good-by; very glad to have made your acquaintance." He nodded to Velchaninov and ran off, apparently in haste to get back before the storm and not to get caught in the rain.

Chapter XV: The Account Is Settled

"Did you see? Did you see, sir?" Pavel Pavlovich ran up to Velchaninov as soon as the youth had departed.

"Yes; you've no luck!" said Velchaninov thoughtlessly.

He would not have said those words had he not been tortured and exasperated by the pain in his chest, which was growing more and more acute. Pavel Pavlovich flinched as from a burn.

"It was because you were sorry for me that you didn't give me back the bracelet, wasn't it?"

"I hadn't time. . . ."

"You felt for me from your heart, like a true friend?"

"Oh, yes, I felt for you," said Velchaninov, in exasperation.

He told him briefly, however, how the bracelet had been given him, and how Nadezhda Fedoseyevna had almost forced him to take it and promise to return it. . . .

"You understand that nothing else would have induced me to do it; I've had enough unpleasantness apart from that!"

"You were carried away and took it?" sniggered Pavel Pavlovich.

"That's stupid on your part; however, I must excuse you. You saw for yourself just now that I'm not the leading person in this affair, but others!"

"At the same time you were carried away, sir."

Pavel Pavlovich sat down and filled up his glass.

"Do you imagine I'd give way to that urchin? I'll make mincemeat of him, that's what I'll do! I'll go over tomorrow without fail and do it. We'll smoke out that spirit from the nursery, sir."

He emptied his glass almost at a gulp and filled it again; he began, in fact, to behave in an unusually free and easy way.

"Nadenka and Sashenka, the sweet little children, he—he–he!"

He was beside himself with anger. There came another deafening thunderclap, followed by a blinding flash of lightning, and the rain came down in bucketfuls. Pavel Pavlovich got up and closed the open window.

"He asked you whether you were afraid of the thunder, he–he. Velchaninov afraid of thunder! 'Kobylnikov has . . .' How did it go? 'Kobylnikov has . . .' And what about being fifty—eh? Do you remember?" Pavel Pavlovich sneered sarcastically.

"You've established yourself here, it seems!" observed

Velchaninov, hardly able to articulate the words for the pain in his chest. "I'll lie down, you can do what you like."

"Why, even a dog would not be turned out in weather like this!" Pavel Pavlovich retorted in an offended tone, seeming almost pleased, however, at having an excuse for feeling offended.

"All right, sit, drink . . . stay the night, if you like!" muttered Velchaninov. He stretched himself out on the sofa and uttered a faint groan.

"Stay the night? And you won't be afraid?"

"What of?" said Velchaninov, suddenly raising his head.

"Oh, nothing, sir. Last time you seemed to have been frightened, or did I imagine it?"

"You're stupid!" Velchaninov could not help saying, and turned his head to the wall angrily.

"All right, sir," responded Pavel Pavlovich.

The sick man fell asleep suddenly, a minute after lying down. His unnatural strain that day in the shattered state of his health had suddenly abated, and he was as weak as a child. But the pain asserted itself again and overcame sleep and weariness; an hour later he woke up and painfully sat up on the sofa. The storm had subsided; the room was full of tobacco smoke, on the table stood an empty bottle, and Pavel Pavlovich was asleep on another sofa. He was lying on his back, with his head on the sofa cushion, fully dressed and with his boots on. His lorgnette had slipped out of his pocket and was hanging down almost to the floor. His hat was lying on the floor beside it. Velchaninov looked at him morosely and did not attempt to wake him. Doubled up with pain and pacing the room, for he could no longer bear to lie down, he moaned and brooded over his agony.

He was afraid of that pain in his chest, and not without reason. He had had these attacks for a long time, but they occurred very rarely at intervals of a year or two. He knew that they came from the liver. At first a dull, rather weak, but irritating pressure developed at some point in the chest, in the pit of his stomach or higher up. Continually increasing, sometimes for ten hours at a stretch, the pain at last would reach such a pitch, the pressure would become so insupportable, that the sufferer began to think that he was dying. During his last attack, a year before, when the pain ceased after ten hours of suffering, he was so weak that he could scarcely move his hand as he lay in bed, and the doctor had allowed him to take nothing for the whole day but a few teaspoonfuls of weak tea and a little bread soaked in broth, as though he were an infant. The attacks were brought on by different things, but always when his nerves were shattered. It was strange, too, how the attack passed; sometimes it was possible to arrest it at the very beginning, during the first half-hour, by simple poultices, and the pain would at once cease completely; sometimes, as with his last attack, nothing was of any use, and the pain only subsided after numerous doses of an emetic. The doctor confessed afterward that he believed it to be a case of poisoning.

It was a long time to wait till morning, and he didn't want to send for a doctor at night; besides, he didn't like doctors. At last he could not control himself and began moaning aloud. His groans waked Pavel Pavlovich; he sat up on the sofa, and for some time listened with alarm and bewilderment, watching Velchaninov, who was pacing the floor of the two rooms with rapid strides. The bottle of champagne appeared to have had an unusually potent effect upon him, and it was some time before he could collect himself. At last he grasped the situation and rushed to Velchaninov, who mumbled something in reply to him.

"It's the liver, I know it!" cried Pavel Pavlovich, becoming extremely animated all at once. "Pyotr Kuzmich Polosuhin used to suffer just like this; it's the liver. You ought to have poultices. Pyotr Kuzmich always had poultices. . . . One may die of it! Shall I run for Mavra?"

"No need, no need!" Velchaninov waved him off irritably. "I want nothing."

But Pavel Pavlovich, goodness knows why, seemed beside himself, as though it were a question of saving his own son. Without heeding Velchaninov's protests, he insisted on the necessity of poultices and also of two or three cups of weak tea to be gulped down, "and not simply hot, but boiling!" He fetched Mavra without waiting for permission, with her help laid a fire in the kitchen, which always stood empty, and heated the samovar; at the same time he succeeded in getting the sick man to bed, took off his clothes, wrapped him up in a quilt, and within twenty minutes had prepared tea and the first poultices.

"This is a hot plate, sir, scalding hot!" he said, almost ecstatically, applying the heated plate, wrapped in a napkin, on Velchaninov's aching chest. "We have no other poultices and it takes long to prepare them, and plates, I swear on my honor, are even better: they were tested on Pyotr Kusmich, I saw it with my own eyes, and did it with my own hands. One may die of it, you know. Drink your tea, swallow it; it doesn't matter if you get scalded; life is too precious to mind . . . such trifles."

He quite flustered Mavra, who was half-asleep; the plates were changed every three or four minutes. After the third plate and the second cup of tea, swallowed at a gulp, Velchaninov felt a sudden relief.

"If once the pain is blunted, then thank God, it's a good sign!" cried Pavel Pavlovich, and he ran joyfully to fetch a fresh plate and a fresh cup of tea.

"If only we can subdue the pain. If only we can make it go away!" he kept repeating.

Half an hour later the pain grew quite weaker, but the sick man was so exhausted that in spite of Pavel Pavlovich's entreaties he refused to put up with just one more "nice little plate." He was so weak he could not keep his eyes open.

"To sleep, to sleep," he repeated in a faint voice.

"To be sure," Pavel Pavlovich assented.

"You stay the night. . . . What time is it?"

"It's nearly two o'clock, a quarter of."

"Stay the night."

"I will, I will."

A minute later the sick man called Pavel Pavlovich again.

"You, you," he muttered, when the latter had run up and was bending over him; "you are better than I am! I understand it all, all. . . . Thank you."

"Sleep, sleep," whispered Pavel Pavlovich, and he hastened on tiptoe to his sofa.

As he fell asleep the patient heard Pavel Pavlovich noiselessly making up a bed for himself and taking off his clothes. Finally, putting out the candle, and almost holding his breath for fear of making a noise, he stretched himself out on his sofa.

There is no doubt that Velchaninov did sleep and that he fell asleep very soon after the candle was put out; he remembered this clearly afterward. But all the time he was asleep, up to the very moment that he woke up, he dreamed that he was not asleep, and that in spite of his exhaustion he could not fall asleep. At last he began to dream that he was in a sort of waking delirium, and that he could not drive away the phantoms that crowded about him, although he was fully conscious that it was only delirium and not reality. The phantoms were all familiar figures; his room seemed to be full of people; and the door into the passage stood open; people were entering in crowds and thronging the stairs. At the table, which was set in the middle of the room, a man was sitting—exactly as in a similar dream he had had a month before. Just as in that dream, this man sat with his elbows on the table and would not speak; but this time he was wearing a round hat with crape on it. "What! Could it have been Pavel Pavlovich that time too?" Velchaninov thought, but, glancing at the face of the silent man, he convinced himself that it was someone quite different. "Why then has he got crape on?" Velchaninov wondered. The noise, the talking, and the shouting of the people crowding round the table was awful. These people seemed to be even more angry at Velchaninov than in the previous dream; they shook their fists at him, and shouted something to him, with all their might, but what it was exactly he could not make out. "But it's delirium, of course, I know it's delirium!" he thought; "I know that I couldn't get to sleep, and that I've got up now because I was too wretched lying down. . . ." But the shouts, the people, their gestures were so lifelike, so real, that sometimes he was seized by doubt: "Can this be really delirium? Good heavens, what do these people want of me? But if this is not delirium, how is it possible that the clamor should not have yet waked Pavel Pavlovich? There he is asleep on the sofa!" At last something suddenly happened again, just as in that other dream; all the people made a rush for the stairs and they were closely packed in the doorway, for there was another crowd forcing its way into the room. These people were bringing something in with them, something big and heavy; you could hear how heavily the steps of those carrying it sounded on the stairs and how hurriedly their panting voices called to one another. All the people in the room shouted, "They're bringing it, they're bringing it," all eyes started flashing and were fixed on Velchaninov; all the people pointed toward the stairs, menacing and triumphant. Now, no longer doubting that this was reality and not delirium, he stood on tiptoe so as to peep over the people's heads and find out as soon as possible what they were carrying up the stairs. His heart was beating, beating, beating, and suddenly, just as in that earlier dream, the doorbell rang violently three times. And again the sound was so distinct, so real, so unmistakable that it could not be a dream. He screamed and woke up.

But he did not rush to the door as he had done on waking then. What thought guided his first movement and whether he had any thought at the moment it is impossible to say, but someone seemed to prompt him to act fittingly: he leaped out of bed and, with his hands stretched out before him as though to defend himself and ward off an attack, he rushed straight toward the place where Pavel Pavlovich was asleep. His hands instantly came into contact with other hands, stretched out above him, and he clutched them tight; so, someone already stood bending over him. The curtains were drawn, but it was not quite dark, for a faint light came from the other room where there were no such curtains. Suddenly something painfully cut the palm and fingers of his left hand, and he instantly realized that he had clutched the blade of a knife or razor and was grasping it tight in his hand. . . . And at the same moment something fell heavily on the floor with a thud.

Velchaninov was perhaps three times as strong as Pavel Pavlovich, yet the struggle between them lasted a long while, fully three minutes. He soon got him down on the floor and, grabbing his arms, held them behind his back, but for some reason he conceived the desire to tie them behind the man's back. Holding the murderer with his wounded left hand, with his right he began fumbling for the cord of the window curtain and for a long time could not find it, but at last got hold of it and tore it from the window. He wondered himself afterward at the unnatural strength required to do this. During those three minutes neither of them uttered a word; nothing was heard but their heavy breathing and the muffled sounds of their struggling. Having at last twisted Pavel Pavlovich's arms behind him and tied them together, Velchaninov threw him on the floor, got up, drew the curtain from the window, and pulled up the blind. It was already light in the deserted street. Opening the window, he stood for some moments inhaling the fresh air. It was a little past four. Shutting the window, he went hurriedly to the cupboard, took out a clean towel and bound it tightly around his left hand to stop the bleeding. At his feet an open razor was lying on the carpet; he picked it up, shut it, put it in the razor case, which had been left forgotten since the morning on the little table beside Pavel Pavlovich's sofa, and locked it up in his bureau. And, only when he had done all that, he went up to Pavel Pavlovich and began to examine him.

Meantime, the latter had with an effort got up from the floor, and seated himself in an armchair. He had nothing on but his underwear, not even his boots. The back and the sleeves of his shirt were soaked with blood; but the blood was not his own, it came from Velchaninov's cut hand. Of course, it was Pavel Pavlovich, but anyone meeting him by chance might almost have failed to recognize him at first glance, so changed was his whole appearance. He was sitting awkwardly upright in the armchair, owing to his hands being tied behind his back, his face distorted, exhausted, and greenish, and he shivered all over from time to time. He looked at Velchaninov fixedly, but with lusterless, unseeing eyes. All at once he smiled vacantly, and, nodding toward a carafe that stood on the table, he said in a brief half-whisper:

"Some water, sir."

Velchaninov filled a glass and held it for him while he drank. Pavel Pavlovich swallowed the water thirstily; after two or three gulps he raised his head and looked intently into the face of Velchaninov, who was standing beside him with the glass in his hand, but without uttering a word fell to drinking again. When he had finished he sighed deeply. Velchaninov took his pillow, seized his outer garments, and went into the other room, locking Pavel Pavlovich in the first room.

The pain had passed off completely, but he felt extreme weakness again after the momentary effort in which he had displayed an unaccountable strength. He tried to reflect upon what had happened, but his thoughts were hardly coherent, the shock had been too great. Sometimes he dozed off for ten minutes or so, then he would start, wake up, recollect everything, raise his smarting hand bound up in a bloodstained towel, and would fall to thinking greedily, feverishly. He came to one distinct conclusion—namely, that Pavel Pavlovich had certainly meant to cut his throat, but that perhaps only a quarter of an hour before had not known that he would do it. The razor case had perhaps merely caught his eye the evening before, and, without arousing any thought at the time, had remained in his memory. (The razors were always locked up in the bureau, and only the morning before Velchaninov had taken them out to shave around his mustache and whiskers, as he sometimes did.)

"If he had long been intending to murder me, he would have got a knife or pistol ready; he would not have reckoned on my razor, which he had never seen till yesterday evening," was one reflection he made among others.

It struck six o'clock at last; Velchaninov roused himself, dressed, and went in to Pavel Pavlovich. Opening the door, he could not understand why he had locked Pavel Pavlovich in, instead of turning him out of the house. To his surprise, the criminal was fully dressed; most likely he had found some way of untying his hands. He was sitting in the armchair, but got up at once when Velchaninov went in. His hat was already in his hand. His uneasy eyes seemed in haste to say:

"Don't begin talking; it's no use beginning; there's no need to talk."

"On your way now!" said Velchaninov. "Take your bracelet," he added, calling after him.

Pavel Pavlovich turned back from the door, took the case with the bracelet from the table, put it in his pocket, and went out on the stairs. Velchaninov stood at the door to lock it behind him. Their eyes met for the last time; Pavel Pavlovich stopped suddenly, for some five seconds the two looked into each other's eyes—as though hesitating; finally Velchaninov waved his hand faintly.

"Well, be off!" he said in a low voice, and locked the door.

Chapter XVI: Analysis

A feeling of immense, extraordinary joy took possession of him; something was over, settled; his awful depression had vanished and was dissipated completely. So it seemed to him. This feeling lasted for five weeks. He would raise his hand, look at the towel soaked with blood, and mutter to himself:

"Yes, now everything is over for good and all!" And all

that morning, for the first time in three weeks, he scarcely thought of Liza—as though that blood from his cut fingers could "settle his account" even with that misery.

He recognized clearly that he had escaped a terrible danger. "These people," he thought, "just these people who don't know a minute beforehand whether they'll murder a man or not—as soon as they take a knife in their trembling hands and feel the spurt of hot blood on their fingers will not only cut your throat, but cut off your head, 'clean off,' as convicts put it. That is so."

He could not remain at home and went out into the street, feeling convinced that he must do something, or something would happen to him at once; he walked about the streets and waited. He had an intense longing to meet someone, to talk to someone, even to a stranger, and it was only that which led him at last to think of a doctor and of the necessity of bandaging his hand properly. The doctor, an old acquaintance of his, examined the wound, and inquired with interest how it could have happened. Velchaninov dismissed the matter with a joke, laughed boisterously, and was on the point of telling him all about it, but restrained himself. The doctor was obliged to feel his pulse and, hearing of his attack of the night before, persuaded him to take some soothing medicine he had at hand. He was reassuring about the cuts: "They can have no particularly disagreeable results." Velchaninov burst into laughter and began to assure him that they had already had the most agreeable results. An almost irresistible desire to tell the whole story came over him twice again during that day, on one occasion to a total stranger with whom he entered into conversation in a confectionary. He had never been able to endure entering into conversation with strangers in public places before.

He looked in at shops, bought a newspaper, went to his tailor's, and ordered a suit. The idea of visiting the Pogoreltzevs was still distasteful to him, and he did not think of them, indeed he could not have gone to their summer cottage: he kept expecting something here in town. He dined with relish, talked to the waiter and to his fellow-diner, and drank half a bottle of wine. The possibility of the return of his attack of the day before did not occur to him; he was convinced that the illness had been over completely at the moment when, after falling asleep so exhausted, he had, an hour and a half later, sprung out of bed and thrown his assailant on the floor with such strength. Toward evening he began to feel dizzy, and at moments was overcome by something like the delirium he had had in his sleep. It was dusk when he returned home, and he was almost afraid of his room when he went into it. It seemed to him that there was something dreadful and uncanny about his flat. He walked up and down it several times, and even went into his kitchen, where he had scarcely ever been before. "Here they were heating plates yesterday," he thought. He locked the door securely and lighted the candles earlier than usual. As he locked the door he remembered that half an hour before, passing the porter's lodge, he had called Mavra and asked her whether Pavel Pavlovich had come in his absence, as though he could possibly have dropped in.

After locking himself in carefully, he opened the bureau, took out the razor case, and opened the razor to look at it again. On the white bone handle there were still faint traces of blood. He put the razor back in the case and locked it up in the bureau again. He was sleepy; he felt that he must go to bed at once—or he would not be fit for tomorrow. He pictured the next day for some reason as a fateful and "decisive" day. But the same thoughts that had haunted him all day in the street continued to crowd and jostle incessantly and irresistibly in his sick brain, and he kept thinking, thinking, thinking, and for a long time could not get to sleep. . . .

"If it is settled that he got up to cut my throat *accidentally*," he went on pondering, "had the idea ever entered his head before, if only as a daydream at a moment of malice?"

He decided that question strangely: "Pavel Pavlovich

did want to kill him, but the thought of the murder had never entered his head." In short: "Pavel Pavlovich wanted to kill, but didn't know he wanted to kill. It doesn't make any sense, but it is so," thought Velchaninov. "It was not to get a post and it was not on Bagautov's account he came here, though he did try to get a post here, and did call on Bagautov and was furious when he died; he did not care a straw about Bagautov. He came here on my account and he came here with Liza. . . .

"And did I expect that he . . . would cut my throat?" He decided that he did, that he had expected it from the moment when he saw him in the carriage following Bagautov's funeral. "I began, as it were, to expect something . . . but, of course, not that; but, of course, not that he would cut my throat!

"And can it be that all that was true?" he exclaimed again, suddenly raising his head from the pillow and opening his eyes. "All that this madman told me yesterday about his love for me, when his chin quivered and he beat his breast with his fist?

"It was the absolute truth," he decided, tirelessly delving and analyzing, "that Quasimodo from T—— was more than sufficiently stupid and high-minded to fall in love with the lover of his wife, about whom he noticed nothing suspicious in twenty years! He had been thinking of me with respect, cherishing my memory and remembering my 'sayings' for nine years. Good heavens! And I had no notion of it! He could not have been lying yesterday! But did he love me yesterday when he declared himself and said, 'Let us settle our account'? Yes, it was from hatred that he loved me; that's the strongest love. . . .

"Of course it may have happened, of course it must have happened that I made a tremendous impression on him at T——, tremendous and 'gratifying' is just what it was, and it's just to such a Schiller, in the shape of a Quasimodo, that such a thing could happen! He magnified me a hundredfold because I impressed him too much in his philosophic solitude. . . . It would be curious to know by what

I impressed him. Perhaps by my clean gloves and my
knowing how to put them on. Quasimodos love the aes-
thetic. Oh, how they love it! Gloves are often quite enough
for a noble heart, and especially one of these 'eternal husbands.' The rest they will supply themselves a thousand
times, and even fight for you, if you so desire. What high
opinion he had of my powers of seduction! Perhaps it was
just my powers of seduction that made the most impression on him. And his cry then, 'If that one, too . . . whom
can one trust!' After that cry one may well become a wild
beast!

"H'm! He came here 'that we might embrace and weep,'
as he put it most abjectly—that is, he came here to murder
me and thought he came 'that we might embrace and
weep.' . . . He brought Liza too. But if I had wept with
him, perhaps he would have really forgiven me, for he had
a terrible longing to forgive! . . . At the first clash all that
was changed into drunken antics and caricature, and into
loathsome, womanish whining over his wrongs. (Those
horns, those horns he made on his forehead!) He came
drunk on purpose to speak out, even while playing the
fool; if he had not been drunk, he could not have done
it. . . . And he liked playing the fool, how he liked it!
And wasn't he pleased, too, when he made me kiss him!
Only he didn't know then whether he would end by embracing or murdering me. Of course, it's turned out that
the best thing was to do both. A most natural solution!
Yes, indeed, nature dislikes freaks and destroys them with
natural solutions. The most freakish freak is the freak with
noble feelings; I know that by personal experience, Pavel
Pavlovich! Nature is not a tender mother, but a stepmother
to the freak. Nature gives birth to the freak, but instead
of pitying him she puts him to death, and with good reason.
Nowadays even decent people have to pay for embraces
and tears of all-inclusive forgiveness, to say nothing of men
like you and me, Pavel Pavlovich!

"Yes, he was stupid enough to take me to see his future
bride. Good heavens! His future bride! Only a Quasimodo

like that could have conceived the notion of 'rising again to a new life' by means of the innocence of Mademoiselle Zahlebinin! But it was not your fault, Pavel Pavlovich, it was not your fault: you're a freak, so everything about you is bound to be freakish, your reveries and your hopes. But, though he was a freak, he had doubts of his dream, and that was why he needed the high sanction of Velchaninov whom he so revered. He wanted Velchaninov to approve, to reassure him that the revery was not a revery, but something real. He took me there out of awesome respect for me and faith in the nobility of my feelings, believing, perhaps, that there, under a bush, we should embrace and shed tears near that innocence. Yes! That 'eternal husband' had to, was obliged at last to punish himself for everything, once and for all, and to punish himself he snatched up the razor—by accident, it is true, still he did snatch it up! 'And yet he did stick him with a knife, and yet he ended by stabbing him in the presence of the governor.' And, by the way, had he any idea of that sort in his mind when he told me that anecdote about the best man? And was there really anything that night when he got out of bed and stood in the middle of the room? H'm! . . . No, he stood there then *as a joke*. He got up for other reasons, and when he saw that I got frightened of him he did not answer me for ten minutes because he was so very much pleased that I got frightened of him. . . . It was at that moment, perhaps, when he stood there in the dark, that some idea of this sort first dawned upon him. . . .

"Yet if I had not forgotten those razors on the table yesterday—maybe nothing would have happened. But is that so? Is that so? Hadn't he been avoiding me before? Why, he had not been to see me for a fortnight; he had been hiding from me to *spare* me! He picked out Bagautov first, not me! Why, he rushed to heat plates for me in the night, thinking to create a diversion—from the knife to tender emotion! . . . He wanted to save himself and me, too—with hot plates!"

And for a long time the aching head of this former "man

of the world" went on working in this way, milling the wind, till he calmed down. He woke up next morning with the same headache, but with a quite *new* and quite unexpected terror in his heart. . . .

This new terror came from the positive conviction, which suddenly grew strong within him that he, Velchaninov (a man of the world) would end it all that day by going of his own free will to call on Pavel Pavlovich. Why? What for? He had no idea, and, with repugnance, refused to know; all that he knew was that, for some reason, he would drag himself there.

This madness, however—he could give it no other name —did, as it developed, take on a rational, as it were, appearance, acquired a fairly legitimate pretext: already the day before, he had been haunted by the idea that Pavel Pavlovich would go back to his lodging and hang himself, like the clerk about whom Marya Sysoevna had told him. This notion of the day before had grown by degrees into an unreasoning but persistent conviction. "Why should the fool hang himself?" he kept telling himself every moment. But he remembered Liza's words. . . . "In his place I would perhaps hang myself, though," he reflected once.

It ended by his making his way toward Pavel Pavlovich's lodging instead of going to dinner. "I shall simply inquire of Marya Sysoevna," he decided. But before he had come out into the street he stopped short in the gateway. "Can it be, can it be?" he cried, turning crimson with shame. "Can it be that I'm dragging myself there, to 'embrace and shed tears'? That senseless abomination is all that is needed to complete the ignominy!"

But from that "senseless abomination" he was saved by the providence that watches over all decent and well-bred people. He had no sooner stepped into the street when he stumbled upon Alexandr Lobov. The young man was agitated and breathless.

"I was coming to see you! What do you think of your friend Pavel Pavlovich, now?"

"He's hanged himself!" Velchaninov muttered wildly.

"Who's hanged himself! What for?" cried Lobov, with wide-open eyes.

"Never mind . . . I didn't mean anything; go on."

"Fie! Damn it all! What funny ideas you have, though. He hasn't hanged himself at all (why should he hang himself?). On the contrary—he's gone away. I've only just put him into the train and seen him off. Fie! How he drinks, I tell you! We tossed off three bottles, Predposylov with us—but how he drinks, how he drinks! He was singing songs in the train, remembered you, blew kisses, sent you his greetings. But he is a scoundrel, don't you think so?"

The young man certainly was a little tipsy; his flushed face, his shining eyes, and faltering tongue betrayed it unmistakably.

Velchaninov roared with laughter.

"So, they did end by hobnobbing over a bottle of wine! Ha-ha! They embraced and shed tears! Ah, you Schilleresque poets!"

"Don't call me names, please. Do you know he's given it all up over *there*? He was there yesterday, and again today. He's a horrible sneak. They locked Nadya up—she's sitting in the mezzanine. There were tears and shouts, but we stood firm! But how he drinks, how he drinks! And, I say, isn't he *mauvais ton*? No, not *mauvais ton*, what is the right word? . . . He kept talking of you, but he can bear no comparison with you! You're a gentleman anyway, and really did move in society at one time and have only been forced to come down now through poverty or something. . . . I couldn't quite make him out, damn it!"

"Ah, so he spoke to you of me in those terms?"

"He did, he did; don't be angry. To be a citizen is better than to belong to society. What I mean is in Russia, nowadays, one doesn't know whom to respect. You'll agree that it's a serious malady of the age, when people don't know whom to respect, isn't it?"

"It is, it is; what did he say?"

"He? Who? Ah, yes! Why did he keep saying 'Velchaninov fifty, but ruined,' why *but* ruined and not *and* ruined;

he laughed and repeated it a thousand times over. He got into the coach and burst out crying—it was simply disgusting; in fact, he was pitiful, the drunk. Oh, I don't like fools! He fell to throwing money to the beggars for the peace of the soul of Lizaveta—his wife, eh?"

"His daughter."

"What's the matter with your hand?"

"I cut it."

"Never mind, it will heal. Damn him, you know, it's a good thing he's gone, but I bet he'll get married again directly he arrives wherever he's going—won't he?"

"But you too want to get married, don't you?"

"Me? That's a different matter. You are an odd fellow, really! If you are fifty, he must be sixty; what is needed here is logic, my dear sir! And do you know, formerly, long ago, I used to be a pure Slavophil by conviction? But now we look for the dawn in the west. . . . But, good-by; I'm glad I ran into you without going in; I won't come in, don't ask me, I've no time to spare!"

And he took to his heels.

"Oh, I've forgot," he cried, turning back; "he sent me to you with a letter, you know! Here is the letter. Why didn't you come to see him off?"

Velchaninov returned home and opened the envelope addressed to him.

There was not one line from Pavel Pavlovich in it, but it contained a letter from another person. Velchaninov recognized the handwriting. It was an old letter, written on paper yellow with age, with ink that had faded. It had been written to him ten years before, two months after he had left T—— and returned to Petersburg. But the letter had never been mailed to him; he had received a different one instead of it; this was clear from the contents of this old yellowed missive. In this letter, Natalya Vassilyevna took leave of him forever, and confessed that she loved someone else, just as in the letter he had actually received; but she also did not conceal from him that she was with child. On the contrary, to comfort him, she promised to find a way of

turning over the future child to him, declared that hence-
forth they had other duties, that their friendship was now
sealed forever—in short, there was little logic in her words,
but her object was clear: that he should no longer trouble
her with his love. She even allowed him to come to T——
in a year's time to have a look at the child. God knows
why she changed her mind and sent the other letter instead.

Velchaninov was pale as he read it, but he pictured to
himself Pavel Pavlovich finding that letter and reading it
for the first time, before the opened ebony box inlaid with
mother-of-pearl which was an heirloom.

"He, too, must have turned pale as a corpse," he
thought, catching a glimpse of his own face in the looking
glass. "He must have read it and closed his eyes, and opened
them again hoping that the letter would have changed into
plain white paper. . . . Most likely he had repeated the
experiment two or three times!"

Chapter XVII: The Eternal Husband

Almost exactly two years had passed since the adventure
we have described. We meet Mr. Velchaninov again one
fine summer day, in a coach of one of our newly opened
railways. He was going to Odessa for his own pleasure,
to see one of his friends, and also with a view to something
else of a rather agreeable nature. He hoped through that
friend to arrange a meeting with an extremely interesting
woman whose acquaintance he had long been eager to
make. Without going into details we will confine ourselves
to observing that he had become entirely transformed, or
rather reformed, during those two years. Of his old hypochondria scarcely a trace remained. Of the various "reminiscences" and anxieties—the result of illness—which had beset
him two years before in Petersburg at the time of his
temporarily unsuccessful lawsuit, nothing remained but a
certain secret shame at the recollection of his fainthearted-

ness. What partly made up for it was the conviction that it would never happen again, and that no one would ever know of it. True, at that time he had given up all society, had even begun to be slovenly in his dress, had secluded himself from everyone—and that, of course, was noticed by all. But he so readily acknowledged his transgressions, and at the same time with such a self-confident air of new life and vigor, that "all" immediately forgave his momentary defection; in fact, those whom he had given up greeting were the first to recognize him and hold out their hands, and, besides, without any tiresome questions—just as though he had been absent, far away on his private business, which was no concern of theirs, and had only just come back.

The cause of all these advantageous and sensible changes for the better was, of course, the fact that he won his lawsuit. Velchaninov came in for all of sixty thousand roubles —no great sum, of course, but of extreme importance to him; to begin with, he felt himself on firm ground again, and so his moral unease was alleviated; he knew for certain now that he would not, "like a fool," squander this money, as he had squandered his first two fortunes, and that it would last him for the rest of his life. "No matter how close the social edifice may come to collapse, and whatever may be shouted from the housetops," he thought sometimes, as he watched and heard all the marvelous and incredible things that were happening around him and all over Russia; "whatever shape people and ideas may take, I shall always have just such a dainty, delicious dinner as I am sitting down to now, and so I'm ready to face anything." This thought, indulgent to the point of voluptuousness, by degrees gained complete possession of him and produced a transformation in his physical, to say nothing of his moral, nature. He looked quite a different man from the "sluggard" whom we described two years before and whom such unseemly incidents had begun to befall—he looked cheerful, serene, and dignified. Even the baneful wrinkles that had begun to appear about his eyes and on his forehead had almost been smoothed away; his very complexion had changed, becoming whiter and ruddier.

At the moment he was sitting comfortably in a first-class carriage and a charming idea was taking shape in his mind. The next station was a junction and there was a new branch line going off to the right. If he were to give up the direct way for the moment and change to a train going to the right, he reflected, then only two stations away, he could visit another lady of his acquaintance who had only just returned from abroad, and was now living in provincial isolation, very tedious for her, but favorable for him; and so he could spend his time no less agreeably than at Odessa, especially as his visit there would wait. But he was still hesitating and could not quite make up his mind; he was waiting for something to decide him. Meanwhile, the station was approaching and that something was not long in coming.

At this station the train stopped forty minutes, and the passengers had the chance of dining. At the entrance to the dining room for the passengers of the first and second class there was, as usual, a crowd of impatient and hurried people, and, as is perhaps also usual, a scandalous scene was taking place. A lady who had emerged from a second-class carriage, and who was remarkably pretty but somewhat too gorgeously dressed up for traveling, was all but dragging after her with both hands a Uhlan, a very young and handsome officer, who was trying to tear himself out of her hands. The youthful officer was very drunk, and the lady, in all likelihood some older relative, would not let him go, probably afraid that he would make a dash for the bar. Meanwhile, in the crush, the Uhlan was jostled by a young merchant on a spree who was also disgracefully besotted. He had been hanging about the station for the last two days, drinking and squandering his money, surrounded by boon companions, without managing to get into the train to continue his journey. A brawl followed; the officer shouted; the merchant swore; the lady was in despair, and, trying to draw the Uhlan away from the brawl, kept exclaiming in an imploring voice, "Mitenka! Mitenka!" This seemed to strike the young merchant as too scandalous; everyone laughed, but the merchant took offense at what he for some reason conceived as a violation of decency.

"Mitenka!" he pronounced reproachfully, mimicking the shrill voice of the lady. "And not ashamed before folks!"

He went staggering up to the lady, who had rushed to the first chair and succeeded in making the Uhlan sit down beside her, stared at them both contemptuously, and drawled in a singsong:

"You're a tart, you are, dragging your tail in the dirt!"

The lady uttered a shriek and looked about her piteously for deliverance. She was both ashamed and frightened, and, to cap all, the officer sprang up from the chair and, with a yell, rushed at the merchant, but, slipping, tumbled back onto the chair with a thud. The laughter grew louder around them, and no one dreamed of helping her; but Velchaninov came to the rescue; he seized the merchant by the collar and, turning him around, thrust him some five paces away from the frightened woman. And with that the scandal ended; the merchant was taken aback by the push and by Velchaninov's imposing figure; his companions at once led him away. The dignified countenance of the elegantly dressed gentleman produced a strong impression on the jeering crowd: the laughter ceased. The lady flushed and, almost in tears, was overflowing with expressions of gratitude. The Uhlan mumbled, "Thanks, thanks!" and made as though to hold out his hand to Velchaninov, but instead suddenly took it into his head to lie down on the chairs and stretched out to his full length on them.

"Mitenka!" the lady moaned reproachfully, clasping her hands in horror.

Velchaninov was pleased with the adventure and with the whole situation. The lady attracted him; she was evidently a well-to-do provincial, gorgeously but tastelessly dressed, and with rather ridiculous manners—in fact, she combined all the characteristics that guarantee success to a Petersburg gallant with designs on the fair sex. A conversation began; the lady spoke heatedly and bitterly complained of her husband, who had "suddenly disappeared from the carriage and so was the cause of it all, because whenever he is wanted he runs off somewhere."

"To answer a call of nature," the Uhlan muttered.

"Ah, Mitenka!" She clasped her hands again.

"Well, the husband will catch it!" thought Velchaninov.

"What is his name? I will go and look for him," he suggested.

"Pal Palych,"[8] responded the Uhlan.

"Your husband's name is Pavel Pavlovich?" Velchaninov asked with curiosity, and suddenly a familiar bald head thrust itself between him and the lady. In a flash he had a vision of the Zahlebinins' garden, the innocent games, and a tiresome bald head that incessantly forced itself between him and Nadezhda Fedoseyevna.

"Here you are at last!" cried the wife hysterically.

It was Pavel Pavlovich himself; in wonder and alarm he gazed at Velchaninov, struck dumb at the sight of him as though he had been a ghost. His stupefaction was such that for some time he seemed not to be able to take in what his offended spouse was explaining in a rapid and irritable flow of words. At last, with a start, he grasped all the horror of his position: his own guilt, and Mitenka's behavior, "and that this 'monsieur' (this was how the lady for some reason described Velchaninov) "has been a savior and guardian angel to us, while you—you are never there when you are wanted. . . ."

Velchaninov suddenly burst out laughing.

"Why, we are friends, we've been friends since childhood!" he exclaimed to the astonished lady, putting his right arm with patronizing familiarity around the shoulders of Pavel Pavlovich, who smiled a wan smile. "Hasn't he talked to you of Velchaninov?"

"No, he never has," the lady responded, somewhat taken aback.

[8] A variant of Pavel Pavlovich.—A.Y.

"Then introduce me to your wife, you faithless friend!"

"Lipochka, it really is Mr. Velchaninov," Pavel Pavlovich began, but broke off abashed.

His wife turned crimson and flashed an angry look at him, probably for "Lipochka."

"And, only fancy, he didn't let me know he had married, and didn't invite me to the wedding, but you, Olimpiada. . . ."

"Semyonovna," Pavel Pavlovich prompted.

"Semyonovna," the Uhlan, who had dropped asleep, echoed suddenly.

"You must forgive him, Olimpiada Semyonovna, for my sake, in honor of the meeting of friends. . . . He's a good husband."

And Velchaninov gave Pavel Pavlovich a friendly slap on the shoulder.

"I was . . . I was only away for a minute, my love," Pavel Pavlovich began making excuses.

"And left your wife to be insulted," Lipochka put in at once. "When you're wanted there's no finding you, when you're not wanted you're always at hand. . . ."

"Where you're not wanted you're there, where you're not wanted . . . where you're not wanted . . ." the Uhlan chimed in.

Lipochka was almost breathless with excitement; she knew herself it was not seemly to carry on like that before Velchaninov, she blushed but could not restrain herself.

"Where there's no need you are too careful, too careful!" she burst out.

"Under the bed . . . he looks for lovers . . . under the bed—where there's no need . . . where there's no need . . ." muttered Mitenka, suddenly growing extremely excited.

But there was no doing anything with Mitenka by now. It all ended pleasantly, however, and they got upon quite friendly terms. Pavel Pavlovich was sent out to fetch coffee and bouillon. Olimpiada Semyonovna explained to Velchaninov that they were on their way from O—, where her husband had a post in the service, to spend two months at their country place, that it was not far off, only thirty miles from that station, that they had a lovely house and garden there, that they were going to have visitors, that they had neighbors too, and if Alexey Ivanovich would be so good as to come and stay with them "in their rustic solitude" she would welcome him "as their guardian angel," for she could not recall without horror what would have happened, if . . . and so on, and so on—in short, as "her guardian angel. . . ."

"And savior, and savior," the Uhlan insisted with heat.

Velchaninov thanked her politely, and replied that he was always at her service, that he was an absolutely idle man with no duties of any sort, and that Olimpiada Semyonovna's invitation was most flattering. He followed this at once with sprightly conversation into which he successfully introduced two or three compliments. Lipochka blushed with pleasure, and as soon as Pavel Pavlovich returned she told him enthusiastically that Alexey Ivanovich had been so kind as to accept her invitation to spend a whole month with them in the country, and had promised to come in a week. Pavel Pavlovich smiled in distress and said nothing. Olimpiada Semyonovna shrugged her shoulders at him, and raised her eyes to the ceiling. Finally came the leave-taking: again a gush of gratitude, again the "guardian angel," again "Mitenka," and Pavel Pavlovich at last escorted his wife and the Uhlan to their carriage. Velchaninov lighted a cigar and began pacing the promenade in front of the station; he knew that Pavel Pavlovich would presently run out again to talk to him till the bell rang. And so it happened. Pavel Pavlovich promptly appeared before him with an uneasy, questioning expression in his eyes and whole countenance. Velchaninov laughed, took him by the elbow in a friendly way, led him to the nearest bench, sat down himself, and made him sit down alongside him. He remained silent; he wanted Pavel Pavlovich to be the first to speak.

457

"So you are coming to us, sir?" faltered the latter, going straight to the point.

"I knew it! You haven't changed in the least!" Velchaninov burst into laughter. "Why, do you mean to say"—he slapped him again on the shoulder—"could you have seriously imagined for a moment that I would actually come and stay with you, and for a whole month too—ha—ha?"

Pavel Pavlovich was all of a twitter.

"So you—are not coming!" he cried, not in the least disguising his relief.

"I'm not coming, I'm not coming!" Velchaninov laughed complacently. He could not have said himself, however, why he felt so particularly amused, but he was more and more amused as time went on.

"Do you really . . . do you really mean it?" And, saying this, Pavel Pavlovich actually jumped up from his seat in a flutter of suspense.

"Yes, I've told you already that I'm not coming, you queer fellow."

"If that's so, what am I to say to Olimpiada Semyonovna a week hence, when she will be expecting you and you don't come, sir?"

"What a predicament! Tell her I've broken a leg or something of that sort."

"She won't believe it, sir," Pavel Pavlovich drawled plaintively.

"And you'll catch it?" Velchaninov went on laughing. "But I see, my poor friend, that you do tremble before your delightful spouse—don't you?"

Pavel Pavlovich tried to smile, but it did not come off. That Velchaninov had refused to visit them was a good thing, of course, but that he should be unceremonious with him about his wife was bad. Pavel Pavlovich winced; Velchaninov noticed it. Meanwhile the second bell rang; from the train came a shrill voice anxiously calling Pavel Pavlovich. The latter fidgeted in his chair, but did not respond to the summons, evidently expecting something more

from Velchaninov, no doubt another assurance that he
would not come and stay with them.

"What was your wife's maiden name?" Velchaninov inquired, making believe that he was unaware of Pavel Pavlovich's anxiety.

"She is our priest's daughter," replied the latter uneasily,
looking toward the train and listening.

"Ah, I understand, you married her for her beauty."

Pavel Pavlovich winced again.

"And who's this Mitenka with you?"

"Oh, he's a distant relation of ours—that is, of mine; the
son of my deceased cousin. His name's Golubchikov, he
was degraded for disorderly behavior in the army, but now
he has been reinstated and we have equipped him. . . .
He's an unfortunate young man, sir. . . ."

"To be sure, everything is in order; the picture's complete," thought Velchaninov.

"Pavel Pavlovich!" The call came again from the train,
and now with a marked tone of irritation in the voice.

"Pal Palych!" came another hoarse voice.

Pavel Pavlovich fidgeted and moved restlessly again, but
Velchaninov took him by the elbow and detained him.

"If you wish, I will go this minute and tell your wife
how you tried to cut my throat, shall I?"

"You don't say, you don't say so, sir!" Pavel Pavlovich
was terribly alarmed. "God forbid!"

"Pavel Pavlovich! Pavel Pavlovich!" voices were heard
calling again.

"Well, be off now!" said Velchaninov, letting him go at
last, and still laughing genially.

"So you won't come?" Pavel Pavlovich whispered for the
last time, almost in despair, and even put his hands before
him with the palms together in his old manner.

"Why, I swear I won't come! Run, there'll be trouble,
you know."

And with a flourish he held out his hand to him—and
was startled: Pavel Pavlovich did not take his hand, he even
drew his own back.

The third bell rang.

In one instant something strange happened to both of them: both seemed transformed. Something, as it were, shook and snapped in Velchaninov, who had been laughing only just before. In an access of fury, he clutched Pavel Pavlovich's shoulder tightly.

"If I—*I* hold out this hand to you," showing the palm of his left hand, where a big scar from the cut was still distinct, "you certainly might take it!" he whispered, with pale and trembling lips.

Pavel Pavlovich, too, turned pale, and his lips trembled too; a quiver convulsed his face.

"And Liza, sir?" he murmured in a rapid whisper, and suddenly his lips, his cheeks, and his chin began to twitch and tears gushed from his eyes. Velchaninov stood before him stunned.

"Pavel Pavlovich! Pavel Pavlovich!" came a scream from the train as though someone were being murdered—and suddenly the whistle sounded.

Pavel Pavlovich roused himself, flung up his hands, and ran full speed to the train; the train had already started but he managed to jump on it, and he made his way into his carriage. Velchaninov remained at the station and only in the evening set off on his original route in another train. He did not turn off to the right to visit the provincial lady of his acquaintance—he was too much out of humor. And how he regretted it afterward!

11E